SINNING IN VEGAS

(VEGAS MORELLIS, #2)

SAM MARIANO

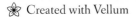 Created with Vellum

1

LAUREL

Four: the number of days I spent with Sin in Las Vegas. Three: the number of times he has called me since realizing I did not, in fact, call Rafe to come get me, but instead booked myself an Uber, bought myself a plane ticket, and flew away from Vegas like a bat out of hell.

Two: the number of days I have spent in Chicago to legitimize the lie I told my sister.

One: the number of nights I have to survive until I can board my flight from Chicago to Connecticut and finally go home.

On one hand, I really wanted to go straight home to my sister from Vegas. My heart is busted up, and no one nurses you through heartache quite like Carly.

On the other hand, I don't want Carly or Vince to know I went there. My lies in Vegas may not have been any good, but the truth is so much worse. My brother-in-law, while wonderful, has a tendency to be overly protective and a bit of a loose cannon. I don't want to ignite his hot-headedness toward anyone in Vegas because I'm realistic, and I understand that's dangerous, whether my heart is broken and my womb has been invaded or not.

I don't need Vince or Carly to handle this for me. I've handled it myself. Now I just have to recover from the unexpected pitfall and get my life back on track.

First things first: I am done with the Morelli drama. I'm done with all of it. The boring life is looking better and better now. Maybe my dinner dates from now on won't be dangerous or exciting, but they won't break my heart and ruin my life in less than a week, either. Underwhelming is underrated. Who needs soaring passion and pulse-pounding excitement all the time? Not me, that's for sure. Nope. Sign me up for Mr. Boring and Predictable. The biophysicist whose biggest point of contention with me is thinking his work is more important than mine? Totally fine with that now.

I need to detox, wallow, mourn my losses, and then go back to Connecticut tomorrow and remember how to be a normal person. No more padded cuffs to keep me tied to the bed while the psycho I'm falling for beats the shit out of people to collect money for my baby daddy. No more kneeling and basking in the glorious power exchanged between us in those moments...

I groan into my pillow, losing steam. God, I miss that feeling. The electrical current that pulses through me, the intimacy of opening myself up for him, giving myself to him in any way he wants me.

Of course, that's the moment my roommate is walking by and hears my miserable, bereft groan.

Sailing into the dark haven of our shared bedroom, she demands, "Okay, that's it. I've tried minding my business, but I can't anymore. What the hell is wrong with you?"

I sigh, peeking out from the comforting fort of pink blankets and pillows I constructed around myself to block out all the light. I'm like a vampire, hiding from the sun's harmful rays in a cocoon of comfort. "I'll be fine. I just need to be alone right now."

Ignoring me, she takes a seat on the edge of my bed. "This looks, smells, and sounds like a break-up, but I wasn't aware you were seeing someone. Tell your roomie what's up. Is this about that Kevin guy? I thought you didn't even like him."

It's laughable that she thinks this is over my last coffee date. Sin could snap my coffee date in half and use a sliver of his broken bones to pick his teeth.

Dammit, that's not helpful. It should horrify me, but it just makes me sigh mournfully. I really liked that stupid, sexy monster.

Patting the bed to get my attention, Daphne says, "Earth to Laurel. Hello? Tell me what I can do to help."

"You can leave me alone and let me be miserable in peace."

With a perfunctory nod, she says, "I've been doing that. Give me something else."

I sigh, squeezing the pillow closer and trying to think of some menial task for her to do so she'll feel like she's helping. I would send her for ice cream, but the thought of eating makes me want to throw up. "How about break-up songs? Can you make me a playlist?"

"Absolutely," she says, with enthusiasm. "What's the break-up vibe? I take it he's the one who fucked up? You're too boring to fuck up."

I can't help smiling. If only she knew. "He's evil. Beautiful to look at, but a soul-shattering demon from the depths of hell. Is that a strong enough vibe for you?"

"Definitely." She holds out her hand, palm up. "Give me your phone. I've got you."

"It's on the night stand," I tell her, burrowing back into my pillow fortress.

A moment later I hear her awe-laden voice as she says, "Holy hell. Is this him?"

I peek back out of Fort Softness. "Seriously? You're supposed to be making me a playlist, not going through my phone."

Daphne thrusts the phone at me, eyes wide. I look at the screen and see the picture of me and Rafe in the Grand Canyon. "Girl, I don't know how you managed this, but let me help you out. I don't know what he did—I'm honestly sad it wasn't me—but forgive him. A guy that looks like this is gonna fuck up from time to time, but if curling up next to *this* every night is an option? You take it. And if you won't, can you put in a good word for me? I'll cry a few tears for him if that's the price I have to pay to get my hands on all this."

"That is *terrible* advice. You give *terrible* advice," I inform her.

"One girl's terrible advice is another girl's mantra. If you don't want him anymore, will you give him my number?"

"He lives in Las Vegas."

"I'm open to relocating," she states. "I can be packed up and ready to go in an hour. This suit looks expensive. Is he rich, too?"

"Your loyalty to me is astounding," I deadpan.

"Hey, I'm suggesting you forgive him first. I'm just saying, if you don't want him anymore, I call dibs. Don't leave this beautiful specimen running around free in the world. Some thirsty bitch is going to take your place while you're here wallowing. Go take a shower and get your ass on a video chat with this motherfucker before he gets away."

"I didn't even say that was the guy," I tell her.

"No, but I see the way he's holding you in this picture, and I know you're not an idiot. If a guy that looks like this is on the table, why even bother looking at any other ones?"

Sighing miserably as memories of Sin's hands locked around my wrists in a vice grip resurface, I tell her, "You haven't seen Sin."

Her eyes widen and she taps my screen, going back to my photos. "Show me. And then tell me where I go to find this bevy of sex gods, because I want to apply for a visitor's pass."

"Trust me, you do not want one. I know where you're coming from. I was on the outside looking in just a couple months ago, wowed by all their beauty. But they're beautiful for a diabolical reason—so they can lure you in and suck out your soul."

"Literally anything of mine Mr. Grand Canyon wants to suck, he has my permission."

I throw a pillow at her. "Go be a ho somewhere else. I'm trying to be sad while I still have a few hours left to indulge. I can't do this tomorrow when I'm back in Connecticut. Carly did everything in her power to stop me from getting involved with these monsters, and I dove head-first into the pit, anyway."

Grabbing the pillow and whacking me with it, Daphne says, "Bitch, I want to dive in, too!"

Bringing up a hand to block her pillow assault, I demand, "Are you going to make me a playlist, or keep snooping through my phone?"

"I'm sending myself this picture. I'm going to Photoshop you out of it and put myself in your place. Full disclosure."

"You're a psycho."

"I'm a connoisseur of fine-looking men, and this one is aces. Show me this Sin guy."

"I don't have any pictures of Sin," I tell her, hit by a swell of sadness as I hear that truth for myself. I want a picture of him, but I'm also sort of glad I don't have one. If I can forget his face and wipe him from my memory completely, that would be much better. "He looks like danger and shadows and passion and power—but sexier."

Daphne's eyes widen. "Damn, you've got it bad."

I nod unhappily. "And I have about 18 hours to get rid of it, so if you're not going to help, can you just leave me to wallow in peace?"

Apparently not, because she fires another question at me. "What's the deal with Mr. Grand Canyon?"

"He got me pregnant," I state.

Daphne's eyes widen to approximately the size of saucers.

Raising my eyebrows, I ask, "Anything else? Can I be alone now?"

"Do you have this whole secret life I don't know about? I'm so confused."

I sigh, burying my face in the pillows and shutting out my roommate. "Go away."

"Fine," she says, standing, and now looking at my abdomen as if it might have popped in the last 30 seconds. "What are you gonna do?"

"Ignore you until you go away."

"I meant about the pregnancy," she specifies.

Sighing, I say, "Ignore it until it goes away?"

"That won't work," she informs me.

"I'm going home tomorrow. I'll work it all out once I have my sister. Now, I'm tired. Let me sleep."

When she thought it was just a break-up, she wasn't willing to let me sleep, but now that she knows a pregnancy is involved, she respects that it's more serious.

Pushing up off the bed, she says, "I'll make you some of that tea you like. How about that?"

"That would be perfect," I say, jumping at an excuse to get her out of my room. "Thank you."

2

LAUREL

The Chicago streets feel grayer today, devoid of the hustle and bustle, devoid of the color and noise. It's a gray day to match my mood, I guess. I can't believe I let Daphne talk me into coming out of my mourning fort, but she guilted me, saying since it's my last night in the city for God knows how long, I needed to come meet her and some friends and actually spend some time with them before they forget who I am.

I already knew it was a terrible, no-good, bad idea to leave the sanctuary of my bed, but it solidifies to a gut-deep certainty when I hear a vaguely familiar voice call out, "Laurel?"

I hate running into people I know even when I'm in a *good* mood, but after Vegas, I am exhausted. The ache in my heart makes just walking around require more energy from me than it should, and now I have to deal with some girl I have barely even spoken to in class out in the real world. Why do people do this? I didn't see her, so she could have easily pretended not to see me.

Forcing a more welcoming smile onto my lips, I turn around to greet her.

My smile falls along with my heart, because that is not a girl from one of my classes. The well-dressed, smiling blonde beauty heading my way with a scarred up bodyguard on her heels is Mia Morelli, the woman whose house I went to for Easter. The woman whose diabolical husband ultimately opened the Morelli portal and invited all these awful people into my life.

Why does she look happy to see me? I haven't seen her since Easter, and to be honest, would not have thought she could pick me out of a line-up. But here she comes, a deep crimson shopping bag dangling from her fingers, a big smile on her face.

God, I'm a mess, too. I didn't put make-up on. Did I even brush my hair? I want the sidewalk to swallow me whole and save me from this interaction, but it doesn't happen.

"It's Mia," she says, in case I don't remember her. "My husband and Rafe are cousins."

"Yes, I remember you," I say, nodding my head.

"What are you doing in Chicago?" she asks, cocking her head. "I thought you were in Vegas."

"I was. Just for a few days. Now I'm back."

Her gaze drops ever so briefly to my stomach, then returns to my face. "Where are you headed? We can give you a ride. It's hot out here. We were just heading back to the car." Now she holds up the shopping bag with American Girl printed in white lettering. "We had to make an emergency doll replacement trip. Westley and Rosalie were playing doctor, and he inadvertently decapitated Willa."

At that, I crack a smile. "Oh, man. That must have been traumatic."

Mia nods. "Ju was quick on her feet and got the doll to the 'recovery room' before Rosalie noticed, but, yeah, real heads were going to roll if she found out."

Gesturing to the bag, I say, "Mom to the rescue."

Mia smiles and nods her head for me to follow. "Come on, we'll give you a ride."

I notice her bodyguard doesn't turn to follow her, but instead keeps an eye on me, waiting to see if I'll follow. I had no intention to even before that, but now I'm damn sure not going to. I've been too trusting with this wily family, and while I got a certain amount of enjoyment from Sin kidnapping me, I also got my heart dinged up. I would rather sweat my ass off walking than get in their air conditioned car and risk ending up entangled with their family again. I haven't even cut the last of the vines from *last time* they pulled me in.

"I'm okay, actually. It was nice to see you, but I really have to get going or I'll be late."

"You won't be late if we give you a ride," Adrian counters, sensibly.

I smile, considering another polite dodge, but I decide just to be honest. "You know what? I'm not going to get into a car with you because I don't trust you. Every time I get into a car with anyone associated with the Morelli family, my life hits a brick wall. It was fun the first couple times, don't get me wrong, but I'm over it. I would like to get back to boring, if it's all the same to you."

A strong arm settles around my shoulders and my gaze snaps to the wall of man suddenly standing beside me. "It's *not* all the same to us, or we wouldn't be here, now, would we?"

I narrow my eyes, staring at the dark-haired, dark-eyed devil beside me. "*You.*"

Alec Morelli nods his head, dragging me along with him toward Mia and Adrian. "Me. Long time, no see."

I try to shrug his arm off me, but his grip is too tight. "Get your hands off me."

Instead, he places the other one on my waist, on the inside of this unwilling embrace so no onlookers would think anything of it. "Why don't you make this easy?" he suggests. "Obviously you're going to get in the car and come with us. I mean, if you don't, I'm going to have to follow you all the way back to your place, knock out your roommate, break into your apartment, and drag you out all by myself. You're on the ground floor, which is nice, but since you're pregnant, I'm disinclined to drug you. That means I'm going to use all my restraint on you and your roommate, so if you struggle and catch the attention of any other helpful onlookers on the way out, I'm just gonna have to shoot them. I'm not in the mood to shoot anybody today. If you would just get in the car with us now, I can avoid all that and take the night off. It's Sunday. I really hate working hard on Sundays."

I glare at Mia, since she's the only one of the bunch who looks remorseful for her part in this trap. "Unbelievable."

"I'm sorry," she says sadly, like we're old friends and she has thrust a dagger into my back. "I was doing a favor for Rafe. I thought you'd come more easily if another woman was here. I know how tired you must be of the men."

"So fucking tired of them, you don't even know."

"No one is going to hurt you. We just want to take you back to the mansion. You can stay for dinner. Rafe is flying in and he wants to talk to you. Apparently you're not taking his calls."

I'm not taking *any* Vegas calls. "Do you know what it means when someone avoids someone else's calls? It means they don't want to talk to them, and they definitely don't want to see them."

"The Morelli men aren't big on taking 'no' for an answer," she informs me.

"How do they feel about getting stabbed? Because I'm feeling kinda stabby."

"Knife play, huh?" Alec asks, winking at me. "Should've told me you were into that when we went for coffee, maybe I would have called you back."

"I hate you."

Alec grins, giving my shoulders a squeeze. "I know. I'm sorry. It's fun to pick on you."

Fun to pick on me, huh? "Well, if knife play excites you, you would really be kicking yourself if you knew all the things I *will* do in bed."

That wipes the smile off his stupid, handsome face.

It brings one to mine, though. I feel a little better about this kidnapping if I at least got a good jab in at red car guy.

Mia grins at me, then shoots Alec a sassy smile. "I don't know what you did to her, but I feel like you deserved that."

"I'm the nice Morelli," he insists.

I slide him a dry look. "That's like being the least harmful demon in hell. No points for you, buddy."

Now a little smile tugs at the corner of Adrian's mouth. "Rafe really pissed you off, huh?"

"Rafe didn't even piss me off, I just can't do it. I can't hang with this family. I can't handle all the mind games and manipulation. You guys are so fucked up."

In his own defense, Adrian points out, "Hey, I'm not a blood Morelli."

"No, you're the Chicago Sin, bending the world to suit the needs and desires of the spoiled asshole you work for."

Mia's eyebrows rise and she slows down to fall in step beside me. "There's a Vegas Adrian?"

"Sin is not the Vegas Adrian," Adrian tells Mia. "I'm higher up than he is. Sin is still just Rafe's enforcer, isn't he?"

"Yes," I murmur, glumly.

"Is he dreamy?" Alec jokes.

"Yes," I murmur, just as glumly.

Mia's smile falls. "Uh oh."

"He's also the devil," I inform her. "A manipulative, heart-breaking monster."

"Uh oh," Alec echoes. "That sounds way too familiar. You know all about those, right, Mia?"

Mia shoots him a dirty look. "My husband is perfect; shut up."

Smirking faintly, Adrian says, "With that description, he is definitely *not* the Vegas Adrian."

Alec concurs, "Vegas Mateo."

"No," Mia says, more adamantly than I would expect, given she has no stake in any of this. "Don't say that. I want to be on Rafe's side; there can't be a Vegas Mateo."

If they knew him, they would understand. Sin isn't a version of anyone but himself. He's one-of-a-kind, irreplaceable. I'll never meet another Sin as long as I live.

Depressed by this new line of thought, I let them drag me back to their Escalade, fully aware that resistance is futile.

When I first encountered Alec Morelli, I had no idea who he was. Hell, I had no idea about the Morelli family, period. The edgiest thing I had ever done was try pot at a party one time; I knew next to nothing about Chicago's criminal underworld.

Then one day a handsome man swept into my life. It seemed serendipitous, a meet-cute from a more innocent time when I didn't know how much of the Morelli experience was just a performance. I met a hot guy at a coffee shop, we seemed to hit it off, and he asked me out to dinner. Day made. Then things got shady. I didn't realize how shady at the time, when he suddenly cut our date short midway through dinner and hustled me out to his red sports car after getting a mysterious phone call. At most, I may have figured Alec for a fuckboy and dismissed the whole experience as a date gone mysteriously wrong, but then Easter happened.

Mateo Morelli, Chicago's leading king of crime, invited me to Easter dinner. That would have been really weird, except my sister was dating his cousin, Vince, and they were coming to town for the holiday. I thought it was nice. A big Italian family extending an invite to come celebrate with them so I wasn't left out. Nothing is ever simple with these people, though. I came for dinner so I could spend the holiday with Carly and Vince, saw Alec Morelli enter the dining room, and got shushed by my sister. Wordlessly, she begged me not to say anything. I figured I would go to her room later and find out why the hell red car guy was at the table—that couldn't be a coincidence, right?—and more importantly, why she needed me to keep quiet about recognizing him, but then the main event rolled in.

Rafe Morelli, then the Vegas up-and-comer, now their very own crime king—and, you know, the man who impregnated me that very weekend. Once he got there and turned his captivating attention on me, I struggled to remember my own name. Forget trying to unravel their secrets, I was more interested in getting tangled up in the sheets with the sexiest man who had ever noticed me. Seducing me was only supposed to be a game to him, a favor to Mateo, a way to piss off my sister for whatever reason, but the game changed when the condom failed, and now look where we all are.

Once I'm in their car, I know I'm not going anywhere unless they want me to. They take me back to their giant, beautiful house. Honestly, house seems a misnomer; this place is a palace. I was blown away by it when I first saw it, but now I harbor too much resentment to allow myself to be impressed.

Alec disappears once I'm safely imprisoned in their house. Adrian sticks around, but now that I'm under their roof, he doesn't even seem as worried about keeping an eye on me. Instead, he takes the shopping bag from Mia and draws out a box. Then the scary-looking Mafioso begins carefully removing the doll from its packaging and tells Mia he'll take it to the playroom.

"Come to my room, we'll get you ready for dinner," she tells me, once we're alone.

I look around curiously. "Am I considered a low flight-risk or something?"

"You're not our prisoner, Laurel," she assures me.

"So, I can leave?"

"Well, no. At least not until Rafe gets here." Attempting a cheerful tone, she says, "Don't think of it as a forced visit. I'm really happy you're here. As soon as Rafe told me you were pregnant, I told him he should bring you here. Are there any other Morelli women in Vegas to help you learn the way of things?"

Her words remind me of Sin's sensual prison. If there were women in Vegas, I didn't even get a chance to meet them. I was swept up in my Sin bubble most of the time. "I'm not sure. I spent most of my time in Vegas cuffed to a bed."

A burst of surprised laughter escapes her. "Oh. Well, I'm sure you had more fun playing with Rafe anyway. I'm not familiar with the Vegas players." Placing an earnest hand to her chest, she tells me, "I do know when *I* first got dragged into this family, I found it extremely helpful when Vince's sister gave me a little introductory course. You met Cherie, right?"

I nod, recalling the beautiful brunette Vince introduced me and Carly to over Easter. "Yep, briefly."

"Between her and Francesca, I had helpful guides to aid me through my adjustment period. Since today is Sunday and you're in Chicago, I can introduce you to a Morelli staple —at least, a Chicago staple. I'm not sure how Rafe runs things, but we always have a mandatory family dinner on Sundays. My husband is very fond of them. I'll warn you, it may initially feel a bit sexist, but I actually really like them. We'll get all dolled up, then we'll head downstairs and make dinner while the men adjoin to the study for pre-dinner drinks."

My eyes widen, images of handsome, well-dressed men in lush leather wing chairs drinking Scotch and smoking cigars floating to mind. It's a mental image from another time, but somehow I can see Rafe enjoying that.

"After everything is done, we will serve our own men. Obviously that means you'll serve Rafe, then sit beside him while we eat."

"I won't kneel on the ground at his feet?" I joke.

"Well, what you do after dinner is your business," she says, slyly.

Sin is the only one I want to kneel for, and he's not interested. I sigh heavily, but Mia misinterprets and offers a tiny, apologetic smile.

"I know the dinner business is a little old-school, but it can actually be kind of sexy. Mateo and Rafe are both into the illusion of a subservient little wife. Fun fact: back when I met

Rafe, within 10 minutes of meeting him, he had me cooking him breakfast. Just because he told me to."

I smile faintly, following her down a long-ass corridor. "Was that in Vegas, or here?"

"Vegas. The only time I've been there."

Since I love my brother-in-law, I don't really *want* to ask, but there will probably never be a better time, either. Normally when I'm around Mia, she has some kind of entourage—whether it's Adrian, her husband, or one of her little munchkins, but right now it's just us. "Can I ask an awkward question?"

Pushing open a white door and gesturing for me to go inside ahead of her, she nods, but I can see reluctance on her face. "Sure."

"Did Vince kidnap you?"

Her eyebrows rise, like that wasn't the question she was expecting. "Oh. Um... yeah, for a few days." Quickly changing the subject, she strides across the room and flings open what appears to be her closet. A closet a small family could *live in*, but a closet, nonetheless. "Anyway, I hope you don't find this creepy, but when Rafe told me he wanted us to bring you to dinner, I was so excited, I went out and bought you a maternity dress to wear."

My eyes widen, her distraction working as I follow her inside the giant walk-in closet. "You bought me a maternity dress?"

Mia nods, grabbing a garment bag and draping it across a marble counter so she can unzip it. "I got you a pair of my favorite maternity leggings, too. Not to wear tonight, they're just my favorite, comfy things, so I thought you should have a pair. It gets hard to feel sexy when you're pregnant, but these stylish little leggings always do the trick. I know you won't be showing for a while, but there's a belly panel for when you are. And I got you these cute shoes to go with the dress," she adds, opening a cupboard beneath the counter and pulling out a shoe box. Patting the box, she adds, "I have a pair myself, and they're really comfortable for heels. Later on in pregnancy, you'll care more about comfort than how pretty your shoes are, but these are the best of both worlds. I have lots of pregnancy pro-tips if you're ever interested."

I take the shoe as she hands it to me, noting the Jimmy Choo tag inside. I don't shop high-end shoes, but I know these *are* high-end shoes. "Why are you being so nice to me?"

Appearing startled, Mia looks at me over her shoulder as she closes my shoe box. "Why wouldn't I be nice to you?"

I bend to slip the shoe on my foot and check the fit. "I know you obviously like Rafe and you're clearly into this whole... idea of us coupling up and having a baby together, but that is not my plan. I left Vegas because I *don't* want to be with Rafe. I don't want this life. No offense. Obviously you have been nothing but nice to me, but this is not what I want. I want to go back to the life I had before I met Rafe, before I met any of you. I just.... I just want to go back."

Sympathy is written all over her pretty features. Dropping the dress and shoes, she turns around and takes my hand, like she wants to offer me comfort. "I don't see that happening. You're pregnant with his baby, Laurel. Even if you don't want to be with him, that means he'll be present in your life. I really hope you'll give him a shot though. I know he can be a little... Rafe-like, but he obviously likes you, and I think he has it in him to be a really good man."

"I'm not saying he's a bad man... although, I mean, that argument could certainly be made."

"They're really not that bad once you get used to them,"

she assures me. "When you're new to the family, the men can be a bit much, but you'll see. They have their quirks, but they are *good* partners. They'll do anything to protect you. They come off a bit old-fashioned, but they honestly treasure you in ways men these days just don't anymore. I know you have your doubts, but I feel like Rafe could make you really happy if you let him."

I can't argue with that. I mean, I *could*. I could tell her what an absolute asshole he was to me when I told him I was pregnant, or about how he let other women flirt with him right in front of me, or the date I had to watch him with at dinner. Hell, I could even tell her Rafe isn't the problem, that the problem is I developed hard-and-fast feelings for Sin, and going back to Vegas means facing him, even if I go with Rafe.

But I can't say any of that, because she looks so damn hopeful, and even though she barely knows me, she's out buying me all her must-have maternity items like I'm already part of the family. Mia has probably been indoctrinated for so long, she doesn't see any other way. Rafe wants me, so I must be his happily ever after.

Rather than rain on her parade, I offer a smile. "Maybe. We'll see what happens."

Her smile comes back and she pats my hand. "As long as you're open to it." Dropping my hand, she's all business again as she tells me, "Now, why don't you go take a shower so we can get you ready for dinner?"

3

LAUREL

After she dolls me up, Mia takes me to the kitchen and introduces me as Rafe's girlfriend.

I stare at her, and she comes back with a blank, "What?"

She's crazy. The other blonde in the kitchen doesn't seem to care whose girlfriend I am; she's in work-mode, and assigns me the job of filling all the water and wine glasses she put on the table.

It's a long table, though not as cramped as it was over Easter. Tonight the chairs are spread out so everyone has a little more room, but as I fill wine glasses, I wonder which seat will be mine. There's no point filling my wine glass since I won't drink it. Considering it just makes me think about the craziness of this whole situation. Dining with mob bosses—not what I thought I would be doing over my summer vacation.

"We're gonna have to get you a maid costume."

The sound of Rafe's voice sends a shiver down my spine. I straighten and turn to face him. Despite myself, I can't help softening when I see him leaning against the arched entryway, arms crossed over his broad chest, a warm smile on his beautiful face. Maybe it's because this is almost exactly where I was the first time I saw him, when the sight of him nearly stopped my heart, but he somehow looks even better in person than in my memory—again.

Now it's not just the command he oozes leaning there, practically bursting out of his well-tailored suit. Flashes of his naked, powerful body moving over mine as he thrust inside me come to mind, along with more casually warm memories, like standing with him at the Grand Canyon, or the way he looked in the glow of the Vegas lights as we walked the strip and devoured strawberry shortcakes.

He can be scary and sexy and sweet.

Oh, and an asshole.

I try to remember that last one as I go back to filling wine glasses, as if unaffected. "You want me to wear a sexy maid costume in front of your whole family? Not sure I'm that kinky, sorry."

"Nah, that'll just be for me." From my peripherals, I can see him push off the wall and head in my direction. "You can wear it when you make me dinner once we go back to Vegas. I'll let you make my bed, and I'll enjoy the view when you bend over. Then I'll toss you on top and we can fuck up the nice, neat bedding."

His casual arrogance draws a helpless smile out of me. "I'm not going back there, Rafe. I'm only here right now because your cousin's wife kidnapped me."

Moving behind me, Rafe settles his hands on my hips like he did at the bookstore. Tension gathers in my shoulders, but I refuse to look back at him. "You seem to be cooperating pretty well for someone who's being held captive, kitten."

I offer a dry smile he can't see, and wouldn't understand

even if he could. "Yes, apparently I excel at being held against my will. Maybe I should start charging a premium for my services."

"There's that Price business sense kicking in." I feel his amusement as he leans in to kiss my neck. "I've missed you."

I didn't expect him to say that, and it makes my heart drop. Maybe because I've spent all *my* time missing someone else. In an attempt to redirect and get his tempting lips off me, I ask, "Why did you tell your family I'm pregnant? We haven't even discussed this yet, and I'm pretty sure Mia is already dead-set on being a bridesmaid in our wedding." I look at him over my shoulder. "She bought me a maternity wardrobe."

Now he chuckles, even more warmth seeping into his tone. "That sounds right. Mia's fiercely protective of her tribe; sounds like you're getting a forceful invitation to be part of it. She probably assumes I'm making a mess and wants to do whatever she can to fix it."

"You shouldn't have told them until we talked about it, Rafe. Now if I don't go through with it, there are even more people judging me."

"No one is judging you," he assures me. "Why do you say that?"

Saving me from having to answer, Mia comes in with two baskets full of bread. She brightens upon seeing Rafe, and he releases my hips to go greet her.

"You're here," she says, putting the bread down on the table and leaning in to hug him.

"I am," he returns, drawing her close and kissing her on top of the head. His hand drifts to her slightly swollen abdomen and he gives it a rub. "How's it going in there, little—" He pauses and looks at her face. "Do you know what it is yet?"

Beaming, she nods. "It's a boy. We weren't supposed to

find out until the next appointment, but the doctor said he definitely saw a penis."

Rafe shakes his head. "Waving his dick around already, huh?"

Mia swats his arm, looking down at her tummy and rubbing. "Tristan is going to be an angel, shut up."

"Sure, with Mateo for his father, how could he not?" Rafe asks lightly.

I move on to the next wine glass. "Dom seems pretty sweet, so it's clearly possible," I remark.

"Dom got all his temperament from his mother, none from his father," Rafe assures me.

"Here's hoping," Mia mutters. "After dinner, you should come play with the babies for a little bit. It made Laurel like you last time," she adds, slyly.

I bite back a grin while Rafe insists he didn't need her baby to help him, but before the debate can go very far, we hear the other men approaching from the hall. Mateo comes in first. Mia sheds Rafe's attention and goes over to greet her husband like she doesn't see him every single day. I can't help watching them, seeing how deeply in love Mia is. Mateo is a lot harder to read. You can definitely see warmth in his brown eyes when he looks at her, in the possessive hand he rests on her hip as he settles her into his side and turns his attention to Rafe. It reminds me of Sin at dinner a few nights ago when Rafe came over, and that just makes my heart hurt. How did everything tumble downhill so damn fast?

Adrian and Alec come in, too, and I linger to see where they're all sitting. Since this is a normal family dinner for everyone but me, there's nothing at any of the place settings to indicate where anyone sits. I know Mateo sat at the head of the table with Mia to his left, but I wasn't sure about everyone else.

Mia and I obviously don't need wine since we're pregnant, but I wasn't sure where I would be sitting, so I just filled every glass but hers.

Alec sits the farthest from Mateo, while Rafe takes a seat opposite Mia, on Mateo's right hand side.

"That's my seat," Adrian tells him.

"Guess you'll have to sit somewhere else," Rafe offers, smiling mildly.

Adrian gives him a dead-eyed look that makes me think of Sin. Apparently sensing conflict, Mia leaves her husband's side and takes Adrian's arm, guiding him to the seat beside hers. "Here, Adrian, sit next to me. I'd rather sit by you than him anyway."

If she wanted to annoy Rafe, she fails. He grins at her and says, "Ah, yes. Between the two of us, Adrian is always your first choice, isn't he, little one?"

For a split second Mia's eyes widen in shock, then narrow with annoyance and she tries to glare him to death. "I take back all the nice things I said about him, Laurel. He's an asshole."

Mateo takes his seat, a self-satisfied smile playing around his lips. "We should have invited Sal and Francesca to dinner. Next time you chase off your flavor of the month and need my help retrieving her, give me a little more notice, won't you?"

"If you like the playboys, Alec is available," Mia tells me, side-eyeing Rafe. "Maybe you two can work out your issues and you can be with him instead. Then you can stay in Chicago."

"You're supposed to be *helping*, not suggesting more competition," Rafe informs Mia.

"And you're supposed to refrain from pissing off pregnant women, but here we are." Turning her attention back to me, she says, "Come on, let's go grab salads. You should bring out Alec's, too."

"Don't you dare," Rafe says, catching my eye.

I would rather spit in Alec's food than serve him, but now that Rafe has said that, I have to. Once we're in the relative privacy of the kitchen, I ask Mia, "Is serving the men some sort of big deal?"

Rolling her eyes, she glances back at me. "You have no idea. When I first encountered this family, Mateo stirred up all sorts of shit simply by making me bring him his food on Sunday. I was dating Vince at the time, didn't think anything of it. It's essentially waitressing without the tip, right? Wrong. I guess it's a respect thing."

"Sounds like a proprietary thing," I volunteer. "I'm not Rafe's property, so... which salad is Alec's?"

Elise stops short, lifting her eyebrows. "Alec? I thought you were Rafe's girl?"

"I'm no one's girl. Tomorrow I'm going back to Connecticut, so none of this matters."

That catches Mia's attention. "How are Vince and Carly doing? Did they ever buy a house? I know Carly told me they were looking to buy after everything settled down."

I nod my head. "They're doing well. They bought a beautiful house with a big back yard. That's where I'm spending the summer. Doesn't make sense to stay by myself in Chicago when I could go hang out with them instead. Plus, Vince got a grill, and he's trying to fatten me up with his mad grilling skills."

Sighing to herself, Mia smiles. "Good. That sounds perfect for him. What did Carly say about the whole baby thing? She didn't seem psyched you spent time in Rafe's room to begin with."

I grimace, considering the conversations I have ahead of me tomorrow after the plane lands and my sister greets me. I'm bringing far more baggage than she's expecting. "I haven't told her yet. To be honest..." I glance up at Elise, since I don't really know her. Not like I know Mia much better, but she exudes a warmth that makes me comfortable talking to her. Elise keeps to herself a little more.

Seeing I don't want to share in front of her, she says, "Oh, okay," grabs two salads, and heads for the dining room.

Once the door swings shut, I decide to tell Mia the truth. "I'm not sure if I'm going through with this pregnancy." I pause, waiting to see judgment cross her features. It doesn't, but her brow does crease with concern.

"Why not?" she asks.

"I went to Vegas to tell Rafe, obviously, but he did *not* respond well. I really don't think he wants kids. His enforcer... it's complicated, but his enforcer started expressing interest in me and we got romantically involved." At this, Mia's eyes go wide, but I keep going. "As soon as Rafe noticed, he wanted me back. I think it was more about stealing a toy from Sin than actually wanting me, so even though he's here right now and I have his attention, I have doubts that it's real. I don't think anything has actually changed in the past week, I think Rafe is just a competitive person who can't stand to lose."

"Oh," she murmurs lowly, as if she hadn't considered that.

I nod. "So whatever he told you, *that* is the actual situation. I'm not playing hard to get here. I delivered myself to Vegas, and while he was initially happy to see me, the second I told him I was pregnant, he turned Arctic and sent me away."

"What an ass," she says.

"Yep."

After a moment of frowning over that, her attention

returns to me. "Well, okay, so you're not completely sold on Rafe. I get that. But does the pregnancy *have* to be tied to being with him? You're already pregnant, so... what does this decision depend on?"

I sigh, shaking my head. Glancing around her kitchen—which is larger than my entire apartment—I know she won't understand my working-class struggles. "I don't know what it depends on, to be honest. At this point, I'm not sure it's even a decision so much as an inevitability. I gave Rafe a chance to speak up if he wanted me to go through with it, and he still hasn't said anything. Weirdly enough, Sin was very adamant that I have the baby, but it turned out he was just manipulating me, so he was full of shit anyway. And, I'm sorry, but I really don't want to do this alone. I already know what life is like as a single mom. Carly basically raised me, and she's only 4 years older than I am. Rather than follow her example and struggle my ass off, I want to keep going to school, I want to finish my degree and accomplish things that will make her proud. I can't do all that and *this* on my own without doing a shitty job at one or the other. I'm only one person."

Mouth downturned like I've just said the saddest thing in the whole world, Mia steps forward and hugs me. "It doesn't have to be like that, Laurel. That's what family is for—to step up and help you out. I don't know how Rafe feels about this because we haven't had a chance to talk about it, but isn't it possible he just needed time to digest the news? He's good with my kids when he's here. I know he's not Mr. Commitment, but he has made comments to me that make me think he is open to a relationship with the right person. Maybe the fact that you're having his baby triggered something for him. It's hard to say for sure in this family. Mateo isn't like that, it wouldn't make a difference for him, but he had an incredibly abusive monster for a father, so he's sort of broken in that regard. From what I understand, Rafe had a healthier upbringing. He may be more normal about that—maybe now that he knows you're having his baby and the surprise has subsided, he wants to give it a shot with you. Would that be the worst thing?"

Dropping her gaze, I look down at the salads. "I don't know. I just don't think it's going to work with him. It's complicated at best, and derails my life at worst."

"Even if it doesn't, that doesn't mean you would have to do this alone. I refuse to believe Vince and Carly wouldn't help you out."

"Vince and Carly live in Connecticut," I state. "I go to school in Chicago and Vince isn't allowed in this city because your husband says so." Guilt briefly transforms her features, so I move along. "I don't just need financial help, Mia. If I had a baby, I would need someone I could trust to take care of it while I go to school and study. I would need a new place to live, because my roommate would in no universe be cool with a baby. We wouldn't have room anyway." I shake my head. "It's just too much. And even if Carly gave me the money to get a place of my own, what is she supposed to do? Leave Vince in Connecticut during the school year and come here to take care of my kid? She has her own degree to work on. It just isn't feasible. I'm not going to let her sacrifice any more for me than she already has. If I did this alone... I would need a lot of help, and she would give it to me, and I refuse to do that to her."

She's quiet for a moment and I shift awkwardly, not accustomed to spilling all my feelings and doubts all over strangers. It's just that since all this started, I haven't been able to talk to Carly, and since she *is* such a big part of my feelings about this, I *can't* talk to her about it. If Carly thought for even a second my decision was based on not wanting to ask her for help, she would kick my ass.

"Carly isn't your only family," Mia finally says.

"Yes, she is."

Her face set with determination, she shakes her head. "Nope. No, she's not. That baby is Rafe's, whether he sticks around or not. That baby is a Morelli. You're our family now, like it or not. I can help you with every problem you listed. I'm a stay-at-home mom with a nanny. So is Adrian's wife. If you need someone to take care of your baby while you're studying, we can do that. I told Mateo I didn't want to have babies until after I finished college for similar reasons, so I *completely* understand your concern. I love babies. I've been raising kids most of my life. Adding yours to the mix would be absolutely no problem, and it comes with the advantage that your baby would have plenty of built-in friends. I think I'm due just a couple months ahead of you, so our babies would be the same age. You've seen our playroom, right? It's kid heaven."

Smiling faintly, I tell her, "That's incredibly sweet, but—"

"I wasn't finished," she interrupts. "As far as everything else, I can't help feeling my husband is partially responsible for this. He's the one who brought Rafe into your life to begin with. If Mateo hadn't been playing games with Carly and Vince, you and Rafe probably wouldn't have even had sex that weekend."

"True. I wasn't mad about the sex; it's the condom-escaping sperm I had a problem with."

Mia cracks a smile. "What I'm saying is, you don't have to do this alone, and you don't have to drag Carly down either. *I* will help you. I'm an excellent person to have on your side, believe me. You could even stay here at the mansion with us if you wanted to. Look at this place; we have plenty of extra room. Many of the main bedrooms are like little apartments unto themselves. You would have your own bedroom, a living area, a bathroom. The only thing you wouldn't have in-suite is a kitchen, but there's this one—and we have Maria to make our meals throughout the week, which would be a nice time-saver during the school year. We could make your life much easier, Laurel. Elise and I will look after the baby whenever you're busy, and we have a library with a comfy couch, chairs, a desk —if you need quiet to study, you could stay in your room or go there, and the baby would be under the same roof, so you wouldn't even have to feel like you're never around. You could take study breaks and play with the baby, then get right back to it. You would probably be asked to come to dinners every Sunday because my husband has a thing about his Sunday dinners, but that's less a job and more being part of the family."

I want to blame hormones for the sudden swell of emotion, but I think it's organic. One thing I've never really felt I had was a family like this—Carly has always been the beginning and end of my support system. Now this woman who only knows me as her ex-boyfriend's new wife's sister wants to open her home and her family up to include me.

The kitchen door swings open, and Adrian is standing there, scowling. "What's going on in here? Did the salads grow legs and walk away?"

Waving him off, Mia says, "Just give us one more minute. Girl talk."

"Can't you girl talk after dinner? Everyone is waiting for you two to start eating."

Sighing, Mia reaches over and squeezes my hand. "Just promise me you'll consider it, okay? I don't want you to make a decision you don't want to make because you feel trapped.

Rafe is not the only one who can be there for you. Even if he is an ass, you're not alone."

I take the two salads she hands me, then balance the third on my arm and follow her back to the dining room. In the eventful few minutes we spent alone, I completely forgot that I wanted to spite Rafe by bringing Alec his salad, but since he's farther down the table, I deliver his first.

As I place his salad in front of him, Alec glances down at Rafe. Looking up at me, he mutters, "Not sure if I should thank you or not."

I can't help smiling. I feel lighter now than I did a mere few minutes ago, like the whole world is full of possibilities instead of struggles. I imagine what it would be like to live here, for this to be a regular part of my weekly routine. Studying throughout the week, relatively stress-free. No more financial woes, no more guilt over how much Carly does for me —I wouldn't even have to feel as badly about getting pregnant in the first place, because while it wasn't in the plan, it also wouldn't ruin my life. I would have a full-fledged support system, and I wouldn't be inconveniencing them, either. This huge house and all its rooms are here, whether they're full or vacant. Mia and Elise already spend their days taking care of kids, so they wouldn't be sacrificing anything by adding mine to their brood. Like Mia said, there would even be built-in socialization since my baby would have all theirs to play with. I know Elise and Adrian have a couple kids, and Mia and Mateo seem to have a whole litter.

Their playroom really is incredible, too. Hell, with all their combined child-rearing experience, they would probably do a better job than I would.

This is definitely worth considering. I'm not sure the rest of the family is as welcoming as Mia—while she seems to be the nicest person I've ever met, I'm not fooled by the calm at the table; I know her husband is another story entirely. I know that while Mateo's suave, debonair looks lead you to believe he's civilized, darkness lurks just beneath the beautiful surface. I know the man at the head of the table thinks nothing of ripping apart lives and stirring up trouble if it suits his needs. He must feel my stare, because his dark gaze catches mine now. I look away, my stomach dropping. Living with *him* would probably be unsettling, but his wife's surplus of kindness sort of balances out the intimidation factor. Plus, I wouldn't do anything to get on his bad side, so he would have no reason to zero in on my life and blow it all to shit.

Of course, I didn't do anything the first time either, when he invited Rafe into my life and landed me in this situation to begin with. I believe he's done playing with Vince's life, though. And Mia did say she's a good person to have on my side; maybe she would look out for me and ensure he didn't get bored and fuck my life up for sport.

I don't know how his supervillain mind works, so I'm not sure how you find yourself in his crosshairs. Intellectually, I am curious about him. It would be hard not to poke and prod at his mysterious mind if I lived here, but knowing the risks, I could probably force myself to refrain. Playing with Rafe is like playing with fire, but playing with Mateo is like playing with the dragon behind it. Step on his toes, and he'll crush you with the reach of his giant foot, have you for dinner, or open his mouth and torch your whole life with one exhalation. Right now he's at peace, calmly heading his family dinner, but I've seen him wreak havoc when he was barely trying—and he upset my life, and nearly wiped out Vince and Carly's whole world. I would not want to see this man operating at full-strength. If I *did* see it, I certainly wouldn't want to be on the wrong side of it.

When I put Rafe's salad down in front of him, I fully expect a reaction to my serving Alec, but his brow is furrowed with concern as he looks up at me instead. "Are you okay?"

Forcing my attention on his face, I nod. "Yeah. Why?"

"I don't know, you seem... off."

Shaking my head, I put his salad in front of him, and mine in front of me. "No, I'm... I'm really good, actually."

He frowns, still watching me, but doesn't push any further.

4

RAFE

As soon as we can feasibly get away after dinner, I haul Laurel to our bedroom. It's the same room we stayed in over Easter—specifically requested to rekindle Laurel's fondness for me. I'm not sure why she ran away from me this time, so it seems I should employ even cheap tricks if they might help my cause.

The first time I understood. I had been a dick.

This time, we were on good terms. We had a great day. I was plenty confident that I could lure her away from Sin. A little less confident when I took her back to his house and she seemed so firmly within his grasp. Right in front of me, even after our nice day together, despite *my* child growing in her womb, Laurel sank to her knees like a sinner before a holy altar, wanting to appease her master.

Luckily, I guess, Sin couldn't be appeased. I knew he was too territorial for a connection between them to survive if I set my mind on killing it, and I was right. Sin saw she clearly still had feelings for me and tapped out.

The confusing part is that after he severed things between

them, Laurel left town. Even Sin had no idea. He showed up at my house the next day looking a little haggard, to be honest. He was only there to get his assignment, but it became apparent Laurel hadn't stayed the night with me. He froze, turned away, and pulled out his phone. We scrambled to find her, but luckily Laurel leaves a blazing trail wherever she goes, so it only took about an hour.

Even better, she came to Chicago instead of Connecticut. Now that Mateo and I are allies, I have a far more aggressive reach in Chicago. She thinks she's going to Connecticut tomorrow, but that's not going to happen. Not unless she intends to show up on Carly's doorstep with my arm around her waist.

That's almost amusing enough to consider, but the long-term negative effects wouldn't be worth the momentary fun. No, I need to get back home anyway. This was not a good time for me to skip town to chase Laurel's little ass around, so bringing her back to Vegas in a timely fashion is crucial.

Right now, Laurel is somewhere else. Physically she's with me, but mentally I feel like she checked out before dinner even started. I need to find out where she went. Since she was with Mia when she disappeared, I catch her wrist and drag into the bathroom for some real privacy.

That catches her attention. Not knowing about Mateo's excessive security, she pulls back, a little hesitant. "Rafe, what are you doing?"

I drag her inside and shut the door behind me, leaning against it. "What did Mia say to you?"

Laurel's blue eyes widen, but she didn't expect me to confront her, and she can't lie for shit when she hasn't had time to rehearse first. "What are you talking about?"

"Something changed while you were in the kitchen with her. Your whole vibe was different when you came back out. If you don't tell me, I'll go ask her. She's an even worse liar than you are."

Laurel frowns at me, but looks down instead of at me. "There's nothing to lie about. I told her that I don't think you really want to have a baby with me, and she let me know you're not my only option if that's what I want to do."

My eyebrows rise in surprise. Mia is supposed to help, not offer Laurel an escape hatch. What the hell? "She's not *seriously* trying to sell you on Alec?"

Laurel rolls her eyes at me. "No, Rafe, she's not trying to sell me on Alec. She's not foisting me off on a man at all—she gave me an alternative, independent of a romantic connection."

I frown, not quite following.

Clearly uncomfortable, Laurel shrugs and turns away, but there's nowhere to go so she circles right back around. "She told me I can live here if I need to. That I can stay in Chicago and she'll help take care of the baby while I'm at school, that way I can still do everything else I want to do in *addition* to having a baby. I don't have to choose. I don't have to leave my life behind and go to Vegas, or get an abortion so Carly doesn't have to help me raise it. Mia said *she'll* help me have both. My life would more or less be uninterrupted this way."

"How helpful of her," I mutter.

Laurel's tone is snippy and defensive, so I back off. "Yes, as a matter of fact, it was."

Up to now, Laurel hasn't expressed a strong preference either way about this whole baby situation. I step forward, sliding my arms around her waist and tugging her close. "I asked you what you wanted to do, Laurel. You didn't tell me."

Still looking down instead of at me, she tucks a chunk of

hair behind her ear and admits, "I'm having a difficult time trusting you."

That's fair. Inconvenient as hell, but fair. Nodding my understanding, I tip her chin up so she has to look at me. "How can I help?"

"I don't know," she murmurs, but her eyes search mine, seeking something stable enough to hold onto. "Tell me what you want."

Simple enough. "I want you."

"Why?" she demands.

"Because I like you. What do you mean, why? I enjoy the hell out of you every time we're together, and I want to explore that. I understand relocation is a hassle, but you don't have to relocate right away. It's summer. Come spend a couple of months with me so we can see if we like each other enough for you to stick around. I realize given my position, you're the one who would have to make most of the changes and sacrifices. I understand that's not fair, but there's really nothing I can do about that. My business is in Vegas." She lets me tug her closer until she's pressed against my chest. "I'll make sure it's worth the hassle of a move, how about that?"

"I don't know," she mutters, but her fingers begin to draw shapes on my chest, so I don't believe her. "Last time you told me you'd make a trip worth my while, you definitely didn't."

"I will this time," I assure her. "Scout's honor."

Scoffing, Laurel cocks an eyebrow at me. "No way in hell were you ever a Boy Scout, Rafe Morelli."

Offering a smile I know she'll find charming, I lean a little closer and trace the curve of her jaw with my finger. "You got me. Still, I mean it. You caught me off-guard before, that's all. Ask anyone. I'm normally much better in a crisis."

My words dull her, if anything. "See, you call it a crisis.

You say you want me, but even if that's true, what if I come with a baby? What if I *do* want to go through with this pregnancy?"

This part is a little harder to sell, given my own conflicted emotions about it, but there's no time for that right now. Laurel is still of a mind to flee, and now goddamn Mia has gone and offered her a golden ticket to get away from me. At least before, I was an advantage. If she thinks she can handle all this on her own without ruining her life... well, then all I have to lure her in with is *me*, and I haven't made that package look very good to her lately.

With far more calm than the mental image of a baby brings me, I tell her, "Then that's what we'll do."

That gives her pause. Her eyes dance with vulnerability, triggering a river of relief pouring through me. I've damaged her trust in me, but she's still willing to open up. I've only fucked this up temporarily; it can still be fixed. "Really?" she asks.

"Really," I verify, nodding once. "You don't need Mia to babysit, I can hire you a nanny."

"Us," she corrects.

I lift an eyebrow in question.

"It's not *my* baby, it's *our* baby. If you hire a nanny, it's for *us*, not for *me*. We need to get a handle on this sexist bullshit right now."

"It wasn't sexist bullshit; it was a slip of tongue."

Not buying *that* bullshit, she says, "No, it was distancing language, and it's stuff exactly like this that makes me nervous about relying on you."

Gripping her shoulders, I look into her eyes. "I won't bail on you. If I'm telling you we'll have the baby, we'll have the baby. If I tell you I'll hire a nanny so you can continue your

studies, I'll hire a damn nanny. I have to be honest; I'm personally invested in you becoming a professor. You've spawned a
series of fantasies where I fuck you on, around, and near your
desk that I'm very interested in bringing to life."

Laurel bites down on her plump bottom lip, trying to hold
back a smile. "Oh, have I?"

"You have," I answer, evenly. Missing a beat, I watch her
for a moment before going on. "Remember how nice things
were between us over Easter? Remember what a nice day we
had before you skipped town? You're having my baby. I realize
it's not ideal because we don't know each other as well as two
people who are becoming parents together should, but we have
nine months to get to know each other, don't we?"

"Seven," she murmurs.

"Hm?"

"Seven months. I'm already 8 or 9 weeks, I think. I'm not
sure. I haven't gone to an appointment yet."

"Well, we should probably do that, then. Should you have
gone to an appointment by now?"

Laurel nods her head.

"We'll do that this week. I'll ask Gio who took care of his
wife when she had their daughter, have him get you an
appointment."

I watch her interest fizzle. "In Vegas?"

"Of course, in Vegas. We have to go back home, Laurel. It's
more important now than ever that I hold down the fort there,
and here I am gallivanting off to fucking Chicago. This is not
where I should be right now."

"That's not my home. It's your home. I don't want to go
back there."

"You liked it well enough a couple of days ago," I
remind her.

Laurel's gaze drops again. She's clearly not enjoying this conversation, but at least she hasn't moved away from me. I can feel right now that she wants to, and it's aggravating, but I can't shake the feeling she's thinking of Sin.

Since being coy when I need to get back to my fucking town isn't going to work, I ask outright, "Is this about him?"

There's only one *him* I could be referring to, so she nods, still looking down. "I know you won't like hearing this, but I had feelings for him and my heart still aches when I think about him. I don't want to have to see him."

She swallows and I can see by the way her chest works it must have taken quite a lot of courage to get that out. I tamp down my baser instincts, ignoring the pull of possessiveness, the irritation that Sin still matters to her so much that she would stay away from me just to avoid him. None of that is what she needs right now, and it won't help me either. I dig deeper and tap into my empathy. Into the logical reasons why it's better she tell me this than keep it a secret, even if it makes me want to punch Sin in the face and spank her straying little ass until she can't sit down.

Instead of giving her the angry retort she's braced for, I cradle her face in my hand. Her gaze jumps to me, her skittish blue eyes widening. "That's all right," I tell her. "Your heart is still tender. You invested some of it in him, and it didn't work out. It was brave of you to even try; most women glean pretty quickly that Sin is a lost cause." I'm losing her, so I switch gears and refocus. "The point is, I'm glad your heart is tender. I'm glad you're strong enough to let people into it regardless. Anyone can be callous and afraid, hiding behind walls and keeping out anyone who may hurt them. It takes real courage to take that risk, to open yourself up to someone like him, someone like me, knowing you could get hurt. Even if you feel afraid, you don't let fear stop you, Laurel. You offer yourself up and you grab for what you want, even if it's scary. I admire the hell out of that. I'm glad that when you offer your heart to someone, you take it seriously." Now I place my hand over her heart. "Because I know the same thing will be true when I'm the one it belongs to."

5

LAUREL

When it belongs to him, he says.

Not if, but when.

I like all his words, but in most of my experience with him, Rafe has always been good at saying the right thing. He's almost *too* good at it, making it hard to trust. Can something that comes so easily be real? I know Rafe can spin bullshit effortlessly—so is he just bullshitting me?

He watches me for a moment, then looks down. "Can I tell you about the last time I gave *my* heart away?"

That surprises the hell out of me. Rafe doesn't strike me as a man who shares his heartaches; he strikes me more as someone who pretends they never happened. A little off-kilter, I nod my head. "Of course."

"Remember the half-naked blonde who was in my house the other day?"

Smiling faintly, I nod my head. "How could I forget?"

"Well, it was her. It was a long time ago, but she's the last person I let myself really fall for. I had instincts early on that I was making a mistake, that she wasn't what she portrayed herself as, but she made me feel things that I... that I just hadn't felt in a long time. I convinced myself that my doubts were just bachelorhood pangs, old issues coming out to play. I dated more before Cassandra. I liked relationships because I enjoyed having a chance to really get to know my partner. Ordinarily, I don't play the way I want to with hook-ups."

"Like with me?"

"I played a little more with you than usual. I wouldn't normally make a hook-up kneel for me. Most women do like it, regardless of whether or not they expect to, but it's just not the sort of thing you do with a woman you won't see again. To me, a good, healthy relationship with a submissive woman takes time to build. There should be an immediate connection, a sense that you could have something with that person, but the most important thing between a dom and his sub is her trust. Everything revolves around that, and two strangers rubbing up against each other in the night can't have that. You need to be together in a relationship to attune yourselves to one another's needs. With a one-nighter, you can experience that spark, that connection, that feeling of synchronicity like something could grow out of it, but without tending, the spark dies. I felt that with you over Easter, that's why I asked you to Vegas in the first place. I wanted to prolong the feeling without committing. I haven't had that with a lot of women since Cassandra. To be honest, as much as I enjoy it, I've avoided it and sought out casual hook-ups with women who weren't right for me. I wouldn't be tempted to keep them. Didn't want to take that risk. To be clear, I was never like that before Cassandra."

I nod my understanding. "Did she break your heart?"

His lips curve up faintly, like it's funny. "Shattered it."

Hit with a wave of tenderness, I reach up to touch his lips, wiping away the smile. "That's not funny. Don't play it off."

"I don't know if she ever even liked me, or I was just the most powerful person she could get her claws into at the time. I do know when a competitor with more power expressed interest, she left me like it was the easiest thing she'd ever done in her life. Like we were partners on a project in a class she no longer cared about passing, rather than two people in a committed relationship. I didn't see it coming, and it made me question my judgment. How could I have such a strong connection with someone who was lying the whole time? I notice everything; how did I miss *that*? I still don't know the answer."

How could I have such a strong connection with someone who was lying the whole time?

Knowing he doesn't know the truth about my time with Sin, I can't believe he said something I relate to so completely. I felt all the things he's mentioning—the spark, the synchronicity, the connection so real I would stake my heart on it... and it all turned out to be bullshit. Absent-minded manipulation on his part, while I was falling in love.

Sighing, I tell Rafe, "Love makes fools of us all. Sometimes you see what you want to see instead of what's there. If you believe something hard enough, it feels like the truth, even if it's utter bullshit."

Nodding once, he says, "Yeah, well, our relationship was definitely bullshit, but it was bullshit I believed in. Since then, I've played my way with women I know like it, but can do it casually, or I have vanilla hook-ups with women I know I won't be tempted to keep. Cassandra was my last serious girlfriend. Anyway, the point is, I survived that and I'm still here, and I'm sure you've survived heartache before. You only knew Sin for a few days. You'll be over him before you know it."

It felt like longer.

I don't tell Rafe that, for obvious reasons. There's little point telling him I had a stronger connection with the jerk who didn't actually care about me than guys I had full-fledged relationships with. Maybe it was just because Sin is more on my level. Maybe my level *is* closer to theirs, and I just never knew. Perhaps that's why I've never been fully stimulated by run-of-the-mill guys. I guess I was just waiting around for a dominant sociopath to notice me.

"What's funny?" Rafe inquires, watching my face.

I hadn't noticed I was smiling, but I guess I am. I shake my head. "Nothing. Just wondering how I got this fucked up."

The corners of his mouth tug upward. "How fucked up?"

"I'm in the house of Chicago's most ruthless criminal, standing in a bedroom with a Vegas boss whose baby I'm carrying, talking about the murderous enforcer I got tangled up with." I don't even bother adding that said murderous enforcer *kidnapped* me, since Rafe doesn't know that. Definitely can't be specific about him tying me to the bed and fucking my mouth.

A pang of arousal strikes me, so I shove those thoughts away. That's not helpful, dammit. I need to stop being turned on by thoughts of Sin. Thoughts of that horrible night should be enough to dampen any arousal, but instead I just think of how I felt when he grabbed my wrists and backed me up against the wall, mid-heartbreak. I still wanted the asshole to fuck me. Even as he ripped my heart out, I wanted him to claim it—and me—for himself.

There's something wrong with my brain.

I didn't want Rafe to fuck me when *he* was being a heartless asshole.

This train is going off-track, fast. Shaking it off, I turn my attention back to Rafe before I start visualizing Sin walking over to the bed to tie me up, that perfect ass on display as he dropped his clothes in the laundry basket. The most mundane shit, and still I miss it.

"Distract me," I tell Rafe.

Cocking an eyebrow at me, he says, "I'm the one who gives the orders around here, kitten."

"Please?" I add, with pointed sweetness.

A smile claims his lips and he steps away from the bathroom door, opening it up and stepping back outside. I don't know why he dragged me into the bathroom to begin with, but before I can ask, he says, "Much better."

He takes my hand and leads me back into the bedroom, but he's not doing the job I need him to do. I understand why he isn't—he's not on solid ground with me right now. Due to his own fuck-ups, he lost all the ground he had, and now he has less than he had the moment he met me.

The problem is, Sin is still in my head, and with Rafe still playing catch-up, Mia's offer looks much better to me than anything that brings me back to Vegas. I'm not completely closed-off to giving Rafe a shot, but I've never been as close to him as I got to Sin, and I'm honestly terrified of how I'll feel the first time Sin walks through the door. They work closely, so I know it will happen. Hell, they're friends. I won't just see Sin once in a great while, I'll see him often. How do I do that? How do I look at him like a normal person now, like a friend of my *boyfriend*, if things actually progress with Rafe? Will the impulse still be there to drop to my knees and worship his body? I know it won't come up, but will I still *want* to? That will be torture.

I've never had to be friends with an ex before, so I'm damn sure not primed for whatever this is. Hell, even adoring Sin, Rafe could stir up some of my feelings. How do you look at someone you've been so intimate with and act like they're nothing to you?

"Laurel."

The sharpness of Rafe's tone and his serious expression lead me to believe he spoke to me, and I must have missed it. "Sorry. What?"

"What would you like to play?"

Play? I don't think I agreed to playing. I know what kind of play he likes—it involves both of us naked and doing things my heart isn't ready for. Purposely obtuse, I brighten. "Cards?"

His tone completely dead, Rafe repeats, "Cards."

I nod my head, even though I don't technically know how to play poker. It seems like a game he would be into. "Sure. Let's play poker. I don't have much money, so you'll have to front me some."

Faintly smirking, he tells me, "I don't think you can afford my interest rates."

"Come on," I say, trying to entice him. "You're Mr. Vegas. You must like poker, right?"

"The fact that you want to play two-person poker makes me think you're not much good at it. Strip poker? You're not wearing much. That won't take long."

I lose a little enthusiasm. "Strip poker? I don't know how to play that."

"Easy," he says, smoothly. "You lose a hand, you remove an article of clothing. Then you don't have to borrow money from the mob—you have all the currency required to play."

"I'm only wearing a dress, panties, and a bra. I don't even have socks."

"Damn," he says dryly.

Trying to lure him away from the end game of getting me naked, I tease him. "I think you're just afraid you'll lose if we play it straight. The big, bad, Vegas boss beaten by a 19-year-old science nerd."

His hands shoot out, grasping my wrist, and he pulls me onto his lap faster than I can blink. My heart skitters, and Rafe situates my thighs around his hips so I'm straddling him. "I feel I should warn you, I don't do well with brats, kitten. You know what brats get? Brats get punished, and you've already racked up quite a debt these past few days."

It's harder to keep a safe distance when I'm straddling his lap, inches from his handsome face. "I have a debt? I didn't borrow anything."

His eyes follow the curve of my shoulder and move along my breasts—then his finger follows the same trail. His light caress is usually relaxing, but it feels a touch foreboding right now. "You didn't borrow anything, strictly speaking, but you gave something away. Something that was supposed to belong to me." One hand settles on my hip and the other moves around the back of me to grasp my ass. "I know you're still sad right now, so I'll be nice. I won't make you pay me back just yet."

My heart pounds harder as he leans forward, brushing his lips tenderly across my collar bone.

"But remember, I have steep interest rates, kitten, so you'll want to start working off your debt soon. Wouldn't want you getting in over your head."

That shouldn't be sexy. Nothing should stir, knowing that while he's only playing with me, he probably means all these things when he says them to other people. The man whose lap I'm in probably ruins lives on the regular—issues hits and takes them altogether, if people get out of line. Why does that turn me on?

I feel like pushing him a little, so instead of keeping quiet or accommodating him, I decide to be a brat. "What if I don't want to pay you back? What if I don't think I owe you anything?"

I don't notice him drawing the material of my dress up around my waist until it's already done and his fingers dig into the soft globes of my nearly bare ass. My panties are so thin beneath his strong hands, so insignificant. He pulls me forward, forcing me against the hardness of his cock. He still has trousers on, but I know how quickly he could shed them.

His voice comes out rough as he drags me across his cock again. "You're testing the limits of my kindness."

I know I'm not ready for this, but my body—once again—is behind the times. I can't help the physical response I have to what he's doing, and for a moment, I wonder if I should just give in. Let him shut my brain off and fill my body full of pleasure. I know he can do it. He's done it before. I don't know how I would feel afterward, but at least while he's inside me I know I'll feel incredible.

Doing my best to resist the temptation even as he rocks his cock against my pussy again, I murmur, "Where did we land on that poker game?"

"Two-person poker isn't much fun," he tells me, running a slow hand up my thigh.

I catch his wrist, stopping him from sliding that devious hand between my legs. "Even strip poker?"

He dips forward and kisses the exposed ball of my shoulder. "That turns into fucking within a few minutes. We could skip the card-playing and get right to it."

Looking at his shoulder instead of his face, I tell him, "I'm not ready."

"Let go of my wrist and I bet I can make a liar out of you," he tells me.

"I don't mean my *body* isn't ready. My body is ready. My heart isn't. My head isn't."

Rafe sighs, but he doesn't break my grasp and push further, which he could easily do. A moment passes in silence, then he says, "We could invite Mateo and Mia."

My eyes widen and I lean back. "Excuse me?"

His eyes dance with mischief. "To strip poker. More fun with more people."

"No way. Are you nuts? I'm not taking my clothes off in front of them."

"Why not?" he asks lightly, his gaze dropping to my chest. His hands follow and he squeezes my breasts like he has a right to.

"Because aside from Mia being gorgeous, your cousin is terrifying. When I catch his glance, I lose a year off my life. My assumption is that nudity draws his gaze move frequently than sitting at the dinner table fully dressed. I'd drop dread by the end of the game."

"I won't lie and say he's not a shit-stirrer, but he only has eyes for Mia. Unless you plan on playing with her, you don't have to worry about snagging his attention."

Biting back a smile, I say, "That suggestion came a little too easily."

He plays at innocence—which is a joke. "What do you mean? I hate watching two beautiful women play with each other. It's just the worst."

I shove him in the shoulder. "I'm not into girls."

"You don't have to be into girls to play with them. Some kissing, some petting... I might be willing to knock down some of your debt for a little supervised playtime."

I shake my head at him. "This isn't going to happen. I'm not even completely sold on *you*, so I'm definitely not going to make out with a girl for your viewing pleasure."

"Hmm," he murmurs, reaching behind my back and tugging my zipper down. "You're not being very playful tonight, kitten." Taking my hand and placing it on his crotch, he asks, "What am I supposed to do about this?"

"Why don't you *imagine* me doing your bidding and get yourself off to that."

His eyes narrow on my face, then he grabs a fistful of my hair and moves me off his lap.

"Rafe..." I begin, as he lowers me to the floor by the hair on my head.

"Quiet," he says, using his free hand to take his cock out.

Tummy taut with uncertainty, I look up at him. My heart pounds wildly in my chest, while a deeper, more primal part of me latches onto the feeling of being where I belong. I'm like a cornered animal, balancing here on my hands and knees with Rafe's firm grip on my hair. My heart knows it isn't ready to do this all over again, but something deeper craves the domination.

Still, I have to object. "Rafe, please, I'm not ready."

My words don't faze him. The sight of his long, thick cock reminds me what it felt like when he first pushed it inside me. The way I cried out and grasped for purchase above me, certain he wouldn't fit. The instant pleasurable friction as his sizable instrument rubbed my walls the way no cock had before. I'd never come so fast, and he hadn't even touched my clit. Prior to that moment, that was the only way I got off.

And that was only the beginning. Not even the appetizer, more a glance at the menu.

Fuck, I am out of my depths here.

Rafe jerks my head forward and I swallow my nerves, biting down on my lower lip as I eye up his dick.

"Put it in your mouth."

I lean forward and open up, taking just the tip between my lips. I forgot his taste, but the salty flavor hits my tongue now as I drag it across his smooth head. I tell myself it's already done, he's already in my body, but something within me still resists.

Sin.

The part that still belongs to him, probably.

Double fuck.

My skin is hot, and I don't know whether it's from arousal, a faint sense of shame, or both. I pull my mouth off Rafe's dick and rear back, but he doesn't let up on my hair even a little bit. In fact, he tugs harder, spinning me around until I'm on my ass with my back pressed against the bed. I see his legs on either side of me, and I fight his hold, tugging my own hair even though it hurts.

"Let go," I tell him.

His chuckle is a low hum in my ear as he leans down, locking an arm around my neck to draw me backward. His mouth hovers near my ear. I gasp in surprise and try to break free, but there's no point. "You only had a taste," he tells me. "You're gonna take more than that tonight, kitten. I want you to kneel for me."

I tip my head so I can meet his eyes when I glare at him. "No."

Rafe shakes his head as if in disappointment, clucking his

tongue. All at once, he releases my hair and my neck, but then he grabs me, lifts me, and dumps my body on the bed.

I go to skitter back, but get caught on the dress. Rafe smirks at me as he kicks off his slacks, then climbs on the bed with me. "Last chance," he tells me.

What does that mean? I don't have time to figure it out. Rafe grabs a fistful of my hair again and turns me over on my tummy. Cool air hits my legs as he drags my dress up, and he runs a hand over my ass. Before I have time to protest, Rafe draws his hand back and brings it down against my ass with a sharp smack.

I gasp, outraged. "Rafe!"

He yanks my hair, pulling me back like a bow. "Yes, kitten?" he answers, calmly. "Are you ready to suck my cock like a good girl?"

"Screw you," I mutter.

"Maybe," he answers, running his hand over the stinging spot on my ass. "I am looking forward to claiming this pretty little cunt again. I don't even have to wear a condom now. I'll feel every silky inch of you this time, won't I?"

My head isn't in the right place, so that feels like a threat. Like a thing to avoid. I know Rafe has no real intention of hurting me, he's only playing rough, but the fear that travels down my spine would seem to indicate otherwise.

Since I haven't amended my bratty behavior, Rafe brings another firm hand across my ass, then another. After the third swat, however, he pushes two fingers between my legs and rubs.

I moan helplessly, not wanting to get lost. I wanted it before. I wanted to submit to all the glorious torment he was putting my body through. I wanted to feel him move inside me, to brace myself on the bed while he fucked me like an animal.

When he rubs me now, when my body responds to him, I feel like a whore, and not in the sexy way. In the way that some confused part of my brain still feels like it belongs tied to Sin's bed. I wouldn't fight him like this—not unless he wanted me to, at least.

While physical pleasure builds from the rhythmic caress of Rafe's fingers, my heart is twisting itself up in knots. Sin's face flashes to mind and I try to crawl away, but Rafe shifts, pinning me to the bed with his knee and sliding a finger inside me. The passage is slick and easy. My breath catches and I try to wiggle my hips away, but a sharp stab of pleasure soars through me instead. I want to object, to make him stop, but my body wants the release more.

"Rafe," I cry, closing my eyes.

He still has my head pulled back, but now he leans down to brush his lips across mine while he finger fucks me. I'm crawling out of my skin from the pleasure, so close I could cry.

"You want to come for me, kitten?"

I keep my eyes squeezed shut, but jerkily nod my head yes.

His tone is hard with displeasure and his grip on my hair tightens. "Is that how you ask?"

"Please. I want..." I grind against his hand, hating myself even as I seek release.

"Say it," he demands. "Tell me who you want to come for, kitten."

"Please don't make me," I say instead.

"I can give you my cock instead," he offers, mildly.

I swallow, still resisting, but when he moves I don't know if his next position will be between my legs, so I give up. "I want you to make me come, Rafe."

He rewards me with a soft kiss on the lips as his fingers

work my pussy. "See, now, that wasn't so bad, was it?" he murmurs against my lips. "Come for me now, Laurel."

I cry out until my voice wavers, ending on a muted scream. Rafe lets go of my hair and I bury my face in the pillow, clutching it with both hands as he draws out my orgasm just to punish me. It's a strange punishment, but it's like he knows right now it's the perfect one. My body needed the orgasm, but now he's just making me fucking revel in it.

I want to hit him, but I don't have the strength. The orgasm finally subsides, but I can't catch my breath. As soon as I do, I'm going to give him a piece of my mind.

Before I can make good on my silent threats, he rolls me over on my back, pins me down with his thighs, and starts stroking his cock, way too close to my face. My gaze darts up at him. "What are you doing?"

"Taking your mouth," he states.

"No," I object, shaking my head wildly. "No."

"Then stop me," he says, easily.

Yeah, right. He has me pinned here like—

Then it hits me. I have a safe word. I can stop any of this, I just forgot. Before I can decide whether or not to utter it, it's too late—Rafe pushes his cock inside my mouth, and then there's no talking. Fuck. I grab onto his thigh and look up at him as he eases his cock about halfway in.

All of a sudden, the fight goes out of me. He has me effectively pinned. He won. My mouth is so full of him I can't speak, and my body is still humming from the spitefully long orgasm he gave me.

There's little point fighting him now. He'll take my throat or he'll let me suck his cock—one or the other is going to happen. Maybe both, because I can't stop it.

Your mouth will be too full of my cock to use your safe word.

Ouch. Tears sting behind my eyes at the memory, so different from this one. Sin's tenderness as he teased me. He ridiculed my safe word, but still reminded me I had one. I didn't need one. I wanted him to invade me—and he did. And he's still there, even though he shouldn't be.

I close my eyes, afraid Rafe will notice them shining. I guess with his dick lodged halfway to my throat is a good time to get teary-eyed if I have to. If I can't keep my shit together, I'll just lean up and take him deep. He'll think it's his cock making my eyes water instead of the memory of someone else's.

This should be an escape. Sex should shut my brain off. It did before, but now the thing I'm running from is stuck here with me. Even halfway across the fucking country, I feel this torn. Sin may as well be standing in this room watching me right now.

If he were, I'd drop to my knees and beg for the chance to worship him. I wouldn't fight his domination like I've fought Rafe's tonight; I would welcome it.

What is wrong with me?

He doesn't even want me. I shouldn't feel this way.

The taste of Rafe's release in my mouth brings me back to what I'm doing, to my mouth working the wrong dick. Thankfully, Rafe wasn't paying attention to any inner turmoil I was experiencing; he was too busy getting his dick sucked. I need to get my shit together, fast.

Rafe climbs off me and drops to the bed beside me, curling an arm around my waist and pulling me snugly against him. "Mm, that was fun."

"Yeah," I murmur, resting my hand on his arm.

I should have at least tried to muster more enthusiasm. "What's wrong?" he asks, carefully.

I sigh heavily, shaking my head. "I don't know. There's something wrong with me."

"Why is there something wrong with you?"

Because I think of your enforcer while your cock is in my mouth.

Can't say that. "Tell me something," I say instead.

"All right."

"You have had sex with *many* women, right? Many of whom you probably still have to see after the fact in a non-sexual capacity."

"Sure, sometimes."

"How do you shut it off?" I ask. "How do you stop thinking about them like that after you've experienced something so intimate together?"

He's quiet for a moment, then he says, "Well, to begin with, it helps not to think of it that way. View it more as a transaction—you're two people who want to get off, so you want the same thing. You find one another attractive, and you can help each other out. You get in, get out, move on. It's not intimacy; it's just a mutually pleasurable physical activity. Like jogging together, but more fun."

"But what if it isn't? What if isn't a cold exchange like that? I'm talking about when you have feelings involved, not... not that."

"Well, then you're generally fucked in a much less fun way," he says, easily. "Catching feelings is a bad idea unless you're in a relationship."

I don't know what to ask now.

Rafe seems to understand. "You'll get over him, Laurel. It's still fresh. You're young and open-hearted, so you let him in much deeper than you should have. You're paying a higher emotional toll than you should have to, but it won't go on forever."

This is so weird. Barely a minute after exchanging our own intimacies, curled up in his embrace, and talking about the heartache I'm feeling over someone else.

"I think you'll ruin me if I go with you," I tell him honestly.

He says nothing for a long while, then his hand drifts down my torso and he splays it over my abdomen. "I think I already have."

6

LAUREL

My phone buzzes for what seems like the millionth time since touching down at the airport in Nevada. My sister has been a good sport, but she's at her wit's end.

I completely get it. I had to ask her to buy me a plane ticket home after I landed in Chicago because I was out of money, and then this morning I had to text her and tell her not to come to pick me up at the airport, because I wasn't ready to leave Chicago.

Her text messages are beginning to look like missives from an angry sailor.

I sigh, turning the phone face-down in my lap and trying to ignore the guilt. I look out the car window as we pass the strip, and Rafe's hand settles casually on my thigh.

"Everything all right?" he asks.

I tear my gaze from the buildings passing by and look over at him. "It's Carly again. She doesn't understand what's going on. I'm going to have to tell her the truth before she loses her mind. If we're going to go through with this, there's no reason to keep lying to her."

Rafe nods his agreement. "We'll call her tomorrow and clue her in."

That sounds good. A tiny weight falls off my shoulders. No, it's not done, but Rafe has said it will be, so I don't have to keep thinking about it. Since I have so much else on my mind, that's a good thing.

"I have a surprise for you when we get home," he tells me.

"You do? I thought I deserved punishment, not surprises," I tease.

His eyes are warm, even as he slides me a dry look. "You deserve lots of punishment, but that doesn't mean I don't want to give you nice things from time to time. Once you learn your place, you'll get plenty more nice things."

"Hmph. Learn my place."

Now he smirks, enjoying getting a rise out of me—even if just a little one. "I have a lot of work to do tonight, so unless you want to tag along, you'll have to entertain yourself. You can unpack whatever Mia sent with you and Juanita will make you dinner."

I perk up. "I'm allowed to tag along?"

Rafe nods. "For some of it. I have a couple errands to run first, so I'll have to go out without you this afternoon, but this evening when I have to go to the casino you can come if you want to. Afterward, we'll grab dinner and finish off the night at one of my favorite clubs."

"All right, I'll tag along."

"Great. You can go shopping this afternoon then, pick out a dress. Unfortunately, I don't have a closet full of women's clothing for you to raid."

He had to go and bring up Sin, didn't he? I've been

stressing enough all morning about the possibility of seeing him today. I hoped Rafe would warn me one way or another, but he hasn't mentioned Sin even indirectly before now. Initially, I was afraid it would be Sin who picked us up at the airport, but it turned out Rafe's car was there, so we didn't need anyone to drive us. Now I'm wondering if Sin will be at the club later.

I just need to get the first sighting over with, that's all. I barely slept all night, despite the warm body curled up with me or the soft, comfortable mattress we were sleeping on. Instead, I wallowed in Sin some more, then around the time the sun came up, concluded that this craving is all in my head. I'm making more of it than I need to because I *am* less experienced with this sort of thing. Look at Rafe—after I had sex with him, I let myself believe I needed to come to Las Vegas to tell him I was pregnant, just on the off chance he'd be romantic instead of practical and tell me to keep it. Even if those feelings weren't like these, even though I never felt heartache with Rafe, I felt enough fondness to want to see him again.

For whatever reason, it's just more intense this time. I don't know why. Maybe because of raging pregnancy hormones?

I should probably stop blaming the baby for everything and take some responsibility. I have made a *mess* of my life, and I have no idea if I'm on track to cleaning it up or making it worse. Logic tells me I should have broken free of this twisted web and hauled ass back to Connecticut. Some other demented part of me said, "Eh, let's see where this goes" and apparently I listened to that crazy bitch instead.

As much as I'm dreading it, I want to see Sin again. I'm hoping against hope that when he appears, I will be fine. Whatever spell I was under will be broken, and relief will pour through me. No longer his captive, I will be free to move on with my life—whether that means giving Rafe a fair shot, heading back to Chicago to let Mia help me out with single parenting, or going home to Carly in Connecticut. Wherever I go from here, I will be able to go without this albatross around my neck. Without the feeling that I'm missing a part of myself, that I left it chained to Sin's bed and I need to go back for it.

The desire to sink to my knees will dissipate, and whatever fever has struck me will suddenly be cured.

I crave wellness, and I don't think I can have it again until I face my demon. Rafe is not my demon; Sin is.

Rafe parks the car in his driveway. This place shouldn't even feel vaguely comfortable to me, but I've been without a home of my own for so long at this point, bounced around from place to place, I'm pretty much open to whatever. Rafe's house is big and gorgeous—though, not as big as the one back in Chicago. Rafe doesn't have a bunch of people living under this roof, though. It's just him, and now I guess me.

He unlocks the front door and thrusts it open, gesturing for me to go inside first. He trails behind with a suitcase. I didn't have a suitcase with me, but before Mia would let us leave, she gave me one of hers, filled with clothing. Some gender-neutral baby clothing none of hers got a chance to wear with tags still on, the maternity stuff she bought for me, prenatal vitamins when she found out I wasn't taking any, and various other things she told me I needed.

This kid needs a closet already, and it has barely made the transition from embryo to fetus.

We head left into his living room, and I halt, gasping, as I see my surprise.

The whole set of blue, leather-bound Brontë books I yearned for at the rare bookstore are lined up on Rafe's coffee table. I turn around, eyes wide. "The Brontë books?"

"Surprise," he says, smiling warmly.

I throw my arms around his neck and give him a big hug for that one. "Holy hell, Rafe. Thirteen thousand dollars worth of books isn't a surprise, it's... I don't know what, but it's a step beyond a surprise."

His arms encircle my body and he gives me a firm hug back, but now all I want to do is look at my presents. Breaking away, I rush over to the coffee table and drop to my knees, this time for something unquestionably worthy—books.

I grab *The Professor* first and flip it open, running reverent fingers over the title page. If he notices, Rafe will probably think I'm a freak, but I don't even care; I lean in and smell the pages, closing my eyes as I breathe in their aroma.

Of course, he notices.

"My God, you are a nerd," Rafe states, clearly amused, as he drops onto the couch and leans back to watch me.

"It's a great smell." I hold open the book like an offering. "Take a whiff, you'll see."

Folding his arms over his broad chest, he shakes his head. "I'm all right."

I explore the books for a few more minutes, wondering that I actually own them. Actually, I'm not sure I *do* own them. More likely, as long as things work out with Rafe, I own them. I'm sure if I leave, the books don't leave with me.

Still, I never dreamed I would own these under any circumstances when we looked at them that day, and I'm feeling grateful. So I crawl around the coffee table, noting the way Rafe's amber eyes warm, and I climb up on his lap. I straddle him like I did many moons ago, bracing my hands on his shoulders. Then I lean in and brush my lips against his. One of his hands moves around to the small of my back, the other settling on my hip and he pulls me closer. I go easily, closing my eyes and letting myself enjoy the moment of tenderness.

As many doubts as I still have, I really don't want to sabotage this before we even have a chance to take off. Rafe and I have never been a couple before; we've never invested in one another. As recently as a week ago, I didn't even know who Sin was, and look how I felt for him by the end of it all.

I'm sure I can do that with Rafe too, but only if I let it happen. Seeing as I'm pregnant with his baby, I might as well give it a shot.

"Thank you," I say again, when I pull back.

"You are welcome," he assures me. "You'll have to check out the library and let me know if there are any more unacceptable missing pieces. Make me a wishlist, and maybe you'll get more."

"Mm, I like book gifts," I tell him, leaning my head on his shoulder. "We should start buying baby books. We could go to the bookstore and pick out one every week, that way when the baby is born, we'll already have a little library going."

"We could do that."

I don't know what kind of parents we're going to be with our mish-mashed lifestyles. I don't know what kind of life we'll have, what kind of love we'll foster between us. Right now so much is unknown, and as positive as I want to be, I can't shake the feeling of there being insurmountable barriers between us and happiness.

I tell myself it's because this is new, and it probably is. I haven't been in a relationship with Rafe before, so literally everything remains to be seen. We took a few steps forward, a couple giant leaps back, and then—oh, yeah—there's the minor complication of my falling for someone else.

I swear to myself if I could fall for Sin in four days, I can fall for Rafe...eventually. After I see Sin and I'm okay. After my heart heals and is willing to open up again.

It's not open right now, and I feel guilty for that. Even though I realize logically I don't owe Rafe anything, I recognize that he's making an effort. Not with the books, but by dragging me here in the first place. By wanting a relationship with me when he just told me last night he hasn't had one since he got his heart broken.

Most of all, I don't want to be the next person he lets in, and also the next person to ding up his heart. If I could give my heart to him to take care of, maybe I would, but I don't possess it just yet. The damn thing is still cuffed to a bed across town, and I can only hope I get it back soon.

7

RAFE

It's going to be a long, probably unpleasant day, so I figured I may as well dive right into the deep end. I'm sitting in my car, looking at the video call I just made as it connects. I called from a blocked number, so I wasn't sure she would even answer, but my screen suddenly fills up with a giant blonde, messy bun and the pretty face of Carly Price—well, Carly Morelli, I guess, now that she's married. Her face loses some of the pretty and turns thunderous instead when she see me.

I offer an obnoxiously charming smile. "Hi, Carly."

Her blue eyes narrow. "Satan."

My grin widens. She fucking hates me. I love it.

Skipping straight to the point, she asks, "Do you have my sister?"

"I do."

Slamming her fist down on some hard surface beneath her, she says, "I fucking knew it."

"That's why I'm calling, obviously."

"Oh, it wasn't for our weekly book club?" she asks sarcastically.

These Price women are not nearly as intimidated by me as they should be. Since there's no way this goes well anyway, I don't waste time greasing the wheels. "Laurel is going to call you tomorrow with some news you're not going to be happy about, and I'm calling ahead to let you know. This way you can process today and adjust your response tomorrow. Regardless of how you feel about it, tomorrow when your sister calls you with this news, you're going to be happy for her. For *us*. You're going to treat it like good news, and offer your support."

Dread has already transformed her face. "What have you done?"

"Laurel is pregnant."

Her face goes blank, then fills up with horror. Carly buries her face in her hands, like I've delivered news of a death instead of an impending birth. It's insulting, but I get it. Given who I am, this is sort of a death—the death of whatever life Laurel might have known before. Where once she may have had normalcy, now she will be forever tied to me. Her fate permanently entwined with mine.

I took over the empire Carly's husband should have inherited, and now Laurel will be at my side. From a traditional standpoint, it's hard to see it going any other way now that she's having my kid. Whether ours is a love for the ages or a marriage of convenience remains to be seen, but she is mine, either way. Even without understanding that part, this is a life Carly didn't want to deal with herself, let alone inflict upon her little sister.

I understand all that from an objective standpoint, but this is all I've ever known. It doesn't seem so bad to me. I think I'm offering Laurel a pretty sweet deal, as a matter of fact. Plenty of women before her have tried—and failed—to earn the position she gets to fall right into.

"This can't be happening," Carly says to herself. "This cannot be happening."

"Now, she's terrified to tell you," I add, once I've given Carly a minute and she's verbal again. "On top of everything else that's stressful for her right now, that's the big one. She knows you don't like me. She doesn't think you'll be happy that she's pregnant by anyone, least of all by me."

Returning her attention to me, she glares. "Of *course* I'm not happy she's pregnant. She is 19-years-old, you son of a bitch. She has her whole life ahead of her—a life that will *not* include you, I'll tell you that right now. No fucking way. No way is my sister getting pulled into the torrential downpour of fuckery that is your family. Nope. Fuck this. I'm calling her right now. This ends today."

"I wouldn't do that, if I were you," I advise her. "See, this is why I called ahead of time, so we could iron out these little wrinkles. Today you can vent your anger at me—I can take it. But tomorrow when *Laurel* calls, you're going to respond with something more like excitement. You're going to be surprised, sure, but ultimately happy. Tap into your love for babies. Are hookers wired with that, or...?"

"Fuck you. At least I got paid. You whore around for free." Her eyes widen and she shoots a look over her shoulder. Probably lost her cool and forgot about Vince. He must not be in the room, because beneath her fury, she looks faintly relieved when she looks back at me. "This is not happening," she tells me.

"It is happening. It's already done. I'm letting you know my expectations of you, and I know you're smart enough not to disappoint me."

"Oh, you know that, do you?" she asks, sarcastically. "Funny, I'm not so sure *I* know that."

"Well, in the event you've forgotten the breadth of my reach, let me remind you that Mateo told me all about your past. I know Laurel has no idea what you resorted to in order to support her, but imagine how devastated she would be if she did."

Eyes narrowed with more than dislike, Carly says, "You don't give a damn about my sister, do you?"

Ignoring her, I go on. "For that matter, I would hate to have to tell *Vince* your secrets. Not the whoring part, obviously. The working for Mateo part. Much worse than whoring to him, don't you think?"

Carly closes her eyes and covers her mouth with one hand, taking a breath. She knows I have her cornered. In an abstract way, she has known that since she came to Vegas and I let her know that I have access to all her dirtiest secrets. Didn't think I'd actually need to use them, just liked fucking with her. Now I'm pretty fucking relieved to have dirt on her. I can collapse her whole life with just a few whispers, and she knows it.

For me, Easter was a vacation. For Carly, it was a trial she barely survived. I got to laze around in bed with Laurel, exchanging meaningless stories and orgasms, but Carly had to fight with all her might just to keep from sinking. Mateo was firing missiles at her life, and Vince was struggling to stay away from Mia's siren call. Not that Mia had any idea she was doing anything to tempt him, of course. She merely existed, and that was enough. Mia doesn't understand or have control over her powers, but damn, that woman really does pull people in. She nearly pulled Laurel in last night, and I didn't think *I* had to worry about that. Mia likes me. She's on my side (as long as I'm on her husband's side, anyway). She just can't help herself.

People crave acceptance, even when they fuck up, and Mia wants to give it to them. Somehow she still hasn't figured out how seductive that is to those of us who fuck up the most.

She's only trying to be nice, but it's damned inconvenient for the people who want to keep what she lures away with her endless well of love. Though I guess it would have been kind of funny if Mia had stolen my girl. I would have had to laugh. Her husband already yanked one from me years ago, so he would've found that pretty damn amusing, too.

Back to the task at hand, I focus on Carly. She still hasn't spoken, so I go on. "This doesn't have to be a disaster, Carly. Laurel can be happy here. I'll take good care of her. You and I don't have to be enemies, either. I'm willing to put all this behind us and start over if you are."

Carly shakes her head, looking down instead of at me. "You have ruined my little sister's life, and *you're* willing to put it all behind us and start fresh. You Morellis really are a noble bunch, aren't you?" she replies, scathingly.

"Look, I'm being nice," I tell her, showing my hands in a gesture of innocence. "I don't have to be. You have no power here. Sure, you could tell your sister you don't approve and make this even harder on her than it already is, but that only hurts Laurel. It's not going to faze me. I'm still going to keep her here; my life with Laurel will go on completely without a hitch. If you want to hurt your sister, by all means, react poorly tomorrow. It will piss me off and I *will* ruin your life as payback, but hey, if that's what you need to do, knock yourself out. It won't change a damn thing."

"I didn't think I could hate anyone more than Mateo for dragging you into my sister's path to begin with, but I was wrong. You've topped my list."

RAFE | 71

Clasping my chest theatrically, I tell her, "You're breaking my heart here, Vivian."

"I hope someone murders you. And not in a badass way, no blazing glory, something really lame, like... they inject some kind of slow-acting poison into your veins, and you drop dead surfing for porn on the toilet."

Smiling, I tell her, "I don't have to surf for porn; I can just go to my bedroom and look at your naked sister stretched prettily across my bed."

Grimacing, she says, "So much hatred. An immeasurable quantity of hatred."

Glancing out my front windshield, I tell Carly, "As much fun as this is, I have to hang up now. I just wanted to prepare you, give you time to work up a convincing performance. Laurel has enough to deal with right now and she doesn't need to add your disapproval to the list."

"What about school? Have you even considered what you're going to do to her life, Rafe?"

"Of course I have. She's having my child; what would you have me do about it?"

Shaking her head and lifting her well-shaped eyebrows, Carly says, "Not this."

I could spend the next ten minutes repeating myself, but that wouldn't do any good. Nothing I say will convince Carly this is a good idea, so I don't waste time trying. "Talk to you tomorrow, Carly."

I disconnect the call before she can say anything more, then tuck my phone away in my pocket and glance up at the exterior of the building I've parked in front of. I've spent far more time at this club in the past week than I would ordinarily spend anywhere connected to Cassandra Carmichael, but what's one more visit? Grabbing the silver gift box, I exit the car and stride into the club Edmund Carmichael owns.

Upon seeing me, a flicker of confusion crosses the face of the first employee who recognizes me. I'd rather not be here longer than I must, so I stride up to her at the bar.

"Do you have a pen?"

The woman hesitates, then nods and reaches beneath the bar. Handing me a black pen, she asks, "Are you here to see Cassandra?"

"No. There's a waitress that works here—college-aged, auburn hair, kinda flighty, not very good at her job, but nice. Do you know the one I'm talking about?"

The bartender nods. "That's Marlena."

"Perfect." I uncap the pen and jot down the name on the card attached to the box. Putting the cap back on the pen, I drop it on the bar and push the box across the surface. "Can you see that she gets this, please?"

The bartender eyes me warily, drawing the box closer as it a bomb might be inside. "Sure, I guess so."

I draw out my wallet and hand the woman a crisp twenty dollar bill. "For your trouble."

8

LAUREL

The casino floor is packed full of felt-covered tables and smiling people clamoring to give Rafe their money. I guess they don't think of it that way, but standing up here on the raised platform, having a basic understanding of the statistical reality of gambling, I watch the pretty waitresses handing out champagne, and I know she's inviting all these people to have a good time so they will bet—and lose—more money. Only in Vegas can you laugh and smile while you're being taken for all you've got.

"Is it fun?" I ask mildly, looking over at the handsome devil beside me.

His hand slides around my waist and he tugs me close. "Is what fun? Gambling? Sure, to some degree."

My smile widens. "No, robbing people and having them thank you for it."

Flashing me a knowing grin, he says, "What are you talking about? This is all on the up-and-up. Aside from the restaurant, this is as straight as my business gets."

"Mm hmm," I murmur, unconvinced.

"These people are looking to have fun. I give them a place to do it," he continues.

"Bunch of suckers," I reply.

"Stand here five more minutes and I'll make enough to buy you a few more books. Still think they're suckers?"

I rock my head from side to side, considering. "Well, yes. But at least I'm doing a better job spending their money than they are."

"That's the spirit," he tells me.

"How are the schools around here?"

Rafe frowns, like he must have misheard me. "What?"

"I was thinking, as much as I *love* my surprise, and as happy as beautiful books make me, what if next time we put that $13,000 to better use? I'd like to talk to the teachers in our school district, particularly the STEM teachers, and see what kind of projects they need funding for. Could I make that my present wishlist instead?"

Still a little blankly, he asks, "You want me to give money to teachers?"

"I'm not asking you to hand over cash directly. I'd like to get a feel for what kinds of materials they need for their class-rooms, then we could buy things for them. Investing in our schools is investing in our little one's future," I tell him, placing a hand on my stomach. "I used to do bake sales and help out with raffles when I was in junior high and high school because we could never afford the equipment to do the really cool stuff. If you're going to throw money around anyway, why not use it to invest in better equipment so that when the time comes and *our* baby goes there, they'll be better equipped to work out this little Price-Morelli brain? Plus, it will benefit plenty of other kids, too. Fueling little brains is always a good idea."

Rafe shakes his head, surveying the floor. "Life with you is gonna be fun, isn't it?"

Smiling faintly, I poke him in the side. "Once more, with feeling."

———

After Rafe shows me around his casino, he takes me out to a quiet dinner, just the two of us. The red, leather booth we sit in is another rounded one, so even though I think it's gross when couples sit on the same side, there are no sides, and I end up right next to Rafe instead of across from him.

I get the impression he is probably one of those gross couples even if there *is* the option of not sitting close, because the man cannot stop touching. If he's not brushing my hand or my thigh or my hip, he's touching my arm or my shoulder or my face. I remember over Easter weekend I loved that, so I don't know why it's bothering me now.

Well, I guess I do. Every time he touches me, it makes me think of the inescapable inevitability of going home with him tonight. Since "I'm not ready" worked so poorly last night when we were in Chicago, I have to assume it's going to be even less effective now that I'm on his turf. Every touch of his hand feels like pressure instead of affection, even if he doesn't mean it that way.

And I really don't think he means it that way. The problem is with me, not him. He's behaving normally for someone trying to jumpstart a new relationship, but I'm still trying to keep a safe distance.

After a delicious dinner and a "shared" tiramisu for dessert (I ate most of it, while he took three bites), we're off to some club Rafe apparently favors. I'm not much of a club person.

Personally, I would prefer to go home, kick off these kitten heels, peel off this clingy dress, and watch some TV before bed. Instead, I'm ushered around a line of prettied-up people waiting to get in, through a back entrance, and into the loud, colorful, beating heart of the club. A huge man in a leather jacket greets Rafe and shakes his hand, then turns and starts pushing his way through the throng of people.

Rafe grabs my hand so I don't get lost in the shuffle, while I murmur apologies to the people glancing back at us as we move past them. These people have probably waited in line for hours being pushed aside so we can walk right in and sail past them. It makes me feel a little like an asshole, but Rafe seems accustomed to stepping right over people.

To my relief, the roped-off area we are led to has a much smaller concentration of people. There are rounded booths over here, but each one is sectioned off to give an illusion of privacy

I hope to find our booth empty, but prepare myself for Sin to be there. The booth we stop in front of is not empty, but I don't recognize the couple already seated there.

Before we take our seats, Rafe keeps one hand securely placed on my hip and uses the other to gesture to the table. "Laurel, this is my cousin Gio and his wife, Lydia."

The man isn't entirely what I've come to expect of a Morelli. He's handsome enough, I suppose, but not Sin or Rafe-level handsome. There's a hard look to him—not the way Sin looks hard and mean, but cooler, more calculation in his gaze. His eyes are blue—another deviation. All of the Morelli men of my acquaintance have dark eyes. He doesn't smile when he sees me. Instead, he appraises me like a new piece Rafe picked up. From the look on his face, I get the impression Gio thinks he overpaid.

When his mouth opens, he offers up a hollow, "Hey, how ya doin'?"

I look to his wife for more warmth, but her smile seems superficial, too.

I decide right away they don't approve. Lydia's gaze drops to my abdomen, and I think I know why. Since these are Rafe's relatives and they don't know me from Adam, they probably think I'm some conniving bitch who got knocked up on purpose to trap him.

Injecting a little more warmth into my tone to make up for their misread of the situation, I smile and say, "It's so nice to meet you. I've only met Rafe's Chicago family so far."

Gio rolls his eyes, apparently unimpressed.

Leaning in to explain, Rafe says, "We haven't been on good terms for very long. It's gonna take a little longer for the rest of the Vegas family to warm up to them."

"Oh. Right." I remember Sin saying something about that, but it's still disappointing. I like Rafe's Chicago family far more than I like these two people so far, and these are the ones I'll have to socialize with if I stay here.

Normally, Rafe urges me to scoot in, but tonight he slides in first and lets me sit on the end. Since I already feel like leaving, I appreciate at least feeling less trapped. If I need to slide out to go to the bathroom—or pretend to go to the bathroom, just to escape the present company—I can do so without a whole production.

Rafe and Gio talk for a couple minutes while Lydia smiles silently. I look around for a waiter. I wish I *could* have a drink tonight; that would probably make this more pleasant.

Since everyone is ignoring me anyway, I pull out my cell phone. Carly hasn't texted or called me at all since this morning, and even though I can't say much to her, it's making me worry. Canceling my flight home today was too obvious. I'm sure I have aroused her suspicions at this point. I hope she isn't trying to poke around on her own; she'll probably get herself into trouble.

On a whim, I close that message and open the one below it —Mia Morelli. She gave me her number, telling me I needed a "mob wife" friend and to call or text her anytime. I told her I'm not a mob wife, but she just patted my hand like I don't know what I'm talking about and started filling her suitcase with baby clothes to send home with me.

I type out, "MW update: not a hit with the Vegas Morelli family."

It only takes her a minute to respond. "Lame! Vegas Morellis wouldn't know a good addition to the family if one bit them in the face." Before I can point out a good addition to the family probably wouldn't be biting any faces, she sends another one. "How is Rafe treating you? Need me to kick his ass yet?"

Smiling faintly, I shake my head. "Rafe is good. He bought me books, so no complaints there. I'm trying to convince him to give all his money away to good causes."

"I do that to Mateo ALL THE TIME," she replies. "If he is to be believed (he's not though) we are giving all our money away and should be living in a box right now."

"That's what they do all that work for, right?"

"Clearly," she answers. "Why else?"

"Have you met their cousin Gio?" I ask her.

"I think I met him briefly at Ben's funeral. Unless there are multiple Gios."

"He doesn't seem very nice," I tell her. "His wife is looking at me like I have a lottery fetus in my womb. I don't think we're going to be besties anytime soon."

"Whatever, screw them. For what it's worth, I also hated the Vegas family members I met. Rafe is the only one I liked. Be glad you never had to meet Ben, he was a complete asshole."

"That's Vince's dad, right?"

"Yeah. Vince never liked him either."

I probably shouldn't ask, but a glance over at Rafe tells me they're still talking shop, so I snap up a sliver of unsupervised girl talk. "Did you meet Sin when you were here? He seemed to know who you were."

"Did he work with Vince? Maybe he mentioned me. I never met a Sin when I was in Vegas, but it's possible I met him here if he came for our wedding or Ben's funeral. I don't remember that name, but I might remember his face. Pic?"

"I doubt he came to your wedding, but he was at the funeral."

I don't know why, I just want to talk to someone else who knows him. He's so much like a shadow, it's like he doesn't even exist. Like he isn't even real.

Mia texts back, "Still thinking about him, huh?"

"I haven't seen him yet, so that inevitability is on my mind."

The sound of Rafe's voice sends a jolt of guilt through me and I close my messages, glancing over at him as he asks, "Who are you texting?"

"Mia," I answer, offering a smile before tucking my phone away. He's paying attention now, so if she texts back and uses Sin's name, he'll see it. Obviously it's no secret Sin is still on my mind, but I'd rather not rub it in his face.

He cocks a golden eyebrow in surprise. "My Mia?"

I cock an eyebrow right back. "*Your* Mia?"

Now he rolls his eyes. "I meant, Mateo's Mia. My family—

you know what I meant. Wasn't sure if you had a friend by that name, or...?"

"Well, I do now," I tell him, with a hint of playful smugness. "*Your* Mia is going to be *my* mob wife friend. She assures me I need one."

"Oh, does she?" he asks, snaking an arm around my shoulder and leaning in to kiss the shell of my ear in one smooth motion.

"Mm hmm," I murmur. It actually feels nice, so I lean into it.

His hand creeps between my legs, caressing my thigh. "Someone to show you the ropes?"

My body responds as his hand creeps closer to the apex of my thighs, but I press his hand against my leg to stop him. "We're in public," I remind him.

"We are," he agrees, but not before nibbling on my ear.

"And we have guests. Or, we are guests. Either way..."

"Hey, people pay for a show in Vegas; they get to sit here for free," he reasons.

I smile, nudging him away with my shoulder. "Come on, I want them to like me. Right now you're making me look cheap."

That catches his attention and he pulls back to look at me. "How am I making you look cheap?"

"Maybe cheap is the wrong word. Common," I amend.

His brow furrows. "Explain."

Glancing at his cousin at his wife while they eavesdrop without even pretending otherwise, I hesitate. Looking back at Rafe, I bring a hand up to caress his cheek. "Can we talk about it later?"

Ignoring my placating gesture, Rafe says, "I'd like to talk about it now."

This is so fucking awkward. With a barely audible sigh, I force myself to offer a pared down explanation. I keep my tone low, but I'm sure they're still listening. "How many other women have sat here and been mauled by you in this booth? Dozens?"

Gio snickers, glancing at his wife. "Dozens, she says."

Lydia tries to fight a smirk, but I feel like the butt of the joke.

Brief irritation flickers across Rafe's face. I think it's in response to them, but I suppose it could be me. I lean in close to his ear so I can talk more quietly. "I just don't want to be one of many. I don't want to be dismissed like the latest temporary exhibit in your museum of conquests. I want them to take me seriously, and they won't if you treat me like all the others."

Instead of getting annoyed at this blatant show of insecurity, Rafe takes my hand and uses his thumb to caress it. "They'll take you seriously when they see you're the one who sticks around. Showing you affection doesn't make you look cheap or common, it makes you look like someone I like."

"You like me?" I tease, wrinkling my nose up in mock-distaste.

"Maybe a little bit," he teases back. "I'll like you even more later, when my cock is buried between these pretty thighs."

I flush, and of course *that* is the moment Sin appears in front of the table.

9

LAUREL

There's no such thing as subtlety—or, you'd certainly think that as I shy away from Rafe and cross my legs, knocking his hand off my thigh. I can feel that he's faintly irritated, but he nonetheless leans back in the booth like he hasn't a care in the world.

"Sin," he says, nodding once in acknowledgement.

It takes a concentrated effort to keep my gaze on the table and off the new arrival, but I'm afraid to look at him. I'm not sure if I'm more nervous to see his facial expression—and if so, what am I afraid to see? His indifference? He's not going to be jealous; he's the one who sent me back to Rafe in the first place —or more nervous about how it's going to feel to see him. Maybe the scariest thing of all is the prospect of looking at him and seeing how he responds to my evident turmoil.

I've been waiting for this moment, and now that it's here, I am too afraid to face it. Sin takes a seat on the other end of the booth, directly across from me.

I rely on my peripherals to get a peek at him. He looks

sinfully sexy in black slacks and a black jacket with a crimson shirt, open at the throat. Sin isn't a tie guy. The temptation to look at his face is too great, and I raise my gaze to his, hoping he won't be looking at me.

Thankfully, he isn't.

It also stings of disappointment. It shouldn't. Why would he be looking at me? I'm nothing to him. I may still be haunted by him, but he is not similarly afflicted. I could have never sent him away to someone else, and he did it with apparent ease. Never kissed me, never fucked me. I lost all my control around him, and he was able to hold everything back.

My heart doesn't understand that, though. It's painfully slow and I wish it would catch up. Instead, it urges my mind to capture his every movement and file them away for later. He greets Gio and Lydia, nods at Rafe, and completely ignores me.

My gaze drops. My heart aches. My stomach hurts.

He's so fucking mean.

One of my last memories of him is worshipping his dick, and the manipulative bastard can't even be bothered to say hello to me.

I'm feeling another mood swing coming on, and I doubt this one is the baby's fault either. Discomfort amongst strangers was one thing, but this is so much worse. Sin isn't a stranger like Gio or Lydia, he's someone I have intimate memories with, and I can't shake the feeling of rejection all over again. Now he's rejecting my very presence at this table.

I should keep my mouth shut, but I can't. "Hi, Sin."

He keeps his head turned so long, it's obviously deliberate. Finally, he looks across the table and meets my gaze. Ice spears me right through the heart, piercing my soul. I shouldn't have asked for his attention. I'm not prepared for it.

"Laurel," he says simply. A toneless acknowledgement, betraying no importance whatsoever. His tone is civil, at least. Not that he has a reason to be anything less than civil to me, but he never has, and he was a jerk to me from the get-go.

Since my stomach is so unsettled I think I may hurl, I don't do anything to further draw his attention. Suddenly parched, I look around for the server again. I see a scantily clad girl in a black latex dress, strapless and impractical for work, but she has a tray full of drinks. Once she finishes putting them on the table she's standing in front of, I catch her eye. She doesn't smile or indicate she's coming, but after chatting up that table for another minute, she slides her tray underneath her arm and approaches ours.

"Hey, how are y'all doing tonight?" With a big, fake smile, she nods at a couple murmured responses she doesn't care about, then asks, "Can I get y'all some drinks?"

I open my mouth to beg for water, but Sin speaks first. "Bottled water, sealed."

"Me too," I say, not caring that I am not next. "And a huge glass of ice, please."

The waitress gives me a smile that's somehow sweet and condescending at the same time. "Well, bless your heart, someone sure is thirsty." I lose her attention as she smiles at Rafe. "And what can I get for you tonight, handsome?"

Grasping his heart theatrically, Rafe asks, "You don't remember my drink? I'm hurt."

Biting down on her bottom lip and flushing, she says, "Of course I remember your usual, but sometimes you mix it up. Stop playin' with me," she says, her tone a little whiny—but cute whiny. Flirty whiny.

"Yeah, yeah, yeah," Rafe continues, shaking his head. "You don't remember. I'm bleeding out over here."

"Rafe," she wines. "You're so mean to me."

My face heats with embarrassment. I'm not sure if I want to stab him so he *actually* bleeds out, tell this bitch to fetch my fucking water, or flee the table. I don't know if he's flirting with her in front of me because he's annoyed that I pulled back when Sin came to the table, or because he's just a dick. Giving him the benefit of the doubt, I allow for it being the first, and I kind of understand that. Not a fan, still profoundly embarrassing, but I get it.

I wonder if Rafe has fucked her. My gaze drifts to her in her tight latex dress, her long, tanned legs, the fake lashes she glued on before coming to work, her perfectly straightened dark hair. Probably. She's gorgeous. Clearly into him. Or maybe they've only flirted. Maybe they haven't fucked—yet. Maybe they will someday. Maybe he'll humiliate me on a level I can't even fathom, and this snotty little skank will be so smug bringing me my water, knowing she's fucked my man, thinking it's some kind of accomplishment.

Lydia finally speaks up. "I'll have a mojito."

"Sounds good, and what can I bring you?" she asks Gio, without the cutesy bullshit.

He orders and the waitress disappears, but not without another coy smile at Rafe that turns my stomach.

I'm not completely sure I even have a right to be, but I am steaming. He better not get touchy feely with me right now; I would rather punch him in the face than snuggle.

In an attempt to abandon the table without physically fleeing, I fish my phone out of my purse to play around on it. My hands tremble slightly from the emotions coursing through me, so I prop it up on the table to steady it.

Rafe leans in. "Are you telling on me to Mia?"

"Nope. I'm asking her if she wants to make out with me in private, somewhere you'll never be able to see it," I answer.

"Oh, come on."

"It's going to be so hot," I tell him. "I may not be able to control myself. I'll be kissing and stroking every inch of her bare skin. She'll palm my breast while we kiss; I'll squeeze her ass. I bet I'll be so turned on, I'll have to fuck her myself."

"Jesus Christ."

I smile wide and look at him. "But never for you. We'll let Mateo watch if she wants him to, but not you."

"What made you this evil?" he demands.

Lydia is slack-jawed and completely scandalized. Well, she's probably never going to like me. Oh well. Fuck her. Fuck all of them.

I flick a glance across the table and catch Sin smirking for a split second before he sees me looking and clears his expression. Was he smirking because I'm being mean to Rafe, or at the mental image of me making out with another girl? Men are so weird. Why is that even hot?

"When I do leave you to go back to Chicago," I tell Rafe, smiling sweetly, "have fun lying awake at night wondering what Mia and I are up to. When Mateo is busy, I bet she'll come to my bedroom and play with me. Tell Mateo to keep you updated so you know what you're missing out on."

"I've never met such a cruel woman," he states, lifting my hand to his lips so he can kiss it.

Since I know this is an unattainable fantasy of his now, I lean in to murmur in his ear, "Imagine how much sweeter that knuckle would taste if I had it deep in Mia's pussy first."

"Sweet lord," he mutters, fisting a hand in my hair and pulling me closer. "Will you marry me?"

"No," I tell him.

"Now I really am bleeding out."

"Good," I say, pulling away from him and going back to my phone.

"Would you even hold pressure on my wound?" he half-jokes.

"Only if you haven't willed everything to me yet."

A little laugh slips out of him. "Jesus, you are ruthless. Maybe I *will* let you run Vegas."

I nod my head. "You should. I'd do a good job."

Rafe shakes his head, smoothing down my hair where he just mussed it and kissing the crown of my head. "I can't wait to train you, kitten."

"Just remember what I do to ducks that piss me off," I advise him, not taking my eyes off the screen. "*Dicks* that piss me off might get the same treatment."

My threat only serves to amuse him. "Severed and served up with roasted veggies, huh?"

"And then a celebratory all-female orgy after the fact. If you don't have a dick anymore, I'll let you watch. That sounds a lot meaner."

"I wonder if I would get a phantom erection?" he ponders.

I can't resist offering knowledge, even though I'm mad at him. "Technically, men who have had their penises amputated do tend to report phantom limb syndrome. Sometimes they feel so strongly that they still have a penis, they have to open their pants and check. I also read somewhere once that a man who had lost that particular appendage could still feel arousal, and if he rubbed the stump..." I pause, catching Gio and Lydia's twin masks of horror. Clearing my throat, I tell Rafe, "Enough with the pillow talk. I wish that skanky waitress would hurry up; I'm parched."

Gio and Lydia are still gaping at me when Rafe turns his

attention back to them. Gio looks at him, as if for an explanation for me. Rafe merely shrugs. "She reads a lot."

I wouldn't say the night is going down in the record books as my favorite night out, but we're all surviving. Rafe has a couple of drinks, he and Gio chat, and Sin just sits there looming over me. The biggest nerd award goes to me, because I keep pace with Sin, that way when he orders another water, he sees mine is empty and orders me one, too.

I didn't know he would, of course, but he does, and that I care is lame, but it also proves he is paying attention to me.

Rafe's hard gaze flickers across the table when Sin orders for me, even if it's just a bottle of water. Sin looks away, not appearing to give a fuck.

"How come you're not drinking tonight, Sin?" Rafe asks, stretching his arm around my shoulder and regarding Sin congenially.

Sin's gaze doesn't leave Rafe's face, doesn't even slip in my direction. "Didn't feel like it."

Giving me a little squeeze to inexplicably pull me into this conversation, Rafe says, "He gets more sociable when he drinks. Doesn't just sit here like a fucking wet blanket."

Sin has maintained a straight face, but now there's a hint of annoyance brushed across the handsome tapestry of his face.

The weird thing is the instinct that kicks up within me, wanting to defend Sin. Rafe's words annoy *me* more than they seem to annoy him. "I have seen Sin drunk," I state, nodding my head. "He was certainly more... sociable."

Rafe's fingers tighten on my shoulder. I should feel bad for intentionally annoying him, but I don't. He shouldn't be mean to Sin. *I should be mean to Sin, but Rafe doesn't have a reason to be.*

The waitress brings our waters and walks away. I lean forward to uncap mine just as she comes back and stops at the head of our table.

"You."

That's not our waitress. I turn my head to investigate the accusing tone and pointed finger of the new woman in a black dress, standing here pointing at Rafe. This one is beautiful, wearing a snug, one-shoulder dress with a pair of tassel earrings swinging out from under her auburn locks. She's not looking at me, though. She's looking—and pointing —at Rafe.

His arm drops from its spot behind me and he leans forward. "What are you doing here?"

"I'm here to see you," she states, glaring at him. "You sent this dress and these earrings to my *work*. What is wrong with you?"

I sink back in my seat, flummoxed.

"I think the words you're looking for might be thank you," he suggests, clearly baffled by her anger.

Her eyes widen at his apparent gall. "Thank you? You got me *fired*! You sent a present to my place of employment and signed your name to it. I didn't even know who you were that night, but you damn sure knew that your psycho ex-girlfriend's father *owns* the club I worked at."

"Oh, wow, this is fun," I mutter. "This is a lot of fun." Turning to Rafe, I demand, "Is this what your life is like? Is this my life with you? You buy me some books, buy her some clothes, everyone goes home happy. Did you buy our southern belle waitress a present, too? Or do I get to find out about that tomorrow night?"

Holding up a hand to halt my anger, he says, "It's not like that."

Ignoring him, I turn to the redhead and gesture to the dress. "When did he send you this present?"

"Today," she tells me.

I laugh. Then I laugh a little more, because why the fuck not? "Okay." Grabbing my purse, I slip my phone inside and scoot to the edge of the upholstered seat.

"Laurel, stop," Rafe says, grabbing my wrist. "This is not what it sounds like."

"It sounds like after we landed *together* in Las Vegas this morning, the errand you had to run was buying and delivering a present for another woman. Did I get any of that wrong?"

He pauses. "Not *technically*."

I shake my head and scoot out of the booth. "This is not for me. I am not interested in this. Do not want. Unsubscribe. Hell no."

Rafe should let me go—he should really let me go, because I want to leave. I want to book myself another Uber and go back to the airport. Since I already played that card, he follows me, grabbing my bicep and turning me back around. "Laurel, it is not what it looks like. I didn't have sex with her. She was just... she was nice to me the other night, and I thought I'd return the favor. Obviously I didn't think you'd find out about it."

I turn back to face him, wide-eyed. "That is your defense? Because if I didn't find out about it, then it would have been fine? Is that the rule? Does that rule go both ways? I assume if you get to do whatever the fuck you want to do as long as you're discreet, I do, too."

That last line irritates him. Eyes trained on my face, he leans back a little. "Yeah, I bet you'd like that, wouldn't you?"

Ripping my arm out of his grip, I fling back, "Maybe I would."

I'm executing a great storm-off when he grabs me, pushes my back against the wall nearest us, and imprisons me with his body. All of a sudden the anger gets pushed down. I look at his massive shoulders, at the muscular wall of man hovering inches from my body—rather intimidating, to be honest. It's easy to forget Rafe is dangerous because he's pretty easygoing by default, but I think I'm about to get a peek at what he's like when he's pissed.

"I've had about enough of this damned mouth tonight, Laurel," he tells me, grasping my jaw in his large hand.

"Remember when you had no complaints about my mouth?" I murmur.

He nods, watching me with his intense amber eyes. "I do. Remember when it hadn't been wrapped around my enforcer's cock?"

Lowering my eyes, I swallow down the jab I want to throw at him. This is not the time. I can smell alcohol on his breath, and he's clearly reaching the end of his good humor for the evening. I don't think Rafe would physically hurt me, but I don't know him all that well, either.

When I don't respond, he goes on, the tone of his voice low and rough. "I see the little fucking looks you keep stealing at him, Laurel. You wanna make me look like an asshole? Is that what you want?"

"I think what makes you look like an asshole is the parade of other skanks you can't seem to shake." I tell him, despite my better judgment. "I don't enjoy going out with you when I don't know how many scantily clad women are going to salivate over you at the table, Rafe. That's not fun."

"At least I'm not salivating over someone else," he says, his voice low with anger.

I ignore his jab and look him straight in the eye. "You flirted with our waitress right in front of me."

"You jumped to Sin's defense in front of my fucking second-in-command."

I did do that. I don't have a good defense for that, so I drop my gaze again. "There's no reason for you to be mean to him. He hasn't done anything to you."

His tone is nearly as sharp as his words. "He made you come, didn't he?"

I flinch less at the crudeness of the question, and more at the memory it triggers of Sin's hands on my body.

Rafe releases my jaw so he can trace the curve of my shoulder. "How many times did you let him play with your pussy, Laurel? How many times did he fuck you? How many times did you let him put his cock in your mouth? I need numbers."

Every word he says is like a new, sharper dagger lodged right in my chest cavity. Dutifully, my heart tries to beat around each blade, but damn, those memories hurt.

"That's none of your business," I tell him. "You give me your numbers and I'll give you mine. You tell me how many women you've been inside, how many mouths your cock has been in. You get back to me with *your* score, and I'll be happy to share mine."

Grabbing me by the throat hard enough that I gasp, he pushes me harder against the wall. "It *is* my business, Laurel. You're my property and he's my employee. I want to know how many fucking bonuses he got."

I glare at him, pushing against his chest. "Get off me."

"No, I don't think I will," he says, pressing a finger to the pulse thundering in my neck. Smiling a slow smile, he leans in to kiss my neck.

"No," I say, shoving uselessly against his chest. "We don't go from 'you're my property' to neck-kissing that fast. Plutonium. Plutonium, plutonium, plutonium."

"You need to stop using that word when your clothes are still on. Maybe you don't remember how safe words work, Laurel. Maybe it's been too long since I last fucked you and you need a reminder."

"I told you I wasn't ready," I say, shoving against his chest with more anger this time.

I certainly haven't gained any strength in the last minute, but this time he eases back enough to look at me.

"You don't listen to me. I told you I wasn't ready, and you ignored me. I told you I didn't want to see him, and you invited him to the club our first night out."

His territorial anger seems to take a backseat as he recognizes real feelings bubbling out of me. "He works for me, Laurel. He's *going* to be around. You've gotta get over it."

"What if I can't?"

I swear, he nearly rolls his eyes. He manages to stop himself, but I see how close he comes. Making a greater attempt at patience, he tells me, "You will. You just need a little more time. A few more days, maybe. It doesn't help that we've had such a rocky start. By comparison, Sin doesn't bring a whole hell of a lot of excitement with him."

I *hate* his subtle putdowns. "Stop saying things like that. Stop being mean to him."

"He isn't yours to defend, Laurel." Aggravation flickers across his handsome features. "If you don't find a way to get over him, I'm gonna have to be a whole lot meaner." Eyebrows rising, he demands, "You need incentive? You want me tell you the only alternative to you getting over it? The only way I *can* make it so you don't have to see him anymore?"

Even before he answers his own questions, my blood runs cold. I can't find the words to speak, so I stay quiet.

Rafe meets my gaze, eyebrows hiked up, knowing he's struck gold. "There is one way. I won't like it, but *he's* not having my baby. You're the one I have to make room for. If you need him out of the way, I can do that. I'm not sure you'll like my method."

"You wouldn't hurt him. He does good work for you."

"He does. But I can't keep him around if the mother of my child can't stop daydreaming about fucking him when we're trying to have a nice night out, now, can I?"

I swallow, staring at his chest. It drifts closer and he hugs me. I don't want to hug him, but I'm presently a little afraid not to, so I wrap an arm around him to hug him back.

His tone is low, almost serene, as he goes on. "I can't have Sin around if I have to worry about him, can I? He's my go-to guy. I need something, he's the guy I call. What am I supposed to do if I can't call him, Laurel?"

"I never said you couldn't call him," I murmur, but without much steam.

"Now, if that's what you need, tell me. If you can't handle being around Sin in social situations, you let me know, and I'll start looking around for his replacement." His big hand caresses my jaw. "But this isn't the kind of work where you get fired and go find a job elsewhere, kitten. When I fire someone, it's permanent."

I meet his gaze warily, my mouth like a cotton field. "It won't come to that."

His tone is falsely attentive, but he knows he's threatening me. Maybe he even likes it. "No?"

"No," I mutter.

"You'll be able to overcome the epic four day love affair you had?"

His mocking tone pisses me off, but I bite my tongue. "I'll get over it."

"Good," he says, pulling me into his broad shoulder, then shifting my weight so he can kiss me. "Get over it fast, because I want to fuck you, and I don't like waiting."

10

SIN

†

Tonight had to fucking suck. There wasn't even an
outside shot it would go any other way.

My fist flexes, wanting to do what it does best—
smash in the face of the person pissing me off. Problem is, the
person pissing me off so much right now is Rafe. A common
occurrence since Laurel came on the scene.

As if it wasn't bad enough having to sit here and watch him
paw at her all night, watching him pay attention to other
women and embarrass her, now as I stand here in the shadows,
I have to watch his hand sliding up under her dress. The
panties she's wearing must be a thong, because I see the bare
curve of her ass right before he squeezes it.

Anger and arousal surge at the same time. I don't want him
touching her ass, but that's a thing I knew I'd have to deal with.
All the rest of this shit, not so much.

Well, okay, sure, I figured eventually it might come up. But
after she already loved the asshole, not right when they first got
together.

He lifts her thigh and guides it until she hooks it around

his hip. Now I have to watch as he presses himself between her legs, pinning her arms to the wall, and kisses the fuck out of her. I'd rather watch a grown man cry and piss himself over the bloody stumps where his fingers used to be than watch this fucking shit—no contest.

I guess I don't *have* to watch this. I could walk away now. Ordinarily I don't get involved in Rafe's love life, but Laurel is full of fire tonight and he's not really used to that. I just had to follow and make sure everything cooled down between them.

I'm stuck here watching him paw at her and I can't fucking walk away. It's increasingly difficult not to walk over there and rip him away from her. To punch him in the fucking face, throw her ass over my shoulder, and haul her out to my car. I should take her feisty little ass back to my house and tie her to my bed, bury my face between her thighs until she remembers how to act.

Nah, what am I thinking? She wouldn't act like that with me. She responded to me very differently than she responds to him.

I like it, but I shouldn't.

Laurel Price isn't for me, so I don't know why it feels so much like she is.

This is going to be fucking hard.

Before I have to watch him fuck her here in the hallway, the bastard finally pulls back. They murmur a couple more things to each other, then she nods and he takes a step back. He has to adjust his pants, but then he gives her hand a squeeze and heads back toward the table.

I keep to the shadows and watch. Laurel sighs and looks down at her shoes, then tips her head back against the wall. Finally, she pushes off the wall and resumes her trek to the bathroom.

I know she's all right so I should go back to the table, but instead I follow her.

The bathroom here is multiple stalls. Single stall, I could follow her inside, but not multiple stalls. Crossing the corridor, I make a snap decision and catch her by the arm.

She gasps and whirls around to see who is accosting her. Her face freezes when she sees it's me. I drag her into the shadows with me, planting her back against the wall. There's a huge potted tree on this corner, so even on the off chance Rafe comes to investigate when he realizes I'm not at the table, he won't see us right away.

I'm not sure how to explain myself just now. Telling her the truth—that I just wanted to make sure she was okay—wouldn't make much fucking sense, but my mind is blanking for lies.

Turns out, I don't have to concoct a reason. Laurel doesn't demand to know what the hell I'm doing accosting her in the halls or pushing her against the wall and standing so close. Her big blue eyes look up at me, so vulnerable, so full of confusion and hurt, but there's something else. It's the something else that's the problem. This girl should hate me, full stop, no exceptions. She should hate my guts. She should want to see me ripped open and disemboweled for using her the way I did.

The way she thinks I did, at least.

The way I meant to, I guess.

Joke's on me this time. Got tangled up in my own damn web.

She doesn't speak, and I don't either. For all the fire and spunk she had toward Rafe back at the table, I still see obedience in her eyes for me. As if no time has passed, no lamps were thrown, no cruel words delivered, Laurel gazes up at me like she belongs to me. I'm half tempted to tell her to drop to her knees just to see if she'll still do it.

I'm haunted enough by that mental image though, so I don't.

Being this close makes me want to get closer. I want to feel her body fitted snugly against mine. It's the last thing I should do, but since I have her pressed against this wall here, I go ahead and push my luck. I take a step forward until I can feel her tits smashed against my chest. Laurel inhales sharply, but instead of telling me to get off her, she touches my sides, then snakes her arms around my back and pulls me even closer.

She hugs me.

His fucking cologne still hangs on her from just a moment ago and my jaw locks. I want to chain her little ass up in my shower and clean every last bit of him off her. Definitely can't do that. I shouldn't even be touching her, but the way she clings to me, she seems to be the one who needs it most. Wordlessly, she buries her face in my chest and holds me close. I don't hug her back because I can't. Because I can hear the sounds of her crying into my shirt, and that alone is turning me to stone.

Maybe I made a fucking mistake. The thought flashes across my mind—not for the first time, but this is the first time I've felt the weight of it. Before this, I felt like I made a mistake because I missed her. Because I could still smell her on the pillow next to mine, because I woke up after she haunted my dreams all night with a hard cock and no pretty little mouth to put it in.

But now she's crying into my chest, and I don't know why. All I want to do is obliterate everything that makes her sad, but I can't because it's probably me.

I can't hug her back because my hands are tied right now.

I gave her back to him. I can't tell Rafe I changed my mind. He thinks he won. He took her public. Even if the embarrassment pisses him off more than losing Laurel would, he's not going to let me take her back now. I crossed the line when I took her the first time. I held that fucking line and didn't back down from it, but I can't just take her back and say, "Sorry, I thought I was done with her but I'm not. I'll find you another one."

Laurel pulls herself together after a minute. She pulls back, sniffling and wiping her eyes. "Sorry," she murmurs.

"Why are you crying?" I ask her.

Her bottom lip quivers and her big blue eyes fill up with tears again. "I wanna go home."

"This is your home now," I tell her.

"No, it's not," she says, shaking her head. "I hate it here."

"Did Rafe do something?"

He better fucking not have. I don't care if he's the king of this fucking city—kings have been toppled before. I helped him take his power, and I could help take it away from him, too. Wouldn't earn me a whole hell of a lot of loyalty points, depending on who I push, but I can't say the thought hasn't crossed my mind a time or two since Laurel happened.

Much to my relief, she shakes her head, not looking at me. "It's not him."

"Then what is it?"

She's quiet for the longest stretch, then she meets my gaze and holds it. "I miss you."

I damn sure shouldn't take her small, soft hand in mine, but I do anyway. "I'm standing right here, aren't I?"

"You know what I mean," she says, glancing down at her hand in mine. "I don't want to avoid your gaze and... I don't want it to be like this. You still owe me Chinese food."

I crack a smile. "Always thinking about your next meal, aren't you?"

"I know I should hate you," she says, looking up at me again. "I should. But I can't."

Selfishly, I'm glad as hell to hear that. "You don't have to hate me."

"I should, though," she insists. "I hated him when he was an asshole, and you were every bit as bad."

My fingers itch to tuck her hair behind her ear. I resist the urge, but just barely. Attempting to lighten the mood a bit, I tell her, "I guess I'm just special."

Laurel cracks a smile, but it's a smile bursting with sadness. "I kinda thought so."

I watch her for a moment, then I lean back and check the hall beyond the potted plant to make sure Rafe isn't around the corner. I was torn on whether or not he would come back here once he saw I wasn't at the table. I might have been escorting the redhead out of the club and laying into the incompetent motherfucker who let her into the VIP section in the first place. That's what I should have done, but I told Gio to do it instead. I'm not the one who should be issuing orders and he knows it, too. The disgruntled look he shot me got the point across just in case I had the intelligence of a brick, but I didn't care.

Rafe made it through Cassandra Carmichael without murdering her, so chances are he can survive Laurel Price. I wasn't taking any chances though.

He's not in the hallway storming toward me though, so we still have a minute. If Gio was back at the table by the time he got there, there's little chance Rafe will come check on us unless we linger way too long. He's not a man prone to emotional outbursts to begin with, and he won't want to give off the impression he doesn't trust me or Laurel. Not even if it's true. Makes him look foolish to keep around people he doesn't trust, and he has to present a strong front for Gio. I'm less concerned about what Gio thinks about me, but if I lose Rafe's trust, I'm more or less fucked. Didn't think I'd be putting my own ass so far over the line when I hatched this idea, but I wasn't prepared for Laurel Price. Didn't think a week or so would be long enough for even a fraction of the feelings shining in her eyes at me right now to develop.

I could kiss her right now and she wouldn't stop me. Hell, I could do more than that. I can visualize dragging her body close, pushing the flimsy straps of her dress down over her shoulders. I can see that pretty head falling back as I bend to take one of her rosy nipples into my mouth. Hear the sharp intake of breath, followed by one of her little moans as she drags her fingers through my hair, keeping me close.

Laurel's voice draws me out of that ill-considered visualization, but not before my cock starts to respond to it. "I have a question. Purely academic in nature, mind you."

That draws a little smile out of me. "All right."

"I know this isn't the kind of job you can quit or retire from, but are you able to transfer? Like, between branches of the family? You obviously work in Vegas, but say you didn't want to work in Vegas anymore. Could you transfer to Chicago and work for Mateo instead?"

The little wheels in her head are clearly turning, alerting me that the hug was as bad an idea as I originally thought it might be. "It's been done before, sure. I am not transferring to Chicago, Laurel."

"Why not?" she asks, wide-eyed at my immediate refusal. "Chicago is great. The family there is... well, different. A little twisted, but they have a nice set-up. Mateo clearly has more money than God, so I imagine he pays well."

I'm already shaking my head. "Based on what I've heard, I can't work for Mateo. I wouldn't be able to do it. Guy's an asshole."

"But you're only hearing what Vegas people say, and guess what? I think the Vegas Morellis are assholes. I'm friends with Mateo's wife and she assures me she's a very good person to have on my side. I bet you if I asked her, she would talk to Mateo about it. I bet you *could* work for him. This guy Adrian does, and he even lives at the house with his wife and kids. I say house, but it's... I mean, it's basically a castle. They have these traditional Sunday night dinners where the guys have drinks in the study while the ladies commiserate and make dinner. It's old-fashioned, but somehow kind of cool and fun. And then the women serve their men. We could make that sexy. I'm not saying you would have to live there, but Mia already invited me to and I bet you could, too, at least until you were used to the city. She said the bedroom she would give me is basically its own apartment, just without the kitchen."

Since she's about to ask me to run away with her, I grasp her shoulders to steady her. "Laurel. No."

Her shoulders sag and she appears to be exasperated with me. "But why?"

"I don't run from my problems, for one thing. You're also having Rafe's baby, so even if I went to Chicago, it's not like you can go."

"Yes, I can," she insists. "I'm considering it anyway. Whether you stay here and deal with Rafe or you make a super smart decision to relocate, I'm not sure *I* want to deal with his shit. I told myself I would give Rafe a chance, but if this is what life with him is like, I don't want it. And I don't have to take it. Mia is my anchor. She told me I don't have to stay in Vegas if I don't want to. She gave me a very appealing back-up plan, and... well, to be honest, it's more my plan A than my plan B right now. If you transferred... things would be different."

I sigh, looking at the wall behind her so I don't have to look at the hope in her eyes. "Laurel..."

"I *know* you started out using me, but don't try to tell me all of it was fake. You wouldn't be standing here in this hallway if you didn't like me at least a little bit."

"Keeping an eye on you is me protecting Rafe's interests."

Her eyes narrow, like she's had about enough of my bullshit. "Oh yeah? Was eating me out protecting Rafe's interests? How about shoving your dick down my throat?"

Damn, she's got me there. Instead of saying that, I respond like the asshole I am. "Well, I don't work for free. I had to get a cut of the profits, didn't I?"

Laurel stares at me, but it doesn't even piss her off. Somehow she deflects my taunts and barbs like they don't bother her—which is odd, since I say them specifically *to* bother her. As if I'm some Romeo she still wants to run away with instead of the dickhead with the mean mouth, she asks, "Why won't you even consider Chicago?"

"You are having Rafe's baby," I say slowly, since she can't seem to get it through her stubborn head.

"You said that didn't matter to you."

"He is *not* going to let you go to Chicago. He's damn sure not going to let *me* go to Chicago with you. There is no chance of any of this happening. Get your head out of the clouds and focus on what you *can* have. It's not me. It's never been me. Nothing has changed."

Futile anger burns in her big blue eyes now. "You drive me crazy. You're a liar and I want to punch you in the face."

Turning my face slightly and patting my cheek, I tell her, "Go ahead. If the slap made you feel better, a good right hook may get you the rest of the way."

Sighing and slouching back against the wall, she scowls at me. "Don't tempt me."

Since she clearly needs a firm hand to push her in the right direction, I offer mine. "Now, you say you're giving Rafe a chance, but this Chicago plan is clearly not something you just pulled out of thin air. Stop wasting your time on me. You and me can't happen. It's not in the cards."

"Fuck the cards," she returns, folding her arms across her chest defensively. "Fuck the dealer. Fuck the deck. Fuck the whole game."

She can be as mad about it as she wants, but it is what it is. She can't force me into a relationship and she can't see inside my head, so let her think it's easy for me. Maybe she *does* need to hate me. I'm not quite ready to push her there yet, but as stubborn as she's being, I might have to. I'll give her a little more time, see if she can get over it on her own.

I'm a permanent fixture in her life if she and Rafe are together, so I really don't want her to loathe me to the point of discomfort when I'm around. That's going to make my life harder. It's going to make Rafe push me away, maybe give his favor to someone else. I should be next in line for a promotion —I was before Laurel—but not if things don't settle down between us.

This girl is fucking up my whole life.

"Give Rafe a chance," I tell her. "You liked him before you met me, didn't you?"

"Yes, I did." She looks me dead in the eye. "But then I met you."

I'm not going to go around in circles with her—I can't. Whether Rafe comes after us or he doesn't, I know without a doubt he's watching and noting every second we're both gone. "I can't do this with you right now, okay? I can't do this with you at all. We aren't exes. We weren't together. Get over it."

Her whole being stiffens, her eyes dimming with hurt. It stings me, too, but fuck, what am I supposed to do? I need her to move on and get past this shit. If she does, I will. Rafe will get over it, our relationship will recover, and someday this will be something none of us even thinks about anymore. Almost like it never even happened.

"I should *want* him to kill you," she mutters, shaking her head and moving down the wall until she has enough distance to storm away from me.

I almost let her, then her words—and her inflection—hit me. My hand shoots out and I grab her arm, dragging her little ass back against me. "What was that?"

She catches her breath, but doesn't speak.

"What did that mean, Laurel?" I press. "Did Rafe say something to you?"

"Oh, now you want to talk to me," she says knowingly. "Fuck you, Sin."

This is not the fucking time for games. I'm not Rafe, I don't get a kick out of her shit, so instead of playing that game, I play my own. I push her against the wall—not hard enough to hurt, just to remind her who's boss—and soak up the sound of her startled gasp. My body follows, my chest pressing against her back.

"Is that how you talk to me?" I murmur, close to her ear.

I hear her swallow, hear her suck in a shallow breath. I

don't know if she's afraid or turned on. There's not a huge difference. It makes me hard either way. Laurel gasps again as I push my cock against her pretty little ass so she knows it.

Keeping one hand on her shoulder, I let the other drift down just above her knee, then I trail a hand up the back of her thigh, catching her dress and dragging it up, too. Laurel's head dips back like she's going to let it fall against my shoulder, but she catches herself.

"Now, I asked you a question," I tell her, releasing the hem of her dress and skimming her ass with my hand.

A little breathlessly, she tells me, "You are the absolute worst, aren't you?"

Smiling faintly, I run my lips along the shell of her ear. "Don't act like you're surprised."

"I know you're using me this time. This won't work now," she tells me.

"No?" I run my hand over her ass again, this time giving it a firm squeeze. "So if I put my fingers between these pretty little legs, you won't be wet for me?"

With relish, she tells me, "If you put your fingers between these pretty little legs, I'll tell Rafe."

"Liar."

"I could tell him to kill you, you know." She can't see my face, but my eyebrows rise in surprise at her casual threat. "You think you have all the power, but guess what? I have some, too. I don't have to protect you. You certainly don't care about hurting me, so I shouldn't care if you get hurt. You're probably just an unhealthy addiction and I should take my meds."

Not sure I like how casually she's referring to my death as the solution to all her problems. This isn't going quite the way I thought it would. It was easy as hell to turn her into something soft and pliable with sex in my bedroom, but I guess now that I've hurt her, she has a line of defense against me.

I fucking hate that, and not just because it makes her harder to bend. I don't like it because even if I deserve it, I don't *want* her to have a line of defense against me. I want her open. When it comes to Laurel, I'm greedy as hell and I want full access.

I guess that's unfair. Impossible. I can't have full access to her if I want her to move on with someone else. I don't *want* her to move on with him, it's just what needs to happen.

I shouldn't draw her deeper into my web, but I also don't want to die. If Rafe has said something to her, I need to know. As it is, I know I need to watch my back, but that sounded specific. If he's already made up his mind to get rid of me, that's information I damn sure don't have. If he hasn't, I don't want to jump to that conclusion. I need information, and I can't use my usual methods of information retrieval on Laurel.

Locking an arm around her waist, I pull her back against my body. I drag my other hand down the column of her throat, trail my fingers lightly over her exposed collar bone, then grab one of her breasts like it belongs to me and squeeze. Laurel gasps, and that time her head lolls back against my shoulder. I have her, I just have to keep her. I massage her other breast and bend my head to murmur in her ear, "You want me to fuck you, don't you? I can't fuck you if I'm dead."

"You're not going to fuck me if you're alive either," she mutters at me with her eyes closed. "You're just a terrible tease."

Can't argue that. "Tell me what Rafe said."

"He said you're an asshole."

I crack a smile, then nibble on her earlobe.

Sighing with pleasure or defeat, I'm not sure which, Laurel

says, "I can't tell you. I don't want him to get hurt, either. I'm sure it's nothing you can't guess. He's keeping an eye on the situation."

I release her earlobe, rubbing her nipples through the dress. "Which situation?"

"He wants me to get over you." Opening her eyes, she looks up at me. "I haven't had sex with him."

Something inside me drops. "What?"

"I mean, since... Obviously I slept with him over Easter, but since I met you, I haven't. I didn't sleep with him last night."

"Why not?"

"I'm not ready," she states.

I try not to feel too pleased as she leans against me, letting me toy with her body, and tells me she's not ready to fuck someone else—especially Rafe. He has a way of drawing in women, making them want him even when they shouldn't. This one *should* want him, but she wants me instead.

"But it's a problem," she adds. "He knows the reason I don't want to sleep with him is because of you, and he doesn't like it."

"Well, sure."

She hesitates. Her gaze drops. Now she's thinking about whatever it is he said to her. "So, while I could try the 'fake it 'til you make it' approach and just pretend to be, it's not that simple. In order to convince him I'm over you, it's not enough that I can be around you..."

I nod my understanding. "You have to sleep with him."

"I think he knows I could fake him out otherwise," she murmurs.

"Could you? You're not a great liar."

"I can lie if I have time to prepare myself, I just can't lie on the spot—and I can't always lie to Carly even with prep time. It's like lying to your mom."

"I lied to my mom," I offer.

"Well, you and I are very different people," she points out, dryly.

Smiling faintly, I say, "That's right, you're a good girl, aren't you?"

Some of the vulnerability I wanted appears in her eyes. "I'm not being very good right now."

"Sure you are." She's just *my* good girl, not his. I won't torture her by saying that. In fact, now that I know he hasn't told her directly he's going to take my ass out, I need to get her back on track. "Did he give you a time frame?"

"He said a few days. He was a jerk about it. Taunted me about my four day love affair."

"Well, he wasn't there."

Her eyes spark, and I realize immediately I shouldn't have said that. I all but admitted there was more to those few days than he could understand.

Brushing past that, I ask, "What did he say happens if you don't get over me in the next few days?"

Dread fills her eyes, verifying my concerns. She keeps her mouth shut though, not wanting to answer me. Not wanting to sic me on him. I don't fucking like it. I don't want her feeling the drive to protect anyone from me—especially him. Her loyalty has to belong to me—all of it. I'm a greedy bastard; there can't be any left for Rafe.

Which I realize is a problem since I'm pushing her to be with him, but I don't fucking care. It doesn't have to make sense; it's just what I want.

I stop caressing her breast and let my hand drift down her

torso. I run my hand over her still-flat tummy, and don't stop until my palm is cupping her hot pussy.

Her voice is strained, her control a delusion. Whether that changes or it doesn't, right now Laurel Price still belongs to me. I could fuck her right here against this wall if I wanted to. I could make her beg me to do it.

Fuck, do I want to.

Good thing one of us has some control.

Rubbing her pussy, supporting her weight as she floats helplessly into my depths, I assure her, "I'll figure something out, okay?"

"What does that mean?" she murmurs.

"I'll buy you more time. You do need to give him a chance, but I don't want you to fuck him because you're worried about me. It needs to be in your time or you'll resent him."

Sighing, she tells me, "This is a weird conversation to be having when you're touching me like this."

"Let's not hate each other," I murmur against the side of her face. "Let's be friends."

She moves her hips, rocking her pussy in my hand, wanting me to do more than rub her. Wanting me inside her. My cock hurts, it's so fucking hard. There's nothing in the world I want more than to give her what she needs, to spread those long legs of hers and bury my cock inside her.

"I don't think Rafe would approve of this kind of friendship," she tells me.

"Probably not," I agree, inching my finger up under the fabric of her panties.

"Oh, God, Sin." She reaches back and winds an arm around my neck, trying to pull herself even closer to me.

I'm so fucking tempted to at least finger fuck her right now, but that's probably not the foot we should start out on. If Rafe *did* walk back here right now, he'd have to shoot me in the back of the fucking head. I wouldn't even be able to blame him; I'd do the same thing.

I don't want to leave her hot and bothered, but I can't get her off, either. Letting my hand drift away from her core and up to her waist, I yank her close and murmur in her ear. "Go in the bathroom. Get yourself off. Think of me while you do."

The yearning is clear in her voice; she doesn't want to get herself off, she wants me to do it. "Sin..."

I hold onto her and guide her upright until I can let go without her falling. She still looks a little lost. I feel bad about it, but those fucking plump lips of her in a light pout are pure torture. My cock throbs, begging me to abandon reason, get her on her knees, and push between those pretty lips so I can find some relief.

There's a reason I don't let my cock run the show; it's a stupid fucking thing that wants to get me killed.

Smacking her on the ass, I nod to the bathroom. "Go."

She takes a couple reluctant steps forward, but looks back at me over her shoulder, her big blue eyes conflicted. I lift an expectant eyebrow, my features unbending. She knows I expect her to listen, and even though she wants more, she obeys me.

Once she's in the bathroom, I consider going into the other one and relieving my own fucking ache, but I can't. I need to get my ass back to the table. Since I probably shouldn't show up with a massive hard-on, I do my best to kill it while I walk back, but it's a struggle. Like Laurel, my mind doesn't want to obey; it wants me to follow her into the bathroom. It wants me to shove open whichever stall she's in and catch her playing with herself, to lick the sweetness off her fingers and shove my cock inside her instead. It tells me we're both so turned on it wouldn't even take long. I could bury myself inside her hungry little body and no one would even have to know it happened. In my mind, I see her helpless with wanting as I batter the walls of her welcoming pussy, as I leave my mark on her so no matter who she goes home with, I'm the one she'll always think about. Her hot, desperate cries would echo off the tiled walls and she'd come for me fast and hard, her sweet pussy squeezing me as her body shuddered with pleasure. My relief couldn't be far behind that sexy fucking show.

Great. My mind and my dick *both* want to get me killed.

I can't tell if I'm more alarmed or relieved when I get back to the table and Rafe isn't there. My steps slow before I approach and I sweep the room. It's a paranoid move, and I don't know why; Rafe would never attack me out in the open like this. He's not a fucking idiot. We do our dirty work in the shadows; our public behavior has to rise above shit like that if we want to stay under the radar. Flying off the handle over private matters would bite us in the ass, and anyone dumb enough not to know that gets killed off before long. Can't have liabilities like that in our crew. This family hasn't survived four generations of rule by being sloppy and careless.

Women sometimes cause waves, though. It's always been the case, and it seems like it always will be.

"Where'd Rafe go?" I ask Lydia, since she's the only one at the table.

Rolling her eyes, she indicates over by the bouncer. "He and Gio are having a word with the bouncer about letting whores in when they're here with the wives." Her lips curve up with a cynical little smile. "He should know better, right?"

Don't really know what to say to that, so I don't say anything. I'm careful not to be more than a distant acquaintance to the wives of the men I work for; makes it easier to mind my own business when it comes to their messy personal lives. Rafe's should have been the ultimate relationship to keep my nose out of, but I can already see that's not going to work. What am I supposed to do if he *does* try some shady shit like Gio? It's hardly a secret that while Lydia is the one here tonight, this weekend it'll be his girlfriend, Carla. Even Lydia probably knows, but as long as she holds her tongue, she can pretend it's not true.

Rafe is far less used to monogamy than Gio, and especially if Laurel resists him too long now that he has her, what if she does lose his interest? It's hard for me to imagine anyone ever losing interest in Laurel—I sure as hell can't stop thinking about her—but then I've always been a one-woman man. Some of the other guys are known for keeping their wives and families in one corner, then having a little something extra on the side. They seem to think it's their right, and sure, I think they're assholes, but I don't *care* when it's them.

There's not a chance in hell I would let Rafe stray on Laurel, and it's not my business. As long as he covers all his bases and takes care of shit, his relationship is his own deal—or it should be.

My gaze drifts to Laurel's empty seat, and I'm hit with fierce dread that I've irrevocably fucked things up here. Even once she gets over me and moves on with him, even if she's never mine again, I'm too invested in her. Instead of keeping my distance and keeping my nose in my own business, I buried it in her pussy.

This can't end well.

For the briefest of moments, I *do* think about Chicago. I'm not much for snow or working for assholes who abuse their power, but am I even going to be *able* to work for Rafe? I told myself our relationship would recover, but shit has already popped up. More shit will inevitably pop up. Even if he never cheats on Laurel, Rafe is a flirt. It's in his nature, who he is. The first time he turns a charming smile on anyone who isn't her, I'll want to smash his face in.

Especially because it upsets her. Watching anything but me upset Laurel makes my insides burn with palpable fury.

While I consider just how fucked I am, I reach for my bottle of water, twisting the cap until I hear the seal break. As I take the cap off, my gaze catches on Laurel's glass. Her new bottle of water is open, half of it already poured. I ordered her an untouched bottle, just like mine, and she hasn't been back to the table.

"What's that?" I ask Lydia, pointing at the glass full of ice water.

She frowns at me, glancing at the glass like she doesn't know what she's looking for. "Huh?"

"Who poured her water?"

"I did," she says, watching me like she doesn't understand what the big deal is.

"Why?" I ask.

"Everyone left me here at the table and I was bored. The waitress brought room temperature bottles of water. I figured since she ordered all that ice, she probably wanted it cold. By the time she got back from the bathroom, it would at least be chilled. Especially since you two lingered so long back there," she adds, lifting her eyebrows and picking up her own drink to take a sip.

That's not fucking amusing. I level her a cold look to let her know it, then I pick up Laurel's glass and inspect it.

"Are you fucking serious?" Lydia demands. "What are you doing?"

There's residue at the bottom of this glass, something

white and chalky. Now, I'm not saying I've never seen this happen before—a dirty glass, maybe some food left stuck to the bottom, a lazy dishwasher who didn't notice or didn't care. Hopefully that's the situation. I had no reason to inspect Laurel's glass before she poured the water herself, so I can't say for sure this glass was clean when she poured the first bottle of water. I know for damn sure it isn't right now, and I hope that's by accident.

Questions pile up in my head. Is Lydia the only one who has been sitting at this table? The chick in the dress Rafe bought her was standing right next to Laurel's glass when she caused a commotion. When Laurel stormed off, Rafe followed right behind her, but that woman lingered. Gio and Lydia were at the table, but I told Gio to escort her out.

Black dress girl said she worked for Cassandra's father. What if Cassandra caught wind of Laurel's pregnancy and sent some floozy to drug her? Since she found out Rafe's in power now, she has been trying to lure him back into her trap. If news has gotten out that Rafe knocked someone up, every skank he's ever fucked is probably realizing she lost her chance to snag him.

Cassandra is vicious. She'll play dirty if it benefits her. If she had her heart set on winning him back and becoming his queen, she wouldn't hesitate to shove Laurel out of her way by any means necessary.

There's no way to tell if this is dirt or crushed up drugs, but it's chalky enough I think it could be the latter. Flicking a glance at Lydia, I ask, "Did you get the name of the woman in the black dress?"

Lydia smirks, clearly not realizing how fucking serious this is. "In my mind, I labeled her Whore Number Two. If her real name was mentioned, I missed it."

My mind drifts to the waitress with the southern drawl. Brandi, I think. I can't remember if he's fucked her—it's too hard to keep track of all of them. Even if he hasn't, it's not impossible someone with more investment could have told her to put something in Laurel's drink.

Fuck, what if the glass had this chalky shit in it when the glass was first brought out?

I'm just about to put the glass down and haul ass back to the bathroom when Laurel walks past me and slides into her seat across the table. Her cheeks are rosy and I remember telling her to get herself off, but it feels to me like a lifetime has passed since then. Now all I can think about is what's in the bottom of this glass, and who might want to hurt her.

My plate is suddenly full. I'm too close to this, and I can't think straight. There are so many fucking potential threats; all I want to do is haul her ass back to my house where none of them can reach her.

Laurel is just now glancing at the empty spot beside her. "Where's Rafe?" Glancing across the table at me, she asks, "Why do you have my water?"

I keep her glass and hand her the bottle I just opened. I know mine wasn't tampered with. "Drink this instead."

Frowning, she says, "It's not cold."

It's not drugged, either, and that's more important.

Instead of saying that and scaring her when I don't have all the information yet, I push up out of the booth, taking her glass with me. "This cup's dirty. I'll go get you a clean glass and some new ice."

11

RAFE

It has been a long fucking day. As much as I usually enjoy going out, I'm glad as hell to finally be home, this day nearly over. I don't like to let a day end like this, though. Some people go to bed depleted after a long day and wake up refreshed, but I'll carry it with me. I need the rest of this night to go a hell of a lot better than it has so far, and that all depends on the lovely brunette in my bed.

Emerging from the bathroom after a hot shower, I find Laurel curled up on my king-sized bed, hugging her pillow as if for solace. She looks sad, and that makes me feel like an asshole.

It drove me temporarily crazy tonight how this girl I once had full access to is so closed off to me, yet when Sin shows up, I sense her opening like a flower, hoping for a drop of his attention. Like he's her fucking *sun*, the nourishment she craves deep down in her soul. It drove *her* crazy when he didn't acknowledge her, and I don't want her to care. Laurel has all the pieces and parts I want, she let me have access to them when we met in Chicago, but now she's closing me out. Now I'm not the person she wants to open up to.

By nature, I am not a jealous man, but this is a different thing. I didn't have Laurel and lose her; I had a *sample* of Laurel, sent it back to the kitchen, and when I changed my mind, a different dish was brought back to the table.

A dish served cold, as it were.

Not being able to reach her is getting to me. I see what I want, it's lying on my bed wearing nothing more than one of my T-shirts, and I can't have it.

But Sin could.

That's the worst fucking thing. I knew Sin was the one who initiated ending things, but I didn't realize she had attached to him more strongly than she had attached to me. Under similar circumstances, when I rejected her, she dismissed me. That's why I can't reach her easily now. If I somehow missed it prior to seeing them at the club, it would be clear now: she still has a thing for him. It's hard to imagine his rejection being less cold than mine, so I don't know what the difference is. Why was she able to cut off her fondness for me so effectively he happened, but after just a few days with him, she's stuck in some kind of mourning period and can't move on with me?

I need to backtrack, that's all I know. If I don't start doing a better job of reaching her, I'll lose her altogether. Given she's having my baby, that's the last thing I need.

I thought Laurel would be easier than this.

As I approach the bed, Laurel's gaze flickers to me, but it doesn't linger long. One thing I can usually count on even when she's not impressed with my behavior is Laurel's physical attraction to me. Right now I'm shirtless, and she barely even looks. She must be really pissed.

The room is dark since Laurel went to bed while I showered. I pull back the comforter and climb in beside her, but she keeps her back to me like we've already been married 20 years, half of those miserable. This won't do at all.

Since she's on her tummy, I advance closer and climb over her ass, straddling her body. I hear her sigh with annoyance, but I know it's because she thinks I'm going to fuck her. Joke's on her; I won't fuck that pretty little cunt tonight even if she begs me to. No, this relationship needs something more than sex—it needs attention.

So, I give her attention. The irritation melts right out of her as I start rubbing her tense little shoulders. I massage her shoulders wordlessly until she feels relaxed, then I lean in and add a few mild neck kisses to the mix.

Some tantalizing sound somewhere between a sigh and a moan slips out of her. "You smell so good," I murmur, before lightly kissing her earlobe.

"Mm, so do you," she murmurs back.

I rub and knead my way down her back. Run my fingertips along her sides, testing her response. I remember most of the things she liked in Chicago, but I need to get reacquainted with her body. Especially if I'm going to piss her off so much. Gotta know which buttons to push to disarm her ruthless little ass.

She's such a sweetheart 90% of the time, but boy, is she a pistol when you piss her off.

Right now she's not a pistol; right now she's my kitten, practically purring with contentment as my hands glide all over her body. Experimentally, I lean in and let her feel my breath on the back of her neck, drop a few feather-light kisses. Her little sighs of pleasure are reassuring. If she genuinely disliked me, she wouldn't enjoy this. Even with her Sin hang-up, this feels good to her. That's a good sign. For all the damage I've done, there's still something here I can work with.

After a few more minutes on her back, I move lower. I run my hands over her ass, but knowing she's not wearing any panties underneath this shirt, I can't resist sliding a hand between her legs. Cupping her pussy in one hand, I use the other to caress the inside of her thigh.

This is harder than I accounted for. Laurel has left me in such a dry spell, and her bare ass looks so fucking incredible. I bet everything I own no one has ever taken her ass before. That makes me want it even more. My cock stirs, trying to convince me to go back on the "no sex" plan. She's letting me touch her, even inched her legs apart slightly when I started rubbing her. A helpless little moan shudders out of her and it's all I can do not to push a finger deep inside her.

Before I can get too carried away, I move lower to massage her legs before working my way back up. After a couple more minutes massaging her neck and shoulders, I reach a hand under her body and turn her over on her back.

"There's that pretty face," I say, smiling faintly.

She narrows her eyes with playful suspicion, but I can see how much more relaxed she is already. Since my next move is to drag her T-shirt up and off her body completely, her suspicion seems warranted. At least she doesn't object. I'm still not going to fuck her; I just don't see the point in her wearing clothes when I could look at her bare body instead.

In case she is less relaxed now that she's naked beneath me, I rub her shoulders again while maintaining eye contact. Her gaze is softer now, more receptive to me. When my fingers lightly graze her collar bone, she sighs with pleasure. When I take both breasts in my hands and start massaging them, her nipples harden against my palms.

The glint of sexual interest in her gaze gets me too hard to hide it. I rock my hips forward so she feels it, then lean down and kiss the corners of her mouth while I squeeze her nipples. Laurel wraps her arms around my neck to hold me close. Since I can feel her wanting me, instead of kissing her deeply like I intended, I run a light finger along the most sensitive areas on her face. Her eyes drift closed when my finger glides over her brow bone, so I kiss her eyelids. Laurel smiles, and there's even more warmth in her gaze when her eyes open. Now I cradle the back of her head and take her mouth. She wants it, so those plump, perfect lips part for me. Our tongues tangle and she sucks lightly on mine in the most tantalizing way. Growling into her mouth, I take her lower lip between my lips and nibble on it.

When I pull back, she arches up to follow, so I know my job here is done.

Laurel is confused when instead of escalating things, I move off her and settle into my spot beside her. At this point, I know it will do me more good to leave her wanting than to fuck her, even if that's what we both want in this moment.

"What's your favorite thing to cook for dinner?" I ask her, wrapping my arm around her abdomen and tugging her close.

"My favorite thing to cook?" she asks, pausing thoughtfully. "I don't know, I like to cook a lot of things."

Running my fingers along her side, I tell her, "You can cook me dinner tomorrow night."

"Oh, *can* I?" she teases. "So kind of you to allow me to serve you, King Rafe."

I crack a smile and reach down to squeeze her ass. "Damn right. You can thank me later. We went out tonight, so we'll stay in tomorrow night, take it easy. I'll show you the library. We'll find a spot for your Brontë books."

"They do need a home," she acknowledges. "If we have a girl, what do you think of the name Charlotte?"

Adrenaline surges through me, but I manage to keep the alarm off my face. "Charlotte Morelli. That could work."

"Charlotte Price-Morelli sounds good, too," she says.

I hike up a disbelieving eyebrow. "You don't seriously expect my child to have a hyphenated last name, right?"

Laurel rolls her eyes. "You're such a brute. If it's a boy, do we have to name him after you?"

"Nah. Middle name, maybe. We don't have to talk about this yet."

With a knowing little smile, she asks, "Am I making you sweat?"

"Of course not. I just proposed to you a few hours ago; you think I scare easily?"

Laurel swats the arm I have wrapped around her. "That wasn't real; it doesn't count. You were all hyped up thinking about me making out with a girl."

"Oh, yes." God, the way my blood stirred when she shocked the hell out of me at the table. "You can continue telling that story if you want to. I especially like your attention to detail."

"It doesn't make you feel in any way territorial to think of the woman you're with making out with someone else? Just curious. I mulled it over, and I definitely would not be cool with it."

"It's another beautiful woman, not just someone else. Obviously I don't want you kissing another man, but if you wanted to kiss a beautiful woman? That's a different story."

"Why?" she asks, curiously.

I shrug. "Because you're not into women, so it's not a legitimate threat, and... you know, two beautiful women playing together... What's the question?"

"I'll be honest, it does nothing for me to think of you kissing another man. Definitely does not turn me on."

It's funny that she's comparing her sexuality and mine. Sex isn't where I wanted to go with this though. Before we can drift back into unpleasantness, I turn the wheel. "Tell me something I don't know about you."

Laurel snuggles into my side, tilting her head back to look up at me. "Like what?"

"Did you have any heroes growing up?"

Nodding her head, she says, "Yeah, but you already know the answer to this one."

"I do?"

"Carly," she says, her voice pointed with expectation, like this is ground we have covered before. "Sacrificed and worked her ass off to take care of me. My sister is my personal hero, no contest. What about you?"

"You wouldn't like my heroes. They're not very good ones. I looked up to them for other reasons, not because they were good people."

Cracking a smile, she says, "Your heroes were the villains, weren't they?"

I hold up my thumb and forefinger with about an inch between them. "Little bit. My dad was the more mild Morelli brother of his batch. There was Mateo's dad—a real sadistic son of a bitch. Vince's dad—a cold-hearted son of a bitch. Those were the ones I couldn't help looking up to when I was young. Granted, I had no idea the depths of their depravity. I didn't see any of that. All I saw was the result. I saw how people wouldn't fuck with them, how they made up their own rules and everyone else followed them."

"So, Mateo is a lot like his dad," I surmise.

Rafe shakes his head. "No, he's not as bad as his dad was. I mean, Mateo is a bastard, don't get me wrong, but his father was a nightmare. There was no love in that man. Now that Mateo has Mia, you can see he is capable of it, but Matt wasn't. When Matt had *his* Mia, he was her monster. He ruined her, crushed her, chased her away, then hunted her down. And when he found her, he didn't bring her back—he slaughtered her and the family she dared build without him."

Regarding me a little warily, Laurel says, "This is your hero?"

"Like I said, I didn't realize all that."

"Well, if you're that crazy, you hide it well. Also, if you kill me, I *will* haunt your ass. You'll never get another erection again. Haunted penis syndrome."

"I wouldn't hunt you down and kill you."

Nodding summarily, she says, "Glad to hear it."

"I liked Ben more than Matt anyway, he had his shit together. Matt let his feelings drive him and make him psychotic, but Ben, he had control. He was ruthless and unbending—he made up the rules and punished anyone who stepped out of line. He was a hell of a boss. Not a great *person*, but a hell of a boss."

Laurel nods, a look in her eyes almost like she's heard this before. Like I'm telling her something she already knows. I certainly never talked to her about Ben during those days in Chicago—I never even told her what I did, since she didn't ask.

Now I can't help wondering if she and Sin talked about him, but that doesn't make much sense. Why would they talk about that? Maybe my mind is just going to Sin because it's a sore subject right now. Since she and Vince are clearly chummy, he could be the one who mentioned Ben to her and

Carly. She was there at his funeral with them, so that makes more sense.

"He and Vince weren't close, though. He wasn't much of a father."

Laurel nods, glancing back up at me. "Yeah, that's what I heard. He didn't really even seem sad at the funeral."

"I'm sure it's harder for the kid who felt abandoned to look at him and see anything worth admiring. I wasn't his son, he didn't let me down, so I looked at it differently. To me, my dad was too soft, so I liked Ben's hardness."

Her gaze drops to my bare chest and she asks, "Do you think you're hard?"

"Nah, that was the simplistic view of a kid. I grew up. Now I realize there's not just hard and soft, strong and weak, there are lots of different ways to be both. Now I know a lot of what people see as strength is just fear, and a lot of what people see as weakness is bravery. There are a lot of intricacies and nuances to people that you miss if you're brushing with broad-strokes."

"I think so, too," Laurel says. "Did you still look up to Ben as an adult?"

"Well, then he was my boss; you have to respect your boss. Years back when he decided to come to Vegas, I made it my goal to join him as soon as I could. I was in Chicago then, but that was Mateo's territory from the time he was born."

"Yeah, your family's weird practice of passing on power by heredity." She nods. "I know about that. It seems like maybe not the best way of doing things."

"I agree, actually. Before all this," I say, indicating her stomach, "it's one of the things I was thinking about trying to change. It always ends up working out, but your brother-in-law is a perfect example of how that could have gone sideways. He and Mia were more like Matt and Belle, but Mia was lucky that the man she loved was Mateo, and he had more power than Vince so he could keep her. If Ben's power had transferred to Vince, he would have abused it to get what he wanted. Would have either ruined everyone else's lives or lost his own if someone with some sense stopped him—probably me. Everyone abuses their power every now and again, but overall you have to be clear-headed. Small minds shouldn't have immense power. That's kinda why I didn't want it to go to Gio. Not to sound like an asshole, but I don't think he's smart enough to be the boss. He's petty about everything, can't let a single thing go to focus on the bigger picture. Can't use his head if his feelings get in the way. He follows his feelings more than a good boss should."

"You don't follow your feelings?"

"Not in business, no. Can't afford to do that."

Laurel nods. "I can see how that would be the case. What about in your personal life?"

"I keep careful control there, too," I inform her, in case she hadn't already guessed. "You came back into my life at a weird time. This crazy ex resurfaced, then I found out you were pregnant, and *that*..."

"Threw you," she finishes, thankfully not looking pissy about it. "Trust me, it threw me too. I mean, I got so carried away with you in Chicago, I wondered if you *didn't* use a condom and I just didn't notice."

Smirking, I tell her, "That's not really something you don't notice eventually. Even if you're slick enough that you don't feel the stretching to fit, there's going to be more of a mess afterward without a condom."

"That makes sense. I don't know, I've only ever had sex with a condom."

Given I know so little about Sin's sex life, I guess I'm glad she made him wrap it up despite being pregnant. I know the doctor will still test her to be safe at the appointment—and draw some blood for a DNA test I'm not going to tell her about, just to cover all my bases—but I like that she's smart about sex. I've always been wary of the girls who seemed eager to fuck bareback; I'm not naïve enough to think I'm the only near-stranger getting that invitation.

Bringing up my sex life is not the way to go after the evening we had, so I don't say any of that. In fact, I don't think we need to say anything more. There are too many hot-buttons for each of us right now, and it has been a long-ass night. As much as I usually enjoy going out, I am certainly looking forward to a quiet night in with Laurel tomorrow. I think that's more her speed, and while I'm not interested in giving up my whole routine, I'll have to bend a little to meet her needs too, or this will never work.

LAUREL

There aren't words for how much I am dreading this phone call.

After a lovely, quiet breakfast with Rafe, now it's time to call Carly. Rafe assures me that my sister loves me and wants me to be happy, but I think she wants me to not have Rafe's baby much more.

"I think we should keep putting this off," I tell him. "There's no reason she has to know right now. We should have second breakfast."

Rafe shakes his head like he thinks I'm overreacting. "We're getting it done now."

"Wanna make out? I have a strong urge to make out with you right now. Let's do that instead."

"As tempted as I am by your offer of avoidance kisses, no."

I pout at him. "You don't like my mouth?"

Sliding me a playful warning look, he says, "Keep it up."

"I'm just saying, if you liked my mouth, you would be much more interested in going upstairs and making out for a while. We can make this phone call any old time."

"We're going to make it now so we can enjoy the rest of the day," he states, grabbing the phone himself since I'm making no move to do it.

"How about *you* make the call and I'll hide behind the couch and listen," I suggest.

He cocks an eyebrow and holds up the cell phone to show me it's ringing. "Better hide fast."

Grimacing, I hide my face behind my hands, but spread my fingers to peek. My sister's face fills the screen. Rafe has the phone aimed only at me right now, so she offers me a big smile.

"Hey, you. How's Chicago?"

This already sucks. Grimacing, I say, "Um, that's actually why I'm calling. I may have been gently massaging the truth when I said I was in Chicago."

"How gently?"

"I'm in Vegas," I blurt.

Her smile falters, but she doesn't flip out. "Vegas? Because you're visiting a certain golden-haired Morelli, or because you're finally pursuing your lifelong dream of legal prostitution? Please say it's the second thing."

Rafe tilts the phone to face him and he waves.

Carly groans and drawls, "No. Be a hooker, Laurel! It's not too late."

"That can't be the answer to everything," Rafe says, lightly.

Carly glares at him.

I might as well get all the bad news out there now. "The reason I came here is..." I hesitate, trying to think of a gentle way to put it, but there *is* no gentle way. "Remember Easter?"

"Like it was a fucking terrorist attack. Never forget."

"Right, well... so, it turns out that, um... Even though we were totally safe and we're not sure how..." I trail off and look

at the screen. I know she already gets it, but she's trying not to.
"I'm pregnant."

She says nothing.

This is scarier than anger and disappointment, because I have no idea what's coming.

Rafe turns the screen back so he's in the frame. "And we're cool with it," he adds. "This is clearly unexpected, but Laurel wants to go through with the pregnancy."

Carly glances down, shaking her head. Her long blonde hair is down today, and as she shakes her head, some of it falls in her face.

"Say something," I prod. "Please don't be mad. I didn't mean for this to happen. I have no idea how it did."

Carly looks back at the screen, attempting a half-ass smile. "I'm not mad, Laurel. Just processing. Sorry." Attempting to rally, she says, "How do you feel about this?"

"I don't know, how do *you* feel about it? I thought you would be more responsive."

"It's not my body, kiddo, it doesn't matter much how I feel about it. Or how *he* feels about it," she mutters. "Sorry, I'm trying."

Boy, would she not like Sin. That makes me sad, too. I'm trying not to think about him while I'm with Rafe in the interest of giving him a fair shot (and, well, because Sin refuses to do more than fuck with my head and toy with my body—no relationship is on offer). My heart won't let me keep him out for long, though. Even though I had a nice night with Rafe once we were in bed last night, and a nice morning with him so far, I can't help feeling a little guilty for it. It doesn't matter that Sin was a jerk, it doesn't matter that he told me himself to focus on what I *can* have and give Rafe a chance. It doesn't matter that he can go from so hot in the hallway, setting my body on fire even though my brain should know better, to so cold at the table afterward, like the interlude in the hall never even happened.

"Laurel?"

My gaze jerks to the phone and I realize I missed whatever Carly said. "Huh? Sorry, I spaced out for a second."

"Are you happy?"

I stare at the phone, unable to conjure an answer. That's a loaded question, and I don't know the answer yet. I'm certainly not the most miserable I've been this week, but I can't say I'm the happiest, either. I was the happiest in Sin's bed, and despite whatever that was in the hall last night, he assures me I won't be going back there.

My happiness doesn't depend on him though, regardless of how it feels at times. So I hope it's not a lie when I tell her, "I will be."

With a tremulous smile, she nods. "That's what matters."

"Please don't be disappointed. I know it's off-plan, but I've got back-up plans for my back-up plans. You know me. I'm not leaving anything to chance. I've got this under control. I'll still finish school; I'm just going to do it with a baby. But on the plus side? Ironic onesies."

Carly laughs a little. "I'll start shopping around for them now."

"Plus, baby shoes are really cute."

"Incredibly cute," Carly agrees. "And the fluffy little sleepers? We're gonna have to go shopping as soon as you find out what you're having."

"Mia bought me a starter pregnancy wardrobe already."

Her smile droops. "You told Mia before you told me?"

"Not on purpose! Rafe told Mateo, who told Mia—then

there was a minor kidnapping situation, nothing to be alarmed about. I had to see stupid Alec again."

Carly frowns, confused. "What?"

"Don't worry about it," I tell her, waving it off. "The point is, I actually did go back to Chicago and I was going to fly home from there, and when I got there, everyone already knew I was pregnant. His doing, not mine."

Carly messages her temples. "I'm getting a Morelli migraine."

"Well, you're married to one and I'm pregnant with one, so we should probably stock up on maximum strength aspirin," I tell her.

Glancing warily from me to Rafe, she asks, "So, are you guys *together* now?"

"No," I say, at the exact time Rafe says, "Yes."

I blink, looking over at him. He quirks an eyebrow. "We're testing the waters," I offer, though I'm not sure if I'm talking to him or Carly. I definitely wouldn't have been able to go to sleep after Sin cornered me in the hall last night if I'd been *with* Rafe, and I would expect him not to be buying other women presents if he thought we were official.

"Testing the waters," Carly repeats.

"To see if we would work in a relationship. Together would mean commitments have been made, and the only commitment I've made is the one to have this baby. Other than that, I'm still figuring things out." I hesitate, but then I decide there's little point holding back. "If things don't work out in Vegas, I'm sort of thinking about taking Mia up on her offer to let me stay at the mansion while I finish school."

"Nope," Carly says.

"See, on that we can agree," Rafe volunteers.

Pointing her finger at him, she says, "Don't you agree with

me, Satan." Pointing at me and lifting her brows, she says, "That's a hard no. Live with Mateo? Has the baby absorbed your whole brain? Do you remember who got you into this situation in the first place?"

"It's a big house; I would probably never even see him except at dinner. And Mia wants to adopt me as a friend. Remember their playroom? If I'm bad at momming, the play-room would totally make up for it."

Rafe interrupts. "I don't know why we're talking about this like it's a thing that may actually happen, because it isn't."

Just because he's annoying me, I add, "Mia says if I come back to Chicago, she'll hook me up with Alec and we can be sisters-in-law. Now that he knows I have a kinky side, he's wishing he hadn't cut our date short."

Rafe scowls. "Your *date*? You went on a *date* with Alec?"

Ignoring him and offering Carly an exaggerated shrug, I tell her, "I mean, I don't *like* Alec, but the only requirement to be my type seems to be 'capable of murder' and Alec assures me he's up to the task, so maybe he could win me over. I could see him sitting through some forced *Smallville* marathons as long as I pay him back once we hit the bedroom. Bonus, I bet he and Vince get along. No family feud if I marry Alec."

"All I'm hearing is you want me to kill my cousin," Rafe states.

I bite back a smile. "All I'm saying is I have a lot of solid options to look at."

"If the Morellis are involved in all your back-up plans, you need to find some back-ups for your back-ups *and* their back-ups," Carly informs me.

Rafe cuts in. "We're just going to focus on the first plan for now."

I nod my head. "Tomorrow is my first baby doctor appointment. Rafe's Vegas cousin got me an appointment with his wife's OB-GYN."

"That's exciting," she tells me. "You better take video if you get an ultrasound."

I look over at Rafe. "That's officially your job."

"Got it covered," he assures me. "Unless of course you'd like to call in Alec. Maybe he'd do a better job."

I shrug. "He might. I've never seen your videographer skills at work."

Rafe shakes his head. "The punishments just keep on stacking up. I'm going to have to spend the rest of my life punishing you at this rate."

"You can try," I tell him with a cheeky smile.

Carly feigns vomiting on the video chat. "You guys are making *me* nauseous."

"Oh, I'm not having morning sickness," I tell her, excited to have a single burst of good news.

"You sure it's a Morelli? They tend to cause as much pain as humanly possible," she replies.

The errant thought flies through my mind that I wish I'd met Sin when he was in Chicago for Ben's funeral that very same weekend. Then it would be his baby, and since he was so adamant about keeping Rafe's, I know he would be a total brute about keeping his. Not that I'd need much convincing in that scenario. Asshole wouldn't be able to cut me loose so easily then, now, would he?

"Um... I was joking," Carly says, watching me. "*Is* there a chance it isn't? Oh, God, please say yes."

Only if I figure out how to time travel. Of course, without Rafe's baby in my womb, Sin won't give me the time of day, but time traveling Laurel will already know he's worth it, so she'll force him to notice her.

Hell, I'll strip naked and cuff myself to whatever bed he stayed in. Watch him ignore that.

Well, I guess he has before.

Why does he have to be so damn elusive? All I want is the ability to time travel and force him to impregnate me so he will be stuck with me forever. Is that so much to ask?

God, infatuation turns me into a psycho. Should I be alarmed that I *have* that scenario at my disposal with Rafe, and I don't care?

Rafe waves a hand in front of my face. "Hello?"

Shaking my head slightly to clear it, I focus on my sister. "Yeah, sorry, I spaced out there for a second. No, there's no chance it's not Rafe's. Sorry."

Now all I can think about is Sin, and time traveling back to Easter so I can get knocked up with his baby instead of Rafe's. What would Daddy Sin be like? I bet it would be sexy. Everything he does is sexy.

I miss his strong arms wrapped around me in bed. Hell, I even miss him cornering me and pushing me up against the wall last night in the hallway. His big, scarred hand skimming my ass. Telling me to get myself off and think of him—like there's even a chance I'd think of anything else.

My chest aches. I want to text him.

This is not how today was supposed to go. I feel like climbing back in bed and wallowing about what an asshole Sin is, not having a relaxing day with Rafe—one of the most handsome men I've ever met, who also happens to have fathered the little cherry-sized being in my womb. I really am going to die alone.

Rafe notices me lagging and takes over the phone call. It's over a moment later since he and Carly don't have much to do with one another. The way he looks over at me, I feel like he knows what I'm thinking, like he can see where my mind went. That's probably me being paranoid, but it brings his words last night back to me. Now that he's not angry and there's no alcohol in his body, I wonder if there's any give. I wonder what would happen if I just told him plainly that I am head over heels in love, regardless of his opinion about how quickly it happened, and I just want to be with Sin. It's not like Rafe and I have some great love affair that can't be replicated. We hit it off over Easter and spent the weekend having great sex—that's every weekend for him. He only wants me because he thinks Sin does, but nobody wins if we don't want each other.

I guess I cannot say I am giving this a fair shot with thoughts like these running through my head. Regardless of Rafe's motives for wanting this, Sin doesn't, and I guess that's the thing that should ultimately shut these thoughts down. There is no choice between Rafe or Sin, my choice is between Rafe and Chicago.

And I do like Rafe. I liked him more a week ago, but I should try to keep an open mind. Maybe last night was an anomaly. Maybe the situations with other women would go away once he was in an established relationship. Everyone here thinks of him as a confirmed bachelor, so my presence at the table didn't mean much. I'm still new. Anyone would have thought of me as temporary.

Of course, he did still buy that girl a present. *Yesterday.*

But Sin just teased my breasts and touched my ass *last night,* so maybe we should clear the slate.

Rafe is silent, watching me, waiting for me to say something.

In the interest of the clean slate, I put on my best smile and say, "Now, how 'bout you show me this library?"

13

LAUREL

I cannot for the life of me understand why, but Sin accompanies us to my baby doctor appointment. When Rafe informed me he would be driving us, I prepared myself for the awkward hell of the ride there, but I was *not* prepared for Sin to get out of the car and accompany us inside.

All three of us stand in the elevator on the way up, staring at the silver doors, not speaking to one another. I'm developing a theory that Rafe is testing me, but testing me when he knows I'll fail isn't cool. Even slightly-inebriated-Rafe gave me a few days, and it has only been *one*.

The elevator dings and the doors slide open. Sin walks out ahead of me and I follow, my steps heavy with reluctance. Rafe walks by my side, so I try to keep my gaze off Sin. Because I'm trying, it's that much harder.

In low tones as I look over at Rafe, I ask, "Are you anticipating an assassination attempt at the baby doctor?"

Rafe cracks a smile. "He wanted to come. I figured there was no reason to say no."

"Is he at least going to stay in the waiting room?"

"You'd have to ask him."

I sigh to myself, glancing up at Sin as he holds the door open for us.

Chairs are set up in a boxy U around the room, then there's a blue, hard-looking couch in the center. That is already occupied by a very pregnant woman in a blue floral shirt with a schlubby-looking man next to her, scrolling through his phone. I see her gaze flicker in our direction as we walk in. Her eyes lower, then immediately snap back up and widen slightly. She's looking at Rafe, of course. It's like walking around with Brad Pitt in his prime, I swear to God. Since she has no idea who we are, after she gets done checking him out, her gaze drifts over to Sin. She looks him over more briefly, more warily, then her gaze snaps back to Rafe. Finally, she lands on me, like she wonders who I am that I warrant this well-dressed, sexy as hell entourage.

Rafe's hand lands on my waist and he tugs me toward the window, a faint smile on his face as he leans down and says, "We can people watch later. Let's get you checked in."

"People watching with you is too hard. You attract too much attention," I tell him.

"Want me to start wearing ugly glasses? You can bring yours, too; we'll both go out in disguise all the time."

"You'd still have this body, wouldn't you?" I mutter. "Glasses won't help. They'd just make you look smarter."

"Hey, it seemed to work for Clark Kent," he reasons.

My eyes brighten and I look over at him. "Do you like Superman? Carly and I have an unhealthy obsession with *Smallville*. Have you ever seen it?"

Nodding casually, he says, "I've seen a couple of episodes. You're a little young to have seen that, aren't you?"

I shake my head at him. "You can stream anything now, Grandpa."

"Keep it up, I'm gonna go steal that pregnant woman from her husband," he tells me, grabbing a pen out of a cup and jotting my name down on a sign-in sheet.

"I don't think you'd have to work very hard at it," I tell him.

"I love not working hard."

I roll my eyes. "I bet you do."

The frosted glass window obscuring the receptionist slides open and a woman with curly blonde hair and glasses addresses us without looking away from her computer screen. "Name?"

I open my mouth to give mine, but Rafe is already speaking. "Rafe Morelli. We're here to see Dr. Clark."

Her fingers halt their mad dash across the keys and she glances up. Smiling like suddenly greeting her patients is her passion, she says, "Of course, Mr. Morelli. Go ahead and come right back." She pushes back, standing. "I'll grab the door for you."

If she seemed annoyed by her job when the window first slid open, now she dotes on me like a loving mother. "You must be Laurel. How are you feeling today, honey? Have you been experiencing any morning sickness?"

I glance back over my shoulder at the pregnant woman and see her spying, but she turns back around when I catch her. I wonder how long she's been waiting? Doesn't seem fair that I get ushered right in.

"No morning sickness," I tell the lady, shaking my head.

"Oh, good."

I glance over at Rafe, a little uncertain, but the special treatment doesn't throw him at all. I guess he's probably used to it.

The woman leads me into a tiny room with a scale, two chairs, and a counter with a sink. Rafe and Sin both remain in the wide doorway, each holding up one side like the wall might fall down otherwise.

The receptionist tells me to take a seat in the chair and the nurse will be right in, apologizing for the size of the room. It wouldn't be so crowded if Rafe and Sin didn't each take up so much damn space. Not even just physically, but the bulk of their presences. It's like having three other people squeezed in this tiny room with me.

The nurse comes in next, not even blinking that there are two space-hogging men standing here guarding me. She runs down a checklist, asking questions, checking my blood pressure. Then she weighs me and marks that down, too.

"All right, if you guys will follow me to the exam room."

Now I expect Sin to fall back. No one is going to murder me in the exam room, right? The nurse has incredible discretion, because she doesn't so much as blink again when both men walk into the room with me.

I have less chill. I am wide-eyed and completely fucking confounded that Rafe is allowing this. Especially after the nurse tells me to undress and slip on this flimsy paper gown and the doctor will be right in to see me.

She leaves the room, shutting the door behind me. I hold the paper gown and stare at Rafe, then glance at Sin, then back at Rafe.

"Yes?" Rafe asks, expectantly.

"I have to undress."

"I heard," he says.

I nod pointedly, looking at the door. "You guys want to step outside?"

Rafe smiles calmly. "We've both seen you naked."

Face flushing, I say, "That's not the point. This is different. This is... weird."

Dismissing my concern, Rafe says, "It's fine. Go ahead, unless you'd also like to strip in front of Dr. Clark."

"You're a psycho," I mutter, stepping out of my shoes. Clutching the paper gown to my chest, I try to figure out how to undress without either of them seeing me. This is unbelievably awkward. It's *worse* because they've both seen me naked. My heart thrums enthusiastically in my chest as I awkwardly try to push down my pants. I didn't have anything of my own to wear, so I put on the smallest pair of black leather maternity leggings Mia sent with me—she sent two sizes, one for now, one for later—and on reflection, leather leggings were not a good choice. They would be annoying to get out of with two hands, but one and grasping a paper gown against me, trying to hide my nakedness from the two last men who have played with my body? Kill me now.

Sin sighs when he sees me struggling to keep myself hidden. He storms over, grabs the paper gown out of my hand, and wordlessly holds it up in front of me like a screen. I steal a wary glance at him, but he's not looking at me. He's in guard mode, completely impassive. That makes me more comfortable though, so before I lose my chance, I make quick work of stripping.

"Thank you," I murmur, as I take the gown and slip it on.

Without acknowledging I've spoken, he eases back to stand next to Rafe.

Rafe has a faint smirk on his face. Lightly mocking, he intones, "Aren't you thoughtful?"

"That's what I'm known for," Sin deadpans.

I hop up on the exam table and the paper rustles beneath

me as I scoot back. There are stirrups on this seat. Oh, God, they're not seriously going to stand over there while the doctor gives me an exam, are they? I can understand husbands being in here for this, but I am husbandless. I don't even have a boyfriend, just these two assholes who don't believe in privacy.

I huff and look over at Rafe, eyes narrowed.

"What's that look for?" he asks me.

"I want a milkshake when this is over."

Sin almost smiles. I see it, but he brings his hand up to cover his mouth and scratch a phantom itch on his face. When his hand drops, his handsome face is carefully blank again.

Whatever, he smiled.

Rafe shakes his head, not bothering to hide his. "I can get you a milkshake. Would you like a lollipop, too? We could stop at the toy store if you'd like."

"That's a cute thing to say to the girl you knocked up," I tell him, nodding my head. "We're all very impressed."

"I didn't say what *kind* of toy store," Rafe states.

Thankfully, he's easy to ignore as there's a knock on the door. A second later, the door opens and a man with thinning gray hair and glasses balanced precariously on his nose comes inside. He stops short, looking at Sin as if startled to see him, then his gaze jumps past him to Rafe.

Rafe steps forward, offering his hand for the doctor to shake. "Dr. Clark."

"Mr. Morelli," the doctor says, glancing uneasily at Sin, then attempting a smile as he looks at Rafe. "These are certainly better circumstances—"

Sin places a hand on the doctor's shoulder, giving it a firm squeeze. "No one needs a history lesson, doc. Your patient's over there."

The doctor looks so uncomfortable, you'd think *he* has to strip in front of Sin and Rafe. Steering right into it, he turns away from the men and walks over to me. He already looks a bit tired as he looks up at me. "And how are you, young lady?"

"Pregnant," I offer.

His lips curve up faintly. "Yes, I heard. Congratulations." Walking over to the sink to wash his hands, he begins asking a slew of questions regarding my medical history. The date of my last period is not a thing I thought Rafe or Sin would ever know about me, but here we are.

At least when it's time for me to put my feet in the stirrups, despite clearly being intimidated by at least Sin, Dr. Clark looks over at the men and indicates the wall over by my head. "Perhaps you gentlemen would like to stand over here for this part."

They both move closer to my bedside and the doctor directs a forced smile at Sin. "I assure you, we're quite safe in here if you feel more comfortable waiting outside."

"Oh, I'm perfectly comfortable," Sin assures him.

"We do have a larger exam room with a curtain partition, at least. We could move over there."

"We're good here," Sin states, smiling faintly while meanness oozes out of his eyes.

The doctor gives up lobbying for my privacy and begins the invasive part of the exam.

At least, I *thought* that was the invasive part of the exam until he grabbed a long gray wand and squeezed blue lube onto it. I realize it must be an internal Doppler, but it looks like a really boring dildo.

"Um, I thought the ultrasound was just... I thought you ran the thingy over my stomach."

"At later appointments, yes. This one has to be done this way."

"Oh, my God." I tilt my head sidewise to look at Rafe. "Two milkshakes."

Rafe smirks, stepping forward and coming over to surprise me by taking my hand. "I'll get you all the milkshakes you want."

The doctor looks like he wants to say something about that, but he holds his tongue. It's still a little startling when he slides this Doppler dildo thing inside me with Rafe and Sin both standing right here. I steal the most fleeting glance at Sin, but he's looking at the monitor. I turn my attention to the noisy white and gray image on the screen. There's a black hole in the shape of an eggplant with a little gray blur inside. The doctor moves the wand inside of me and the shape changes.

"Okay," the doctor says, pointing to the little gray blob. He moves the wand slightly and all of a sudden, it's baby-shaped. There are little legs, little arms, and a bulbous head. My hand flies to my mouth, all thoughts melting out of my brain except for one: that's my baby.

My heart beats strangely, my stomach rocking like this is the first time anyone has ever bothered to tell me I'm pregnant.

"He's wiggling a little, let me try to get a picture for you," the doctor says.

"He's wiggling?" I question, my eyes darting to the little movements. Oh, my god, it *is* wiggling. "Oh, my god, it's so cute," I gush, unable to help myself.

The doctor smiles faintly, pointing to a spot on the screen. "The heart is right here. Looks good. You want to hear the heartbeat?"

"Yes," I say, nodding vehemently.

The baby wiggles along the side of the sac like it's snuggling me.

"Oh, my god." I can't take my eyes off the screen, so I reach a hand in Rafe's direction. "Are you seeing this? Do you see how cute this is?"

"He's an active little guy," Rafe says.

"Or girl," I offer, glancing at the doctor. "Right?"

"Of course, too little to tell. At the 20 week appointment you should be able to tell. Sometimes the 16, but we like to wait until 20 to say anything."

I glance over at Rafe, remembering belatedly that Carly asked me to record this. My mind completely blanked the minute I saw the baby, but thankfully it's covered. By Sin. Face impassive, he stands beside Rafe, holding up a phone and recording all this. My stomach sinks and I look back at the gray monitor.

"Now, if the heartbeat cuts in and out, don't worry," the doctor says. "Since he's moving around so much, that might happen. It doesn't mean anything."

The sound of a rapid little heartbeat fills the room, and I clutch my own, certain it's going to either race out of my chest or drop out of my body.

"There we go, there's baby's heartbeat," the doctor says. "Sounds good." He measures something on the screen to get the beats per minute, then switches the screen back to the live view. Baby is dancing around again, then it snuggles me.

It's the cutest thing in the whole entire world. "I want to stay here forever and watch its cute little dance moves."

The doctor smiles and flicks a glance back at me. "I can make a DVD for you, if you'd like."

"Oh, yes, I would like. Thank you."

"Of course. I'll take a few more photos, too."

"You are my favorite OB-GYN ever, hands-down."

I moon at the screen the whole time. I might have thought it would get old watching the same few inches of space over and over, but it doesn't. I could move into this room and spend all of my days watching the baby dance to its own little beat, then snuggle me.

That's probably not what it's doing, but I don't care. That's what it looks like, and that's what I'm going to believe.

I didn't think I'd fall in love once in Vegas, let alone twice, but here I am—completely in love with the little wiggle worm snuggled up in my womb.

It would be nice if the first time had been with its father, but hey, life isn't perfect. As happy as I am, it's easy not to look at Sin right now. I don't want to worry about how he feels or what he's thinking. I refuse to feel guilty that I've been holding Rafe's hand this whole time. I ignore their drama and focus on the most important thing in the room—my little wiggle worm.

I'm in a daze now, removed from this earthly plane, floating on cloud nine. It's funny that as recently as a half hour ago, just thinking about it as a baby was vaguely stressful. Everything has changed. The doctor gives me two long strips of photos to look at and tells me come December 23rd, everything will change even more.

I'm gonna be a mommy.

The doctor is still talking. I assume Rafe is paying attention, because I'm not. All I can focus on now is my pictures. I touch my tummy and know this adorable little thing is nestled away in there. I'm much less mad at Rafe and the condom company about this situation now. Ideal? No. But holy cuteness, I can't be mad about it.

Thank God Sin kidnapped me.

Rafe is talking to the doctor, so I steal a moment to look

back at him, hanging back against the wall. There are no shadows in this brightly lit room, but he still tries to keep to them. He's watching the doctor and Rafe. I hold up the ultrasound pictures to get his attention. My movement causes his gaze to flicker in my direction and he takes a tentative step forward. I nod and wave him over.

"Look at this," I tell him, handing over the strip.

Smirking faintly, he says, "I just saw. I was standing right here, remember?"

"How freaking adorable was that?"

He rolls his eyes and his tone is dry, but I know he means it, the big brute. "So adorable."

Now that I'm firmly decided and I would take a bullet for the tiny little nugget that couldn't even survive outside my womb, I feel like a jerk for saying it was a pregnancy I didn't want. I mean, it *was*, but it's not now. I know logically it couldn't hear me, but still.

"I normally wouldn't want to say this and further encourage your pushy, oppressive, caveman bullshit, but thank you. I was leaning in the direction of not doing this, and... well, I'm glad now that I had a little extra time to consider my options first."

"You like my pushy, oppressive, caveman bullshit," Sin mutters, handing back my photo strip.

"I really don't. Not philosophically. It's why I dumped you."

Snorting in amusement, he says, "Is that how that went down?"

I nod confidently. "Yep. All my idea. I hope your feelings weren't hurt too badly."

"I'll try to survive," he assures me, dryly.

"Laurel."

Rafe's voice pulls my attention to the foot of the bed, where he stands and talks to the doctor while I joke around with Sin. The serious look on his face startles me and I sit up. "What's wrong?"

"It's not the baby," the doctor assures me, flicking a glance at Sin. He's probably wondering why he's the one standing at my side now. Rafe could move back into that spot, but Sin doesn't move.

"Then what is it?" I ask.

Rafe cracks a smile and shakes his head. "You have a weak uterus."

"What?" I frown, glancing from Rafe to the doctor, then back to Rafe. "This is funny? Why are we amused? What does that mean? Is the baby safe? How do I fix that?"

"You'll be all right as long as you're careful," the doctor rushes to assure me. "It's nothing to stress about. Rafe has my number, should you experience any bleeding or cramping, you can call me straight away, but this isn't something to get yourself upset about." His gaze flickers to Sin again and he pauses, awkwardly. "There's just a minor inconvenience, and it may not last the entire pregnancy. I'll check you again at your next exam in four weeks."

"What's the inconvenience?" I ask, though I don't much care. Whatever it is, I'll do it.

Rafe answers for him. "We can't have sex."

My eyes widen. "What?"

The poor doctor, clearly not happy to have to deliver this news, rushes again to assure me, "It could be a short-term situation. I'll be sure to examine you again at your next appointment. But until then..."

Amusement bubbles up within me, but I smother it down. I shouldn't laugh. This is *not* funny. If my uterus is weak, that pisses me off—not because of the sex thing, but because I don't want there to be any risk to the baby, no matter how small.

It's just that not being able to have sex with Rafe for at least a month being the only way to protect the baby? Kinda funny.

14

RAFE

It has been three days since the baby doctor appointment, three nights of sexless sleeping. I'm not excited about it. After two nights of warming Laurel up, I expected her happiness at the doctor's office to have a very different result. As she squeezed my hand and squealed over the wiggling little thing on the screen, I was pretty sure I was going to have a very good night.

Instead I got "no sex for at least four weeks."

Fantastic.

At least Laurel is happy. She's been softer and dreamier since the appointment. Every day, at least twice, she watches the DVD. Any doubt or hesitation has evaporated completely.

After four nights in, though, I'm itching to go out. While I'm out today, I decide to pick up a new dress for Laurel. A surprise might lure her out. She seems perfectly content to spend each and every night at the house, but I'm starting to feel claustrophobic. Maybe it wouldn't be so bad if we could spend part of those days in bed, but it's a little more challenging living like a monk. I would have thought we could at least fuck around, but the goddamned doctor told me—in front of Laurel—that even oral would have to be gentle and infrequent, as she really needed to rest as much as possible.

Neither of us can find much to get excited about in a "gentle and infrequent" potential blow job, and Laurel is in protective mama bear mode, so my libido is not high on her priority list.

Long story short, no sex is happening. Not any kind of sex. We can kiss and touch, but knowing I have no outlet for it, I don't take the touching too far.

I've also kept her away from Sin, though I'm thinking less about that with her in baby mode. Her love life seemed to be a bigger priority before the first wiggle. After that, she was a goner. Sin might have been able to compete with *me*, but he can't compete with *that*.

She's probably less appealing to him now too, knowing she can't fuck. Not to be an asshole, but it's not an unimportant part of a relationship, and it's off the table indefinitely right now. I'm hoping she gets cleared at the next appointment, but there's no guarantee. When I asked the doctor about the chances, he hemmed and hauled and couldn't say anything concrete.

Putting my car in park and killing the engine, I look up at the apartment building in front of me. I remind myself I'm not doing anything wrong, but I don't know why I need the reminder. Probably the fact that I haven't had sex in five million fucking years.

It's a derelict building with absolutely no security. No buzz required to get in, no bumbling security camera fixed above the door to see who comes and goes. Doesn't appear to matter in this building. I open the door and let myself in like any of the tenants, then I head up two flights of stairs. Stopping in front of room 307, I rap on the door.

A minute later it swings open. Marlena stands on the other side, frowning at me. "What are you doing here?"

I smile faintly. "Nice to see you, too."

Leaning against the doorframe, she looks up at me. "You want me to lie? It's not that nice to see you. I'm kind of busy right now."

My gaze flickers past her to the interior of her apartment. "Boyfriend over?"

"I expected more subtlety from an accomplished player like yourself," she states, clearly unimpressed.

I offer her a slow smile, the kind I've used to melt a cubic fuckton of women before this one. "Honey, I don't need subtlety."

Losing a little of her cocky demeanor, she shifts and looks away. "You shouldn't be here."

"I say otherwise. I'm gonna come in," I tell her, pushing on the door.

She huffs, but takes a step back and lets me waltz into her apartment anyway. I frown when I see boxes all over the place. The whole apartment seems to be packed up—all but a couch and the ugliest fucking yellow chair I have ever seen in my life. It looks like someone plucked it straight out of the 70's and dropped it into her apartment.

"Moving apartments?"

"Moving, period," she states. "I don't have a job, and my landlord has this weird insistence on being paid to house me."

"What an asshole," I say lightly.

"Right?" She glances around, crossing her arms awkwardly. She's slightly uncomfortable with me being in her apartment, but it's because she's attracted to me.

"Where are you moving?"

Her gaze drops along with her tone, alerting me to a drop in mood. "Arizona."

Surprised, I look back at her. "Arizona? I thought you were in school."

"Can't pay for that without a job, either. I have enough to pay for gas money back home, but not enough to pay another month's rent while I try to find a job. Failing a miracle, I don't see that changing. I've applied everywhere with unbecoming desperation, and no bites."

"You don't need a miracle, you need money." Reaching into my back pocket and drawing out my wallet, I ask, "How much is your rent here?"

Frowning at my wallet, she says, "I don't want your money."

I pinch a stack of 20's, looks like a little over $2,000. Holding it out, I tell her, "Here."

"I'm not taking your money," she states again.

"Why not? You need money. I have money. What's the problem?"

Her blue-green eyes widen in disbelief. "The problem is I don't want to be in debt to the mob. Are you kidding me?"

"The mob isn't loaning you money. I am."

Eyeing me warily, she says, "Well, I have a feeling I don't want to be indebted to you either."

"You're not indebted to me," I tell her, shaking my head. "Think of it as an advance. I'm going to give you a job."

Warily stepping closer, she eyes the money, but her distrustful gaze returns to my face and she still doesn't take it. "Doing what?"

"Waiting tables. You're a waitress, right? I have a restaurant. Nicer than the shitty place you worked at anyway, better customers, better tips. Better management," I add with a wink.

That makes her smile, but she's looking down again. She does that a lot. "I'm not sure your girlfriend would like that."

"Well, she doesn't know. And... she's not exactly my girlfriend." I don't know why I add that last part. Or maybe I do, because my gaze is less of a liar and it drops to those pretty plump lips. The waters are too murky to do anything about it right now, but I can't honestly say I haven't pictured catching that plump bottom lip with my thumb, seeing vulnerability in those blue-green eyes as she looks up at me.

Regarding me with perfectly reasonable suspicion, she asks, "Why?"

"Why isn't she my girlfriend?"

Marlena shakes her head, nodding at the money. "Why do this? Why give me money? Why give me a job?"

"I got you fired, didn't I?"

Rolling her eyes, Marlena says, "Yes."

"So I only have to ruin a set amount of lives each month, and I've already met my quota for this one. I can afford to do a nice thing just this once."

Fighting a smile, she meets my gaze. "Oh, can you?"

I nod, giving her a playfully hooded look. "Just don't tell anyone. Gotta protect that reputation."

Her plump pink lips stretch into a nice smile. Her guard is down and she moves closer. I think to take the money, but she just touches my shoulder, then walks past. "I'm going to grab a drink out of the fridge. You want anything?"

Instead of answering, I follow her. She opens the refrigerator door and leans down. My gaze drops to the curve of her ass for a split second, then I move up behind her to peer inside. "Sure, grab me a bottle of water."

She does, but she straightens more slowly than she bent over, clearly cognizant of me behind her. I let a hand rest on her hip and I hear her hastily inhale. Pulling her back against me, I push the refrigerator door open and murmur, "Don't want to leave that open."

Turning around, she neatly moves my hand off her and holds out the water, swallowing. "Here. I appreciate the job offer, but I can't take it."

I frown at her. "Why the hell not?"

"Because I am very much attracted to you, and I think you're attracted to me. I won't believe you if you tell me you're not, and if you think that's arrogant, fine, but I have my principles."

"Your principles?" I echo.

"I don't know what that girl is to you, but I know she was upset that you bought me a dress, so I don't think she would be any happier that you're giving me a job at your restaurant. Arizona isn't the end of the world. I won't sell my soul to stay in Vegas."

I can't help smiling. "Sell your soul? That's a little dramatic, isn't it?"

Pulling herself upright, she tells me, "No, it isn't. She's having your baby, isn't she?"

That knocks the smile off my face. I hesitate, knowing this will be a dealbreaker, but I won't lie to her, either. "Yes."

Nodding once, eyes dimming, she says, "So, that's a mess I'm not going to get involved with. I'm sure you can find plenty of side dishes around town, but I won't be one of them."

"Side dishes? That's not what this is."

"Then what is it?" she demands.

Eyebrows rising, I tell her, "All I offered you was a job, Marlena."

Unconvinced, she says, "And you had to do that yourself? You couldn't have sent someone in your stead? Or, hell, had the manager of your restaurant call me with an offer? Does your not-girlfriend know you're here? Is she okay with this?"

Maybe it shouldn't agitate me that she suggests I should run everything by Laurel before doing it, but it does. "I didn't ask permission. I'm not—" I stop short, realizing anything I say here will only make her scowl harder at me.

Shaking her head, she tells me, "I'm sorry. I'm not that kind of girl. I'm not interested in your job or your money. Thank you for the offer, truly. Especially because you already know I'm not a very good waitress, it was nice of you to offer, but the answer is no."

"I am not *cheating* on her. There's nothing untoward going on here. I'm offering a job, no strings. I'll rarely even see you. If I *do* ever see you, it will probably be when I'm there eating with her. Does that make you feel better?"

"I can't," she insists, shaking her head. "I'm not blaming you, I just... I can feel that this is a bad idea, and I'm going to listen to my instincts on this one."

"No, you're not," I state. "This is stupid. I'll take the money to your landlord myself. Trust me, you won't be evicted." Then, reconsidering, I look around her apartment. It's clean enough so she clearly takes care of the place, but damn, is it small. In fact, looking into her living room, I notice the bedroom isn't even completely closed off—merely hidden behind a bookcase that acts as a wall. She doesn't even have a bedroom.

I'm also realizing I haven't had sex in an eternity and I'm this close to a woman I find attractive and her bed. Damn, I do need to leave this apartment. Not until she stops being a pain in the ass, though.

"Actually, you're already packed up. How about this? I own an apartment community in town. It's a nice one—a hell of a lot nicer than here. I know for a fact there are some vacancies. Let me see what they've got, we'll move you into one of those instead."

Eyes widening, she demands, "How did you get to 'move into an apartment I own' from my refusal to take your job offer?"

"I'm a presumptive bastard," I tell her. "And you're moving. I've decided. You can get on board or not, but I'm having men move your stuff this evening."

"Like hell you are," she says, eyes blazing.

"You think you can stop me?" I ask, eyes dancing with amusement. "This apartment is closer to the restaurant where you work now anyway."

"I do *not* work at your restaurant."

Placing the bottled water down on her counter, I reach for my pocket to put the money away. I like this plan much better anyway.

Glaring at me, she asks, "Is it also closer to wherever you live, by any chance? Late night driving distance if you get bored at home?"

I can't help smiling. It's starting to amuse me how angry she's getting at my perceived bad behavior. "You can believe me or not believe me, doesn't matter. You're not going back to Arizona and you're not staying in this closet." Pointing to the ugly-ass yellow chair, I tell her, "You can leave that, though. It's older than I am."

Now she looks offended on behalf of the chair. "You be nice. That's my favorite studying chair. I've had it since junior high and it goes where I go."

"It's ugly," I state.

"It's mine and I love it," she says, planting a hand on her hip and mean-mugging me.

Damn, she has a cute mad face. Good thing, since she's been mad at me half the time I've known her. I wanna bury her little angry ass in the mattress, though, so I really do need to leave. Grabbing the bottle of water, I make my way for the door.

"My men will be by this evening. Don't leave, or I'll follow your ass to Arizona. And then I'll be annoyed, and you have a hard enough time dealing with me nice."

"You are an overbearing jerk, has anyone ever told you that?" she says, following me.

"I've heard much worse," I assure her.

"You can't just make me move. You can't make me work for you. You can't just take over my life like this."

I pause with my hand on her doorknob and glance back at her. "You wanna bet?"

She must know better than to challenge me on that. She still scowls at me like I'm the biggest pain in the ass she has ever encountered, but she doesn't argue. "I don't even know where this apartment is."

I won't gloat too loudly, but I can't help smiling. "Don't worry, the guys will escort you." Holding up the cheap bottle of water, I tell her, "Thanks for the drink."

15

SIN

Fury burns through my veins as I pound on the front door, then remember there's a doorbell. I envision Rafe answering the door. I *hope* Rafe answers the door, because I'm going to lay the motherfucker out. My hand flexes into a fist, then releases, flexes, then releases. Open the goddamn door, asshole.

Juanita answers the door, her brown eyes wide with mild alarm at the ferocity of my knocking. Her alarm ratchets up another notch when she sees how fucking angry I am.

"Where is Rafe?"

She points toward the living room.

I storm right past her without another word.

I get just a glance at the scene before I disrupt it. Laurel and Rafe are sitting on the couch watching television, a bowl of popcorn between them. His arm is stretched across the back, draped over her shoulder. She's laughing at something on the television, but he doesn't look as impressed.

Her smile dies as I storm into the room. Rafe's arm abandons her shoulders and he eases forward, regarding me warily.

Struggling to keep a lid on my fury, I clench my fists again and take a breath. Unlocking my jaw, I tell him, "I need to talk to you alone."

Easing up off the couch, he glances back at Laurel. "I'll just be a minute."

He shows me to the foyer, but that's not far enough. I walk back outside and wait for him to follow. Still eyeing me as he shuts the door behind him, he asks sarcastically, "Is this far enough away, or should we walk down the street?"

"What the fuck do you think you're doing?" I demand.

Like the smug son of a bitch he is, he lifts his eyebrows and says, "I think I'm having yet another quiet night in with Laurel. Why?"

Jabbing a hand angrily out at nothing, I ask, "You wanna tell me why *your* men are moving that fucking waitress into one of your apartments right now?"

Rafe rolls his eyes and falls back a step. "Oh, good. The morality police dispatched another fucking officer."

"This is not a fucking joke," I tell him.

"This is not your business," he counters.

"It absolutely is my business," I fire back. "You fucking up the relationship I handed you on a goddamn silver platter? That is my fucking business. I'm *making* it my business. You have been with her for a week, and you're already fucking around on her?"

"First off, I am not *with* her. Laurel made it very clear to me and her sister that we're only 'testing the waters' to see if we want to be in a relationship. I can't even *fuck* her because she has a defective fucking uterus. This is not cheating. Secondly, her name is Marlena, not 'the waitress' and I am not fucking her either."

"I don't give a fuck what her name is."

Pointing his finger at me and lifting his eyebrows, he says, "*Lastly*, it is not your motherfucking business. You didn't hand me anything, and I am not wronging Laurel. All I did was repay a little kindness to a woman who was nice to me for no reason. That's it. I'm not moving Marlena into the apartment so I have unfettered access to her. That is not what this is. In case you didn't notice when you stormed into my house, *Laurel* is the one I'm spending the evening with. Laurel is the one I had dinner with, and Laurel is the one I stayed in with when she said she didn't feel like going out tonight. *Again.* Laurel is the one I will go to bed with tonight and the one I will wake up with tomorrow. I am not going to abandon Laurel."

"That doesn't mean shit," I say, shaking my head. "You have the financial resources to take care of her; I'm not worried you're gonna abandon her. I'm worried you're not respecting her, and I've gotta be honest, that really pisses me off."

"Well, that sounds like a personal problem you need to take care of," he tells me. "Laurel's mine, not yours. You don't decide how I treat her. And she has no complaints, so—"

Gesturing at the front door, I ask, "She knows, then? If I go in there and tell her you're moving the woman you bought a dress for into an apartment, she won't be surprised?"

The look on his face tells me that is not the case.

"This is bullshit," I tell him, shaking my head. "You like Laurel. Why are you doing this? Why are you fucking it up?"

Sighing and raking a hand through his hair, he tells me, "It's one thing after the next, Sin. Yes, I do like Laurel. I like her a lot. But it's one fucking struggle after the next. This isn't a relationship, it's a damned ordeal. First I'm an asshole and I fuck it up, I fully admit fault there. Then you get in the way and she leaves. I make her come back physically, but she's still stuck emotionally, then we can't even work through our shit. She doesn't like to go out, and I don't want to stay in all the damn time. At the end of a long day, I can't even fuck her. It's just... this isn't fucking fun. I'm sorry, but you wouldn't be having fun either."

"Bullshit," I say. "I *did* have fun in the same fucking circumstances. If the only ways you can have fun with Laurel are going out or having sex, I feel sorry for you. She can't have sex with you because she's trying to carry your child, you asshole. Give her a few weeks."

"It may not just be a few weeks. It could be the whole pregnancy."

"So what? You can't have sex for a few months and she's not worth having?"

"You're putting an awful lot of words in my mouth, Sin. I am trying to make this work. I'm doing my best. It just isn't easy, that's all. It's one obstacle after the next when it should be the easiest. This isn't our seventh year of marriage, this is a new relationship. It should be fun at this stage, and when it isn't fun, there should be memories of when it was. I have a few damn days of nice memories—that's it. We don't have enough of a foundation to weather this kind of crap."

He's not wrong, but it still feels like an excuse to me.

"Tell me you don't want to fuck the waitress."

His eyes narrow. "I'd like to fuck *someone*, sure. *Laurel* has had sex more recently than I have, and now she's closed for business."

"No, she damn sure has not. Laurel hasn't had sex since Easter."

He rears back briefly, then frowns at me. "What are you talking about?"

"I didn't fuck her. She didn't tell you?"

Clearly, she did not, because he laughs. Not with real amusement, but a tired half-laugh. "Yeah, okay."

"I didn't. We fooled around, that's it."

Seeing I'm serious, he stares at me. I expect relief to follow, but this seems to piss him off more. "Are you fucking kidding me? You didn't even have sex, and she's this hung up on you? I fucked her for three days straight and she cut me off the first time I was mean to her. I gave her the first vaginal orgasm of her life, and you..." He trails off, shaking his head. "What the fuck?"

I know I would be more relieved in this scenario than he is, but his sincere surprise knocks a little bit of the wind out of my sails. I don't know why Laurel didn't tell him that. I specifically told her to.

When I paid the doctor a little visit and persuaded him to feed them the weak uterus bullshit, I figured it might make things a little hairy, but Laurel needed more time and I didn't want to risk Rafe steamrolling over her.

I know he has to sleep with her if this is going to work, but knowing that doesn't make it any easier to swallow. I guess I can't claim complete selflessness here, because there was no reason to add the part about how they shouldn't fool around either except that I didn't want them to.

"I'm in the way," I say more calmly.

Rafe sighs, but he seems calmer now, too. "You are, but that's not all it is. I thought that was it at first, but it's more than that. I'm trying to build a relationship with just the broken pieces. Most people having a baby together get a chance to fall in love first. We didn't get that. I never even wanted any of this in the first place, and *maybe* I could get on board with it with someone I loved first, but Laurel and I barely knew each other. The timing here is not good. We skipped right past falling in love and fell straight into the kind of rut it should take people years to sink into. It certainly doesn't help that I look at her sometimes and I can *see* her thinking about you. She might as well be projecting her thoughts onto my wall for how clearly I can see it."

"Do you want this to work?" I ask, simply.

"I don't know," he admits. "I like Laurel. It's not... she has plenty of appeal, the problem isn't her. It's everything, and everything is a lot to deal with."

"You have to want it to work," I advise him. "It won't work if you don't. You're just wasting each other's time at that point."

"Yeah, well... I don't think *she* wants it to work. She was open-hearted when she came here, but bit by bit, we've closed her off."

I notice he says we, not letting me off the hook, and he doesn't even know how much I contributed to that. I do, though. I know exactly how much I contributed to it.

"She'll open back up if you work at it," I tell him. "It's still fresh. She'll come back around if you earn it. The ball is in your court at this point, but... you're right, this isn't my business. I need to take a step back. We need to give Laurel a break from me. If you and I need to meet up, let's do it away from the house for a while. If you two go out, don't invite me. Give her a chance to clear me out and make room for you. And be nice to her. Don't do shady shit like this. You need to stay away from the waitress. I'll stay away as long as you do, but this won't work if your eye is already wandering. You have more focus than that. Laurel is great, and she deserves your full attention, not whatever scraps you can cobble together at the end of the day."

He's not angry now, but I can see my words still irritate

him. "That is not what I was doing. But yeah, that sounds like a good idea." He misses a couple beats, and I don't say anything either, so he adds a far too knowing, "You still want her, don't you?"

There's little point answering such a stupid fucking question, but I do anyway. "Of course I do."

Since I've said far more than I meant to and I have a shit-load of work to do, I turn and leave without another word.

16

LAUREL

Over the next few days, more things change. The doctor called me to say he was reviewing my chart and he found an anomaly in what he had written down, so he needed me to come back in for an exam. Rafe brought me, this time without Sin, and the doctor let me see the baby on the ultrasound screen again. Added another few minutes of runtime to my DVD and made me a happy girl. He also gave me another pelvic exam and discovered, somehow, what he had taken for uterine weakness must have been something else, because my uterus was strong, healthy, and fully capable of holding the baby safely if I wanted to start having sex again.

That should have been a relief. It certainly was for Rafe, but while he looked like a dying man someone had just healed, I felt dread sink inside me. The weak uterus bought me several days, but I thought it was going to buy me several weeks—at minimum. I had a whole plan in my head, and I budgeted the time. No longer racing against the calendar, I could go at my own pace. I would surely get over Sin—since I only spent *days* with him—in a few *weeks*.

But suddenly, I have no more days. Rafe was immediately more affectionate, but that sort of annoyed me. Sex is great, but it isn't everything. These past few days when he knew he wasn't getting sex, he has been markedly less affectionate with me, and I definitely noticed. Sin knew he wasn't getting sex out of me (his choice, not mine) and he found me no less interesting.

So, while a few nights ago I felt closer to wanting to sleep with Rafe, the days since the first doctor's appointment have made me want him *less*, not more. I also really wanted him to be more excited about the baby after that appointment. It changed everything for me, and if he had responded with some kind of eagerness at the prospect of us having a baby together (and kept up the same affection, like the night he gave me the massage and talked to me in bed) then I think I *would* be willing to sleep with him now that the doctor has cleared me.

But he didn't.

If it all comes back now that he can have sex with me, it will feel insincere. Will he lose interest in me all over again when the baby is born and I can't have sex for several weeks? His interest now just doesn't feel real or dependable, and as much as I try not to compare him to Sin, I can't help comparing. Back in Chicago after Easter, I compared the guys I met to Rafe and found them lacking, but now I compare Rafe to Sin, and... well, he doesn't stack up. As a man, yes, Rafe is absolutely appealing. If I had never met Sin, or I hadn't met him until I was already in love with Rafe, maybe I wouldn't feel this way. But I did, and I do. At the end of the day, no matter how attractive Rafe is, I don't think he will ever compare to Sin in my eyes.

Because of all that, I no longer want to sleep with him, and I can already see that's going to be a problem.

So, on the way home from that appointment, I text Mia. I tell her that I don't think things are going to work out in Vegas, and ask if she is *positive* about her offer to let me stay at her house for fall semester. I already sent her the video of the ultra-sound and she freaked out about how cute it was with me. I guess you just need a fellow girl for that, because neither of the guys were adequately excited. She didn't find it at all odd that Sin was at the appointment with me to record the video, but when I sent it to Carly, she did.

"He invited one of his thugs into the exam room with you??" she demanded.

With misplaced indignation, I informed her, "Sin is not a thug!"

Which I guess is a lie. Sin *is* technically one of Rafe's thugs, but he's so much more than that, so it feels like an insult to refer to him that way.

I have yet to explain Sin to my sister. I don't think she would like him, and I will want to jump all over her about it, so I'm just avoiding telling her. Not to mention, as much as Sin still occupies so many of my thoughts and so much of my heart, it doesn't seem to matter. We have no future together, so it's irrelevant.

My future is in Chicago, apparently.

Maybe I really will end up with Alec.

The thought makes me smile with wry amusement, but men are the last thing on my priority list. If Chicago ignited my interest in them, Vegas has just about cured me.

"Who are you texting over there?"

I glance at Rafe in the driver's seat. "Mia."

"Are you two best friends now, or what?"

I shrug. "She's easy to talk to. Normally I talk to Carly about everything, but I can't talk to her about you. She already doesn't like you, so she's too biased. Mia likes you, so I don't feel the need to protect you when I'm talking to her."

His lips tug up in a faint smile. "So, you're complaining about me. What did I do now?"

"I didn't say I was complaining about you."

"I'm not a moron, so I was able to deduce that from what you just said."

I sigh. "I'm not complaining about you." I'm not sure now is a good time to tell him I'm hauling ass back to Chicago, but I have to offer him something. "You've been less attentive since the doctor told us we couldn't have sex. I was inquiring as to whether or not Mateo loses interest in her in the post-baby days when she can't have sex, and if so, how does she not resent him for it. Turns out, he likes her whether he can fuck her or not, so she can't help me."

His smile falls and he looks caught somewhere between alarm and offense. "I did not lose interest in you because I couldn't fuck you."

I hike up my eyebrows. "Really? Sure felt like you did."

Now he frowns slightly, reaching over and resting his free hand on my thigh. "No, of course not. I'm not *that* big of an asshole."

"Well, that's how it felt. Don't take this the wrong way, but if you don't agree with me, this is not the first time since I arrived in Vegas you have been in denial. Remember when I told you I was pregnant and you didn't believe you were the daddy? I'm not really an insecure woman, and I have felt distance from you since that appointment. If it wasn't the sex, maybe seeing the baby freaked you out. Maybe it's something else I'm just not privy to. I don't know. Something happened.

You backed right off. You can deny it all you want; I know what I've felt. I know how guys act when they withdraw, and I know when they deny acting that way, they're just being dicks. You aren't the first guy who has ever made me feel unwanted, just the first one I didn't dump immediately when I realized how shitty he was making me feel about myself."

Rafe is quiet for a long time after that. Men hate being called out on their shit, so I'm not surprised. I'm not even disappointed. It is what it is, I'm just not going to sit here and keep my mouth shut so he can put all the blame on me later for this not working out.

I'm not sure the blame needs to be on either of us, honestly. I think this isn't working for bigger reasons than incompatibility—I actually think we *are* compatible on many levels, and under different circumstances this relationship might have blossomed into something great. Namely, if I had fallen in love with him. The ability to tolerate the ugly side of a person and still love them only comes after you've *fallen* for them. I know Sin is an asshole who plays games with my mind —which should make him far worse than Rafe, who simply loses interest in my company if he knows I'm not going to get him off—but it doesn't change my feelings for him. Seeing Rafe's ugly side *before* falling for him has made falling for him much harder. This is the opposite of how dating and relation-ships should work.

I read a book about the nature of love once, so I know it's not magic, I know there are logical, scientific explanations for the way I'm feeling or not feeling, they just don't matter. You can't logic yourself into love, you have to fall, and Rafe is not touching my triggers. There is no release of dopamine in his company. His hand on my thigh doesn't rain oxytocin down upon me. Meanwhile, if I hear Sin's *name*, I feel a clenching in my heart, like it's trying to hold onto even the mere mention of him.

I'm super fucked, and not in the way Rafe wants me to be.

I just have to figure out how long I can reasonably stay here pretending to give this a shot. Now that I've called Rafe out on his disinterest, he will probably grow even more distant. A few more days of distance, and he probably won't object when I tell him I want to go home.

It's a cowardly escape plan by normal relationship standards, but when dealing with a mob boss who has proven spiteful and territorial in the past, one has to tiptoe out of the non-relationship.

When we get back to Rafe's house, he is the one on his phone. I don't know who he's texting, but the way he smiles before catching himself makes me think it's a girl. Fuck him. Since I'm completely wasting my time in Vegas, I decide to waste it in a more fun way. I head to the library with my ultrasound DVD. Rafe has a computer set up at a desk in here and the office chair behind it is actually really comfy. Plopping down on the chair, I fire up the computer and pop in my DVD. I've watched it a million times already, but now I have a few minutes of new footage. I figure I'll pick out a book to read, and when I glance up between chapters, I'll see my wiggle worm on the screen. That'll make me smile.

As I peruse the shelf, I wonder what Mateo's library looks like. When Rafe showed me his, he told me his cousin has a much more impressive library in Chicago. He said he would show it to me next time we visit, but I already knew about its existence, since it was one of the selling points Mia mentioned. I grab my phone and text her, asking if she can send me a picture of it next time she's there so I can envision my future study spot.

I'm kind of excited about it, really. If I can't have what I want, I'll just want something else.

My mind drifts to Sin's house. He certainly didn't have a library, but he did have three empty bedrooms and a room with a fireplace that was probably supposed to be a family room, but could easily be turned into a library. I don't know why he has such a big house for just him and his three pieces of furniture. He seems like the kind of man who could live in a studio apartment and be happy. I could be too, if I lived there with him.

Ugh, stop it, Laurel. He doesn't want you! Get your shit together.

I'll be glad to get back to Chicago and get my head right. I'm eager to see what life after Vegas will be like for me. No more Sin, no more Rafe. I'm sure I'll see Rafe on occasion when he comes for holidays, but that doesn't bother me. Even though he's probably downstairs sexting some other fucking girl right now, I know I won't be bitter about Rafe. I don't feel for him deeply enough for bitterness to take root. Meanwhile, if I had to endure holidays with Sin and the woman he goes on to fall in love with, it would turn me to stone. Probably another reason there's no chance for me and Rafe. Being with Rafe would mean Sin would always be in my life, but never within my grasp. Someday someone will unlock him, and he will get married or have babies... and I want all that for him because I want him to be happy, but I don't want to witness it, because that would make me absolutely miserable.

This is making me sad. I don't want to think about this. Grabbing a piece of paper from a note cube on the desk, I mark my place in the book I'm reading and head downstairs to make myself some lemon tea.

Juanita is cleaning up in the kitchen. She should be starting dinner, so I don't know why she looks like she's finishing up for the day. Maybe it's one of her nights off. I haven't quite figured out her schedule. It seems to change around Rafe's whims. If she's not making dinner, I assume that means he isn't staying in either. Maybe now that I've had the nerve to notice his dip in interest, he's given up on me completely. Or maybe he thinks to punish me like he did by flirting in front of me by openly going out with someone else.

Joke's on him; I don't care anymore.

Stirring my tea, I glance up at Juanita. "Taking the night off?"

She appears startled that I've spoken to her. "*Si*, yes."

"I speak Spanish if you prefer that. Just don't talk too fast or I can't keep up."

Smiling faintly, she says, "Is okay, I speak English."

"Do you like working for Rafe?"

Nodding her head, she says, "Yes, he is good man. Bad taste in woman, but good man."

A little laugh of surprise shoots out of me. "Thanks, Juanita."

"Oh, not you," she says quickly, rushing over to pat my arm. "*Lo siento.* Not you."

"She means Cassandra."

I spin around, startled to see Rafe leaning in the doorway. "Eavesdropper," I accuse.

"I love to eavesdrop. I do it every chance I get," he tells me, completely unapologetic.

I turn back to my tea as he pushes off the wall and heads in my direction. "I do too, actually. Not people I know, but like, when I go out to eat by myself? Unapologetic eavesdropper. I like observing people."

He's closer than I expected him to get, but his arms encircle my waist. My hair is tucked up neatly into a bun leaving my neck exposed, and he takes advantage to bend his head and kiss that sensitive swatch of skin. "So do I," he murmurs. "We should make a date of it one of these days."

I can't help smiling faintly. "An eavesdropping date? I wouldn't say no to that. We should invite Carly and Vince, make it a double. He's not much good at it, but Carly is a blast to people watch with."

"I think I'm the second to last person Vince wants to go on a double date with," Rafe tells me. "Also, Vince isn't allowed to come here, and I have no desire to go to Connecticut."

"You don't have any coupled up friends, do you?"

"Not really. Gio, but he's not much fun."

Wrinkling up my nose, I shake my head. "I don't like double dates with them. His wife doesn't like me. I don't think he does either."

"I'll lure Mateo and Mia out here one of these days, we can have a couple date with them."

"He's too scary," I tell him, shaking my head. "I like Mia, but he makes me nervous."

"Fine, we'll leave him home and you and I can take Mia out. I like that even better."

Biting back a smile, I tell him, "Yeah, I bet you do. You need to give up on this fantasy, it isn't going to happen."

"I think Mateo wanted to give me Mia if anyone ever took him out. Since you two get along so well, how do you feel about potentially having a sister wife?"

That makes me laugh, mostly because I don't think he's kidding. "I'll take Mia for a sister wife, but only if I get a second husband. Every night you spend with her, I spend with him. Yep, I'll take that deal."

His tone is dry. "Sorry, Sin doesn't play well enough with others for an arrangement like that."

Mentioning Sin makes the joke far less funny, and my smile melts right off my face.

He must feel it, because he swiftly drops the joke and changes the subject. "Juanita is taking the night off because I'm taking you out. I figured we could grab dinner, then stop by the casino so I can check in. I reserved a suite for us so we can stay on the strip like tourists."

Reluctantly delighted, I glance back at him over my shoulder. "You did? I love being a tourist."

Rafe smiles. "I know you do."

"This is not what I was expecting to follow our conversation in the car. Usually men get pissy when you tell them they've done something wrong."

"I try to be reasonable," he tells me. "Whether I think I've backed off or not, you obviously do, and that's what matters. That was not my intention, so if it came across that way, I'm sorry."

Sighing, I let my head fall back against his strong shoulder. "You're such an adult sometimes. It's pretty sexy, I'm not gonna lie."

"You keep me on my toes, you know that?" he asks me.

"Yeah? Is that a good thing or a bad thing?"

"I haven't decided yet." He kisses my neck one more time, then lets me go. "Go upstairs and get dressed. I picked out an outfit for you, it's on the bed."

RAFE

Laurel looks lovely tonight. Her hair hangs down around her shoulders, the black dress I had sent over looks lovely on her. She doesn't complain, but I don't think she loves the heels. Probably should've gone with kitten heels. I'll make a note for next time.

I can't decide if I like or dislike how little I affect her right now. On one hand, I should have much more power over her than I do. I have yet to even recover as much control over her as I had at Mateo's house over Easter, and for a relationship to work, I'll need at least that, probably more.

On the other hand, I haven't earned it. She's right. Sin was right. I didn't see myself doing it, not even when Sin said I was. It wasn't until Laurel called me out on it that I admitted my interest *had* dipped. Given what she said to make me realize it, I couldn't fully admit it to her.

I wish Laurel had a more forgiving nature. She doesn't know the story of Mia and Mateo's relationship, but I know if Mia *had* lost Mateo's interest for a little while, she wouldn't have resented him for it. It would have made her sad, of course, but she wouldn't be ready to jump ship over a rough patch. Once they worked it out, she would sail right past it and go back to adoring him. In turn, he would remember what a great thing he has, and shower her with emotional and material rewards to show his love and appreciation.

Laurel does not have Mia's emotional elasticity. When Laurel gets sick of my shit, she gets sick of *me*. I don't bother pointing out that I'm not the only one who has withdrawn. Even though it's true, confronting her with it would be pointless. Trying to draw her out of it is more effective. I already knew that, but then Mia texted me with a, "Psst, can I give you some advice?" and I knew Laurel must be really annoyed with me.

I don't love having to be on my A-game all the time to keep her interest, but maybe once we're settled into a relationship she'll get easier. Sin is damn sure not on his A-game all the time, and she clearly liked him.

Regardless, tonight I can step it up. I brought her out to my restaurant, reserved my favorite booth with the view of the city. Laurel likes food, so feeding her is always a good idea.

Leaning in, she points to the menu. "I can't decide what to order. Do I want pesto or alfredo?"

I grab her menu, closing it and putting it on the table. "I'll pick for you."

Smiling, she snuggles into my side. "Good deal."

My arm tightens around her and fondness washes over me. I *don't* like always having to work so hard for her little ass, but I *do* like the results.

Of course right then is when the servers come over. Servers, plural. When I requested my usual waitress, I completely forgot that I told them to train Marlena with her. Knowing Marlena's waitressing skills aren't quite up to snuff and not wanting my waitstaff to suffer from my good deed, I figured retraining her with my best waitress was a solid plan.

It is, but I also look a lot like a liar when she walks up to the table I'm sharing with my not-girlfriend and Laurel is *snuggling* me.

Marlena's lips thin like she's thinking the same thing, but she writes on her orderpad to avoid looking at me.

The snuggle ends the second Laurel recognizes her.

Turning to look at me with wide eyes, she asks, "What is she doing here?"

Had I been thinking far enough ahead, I might have been able to come up with something better than the truth. "I hired her."

Laurel's jaw drops open and she looks at me like she cannot believe my gall. Then she starts laughing. I'm starting to think Laurel laughs when she wants to murder me.

Before she can jump to the same conclusions Sin did, I say, "I got her fired. I had to make reparations."

"I can't believe no woman has murdered you yet. Is that why you stay single? It's the only way to stay alive? Good strategy. At least you're self-aware."

Marlena's face is flushed and my favorite waitress stands there with her eyes wide and her pen poised over the orderpad, not having a clue what the hell is going on. I hadn't made it public knowledge in the restaurant that I specifically made them hire Marlena, because I didn't want anyone she would be working with to draw inappropriate conclusions.

Everyone is drawing inappropriate conclusions.

Laurel shrugs my arm off and scoots away, but she must figure she has to eat, because instead of trying to leave, she tells the servers shortly, "Ice water to drink, chicken alfredo for my entrée." Glancing at me, she says, "I'm going to the bathroom."

Marlena backs up as Laurel scoots out, but Laurel turns to face her anyway. Marlena flushes even deeper as Laurel stares her down, then wordlessly turns and leaves the table.

My regular server is a champ, so she pretends none of that just happened and says, "And for you?"

I sigh, glancing after Laurel to see if she's actually heading to the bathroom. After the sneaky exit she pulled over *Sin*, of all fucking people, I'm a little wary about trusting her. I wouldn't put it past her to order just to throw me off, then leave me sitting here like an asshole while she flees the scene.

Since she *does* appear to be heading for the bathroom, I look at Marlena.

"I told you this was a bad idea," she informs me.

"It's fine," I tell her.

"Clearly."

Glancing at my favorite waitress, I tell her, "Don't mention this to anyone else."

Her discretion is a given, but she nods anyway and assures me, "My lips are sealed."

"If she doesn't come back in a few minutes..."

Nodding, she says, "I'll go make sure she's in the bathroom. Gotta wash my hands all the time anyway, you know."

I'm going to give her a really big tip tonight. "Thank you, Virginia."

She smiles faintly, gives me a thumbs-up, then heads for the bathroom to make sure my date hasn't run away.

18

LAUREL

Bracing myself on the sleek brown vanity and peering into the mirror, I contemplate whether or not Rafe will be standing outside the bathroom waiting for me when I open the door. I shouldn't have come to the bathroom. While he was busy with the skank he bought the dress for, I should have high-tailed it out of this godforsaken restaurant.

My purse is on the countertop beside the sink. I open it and draw out my phone, opening my messages and starting a text to Sin.

"I hate Rafe. Come get me before I kill him in public."

The message makes me feel a little better, but I backspace all of it. Obviously I can't send that.

I type a new message, this one reading: "Is your house still equipped for a live-in hostage? Are you taking applications? I have references."

I don't delete that one, but I don't send it, either.

The bathroom door swings open and I automatically shuffle over to the next sink as a woman with a brisk walk approaches the counter. I don't look directly at her, so I don't realize it's the waitress—not the whore waitress, but the one who remembers my drink order from two months ago.

"You okay?" she inquires.

Avoiding her gaze, I nod my head and look in the mirror. I need something to do, so I reach into my handbag, depositing my phone and drawing out a tube of lipstick. Uncapping it, I run it over my lips, smacking them together and flashing her a smile. "I'm fine, thanks."

"You don't have to bullshit me," she says. "I'm like a priest at confession; whatever you say goes into the vault and doesn't come back out. If you need to vent, go for it."

"I'm honestly fine. No venting needed. Just rethinking every life decision I have made over the past couple weeks, no big deal."

The dark-haired waitress leans against the wall, nodding her head. "Understandable. I'm not privy to all the details, but between the tug-of-war with Rafe and Sin when he brought you to dinner and Miss Cotton Candy's sudden appearance, it seems like Rafe is being a pretty enormous shithead."

"Miss Cotton Candy?"

Nodding decisively, she says, "Marlena. Don't worry about her. Dump a glass of water over her head and she'll disintegrate. She's boring as fuck; she just has Bambi eyes and a nice ass. I don't think he'll cheat, he just... he's a flirt. I don't think he can help it. I don't think he'll ever stop. It's just a part of who he is. Always has been." Her gaze drops to my stomach. "Are you pregnant?"

My eyes widen at the boldness of her question, but I detect a faint hint of resignation, too. I'm not entirely sure what to make of it, but there's little point denying it. "Yeah."

She nods. "Kinda figured when you stopped drinking

alcohol and Rafe became a raging douche nozzle. He doesn't want kids."

I'm not sure how I should feel about the authority and familiarity with which she speaks about Rafe, like he's a topic she has spent an enormous amount of time studying, and now she is the leading expert on the subject. "Yeah, I kind of picked up on that when I told him I was pregnant and he threw me out of his house."

Grimacing, she says, "Ouch."

"Yeah," I mutter.

"He's a really big dick sometimes. Not usually. This is not... I don't know how long you've known him, but this is not how he is all the time. It's just that sometimes he gets mean when something happens that throws him off, something he wasn't entirely prepared for. Or if he gets bored and feels stuck. Or when his heart is broken. Okay, so there are a few scenarios during which he becomes a major asshole."

Turning my back to the mirror, I lean against the sink and look her over. There's a pink tint to her cheeks, a faint reddening around her ears. She's pretty—not sex-pot pretty, like so many of the women Rafe surrounds himself with, but comfortably pretty. She looks no-nonsense and authoritative in her severe black button down and slacks, but she seems nicer than she looks—even as she tells me what a giant douche Rafe can be, I hear a silent "but" coming.

"But," she finally says, crossing her arms over her chest, "Rafe can also be really, really great, and he is so much of the time, it makes it easier to handle him when he sucks. He's a guy; they all suck from time to time. At least when he sucks, you know he'll come out of it. Rafe's shitty side is like a storm that always clears up. He doesn't stay a massive douche for long, and if you let him know he's hurting your feelings, you'll get more of a response. If he thinks you can handle yourself, he'll let you, but if you express that you need him to be nicer to you, he will. I made the mistake of thinking he would respect it more if I held my tongue and kept a stiff upper lip, but I was wrong. He doesn't value that. If you open up to him, he's just... a waterfall of understanding. He'll stop being a dick, all you have to do is ask—and I know, you shouldn't have to ask, it should be a given, but... it's just how he operates. For all that Rafe notices, the man closes his eyes to what's right in front of him if he doesn't want to see it. He's really not a horrible person, though, I swear. I know it might feel that way to you right now, but... he isn't. He's really great."

"You like him."

It's not a question because I'm not a moron, but she shakes her head, looking at me like a deer caught in the headlights. "What? No. Of course not. I mean..."

Offering a smile, I shake my head. "It's fine. I wasn't accusing you of anything. In my experience, *every* woman in this damned city likes Rafe, so... I won't scratch your eyes out, no worries. How long have you known him?"

"Four years."

My eyebrows shoot up. "Four years?"

She shrugs, glancing down. "Just working here at his restaurant, we're not best friends or anything."

"Are you one of the three women in the city he hasn't slept with?"

Smiling helplessly—like it's adorable instead of gross—she nods her head. "I am one of those three, yes. It's an exclusive group. We have membership cards. Meet-ups the second Friday of every month. It's just me and two cat ladies. We have fun."

I shouldn't feel so laidback with someone who basically

just admitted she likes my baby daddy, but there's something about her I trust. Hers seems more like a quiet crush, subdued, probably something Rafe himself doesn't even know about—which is shocking in and of itself, since he's so damn full of himself.

"I don't want to be with a cheater," I tell her quietly, looking at the tiled floor instead of her.

"He isn't going to cheat on you," she tells me, so adamant I nearly believe her.

"You can't know that," I state.

"I can now," she insists. "He employed the dumb bitch here. If I start picking up on any vibes, I'll just dunk her in a sink full of water and she'll disintegrate."

Cracking a smile, I say, "Miss Cotton Candy. I like that."

"Don't worry about her. If he actually spent any time with her, he would be bored in ten minutes. I've been training her tonight, and every time she opens her mouth I want to stab myself in the temple and end it all."

"Don't do that. You're the best waitress I've ever had."

Sighing as if put-upon, she says, "Yeah. I have an eidetic memory. The orderpad is a prop. I could tell you what Rafe ordered the second Thursday of last March if you asked."

Intrigued, I cock my head in consideration. "Really? That's awesome. That must make studying way easy."

"It did. I'm done as of a year ago, but... yeah, easy peasy."

"What'd you go to school for?"

After a brief pause, she says, "Not waitressing."

"Then how come you're still waiting tables?" I inquire.

"I make questionable decisions."

A little burst of surprised laughter shoots out of me. "Yeah, I feel you there."

"Rafe's a good decision," she assures me, her faintly

resigned smile making me feel guilty, even though I don't have a reason to. "Just hang in there. The storm will clear. The cotton candy will go away."

"There will always be more cotton candy."

"But he won't always be in crisis," she states. "Once he's steady again, he won't be looking for cotton candy. Trust me, if the man is in a committed relationship, you could strip naked and straddle his crotch and he wouldn't do anything about it. He's a damn good man, just give him a little time to come around."

I struggle to accept the confidence of a woman who clearly likes him, but she has known him much longer than I have. The way she talks, she must have witnessed him on the inside of a relationship, so she must know more about that side of him than I do.

The problem is, I'm struggling to muster the interest in *being* in that relationship with him. Maybe she thinks his wandering eye and magnetic personality is worth dealing with, but all it does is turn me off. For all that she's convinced there's a shiny diamond beneath the dirty surface, I'm not, and I'm not about to spend my life dusting him off every time the man gets bored.

I can't say any of that to her, but I do feel a little better now that she's talked me down. Miss Cotton Candy. I'm going to picture a pink sugar cloud every time I look at that dumb skank from now on.

I can't believe he fucking hired her.

Before I can get worked up again, I offer a smile to the waitress. "What's your name? There are too many waitresses to keep track of, I swear to God."

"Virginia," she tells me, pushing off the wall. "I think Rafe likes waitresses. Something about them serving him appeals to his interests."

Rolling my eyes, I tell her, "You know what? That makes perfect sense."

Virginia flashes me a smile. "I better get back out there, make sure Marlena isn't playing in the sink. Don't want her to die."

"Are you sure?" I ask innocently.

"Well... if you need someone to kill her, Rafe knows people. Sin would probably take care of it for you; just tell him she's a troublemaker. The Morelli outfit is a real boys' club, but Sin has a personal vendetta against cheating hoes. Ask nicely and he'll probably clean up that cotton candy mess for you. Burn all her stuff and tell Rafe she went back to Arizona. Problem solved." The mention of Sin drains my smile, so she adds, "I was kidding. Kinda. Not really. We can pretend I was kidding if that makes you feel faint."

"No, I have a strong stomach. Killing troublemaking hoes doesn't nauseate me."

With a nod that's all too-knowing, she says, "Is it Sin?"

Considering she is an agent of Rafe's, whether he knows it or not, I don't offer anything on that subject. With a smile I hope indicates I'm done talking about this, I say, "Thanks for checking on me, Virginia."

She nods once, accepting her dismissal. "Anytime." Then, without another word, she backs out of the bathroom.

19

RAFE

After a rough start to the night, things get even worse when I take Laurel to the casino and Gio is hanging out there with his girlfriend, Carla. As soon as I see them, I almost turn around and tell Laurel never mind, let's just walk the strip, but he spots me and waves, and then it's too late.

To say Laurel is unimpressed by his flagrant adultery is an understatement. To say she is unimpressed with my casual acceptance of it is an even bigger understatement.

This night was supposed to bring us closer together, but I think it's driving us apart. Laurel already told me her main issue with me is that she doesn't think she can trust me, and I am clearly not helping her do that.

I have to get out from under all this and allay her suspicions. I can't do that with the truth, since even Sin accused me of being shady as fuck, but I do have an idea. I'm not sure if it's a *good* idea, but it's all I've got right now. It's not what Sin wanted—or what I wanted—but I need a viable bail-out if I want Laurel to like me again.

So, I text Sin. I fill him in on what just happened at the restaurant, and tell him I need him to do me a big-ass favor.

I get us away from Gio and Carla as fast as possible, check in with the casino manager, and then tell Laurel we're on to our next planned stop—one of the clubs I like to go to. Even on nights she likes me, she isn't thrilled about going to my clubs, but despite her lack of enthusiasm, she nods her agreement. Now she's probably just eager to stay out as late as possible so she doesn't have to spend much time alone with me in the hotel room afterward.

The club is busy and loud, but we head right in. I wrap an arm around Laurel's waist to keep her close, but her expression doesn't change. She possesses the bored beauty of a model. Never much liked that when I went out with the three models I did date, but I'm pretty sure Laurel gives zero fucks about my opinion of her facial expressions.

Since I'm watching her so closely, I get to see the exact moment her gaze lands on Sin. She stops walking though, so I guess I couldn't have missed it. If the world beneath her feet opened up and swallowed her, I don't think she would notice. I didn't intend the pain I see immediately transform her features and I have to look away from it.

I look where she's looking and see Sin seated at a table across from Marlena. They're off in a corner booth, and he's sipping a beer as Marlena talks animatedly.

"Aw, shit," I mutter, raking a hand through my hair, playing at obliviousness.

Laurel can't seem to breathe properly, but my voice tugs her out of the bubble of horror she seems to be living in. "What is going on?"

"I didn't know they were coming here. I'm sorry."

"What the hell are you talking about? Why....?"

Sighing, I drape an arm across her shoulders and steer her away, back toward the VIP section. "I didn't want you to see that unless it turned into something, I'm sorry."

Shrugging my arm off, she looks at me, demanding an explanation. "See what? What the fuck is going on?"

"Marlena isn't for me. I met her and thought she seemed like someone Sin would like. Since he's clearly ready to get back into the dating pool and it will be easier for everyone once you move on, he let me set him up."

"They're on a date?"

Considering she thought *I* wanted to fuck Marlena an hour ago, you might think she would look relieved. Judging by the look on her face, I think she would strip my clothes off and thrust my naked body at Marlena in a split second if it would get her away from Sin.

I wasn't entirely confident this would work, but she definitely believes it. I guess Sin is so damned appealing to her, she finds it easy to believe Marlena would go for him. I was a little less confident she would buy Sin going for any woman, period, but Laurel doesn't know that Sin. She doesn't think of him as the perpetually single, as being completely disinterested in dating. To me, it is utterly ridiculous that Sin would go out with a beautiful woman I suggested he go out with, but Laurel fell into his bed the same night she met him, so she clearly doesn't see him the way I do. All she can see right now is that Marlena *is* romantically linked to a man she likes, but it isn't me.

Poor Marlena. Laurel is going to be throwing flaming darts at her picture before I'm done here. Actually, judging by the hateful look on Laurel's face as she looks back at their table, she might just throw flaming darts at *her*.

"We can leave if you want to," I offer.

"We should go sit with them," she says.

I freeze, unprepared for that suggestion. "Uh, what?"

"Is this a first date? First dates are awkward. We should go sit with them, keep them company, see how it goes. Maybe it's going terribly and they need help."

"Or maybe it's going well, and we would be intruding."

Laurel shakes her head adamantly. "He doesn't look like he's having fun."

I'd like to control myself, but I can't help asking, "Think that might just be wishful thinking?"

Glaring at me, she says, "No. I know what his face looks like when he's enjoying himself, and that is not it."

Well, this is backfiring quickly. The last thing I want to do is go sit next to Sin and Marlena on their fake date and watch Laurel moon at him like he's the greatest thing since sliced fucking bread. Also, she'll be mean to Marlena, and I've brought enough shit on that poor girl.

"No," I say, firmly. "They're on their date, we're on ours."

Ignoring me, she shrugs out of my hold and ducks behind me, heading for their table.

"Laurel. Goddammit." I turn and head after her, but the six-inch heels I bought her don't seem to be slowing her down now. Normally she is considerate; I've even noticed her apologizing to people I've brushed past, but right now she plows through them on her way to interrupt Sin's date.

Well, this is probably going to blow up in my face. Knowing Sin the way I do, I can't imagine this date is going well. In fact, I figure it's probably terrible, and I was planning on sending Marlena a bouquet of apology flowers tomorrow. I was relieved she had agreed to it, but she's sweet and wanted to help me cover my tracks so Laurel wouldn't be hurt, even though Laurel would currently like to see her murdered, ground up, and stuffed into a dog food can.

Marlena's laugh sounds authentic as we get within earshot. I wouldn't have taken her for much of an actress, but hell, I'm convinced she's having a good time.

Sin has better instincts, so he notices Laurel first. Marlena looks up, startled, and the happiness drains out of her face.

"Hi," Laurel says. The brightness of her tone is so aggressive, I half-expect to see a look of pure madness on her face, but she's managing to smile.

Sin shifts, looking down. I already know he has good control of his facial expressions, so I'm less impressed that he looks like someone who legitimately got caught out on a date by his ex.

"Oh, hello," Marlena says, forcing a smile.

"You were just working. Weren't you just working?"

Marlena nods, tucking a chunk of hair behind her ears. "Yeah. Sin picked me up when I got off, brought me over here."

Laurel looks a little like Marlena just punched her in the gut. Laurel's gaze drifts to Sin again, but he will not look at her. I've never known him to avoid conflict the way he is right now, but he is very obviously unwilling to look at Laurel. I have to wonder why. Is it because he thinks that's the way to play it, or because he won't be able to pull it off if he looks at her? Is he afraid to see the pain he might be inflicting by helping me out? He's clearly inflicted a good deal already, because Laurel's chest is working way too hard.

Laurel's mouth opens like she wants to say something, but then closes, like she can't find her words.

Marlena clears her throat uncomfortably, looking up at Laurel. "Um, did you guys want to join us?"

"Yes," Laurel says. Without waiting for agreement from anyone else, she takes a step to the left and sits down, practically right on top of Sin. He quickly scoots down, but only one spot.

Sighing, I take a seat next to Marlena, who scoots closer to Sin to make room for me. Laurel watches the distance shrink with dread. If Marlena touches Sin, I think Laurel is going to launch herself across the table and claw her face off.

What a wonderful fucking date.

Marlena either doesn't remember that I told her Laurel and Sin were once involved, or doesn't care. She sells the date, turning a smiling gaze on him. "We were just talking about—"

Sin interrupts. "We were just talking about how rude it is when women approach men they clearly want to sleep with while they're out on dates with other people." He pauses just long enough to laugh a little, then he says, "Oh, wait, no." He looks over at Laurel. "That was you that said that, wasn't it?"

Laurel glares at him. "Oh, you weren't talking about how you don't date, ever? That's a fun topic." Elbowing him with exaggerated good-nature, she tells Marlena, "Forever alone, this one. He'll fuck with your mind, but don't expect him to fuck anything else."

"Keep it up," Sin tells her, grabbing his bottle of beer and tipping it back.

"I will," she states, not at all worried that she's coming off like a crazy person. "What kind of sex are you into, Marlena? He likes to tie girls up so they can't leave. Not just during sex, either. I hope you have captivity fantasies."

With such smooth cruelty that even I'm impressed, he says, "If she doesn't yet, she will by the time I'm done with her."

He wins that round. Laurel loses her crazy mean-face and

looks like she just took a fatal blow. Fuck, that's not fun to watch.

Even Sin looks away.

Marlena oozes discomfort.

Laurel's breathing is actually starting to worry me. I think she's near hyperventilation. Concern leaps when she pushes up out of the booth and hustles toward the door.

I sigh, standing up and following her. "Laurel."

She ignores me and doesn't stop until she's outside the club. By the time I get to her, she is, in fact, bent over with her hands braced on her thighs, struggling to draw in breath.

Well, this is not how I saw tonight going. Fantasies of feeding her chocolate covered strawberries and making her come are dying swiftly as she hyperventilates over the sight of Sin on a date with someone else. I have sat right next to Laurel while out on a date with someone else, and she had maybe one or two fucks to give. For the most part, she was fine. Conversed pleasantly with Jayla, smiled and joked around with Sin, caressed his arm and his thigh. I assumed from that experience that Laurel could play it cool, but what I'm seeing right now is far from playing it cool.

I don't really know how to respond to this. I've never seen a woman fall apart over someone else while out on a date with me. When she stands upright, I pull her into my chest, since that's all I can think to do.

She accepts the comfort. I wonder if there's any possible way to build on this. If she were falling apart over some random man, I might not consider this a lost cause yet, but I don't know what to do about it being Sin.

Once she settles down, Laurel surprises me by taking my hand and dragging me back in the direction of my car. "Let's go to the hotel."

"Okay," I say, though I'm not entirely sure I'm following. "Are you all right?"

"I'm great," she mutters. "Are any bakeries still open? I need some sweets."

"This is Vegas. Of course there are bakeries still open."

"Good. Let's go buy all the dessert."

LAUREL

As I lie tummy-down on the bed, eating macaroons and watching TV, I decide I haven't been giving Rafe enough credit. Despite not being one for sweets, and despite watching me break down over Sin being on a date with someone else, he took me to the bakery and bought me two boxes full of macaroons and two slices of fruit-covered cake. Knowing I was in pain over another man, he still hauled me back to this hotel room and promptly ordered an entire season of *Smallville* for me to watch while devouring all the desserts. Through all of it, he didn't even act a bit resentful.

He comes out of the bathroom now, stripped down to a pair of pajama pants. I know this is not the date night he had in mind, but he doesn't complain. I'm also pretty sure he didn't want to spend tonight watching *Smallville*, but he climbs on the bed and folds his hands behind his head, turning his attention to the TV.

"What did I miss?"

Pushing up to my knees, I crawl up next to him and snuggle into his side. "Only everything. Clark looking dreamy as he looks out the barn window at Lana's house, then he took the necklace back over there. She heard noise on her front porch and thought it was Whitney, so he left the necklace on her door for her to find and sped away."

"He's a swell guy, that Clark."

I nod my agreement. "Too swell. I ship Lex and Lana hardcore, but with that jaw, I understand why she would be attracted to him even though he's a major goody-goody."

Rafe smirks, tugging me close. "Yeah, good guys are not your type."

"So boring. I'll probably marry one, but God, why?"

"Hey," he says, offended. "Maybe you'll marry me. I can save you from the good guy."

"How twisted. I like it." Tilting my head up to look at him, I say, "Tell me something. And don't lie."

"Okay," he says, warily.

"What kind of marriage do you see yourself having? Are you like Gio, with a wife and kid, but a mistress on the side? Or are you faithful once inside a committed relationship?"

"I don't cheat when I'm in a relationship," he tells me. "If I didn't want to be in the relationship, I wouldn't. At least, that's how it always was before. I guess the wiggle worm made this a little more complicated for me."

I nod my understanding. "I get that. We have had a bizarre courtship."

"We definitely haven't had *The Calling* singing in the background during our tender moments," he says, nodding at the TV.

"Who?"

Cracking a smile, he says, "God, you're just a baby, aren't you?"

I smack him in the stomach. "Shut up, grandpa. I'm not

a baby."

"If we do get married, this is going to be our first dance. I'm calling it."

I can't help smiling. "You think there's even a remote chance of us getting married?"

"You don't?" he questions.

"I think I was more ready to marry you our first night in Vegas, with Vince and Carly, than I am now. No offense."

Chuckling and shaking his head, he says, "None taken."

I like him relaxed like this. A less secure man wouldn't be this relaxed after the scene he just witnessed. Seeking to reward him, I grab one of my pink macaroons and bring it to his lips, feeding him a bite. He takes a small bite and it reminds me of Easter. The way he smiled at me when I was feeding him jelly beans. Some of that tenderness comes rushing back as his eyes meet mine with the same amused fondness they held then.

"Good, aren't they?" I ask.

"Delicious."

I take a bite of the same macaroon, my gaze dropping to his lips. "Tell me something. You clearly have loads more experience than I have at... well, everything."

"Yes," he agrees. "Perks of being a grandpa."

I crack a smile. "So, you know how they say the quickest way to get over someone is to get under someone new? How true is that?"

"Oh boy. I'm gonna have a hard time finding objectivity here, you realize that, right?"

"Hey, I am relying entirely on your wise guidance. Tell your libido to slow its roll so your brain can give me good advice."

"Why don't you ask your sister? She's probably better

equipped for this one."

"I can't. She doesn't know I was ever under anyone but you, so if I ask that, she won't be unbiased either. She will enthusiastically assure me that I should definitely get under someone else, thinking that she's advising me *away* from you."

"Good point."

"I could ask Mia," I suggest.

"She won't be any help on this. All right, let me work this out. The answer isn't the same for every person. It is true for some people. Sometimes we build people up in our minds, especially after a break-up. We gloss over the bad and focus on the good, rewriting the history and giving ourselves more to be sad over. If you wallow, you will be sad. If you legitimately want to get past that person and you go out, then yes, getting under someone else can be an effective way of moving on. That said, if you're still wallowing and fucking someone else is a desperation move, you're more likely to feel like shit afterward."

"Huh."

"Yeah."

"Well, that's not super helpful. Maybe I'll text my roommate."

Cracking a smile, he grabs the remote. "Let's just watch the next episode of *Smallville*."

"That's always a good answer to life's problems," I say, turning my attention back to the television.

S omewhere between episode two and episode three, I fell asleep.

When my eyes open again, I am still fully dressed and

tucked under the covers. The room is bright from the sun streaming in through the window. I don't immediately understand why I dread the daylight, but then I remember Sin's date last night. If it's daylight, that means Sin may have taken that goddamn waitress back to his house. She could have woken up in my spot this morning, his muscular, tattooed arms wrapped around *her* waist. His scarred, rough hands may have traveled every inch of her skin. That beautiful mouth may have been places even more intimate.

I want to throw up, and I don't think it's because I ate dessert for four last night.

The bed dips as Rafe takes a seat. "Good timing. I was just about to wake you up."

"You were?" I ask, pushing myself up in the bed, then giving up and falling back down.

"I was. We didn't get to enjoy the room service since we brought 18 desserts last night. I ordered last night's plan for today, if you're up for it."

Bet he didn't think he signed up for nursing his baby mama through heartache. Poor guy. Sin is fucking someone else, so what the hell? I should, too.

Throwing back the blankets, I sit up. "Sure, let's do this."

I don't know what we're doing, but I don't really care. After the emotional toll last night took on me, I am pretty numb today. If I think about anything too hard, I'll probably cry, so I'll let myself get swept up in whatever Rafe has planned.

Turns out, Rafe has pretty sweet plans. He takes my hand and leads me into the bathroom. He ran a bubble bath. In the corner by the window, an open champagne bottle chills in a bucket of ice with a towel thrown over it and two champagne glasses stand on either side of it.

"Are you forgetting something?" I ask, placing a hand on my tummy.

"I am not," he states, leaning forward and reaching into the bucket of ice. Obscured from view by the towel is a bottle of water. He puts it back down and indicates one of the glasses, which I'm now realizing is clear instead of champagne-colored. "This one is yours."

I grin at him. "You think of everything, don't you?"

"I hope you're not sick of dessert yet."

I turn my attention to the plate of strawberries and the chocolate mousse-looking dish next to it. "I am never sick of dessert."

Stepping behind me, Rafe grabs the zipper on the back of my dress and draws it down. I swallow down my reluctance and tug down the ¾ sleeves, pulling on the dress until it falls to the floor. I'm wearing a burgundy bra and panty set underneath since that's what Rafe laid out for me the night before, and he's still wearing only pajama pants. Sadness overwhelms the numbness as I recall Sin standing behind me, taking my dress off me. I don't want to be in this hotel room being undressed by Rafe, I want to be in Sin's bedroom, letting him take off my clothes.

Only he probably already took someone else's clothes off in my place just last night. Sure, it was only a first date, but he wasn't just using her to play games with Rafe. He probably doesn't take so long to fuck someone he's dating for fun. It's hard for me to imagine that damn waitress making it to the end of a date and not wanting to go home with him. By the time he got her back to his place, he probably had her begging. When they got inside, he probably made her kneel for him.

My heart hurts. I eye the champagne I can't drink, the food

I don't want, then turn around and look at the only mind-altering substance in the room I *can* have: Rafe.

"Get your head out of the clouds and focus on what you **can** *have. It's not me. It's never been me. Nothing has changed."*

Looping an arm around Rafe's neck, I take him by complete surprise by rising up on my tiptoes and kissing him. His big hand comes to rest on my waist and he tugs me close, then cradles the back of my head in his palm and pulls me in for a deeper kiss.

It's a relief how easy it is to get drawn into him. My feelings may not be where they once were, but the man is skilled. He knows just how to kiss you to make your knees weak, just how to touch you to make you feel loved, even if you aren't. I know from our talk last night he's no more sure than I am that this is going anywhere, but as his hand drifts from my waist down to my ass, as he squeezes and yanks me against him, there is no hesitance, no uncertainty. That's what I need, Rafe to take control. I gave my power to someone else, and he didn't take care of it. If I ever give it away again, it needs to be to someone who will.

I'm not sure that's Rafe, but I'm not sure it isn't, either. Just because the road has been rough doesn't necessarily mean it's a dead-end. Maybe we're going through all the hard stuff first. Maybe I'll fall for him in the wrong order, after seeing how well he pulls me through the heartbreak Sin dealt me.

Regardless, it can't make things worse. Things are about as bad as they can be. Even Sin told me to sleep with Rafe, so I'm saying no for no reason. If I end up going back to Chicago, it's not like I'll regret sleeping with Rafe here. I've done it before. It will be fine. I'm making too much of it.

When he breaks the kiss and pulls back, I offer a smile and

reach back to unhook my bra. "Let's get in this bath while it's still hot."

My heart beats wildly now that the invitation is out there. I turn away from him to take off the last couple items of clothing, looking out at the strip while I step out of my panties. For a surreal moment, it hits me that the man undressing behind me has power over this whole city, but he's waiting for me. Maybe not patiently, but he is waiting. He doesn't have to. Women who would love to slide into bed with him are crawling all over this city, and while he has frustrated me with them, I don't think he's actually had sex with any of them since I came to town. It's not like we were committed to each other, so if he had, he wouldn't have been wrong.

His arms slide around my waist from behind and he bends to kiss my neck. I close my eyes, tilting my head in the opposite direction to give him an unobstructed path. While he kisses my neck, one of his big hands comes around to caress my breast, setting my nerve endings off and making them go wild. The guilt that follows is worrisome, but I ignore it. I have no reason to feel guilty. Sin's face pops up in my head—the worst possible memory of his face: the evening I came back from the marathon "date" with Rafe. His head hanging, the look on his face, the sadness I swore I felt. Surely fucking Rafe would bring more sadness than that.

Dammit, I don't belong to Sin.

Yes you do.

My brain is my enemy, and I ignore it, bringing my hand up to caress Rafe's as it squeezes my breast. Fuck you, brain. Fuck you, Sin. Nobody owns my ass. I'm as free as a fucking bird, and I'll do what I want.

Struck by rebelliousness, I turn around and loop my arm around Rafe's neck again, pulling myself up to kiss him. His hands slide under my ass and he lifts me. I secure my legs go around his waist and crush my breasts against his chest.

God, he is sexy. I've been ignoring it, but right now, that's impossible. He's bare ass naked, his hands cupping my ass. He walks forward, pressing me against the floor-to-ceiling glass window.

I gasp, hanging onto him tighter and pull back. "The window is a bad idea. A wall I could accept, but my luck this is a weak window. I don't want to plummet naked to my death."

"Plummeting to your death is only acceptable if you're fully dressed?"

"I would actually prefer to avoid it altogether, if at all possible."

Shaking his head, he says, "So high maintenance."

"Yep. Sorry."

He lowers me back to the ground, but he's not too disappointed, because then I grab the black elastic band off the sink, pull my hair up in a bun, and climb into the tub. Luckily it's a huge tub. He climbs in on the other end and stretches his long legs out. I scoot to accommodate him, then reach behind me for his champagne and lean across to hand it to him.

"Thank you."

"Mm hmm. Remember when I had only known you for like 35 seconds and you already had me fetching your wine?"

Rafe smiles, taking a sip of the champagne. "I do. Remember when you had only known me for 35 seconds, but you were eager to serve me? Maybe I need to wipe your memory and start over."

Shrugging unapologetically, I reach back and grab my champagne glass full of water. "I wanted a ride on the Rafe train, what can I say?"

"You got one."

"I sure did. And a bonus baby—I didn't even check that box."

"Getting involved with a Morelli usually means getting much more than you bargained for."

I nod my head, taking a sip of my water. "Carly tried to tell me that, but I was blinded by your general hotness and didn't want to believe her."

"A common blunder. Pretty sure every woman who has ever gotten involved with one of us has been warned off at least once. We were designed to make women ignore good advice and pursue relationships with us anyway."

"And if that doesn't work, kidnapping?"

"I've never kidnapped anyone," he says, slightly confused.

"According to—" I stop short of saying Sin and amend my statement. "From what I've heard, kidnapping is an accepted part of Morelli relationships."

Nodding, he acknowledges, "True for some. I've never had to, but I have more difficult relatives."

"Like Vince?"

He regards me curiously, but nods. "Like Vince."

I'm not sure I actually want to know, but with this opportunity to learn more about an integral part of my life, I can't resist asking, "Did he kidnap Mia when she was already married to Mateo?"

"Not married, no. They were engaged."

I look down at the water in my glass, hesitating before I ask the rest. "Did he hurt her?"

Rafe clearly knows the answer to this question, but instead of answering me, he watches me for a moment. "Do you care for Vince? He's married to your sister. You like him?"

"I do."

"Then why don't you leave these particular skeletons in

the closet," he suggests. "He and Mateo did some not-so-nice stuff to one another, and Mia was often caught in the crossfire. Mia and Vince both got hurt, they both hurt each other, and they're better off apart. That's the important takeaway. That's all you need to know."

"I don't want my sister to get hurt," I tell him.

"She won't," he says. The confidence in his tone, like there's no chance of that happening, makes me feel a little better. "Trust me, your sister is scrappy as hell. She handles Vince like a pro. She'll be just fine. If he ever crosses her, she can just kill him and keep all his money."

Laughter bubbles up and I take another sip of water. "I don't think my sister would murder anyone."

"She wouldn't have to," he says, dryly. "If Carly ever wants Vince dead, all she has to do is make a single call. If she has your ruthlessness, Vince better treat her well."

"That's good to know, I guess. Maybe not so good for Vince."

"She seems to like him, I'm sure he'll be fine," Rafe says. "Either way, the kid has escaped death at least a dozen times at this point, so if he dies, he dies."

Because I can't help being curious, I ask, "Have you ever killed someone? I don't mean hands-off, commissioned a hit, but like..."

"Dirtied my own hands? Yeah, of course."

Of course, he says. I guess they probably wouldn't let him be boss if he hadn't proved himself somewhere along the line. "More than once?"

Smiling faintly, he says, "Yes, more than once."

"That's so weird."

"Considering my position, I think it would be weirder if I hadn't," he tells me. Then with a nod, as casually as if we were discussing the weather instead of his murder record, he says, "Give me a strawberry."

I turn to grab a piece of fruit. "With chocolate, or no?"

"Sure, what the hell?"

I dip the strawberry in the chocolate mousse and lean over to hand it to Rafe. He makes no move to reach for it, instead curving his finger and beckoning me closer.

Ah, he wants me to feed him.

Well, I like feeding him, so that's fine. I take a sip of my water and put it down on the ledge, then glide over to him. It's a big tub, but he's not a small man, so I still have to sit mostly on his lap to fit over here with him. I loop my free arm around his neck for increased comfort, bringing myself closer. Then I bring the strawberry to his lips, holding his gaze as he bites into it.

"Are strawberries your favorite fruit?" I ask, since this is the second strawberry-related treat I've had with him.

Rafe nods, one hand coming up out of the water and catching my hand. He brings it back to his lips, devouring the rest of the strawberry, then grabbing the back of my head and pulling me close. My loins stir and I close my eyes just in time for our lips to meet. He tastes like strawberries and chocolate, as if I didn't already like kissing him enough. Grabbing my hips, he resituates me so I'm facing him, straddling his body. His hands slide up my back and he pulls me close, bending to catch my nipple in his mouth. I gasp, my body arching as his tongue circles the hard nub, one of his hands coming around to squeeze the other one. Sensation takes over, and for the first time in a while, I get caught up in the pleasure. He takes his time, nibbling and sucking, drawing sighs out of me. He turns his attention to the other breast, giving that nipple the same thorough attention. His teeth graze the sensitive nub and I jump, arching my back and pushing my fingers through his hair.

It's a different texture than Sin's and the thought stabs me in the heart. I do my best to ignore it as Rafe's hands move to grasp my hips, pulling me flush against him. I feel his cock pushing against me, and instead of wanting it inside me, I panic.

"Wait. Wait, I'm sorry. I can't."

Rafe sighs, his head falling back.

"I'm sorry, I'm not trying to be a tease, I swear. I thought I could, but I can't. I don't want to be the person who feels like shit afterward."

"You're killing me."

"I'm sorry," I repeat. "I really am. Just... I need to know he fucked the waitress first. I'm so sorry, but I have to. If he did, then I'll know it's over. I'll have closure. But I have to know. I can't be the one who ruins it, I need it to be him. I'm sorry; I know this is... not what you want to hear."

Instead of looking angry, he looks relieved. "That's it? You only need to know he fucked someone else?"

"Yes."

"And you'll let go?"

I nod. "I'll cut the strings of that attachment so fast, you won't even see it."

"Huh." He cocks his head. "Okay. I can handle that."

"Yeah?"

"Sure." His hand comes up out of the water again to cup the back of my neck and draw me closer. It's a Sin move, one that cuts deep *because* it's a Sin move, but right before he gives me another kiss, he says, "He probably fucked her last night, so I won't have to wait long."

21

LAUREL

Rafe wanted to go out tonight, but I was exhausted so I told him to go without me. He didn't seem overly enthused, but I swear, sometimes since this pregnancy started I feel like I could pass out at 6pm. Today is one of those days.

Since I can't *actually* go to sleep at 6pm, I curl up on the couch and resume watching *Smallville* by myself. I feel vaguely guilty, so I text Carly to tell on myself and she starts watching with me so we can text about it.

We only make it through one episode, then the doorbell rings.

I sit up, alarmed. I don't know if I'm allowed to answer the door, and Juanita is already off for the day. I walk into the foyer, holding my phone like a weapon. An ineffective weapon. If anyone on the other side of this door means me harm, I would do better to walk over and grab something out of Rafe's weapons armoire.

Of course, if they meant me harm, they probably wouldn't be ringing the doorbell. I open up my text messages to Rafe to ask him if I should answer the door, and see two texts from him I must have missed while I was texting Carly about *Smallville*.

Hey, Gio's babysitter canceled on them, can you watch Skylar?

Told Gio and Lydia you could watch Skylar. Figured you'd appreciate the practice. ;) Hope you're awake, they're on their way.

Awesome.

Now that I know there's nothing more lethal than Gio's spawn on the other side of the door, I walk over and flip the locks one at a time, then ease it open.

A mountain of baby things greets me on the other side. Gio is hidden behind them somewhere, while Lydia is dressed up and lugging a baby carrier.

"You are a lifesaver," she tells me, inviting herself right in. "You know, I wasn't so sure about Rafe knocking you up at first, but I'm coming around to it. I swear, you cannot count on people these days. What did I say?" she asks, glancing back at Gio. "Didn't I tell you she was going to leave us high and dry one of these days? That boyfriend of hers. Don't even get me started."

I don't know which one of us she's talking to, but I take a step back and look down at the sleeping baby sucking on the pacifier. A faint smile steals across my face. "Aw, she's adorable."

Distracted giving Gio directions, she tells him, "Take that to the living room and set it up for her. Where's the bear? Did you bring in the lasagna?"

Sighing, Gio traipses past me muttering, "Yes, I brought all of it."

I guess I'm glad Rafe isn't here to see this. I'm not terrified of domesticity, and this scene right here would not make me eager to procreate with someone.

Lydia pats me on the arm as she follows after Gio. "I brought you some lasagna for dinner. Rafe said you didn't feel like going out and I wanted to thank you. My mother's recipe. Delicious."

"Thank you, that was nice of you," I tell her, following her back into the living room. *Smallville* is paused, Tom Welling gazing dreamily off at nothing. Gio glances at the screen, then looks at me and cocks a skeptical eyebrow.

"Not a Superman fan?" I ask.

"Do I look like I root for the good guys?" he asks.

"Ignore him," Lydia tells me. "He's grumpy." Bending to put down the baby carrier, she says, "She should sleep for you a good hour or two, you won't even have to do much. When she wakes up she'll probably be hungry. I have two bottles in here. Make sure you warm them up, but not too warm. Test it on your wrist. It shouldn't be chilly, but in the meantime, put it in the fridge. Diapers are in the bag along with two changes of clothing." Reaching over to retrieve a teddy bear from Gio, she places it on the coffee table. "She doesn't really play with this yet, but she likes to have it around so she can look at it. I packed her play mat. She likes to look up at the little mirror at herself if you hold it over her head. After she eats, burp her. I think that's it. You know how babies work, I assume?"

I thought I did, but my head is spinning. It can't be too hard to figure out, so I nod my head, since that seems to be the expected response.

"Good. We're going to a movie, then dinner. If you need to reach us, here, let me give you my cell phone number."

I hand over my phone and she taps the screen, then hands it back. "There you go. I hate to drop her and run, but the stupid fucking babysitter really set us back, now we're running late. Enjoy the lasagna!"

I don't even get to say goodbye, she's already grabbing Gio's arm and hauling him back into the foyer and out the front door.

Now that they're gone as quickly as they came, I dig through the diaper bag to find the bottles Lydia mentioned so I can put them in the refrigerator. I hustle back, not wanting to leave the sleeping baby alone, and look around at everything else. Gio set up some kind of portable bassinet type thing. There's a square, colorful mat spread out on the floor.

A tiny little sound grabs my attention and I turn around to see a pair of big blue eyes looking up at me.

"Uh oh, your mommy said you were going to sleep for a couple hours."

She starts to wiggle around and her binky pops out of her mouth. Immediately, she starts to fuss. I crouch down in front of her seat, unsure whether or not I should take her out. Will she go back to sleep? I should probably hold her. If she does fall asleep, I can put her in the bassinet thing and she will probably be more comfortable than in the car seat anyway.

I pop her binky back in her mouth and peel back her blanket, unfastening her harness and reaching under her tiny arms to pick her up. "Well, hello, cutie. My name is Laurel, and apparently I'm going to be babysitting you tonight. How does that sound?"

She lets out a string of noises that sound vaguely like a complaint.

"Well, I think we'll have fun," I tell her, lifting her up. "Your mommy and daddy left us all kinds of cool stuff to play with. How old are you?"

Naturally, she does not answer me. I wish someone had

told me how old this baby was. If I need any mom tips, I could text Mia for emergency help on how to keep a baby of this age busy. She's really small, but that's not much help.

I'm not sure what to do with her, so I just walk around, gently jostling her while I try to figure it out. Since Lydia said she should nap for a while, I assume she has been fed and diapered recently.

"How about your mat?" I ask her. "Your mom said you like to look up at yourself, let's try that."

Holding her close to my chest, I drop to my knees next to the mat Gio laid out for her. I support her neck and put her down on her back, but the minute her back hits the mat, she starts fussing.

"Wait, wait, wait," I tell her, darting over to grab the diaper bag. "Hang on, you know what I see?" I grab the round reflective toy and hold the mirror up over her head and gasp. "Look at that! Do you see that pretty baby right there?"

For about a second and a half, she looks at the mirror.

Then her little face crinkles up and she starts screaming bloody murder.

I try again to get her attention, to show her the reflection in the mirror, but she is *not* having it. Her little downturned mouth and mournful cry are so heartbreaking, I can't stand it. I give up and put the mirror aside, grabbing the teddy bear and holding it up to show her. "How about Mr. Bear? Is that his name? That's not a very creative name, is it?"

Still, she screams, so I put the bear back on the coffee table and pick her up, gathering her against my chest, rocking and shushing her.

That does not work. Apparently she finds it offensive that I put her down in the first place, and outraged by my perceived abandonment, she now wants no Laurel cuddles.

"I'm sorry, I thought you would want to play," I tell her. Her screams of betrayal tell me I thought wrong.

Thinking to walk around and distract her with something else, I stand and look around for something to show her. Rafe doesn't have anything she would care about, but there is a large silver mirror on the other side of the room, so I walk over and turn so she can see her own reflection.

"Look, you see there?" I ask, pointing.

Her head wobbles on my shoulder as she looks up, but then her face crumbles and she shoves her fist into her mouth, sobbing inconsolably.

Damn.

I walk around for the longest few minutes of all time, but she does not stop crying. Not once, not even to catch her breath. My nerves are already shot as I try desperately to think of what could be wrong with her.

"Are you hungry?" I ask. "Your mom said you wouldn't be hungry for a couple hours." She is chewing on her fist though, so maybe her mom was wrong? Maybe she only figured she wouldn't need to eat because she would be asleep.

Walking back into the living room, I grab my phone and text Lydia to ask if there's any chance Skylar might be hungry. It takes her a few minutes of screaming to text back, and when she does, it's simply, "Yeah."

I try putting Skylar down in the bassinet so I can go make her bottle, and boy, does *that* piss her off. Now she is doubly offended—not only did I put her down once, I repeated the offense. This baby has clearly had it with me, and I've only had her for roughly ten minutes.

I pick her back up and try to stop the wailing, but to no avail. My insides are shaking as I haul her into the kitchen and dig out a bottle. Rafe has a Keurig machine, so I grab a boring-ass coffee mug and fill it with hot water.

I make a mental note that his coffee mug situation needs to be fixed. He has white ceramic mugs and black matte mugs, and not a single funny saying on any of them. I can't live this way.

"We need to buy Uncle Rafe some cool coffee cups." Frowning, I reconsider, "Wait, is he your uncle? No, he's your second cousin, isn't he? You Morellis have way too many babies. Do you know that? I realize I myself am contributing to the problem, but sheesh."

Skylar does not at all appreciate my commentary on her family's reproductive habits, and she screams her little head off until she can't breathe to let me know it.

Now she's starting to worry me. It was bad enough she was crying, but now she's crying so hard her little body shudders as her breath hitches.

"Why are you so mad?" I ask, rocking her as I dip the bottle into the coffee cup. "I'm so sorry I put you down, I'll never do it again. Never ever. I'll learn to sleep standing up, and steal you from your mommy and daddy to prevent such a thing ever happening again. Will that make you happy?"

While the bottle is warming up, I take her back to the living room to try her binky again. She seemed to like that thing while she was sleeping. Retrieving it from the carrier, I bring it to her mouth, but she's too busy freaking out to take it. She begins to calm down and starts sucking on it, but within several seconds, she stops sucking it and wails again, like it has only added to her disappointment.

Giving up, I toss that back in the carrier and haul her back to the kitchen.

The bottle isn't warmed up yet, but after a couple

desperate minutes of rocking and humming while we wait, it's finally warm enough—I think. Popping the bottle in her mouth seems to work for five hopeful seconds, then she turns her head and rejects my offering.

"Skylar, I don't know what you want. I don't know what to do here."

Letting her scream can't be the answer. I put the bottle back down and trail back into the living room, but much more hopelessly than I was a minute ago. This is going to be a long few hours if this is what she's going to do, and why is this happening? Am I horrible with babies? Is my own baby going to come out, take one look at my ineptitude, and cry for the rest of its life?

That's all I can think about, then Skylar distracts me, burping and then throwing up all over me. I go rigid, looking down at the white baby vomit now covering both of us.

Oh, my God.

Now big, wet tears make their way out of the corners of her eyes as she screams.

"Does your little tummy hurt?" I ask uselessly, watching a white trail drip off me and onto the floor. "Oh, God, this is so gross."

I need help.

Juanita left for the evening though, so I'm on my own.

"Okay, we need to get you undressed," I tell her. Only I don't know where to put her down. I don't want to get her mat dirty, I have a hunch Rafe will murder me if I put a vomit-covered baby down on his couch, and I don't want to get her baby carrier or bassinet thing dirty, either. Digging in the diaper bag, I look for an extra receiving blanket. Once I find the only extra Lydia packed, I spread it out on the floor and put Skylar down on it.

The baby shrieks louder, her little body rigid with anger or discomfort, I'm not sure. "I don't know what to do for you," I tell her, desperately, as I pull the little polka dot pants off her legs. God, it's everywhere, even on her socks. I pull those off, too, but before I can start on the onesie, more of the baby puke starts spewing out of her mouth.

"Oh, crap! I'm sorry," I tell her, picking her up, not wanting her to choke on it. I cradle her against my chest, grimacing that she's resting against the last batch of vomit.

I feel badly that she's crying, but I want to cry, too. This is horrible. I feel so helpless and I have no idea what to do. Reaching for my phone on the table, I text Lydia and tell her the baby has thrown up everywhere and I'm not sure what to do. I wait two minutes, and no response. I move on to the next person—Rafe.

"Can you come home? Skylar is flipping her shit and I don't know what's wrong with her."

I put the phone down and grimace at Skylar, digging in her diaper bag for a burp cloth. Optimistically, her mother only packed one, and now I have to use it to clean baby vomit off her chin.

My phone buzzes. "I'm afraid I wouldn't be much help there, kitten."

Glaring at the phone, I say, "Are you freaking kidding me?" I want to tell him to get his ass here right now, but then I envision that happening, and it only ends up making things worse. If he doesn't help me and just stands there, I'll murder him. Then Sin will have to help cover up that I murdered the Vegas boss, and it'll be a whole thing.

Sin.

That's a crazy thought, but I don't have anyone else to call. I don't know anyone in Vegas. Sin murders people, so he has to have a strong enough stomach to face down some baby vomit.

The situation is so dire that instead of texting him, I make a phone call.

I can barely hear his low, "Yeah?" over Skylar's screams.

"Are you doing anything important right now?" I ask him.

Hearing the shrieks, now he sounds more alert, but confused. "Not really. What's going on? Is that a baby?"

"Gio and Lydia needed me to babysit, but the baby is so mad and I don't know why, and she threw up all over the place, and when I was trying to clean her up, she threw up again, and now there's baby vomit everywhere and all over both of us. I don't know what to do and Lydia won't text me back, and I'm not good at this, and I don't know what to do," I wail.

"Okay, calm down," he says, his tone level, like this is not the crisis it feels like. "Are you at the house?"

"Yes, I'm all by myself, Juanita isn't even here, and I need help."

"Give me five minutes," he says.

22

LAUREL

I t takes him seven minutes, and by the time Sin appears soundlessly in the living room, I am crying almost as hard as Skylar is.

Without a word, he walks over and takes the noisy baby from me, glancing down at the mess on the floor. I am kneeling, but there is nothing sexy about it. I draw in a shuddering breath, embarrassed by my own failure. I'm certain now he will see that I am not good at motherhood, and he will immensely regret encouraging me to have a baby.

As if the screaming child does not bother him in the least, he tells me, "Go get yourself cleaned up. Take your time. Take a shower. I've got this."

"She's possessed," I inform him, scrubbing at the tears on my face.

Sin cracks a smile. "Just go take a shower and calm down. When you come back, the mess will be gone and hopefully I'll have exorcised her."

Shaking my head, not getting up off the floor, I tell him, "I'm not good at this. Is this what it's going to be like?"

"No," he says, firmly. "You will have plenty of time to adjust to your baby. You just got this one in the midst of a fit. Babies cry. That's what they do."

"She threw up everywhere. Is she sick?"

He puts the back of his hand against her forehead. "Probably not. Babies spit up. Another fun feature." He glances down at her, noticing she starts to quiet down when he touches her face. So he cups her face in his giant, scarred hand and uses his thumb to rub the side of her face. The baby wiggles and he asks. "You like that, shortcake?"

Of course now that he's here, she quiets right down.

I blink, pushing up off the floor and standing. Her big blue eyes are focused on Sin's face now. She seems to like his attention as much as I do, and now that she has it, she blinks up at him like a little angel. Then she reaches her tiny hand up, trying to touch his face, but she can't reach.

"Oh, God, she's cute again," I murmur quietly.

Sin cracks a smile and looks up at me. "See? I told you I could settle her down."

"You're magical," I tell him.

Sin shakes his head, looking down into Skylar's face. "No magic, you just have to show 'em who's boss. Babies look all sweet and innocent, but they're like dogs; they can smell fear. Gotta let 'em know you're in charge and you're not going to tolerate their bullshit, then they'll know they're in capable hands. Then they can relax and be cute."

"I'm not sure that would work for me," I mutter, looking at Skylar.

"Then maybe you need to step up your game. Just pretend she's on a date with me and you should be able to muster some dominance."

Flushing, I smack him on the arm. "Not funny."

His lips tug up in a little smirk. "Maybe not for you."

I look down, shaking my head. "You're such a jerk."

Cocking an eyebrow, he says, "Want me to leave you here with this baby?"

I hold my hands up in surrender and slowly back away. "No. I'm going to clean the baby vomit off myself. You stay right here and be magical."

Now that Sin is here to help, I escape upstairs to Rafe's room so I can shower and change into something clean and comfy. The little devil on my shoulder and the little angel are in cahoots tonight. I know I'm supposed to be open to Rafe, but Rafe is sitting in the VIP section at a club right now and the man I'm crazy about is the one who rushed over to help me clean up baby vomit. So, maybe fuck Rafe, and not in the literal sense.

Rather than putting on actual clothes, I listen to the devil. I slip on a matching white bra and panty set. Instead of slipping a sleep shirt on over them, I pull on my pink satin robe. This will be much easier to shuck if Skylar throws up all over me again anyway, so in addition to being sexy, it's practical.

I apply a quick layer of make-up—nothing major, just some eyeliner, mascara, and subtle lip gloss. I make quick work of blowing out my hair and tousling it, since I don't want to look like I've done this much work. Lastly, I slide an elastic band on my wrist, just in case things get messy again and I need to put my hair up in a bun to deal.

As I head downstairs, I'm feeling much lighter than I have. Icky thoughts keep trying to bring me down, flashes of memory from last night, Sin sitting across the table from that damn bimbo. I want to set her on fire. If he went home with her last night, I'm going to. My pregnancy hormones are harder to control, and I'm a territorial person to begin with. If she wants Rafe, she can have him, but Sin is mine, goddammit.

Well, I guess he isn't, but if he's going to move on, he needs to wait until I'm back in Chicago so I don't have to witness it.

All thoughts of Chicago fly right out of my mind like birds from an open cage at the sight of Sin relaxing on the couch with a sleeping baby snuggled up on his muscular chest. My heart nearly gives out, then goes into overdrive. Sin senses me in the room and glances my way, but his face shifts from congenial to something much less platonic at the sight of me. I linger where I am for a moment, letting him look me over while the tempting image of him with a baby emblazons itself on my brain.

The way he looks at me, he finds the picture I present just as enticing as I find him right now. My legs go on forever in this robe, and the way I tied it, a swatch of my bra underneath is visible. Sin's eyes take their time perusing me, then his hot gaze meets mine.

His tone is faintly accusing. "That's what you're wearing?"

"Easy to take off," I say, pushing off the wall and heading toward him.

His dark eyebrow rises, and I realize how that sounded.

"I meant, in case Skylar makes another mess," I add, hastily.

Smirking faintly as I drop onto the couch next to him, he says, "Yeah, I bet you did."

"I totally did. I'm so sweet and innocent, you don't even know," I add, sinking into the couch and leaning against his side.

"Yes, I remember how sweet and innocent you are," he says, dryly.

"I didn't hear any complaints." Grabbing the remote control, I ask, "Wanna watch *Smallville* with me?"

"I think Carly will be peeved," he replies.

I frown, cocking an eyebrow at him. Before I have a chance to ask what he means by that, he picks up my phone from the other side of the couch and hands it back.

I sigh, taking it from him. "Did you really go through my phone again? I'm not even your captive anymore, you really shouldn't do that."

"Rafe texted you, wanted to know if everything was going okay. I didn't want to take the chance he'd rush home when you didn't respond, so I told him all was well."

"Kind of him to inquire," I mutter, opening up my text messages to review the ones he already checked.

"You and your sister don't talk about him," he remarks.

I raise an unimpressed eyebrow at him. "What purpose did going through my messages to my sister serve?"

"I was curious."

I love how he says that like it's the only justification he needs. He knows by now it doesn't bother me, but our circumstances are not what they were last time I was an open book for him, so he really shouldn't be taking the same liberties. "I don't think your *date* would approve of you being curious about what's in my phone."

"You are an aggressively jealous person, you know that?" he asks.

"You think I'm aggressive now, wait until next time we're at the restaurant and I accidentally stab her with my steak knife. Get up to help her, accidentally stab her in the eye socket with the heel of my shoe. You haven't seen me aggressive yet."

"If you're going to kill the waitress, can you not do it at the restaurant? That's going to be a hell of a mess to clean up."

"I haven't decided if I'm going to kill her yet. I might leave her alive and chain her up so I can torture her. I'm gonna need those tricks you use to deal with blood, because I have grisly plans for this bitch."

As if my unexaggerated homicidal intentions toward Slutty McBitchFace greatly amuse him, Sin smirks. "You're crazy."

"Wait until I wind a corkscrew into her abdomen and pull out her intestine while she screams. Then you'll see crazy."

"What has this girl done to you to deserve this kind of loathing?"

Cocking my head innocently, I ask, "Did you sleep with her?"

His amusement wanes slightly and his dark eyes meet mine. Maybe I don't have a right to ask, maybe I don't have a right to care, but I do. My insides feel as wobbly as gelatin in this eternal moment, the question out there in the universe so it's real, but I don't yet know the answer. The idea of him naked on top of another woman makes me feel things I don't even know adequately awful words to express.

Finally, ending this horrible stretch of torture, he answers me. "I did not."

Despite the joking demeanor, I feel like an entire building just lifted off my shoulders. Breathing a quiet sigh of relief, I nod. "Good. I'll probably let her live, then. Pick out a nice eye patch for her—something stylish, to say I'm sorry. I won't be, but, you know."

Sin grins, shaking his head at me. "You're a little psycho."

"Well, you shouldn't have kissed her," I state, smoothing down the satin of my robe.

"I *didn't* kiss her."

Flashing him a victorious grin, I say, "Ha! I got more information out of you. Better be careful, I'm getting good at this; I might steal your job."

Sin rolls his eyes at me. "Yeah, because I was being so secretive."

I'm so happy, I can't hide it. Hugging his arm and resting my head against his muscular bicep, I tell him, "You were mean to me last night."

"I'm mean sometimes," he states.

"I know," I murmur, absently running my fingers over the black ink peeking out from beneath his black T-shirt. He's dressed casually tonight, a tee and dark jeans, not his usual work gear. "What were you doing when I called you?"

"Not cleaning up baby vomit," he says, dryly.

Smiling faintly, I tell him, "You look really good with a baby. Like... really good."

His gaze drifts down to the little swatch of bra peeking out from beneath my satin robe, but he doesn't say anything.

In the interest of playing fair, I turn my attention back to his tattoo. Given he slept naked in his bed and I slept on this side of him, I have seen it before, but I've never asked about it. I can only see the bent legs right now, but the whole tattoo appears to be an angel kneeling on the ground.

"Are you religious?" I ask him.

"If I am, I must be really excited about my inevitable descent to Hell."

"Well, if you're going to Hell, at least you know all your friends will be there," I tell him.

"Are *you* religious?"

I shake my head. "Not really. I know you can't tell by the whole 'I'm falling in love with you after four days' situation, but I tend to run more logical. I like things that can be studied and proven, not things made up entirely of myth and belief. But agnosticism aside, I've let a mob kingpin impregnate me and given many blow jobs to a man I know to be a killer, so I think I'm a little too scandalous for the pearly gates crowd. If you die first and Hell does exist, make sure to pick out a nice torture pit and I'll come keep you company once I get there."

"No peace and quiet, even in death," he says lightly, shaking his head.

"I mean, we might just be worm food. Who knows?" Glancing back at the tattoo, I ask, "So, if you're not confessing your sins on Sundays... how come you have an angel on your arm?"

It doesn't seem like a difficult question, but as his gaze shifts to the ink on his arm, he says nothing. His gaze drifts away, across the room. He looks off at nothing, and the solemnity of his features gives birth to dread. I can't help wondering where he mind is, who it might be with. I look at the tattoo stretched across his muscular bicep again and think about the closet full of clothes Sin has in his bedroom.

I almost wish I hadn't asked, because his reluctance to tell me makes me want to know even more. Softly, I ask, "Did you lose someone you loved?"

Still, he says nothing.

My curiosity deepens, grows roots and wraps itself around me. If he got a tattoo over some woman, where is she now? It's an angel, so did she die, or is it more figurative? Was she *his* angel? The thought makes my stomach sink. I'm jealous of a woman who might be dead, who might not even exist. Maybe it's not about a woman. Maybe he had religion once, before this life. Perhaps the weight of all his sins grew too heavy, so he stopped believing in order to cope. Or maybe the tattoo doesn't mean anything significant at all. Maybe he just liked the design.

Of course, if he just liked the design, that would be easy enough to say, wouldn't it? The religion thing seems like a simple enough explanation, too. It only gets hard if there is some personal significance, something he doesn't want to share with me.

I would share anything with him, so I don't want there to be something he won't tell me.

Instead of sating my curiosity, he lifts his hand to rub the baby's back, knocking my hand off his arm in the process. The tenderness of this lethal man lovingly stroking this sleeping baby's back is an incredible distraction. He is so damn good at distracting me.

I sigh, leaning my head on his shoulder and watching him love on Skylar. It gives birth to new torturous mental images, like him holding my baby the same way. It also calls back memories of his hands on my breasts, his breath on my skin, his beautiful, lying words on his lips, convincing me this could be our life together if I kept Rafe's baby.

The doorbell rings, swiftly pulling me out of my Sin stupor. I shoot upright, alarmed. "Did Rafe say anything about coming home early?"

Shaking his head, Sin shifts, keeping one hand on Skylar's back as he lifts his ass off the couch. "Grab my wallet. I figured you'd be hungry, so I ordered us dinner. Charged the food to Rafe's account, but you need tip money."

I'm not going to turn down a chance to touch Sin's ass, even if it is only to fish a wallet out of his pocket. My face flushes as I reach into the back pocket of his black jeans and I can't help meeting his gaze.

This is so much more appealing than I want it to be. An

evening in, cuddling babies and talking, ordering take-out. I want this. I want all of this, and I want it with him. I guess he can keep his secrets if he needs to. I like to believe someday he'll trust me enough to share his past with me, but it's his future I want.

23

SIN

This skimpy fucking robe is a nightmare. Cash in hand, Laurel climbs off the couch and heads for the foyer to greet the delivery guy. As much as I know I shouldn't look, I can't keep my eyes from following her, from trying to steal a peek as the fabric moves against her long legs. Is she wearing panties? If she is, I want to drag them off her and get another peek at her ass, her pussy. I want to spread her thighs and have *her* for dinner.

Instead, we'll have to sit here and try to pretend we don't want to fuck each other while we eat Chinese food.

Goddamn Rafe.

I really shouldn't have come here tonight. I didn't even want to answer the phone when she called, but I couldn't ignore it. A text message could have been ignored, but if she was calling, something might be wrong. I still haven't found any evidence that anyone *did* try to drug her, but it's been on my mind ever since. I'm probably worrying my life away over a dirty fucking glass.

Laurel comes back in with two paper bags stuffed full of

food. She's grinning like she has Christmas presents instead of nourishment.

"I love you for ordering this much food," she informs me, putting the bags down on the coffee table and ripping into them.

"I know you like food," I remark.

"I do. Lydia actually brought me some ziti or lasagna or something like that, some kind of leftovers as a thank you for watching Skylar. I was going to warm that up and eat by myself, but then Skylar became possessed and you know the rest of the story."

Frowning, I watch her open up a white container of rice. "She brought you food?"

Flicking a glance my way, she nods. "Yeah."

"You didn't eat any of it, did you?"

"No, not yet. Good thing, now we can eat together." She offers me a smile, but it drops when she sees me scowling. "What's wrong?"

"When we're done eating, I want you to throw out whatever she brought. Tell her you ate it, but don't. Don't eat anything she gives you, her or Gio. Don't drink anything the southern waitress from the club brings you either, and don't eat *or* drink anything Marlena has had access to."

Laurel's eyes widen. "What?"

I don't want to alarm her needlessly, which is why I haven't said anything before now, but if Lydia is bringing her food now, I have to say something. Until I am reasonably sure it was just a dirty glass at the club that night and not an attempt to hurt her, everyone at that table is a suspect. "Don't worry about it, just do as I say. I'm being overly cautious, but just... do it and don't ask questions."

"I already ate something the slutty waitress had access to," she tells me. "Rafe and I went to his restaurant to eat last night before your..." She halts, her voice a little tighter with dislike as she continues. "Your *date*. She was training with Virginia." Now scowling at me, she demands, "Why are you going out with someone you don't even trust to be around my food? Is this Rafe's doing? He's fucking around with her and he wanted to throw me off his scent, didn't he? You didn't really want to go out with the waitress."

"That's wishful thinking," I murmur.

"Is it?" she asks, sharply. "Don't do the bro code bullshit and keep this from me, Sin. This is my life. I deserve to know who he is. And if he *is* into the waitress, maybe he would be cool with it if you and I got together. Then he's free to have her without lying and sneaking around. We all win—I mean, except the waitress, two weeks from now when he gets bored with her, but then I'm pretty sure it's on to the next for him. The point is, if he thinks the sun sets between her legs right now, let's use that to get me out of this house and back to yours."

"Let's not do this, okay?" I ask, nodding at the food. "I want some of that teriyaki steak on a stick. Bring me a skewer."

"I'll bring you a skewer, all right," she mutters.

I can't help grinning. She's such a fucking trip, with her little bullshit murderous tendencies. "You gonna stab me with it?"

"I should," she informs me, as she grabs a skewer of meat and comes over to deliver it to me.

As Laurel contemplates murdering me, my mind wanders back to the fact that she ate at Rafe's restaurant last night and Marlena had access to her food. If Virginia was there too, she probably would have noticed anything off, but with Laurel's well-being at stake, I can't be too cautious.

"Did you feel okay after you left the restaurant? You weren't sick or anything?"

Laurel shakes her head. "No, I felt fine. Why would she mess with my food? It's Rafe's fault, isn't it? She doesn't know I'll give him up without a fight. She's probably trying to get me out of the way so she can have him."

"I don't think that's what's going on. I'm the one who went out with her, not him. Why would she want Rafe when she can have me?" I half-joke.

Only that joke doesn't land at all. Laurel looks like I just shot her dog. "Did you really order all this food just to make me lose my appetite?"

"It was a joke," I offer.

"No, it wasn't. Jokes are funny," she informs me, sticking her nose in the air and rising, going back to the coffee table to get herself some food. Stealing a glance at me as she shoves a spoon into a bowl of rice, she asks, "Do you really like her? If you're just covering Rafe's ass, you can tell me. I honestly don't care."

That's not what Rafe said. "How about we drop Marlena for the night?"

"Drop her from where? Somewhere high?" she asks innocently. I bite back a smile, but Laurel is still going like a dog with a bone. "Are you planning to see her again?"

"It's not really your business, is it?" I ask mildly.

I'm not trying to make her feel shitty; I just really don't want to talk about it. I don't know what the hell Rafe is up to with the shitty waitress and I don't *like* covering his ass, but it's already done now. Admitting I couldn't give less fucks about the waitress would feed Laurel's hopes that I never wanted to go out with her in the first place. It will feed her dead-end hopes about getting with me, and it will turn her off Rafe to know he was doing whatever shady shit he was doing before I intervened and reminded him not to be a bastard.

This is a fucking mess. I know I helped make it a mess, but fuck, I need to wear a hazmat suit just to wade through all this shit.

"How are things with Rafe?" I ask her.

"That's none of *your* business, is it?" she shoots back.

"It kind of is."

"Doesn't matter," she tells me. I wait for further explanation, but I don't get one.

We eat quietly for a few minutes. Well, she eats. I finish the steak on a stick, but I can't really eat the rest of it with Skylar sleeping on my chest. I'd put her down, but I don't know if she's a light sleeper and I don't want to wake her up.

Eventually Laurel sighs heavily and catches my attention. She's giving me a surly look, but she walks over and sits next to me, holding a plate of food and a white plastic spoon.

"Open up," she tells me.

I lift an eyebrow. "No chance."

Rolling her eyes, she says, "Don't be a baby. You can't hold the plate and eat. Just take a bite."

"You're not feeding me," I inform her.

"Why not?"

"Because I am not 5-months-old."

Shrugging, she leans forward and puts the plate down on the coffee table. "Fine, starve then." That lasts three seconds, then she asks, "Want me to take her so you can eat?"

I shake my head. "I'm fine. Don't worry about me."

"I'm straddling the line between worrying about you and wanting to stab you—would you like me to step back over to the other side?"

"You know you're only allowed to be possessive of things you actually possess, right?" I ask her, just to be a dick.

It's mean, so her eyes narrow at me. "Oh, yeah? So you never have any possessive feelings about me then, huh?"

I consider telling that bold-faced lie for a split second, but in the end, I decide not to. It's too obviously bullshit. Just seeing her sit close to Rafe at the club, knowing he was the one going home with her, made me fucking crazy. After six years of serving this family and never once wavering, since I met this girl, I've considered betraying everything I stand for just about every goddamned day.

She doesn't know any of that, and God help me if she ever figures it out. Her ruthless little ass would probably encourage me, convince me to raise an army against Rafe—and hey, why stop there? Just overthrow the Morelli family altogether and take the reins myself. I certainly know all the important players in this town.

Actually, no, she still doesn't want me to hurt the fucking bastard, so that's probably more my fantasy of what Laurel would say than what she would actually say. If it came down to a choice between his safety or mine, I think she would pick mine, but she doesn't *want* anyone to get hurt because she likes impossible things.

At least, I'm fairly certain she values my well-being—until she keeps talking.

"When you see Rafe's hand on my inner thigh, I bet you don't think about how he could push his long fingers between my legs and touch me right there at the table. You like Marlena now, right? So you don't care if Rafe finger fucks me right in front of you. You don't care how many times he makes me come. You don't care if he takes me home afterward, strips off all my clothes, drags his lips over every inch of my naked body the way you did once. You don't care if he pushes me down on his bed, climbs on top of me, and drives his cock deep—"

I reach out and grab a fistful of her satin robe, yanking her close. "Stop talking."

All innocence, she asks, "Why? Feeling possessive?"

"That goddamn mouth of yours is going to get you in trouble one of these days," I inform her, forcibly unclenching my fist and letting her go.

Only once I've released her she doesn't lean back. She stays close, because she likes to fucking torture me. Because for all her brain power, the damn girl doesn't have a lick of sense when it comes to keeping her distance from dangerous assholes. "So I keep hearing. What are you actually gonna do about it though, Sin?" she asks, lifting a dark eyebrow. "Not a damn thing, that's what."

Motherfucker.

I've been reluctant to move, not wanting to wake the baby, but I can't just let this fucking girl sit here and call me out like that.

Well, I guess I could. I definitely *should*.

Instead, I rise up off the couch, shifting Skylar on my chest, and walk over to the bassinet. I put her down gently, but she still shifts. Her little arm shoots up in the air briefly, then settles on her tummy. The ache in my chest as I look down at her almost makes me forget why I stood up in the first place. This whole night is part fantasy, part nightmare, and it doesn't get any easier when I turn around and see Laurel sitting on the couch, her long legs curled up behind her, watching me with undisguised interest. There she sits, looking like everything I've ever wanted and belonging to someone else.

The thing I should do is turn and walk right out the door. The baby is settled, the mess is cleaned up, and Laurel is fed;

my work here is done. I shouldn't respond to such obvious bait, but it's different now. It's different because she's not taunting me with what *might* happen, she's taunting me with what *did* happen. There's no way in hell that after seeing me out with Marlena last night, she didn't fuck Rafe when they went home, even if only to spite me.

The night at the club she floored me, telling me she hadn't slept with him yet. The greedy, possessive side of me wanted that to mean she wouldn't, but I knew that couldn't last forever. Deep in my selfish heart, I was relieved that she wasn't ready. When I showed up at the doctor's house, I was all too happy to threaten his ass into lying. Anything that kept Rafe's hands off Laurel longer was a plan I could get behind.

I knew it ran counter to getting them together, but it was a nice fucking fantasy. Women have flung committed relationships out the door for the chance to screw around with Rafe, and here's this one who—by all rights—should be his, but I'm the one she wants. That she was telling him no even when I told her we couldn't be together was seductive as hell. I like that kind of single-minded devotion. I like it a whole hell of a lot.

I don't hold it against her that she finally fucked him, but I sure as hell don't want to hear about it. It was bad enough when Rafe baited me at the restaurant, telling me what she looked like kneeling for him, but to hear it from Laurel's lips really pisses me off. Even if she should want to hurt me, even if I deserve it, I don't like her saying shit like that to me.

Even if it makes both our lives harder than they need to be, I like Laurel wanting me. It's selfish as hell, but I don't want her to stop.

I walk slowly to stand in front of the couch, my eyes trained on her the whole way. When I get there, I reach back and grab my T-shirt by the neck, tugging it off and tossing it on the floor. Laurel's blue eyes widen as they drop to rake a glance over my bare chest, then dart back to my face. She swallows, looking up at me with a sort of fascinated unease—like I'm the big bad wolf, but she *wants* me to eat her whole.

"This what you want?" I ask her, putting a hand on her chest and shoving her down on the couch. I don't know why I expect a little struggle; I don't get one. She lets me push her on her back, then watches me climb on top of her. Her big blue eyes never move away from mine.

Once I have her body pinned beneath me, the breath rushes out of her and she swallows, but doesn't speak. Like she didn't expect that to work, and she's afraid to trust it. Smart girl.

Well, not *that* smart, because she thinks it's a good idea to antagonize me into fucking her, and it isn't. That is a bad fucking idea, and the damn girl needs to get that through her head.

Now that I'm on top of her, I twine my fingers together with hers like I'm gonna hold her hands, but instead I push them over her head. Her godforsaken robe falls open so I can see her belly button, so I can see the pretty bra and panties she put on to come down here and tempt me with.

"You want me to fuck you, Laurel?" I ask, leaning in to press my lips against her neck.

She sighs with pleasure, her head drifting to the side to make room for me. "Yes."

"Right here? We're on Rafe's couch. That doesn't bother you?"

"You can fuck me on his bed, if you really want to," she tells me.

Damn, that's fucking brutal. I can't help smiling a little, my tongue darting out to taste her skin. "I don't know, you didn't ask very nicely," I tell her.

"Please," she whispers, holding me closer. "Please fuck me."

"You don't know what you're asking for, pretty girl," I murmur, dragging my lips across her jaw.

"I don't care," she says, eyes closed, her chest already working. She is so fucking hot for me. God, it's impossible not to want this woman. "I'm not fragile, Sin. You can be as rough as you want. I love when you're rough with me. I want all your violence."

Jesus Christ, this woman is going to be the death of me.

I growl, releasing one of her hands so I can grab a fistful of her hair and tug her head back. I lean in and kiss her jawline, then kiss her neck more roughly, nipping and sucking before I realize I can't do that. I can't leave a mark on her, because Rafe will see it.

Fuck. I pull back before I get too lost in this moment to remember to pull myself out of it. Laurel damn sure doesn't help, spreading her legs for me, hooking one around my hip so I can fit myself right up against her barely covered pussy.

"Sin," she says on a sigh, wrapping the arm she has free around my neck and pulling me into her.

"Is this what you want, Laurel?"

"Yes. Yes, please," she adds, remembering her manners. "Please give it to me, Sin. I want this. I want it so much."

I run a hand along her face approvingly, but I keep from verbalizing it. "Yeah? What will you do for it?"

Her response is hungry and eager, her blue eyes dancing with arousal as I grind my cock against her. "Anything you want. I'll do anything."

I lean down to kiss her forehead and her pretty eyes drift

closed. I almost feel bad for what I'm about to ask, given how peaceful she looks right now. "Do you know what it'll cost, Laurel?"

It takes a moment for my words to land, her mind and body already too far gone. Her eyes open when it hits her and she sighs again, but this time with something closer to exasperation. "Dammit. This is a trick, isn't it?"

My rigid cock testifies it's not *purely* a trick, but I know I can't fuck her. No matter how much my stupid cock wants to get inside her hot pussy, I can't afford to make a move like that. Rafe isn't going to kill her for straying, but he *will* kill me for fucking his woman. Or I kill him before he sees it coming, and that opens up a whole new world of problems.

Despite her words, despite figuring out I'm toying with her again, the hand I still have pinned above her head squeezes mine. It's almost a reflex, like she can't help it, and I get it, 'cause I can't help squeezing her back.

"If I fuck you, somebody has to die," I tell her simply.

She shakes her head in denial, her long dark hair moving against Rafe's couch. "That's not true. I told you, we could go to Chicago. We could be happy there."

"And I told you, Chicago won't work."

"Chicago is a great plan. I worked it all out," she informs me. "You can work for Mateo, Mia and I can raise babies together, I can go to school, and the best part? You can fuck me as much as you want. No Rafe, no problems."

"Rafe will not let that happen," I state.

Laurel shrugs like she's not convinced, her gaze dropping to my chest. "We don't know unless we ask."

Now that I'm not actively mauling her, she takes a moment to look me over. Her gaze is full of tenderness, like she's spent an eternity missing me. I know it's only been a few days, but I get it. I've missed her the same way. I didn't know I'd let her get so close when I had her at my house, not even the night I chased her off. It didn't hit me until afterward, when the solitude I needed to live before her suddenly felt like loneliness. When I dreaded going home to my bed at night because I knew she wouldn't be there waiting for me.

It's so hard to look at her now, wanting all the same things I want, and tell her she can't have them. The injustice of it all pisses me off, but I remind myself it's my fault. I'm the one who set her free in the first place. I may not have had rights to her, but I took them, and I gave Rafe a fair shot first. He could try to steal her from me, but I had played fair.

Wouldn't have mattered once the DNA test came back positive, though.

Wouldn't have mattered if he played the long game, waited for my newness to wear off, then swept in, swept Laurel off her feet, and stole her back from me.

One thing I've learned in life—most people don't know what it is to love forever. As soon as it isn't explosive anymore, they get bored and go looking for new excitement. I'd like to believe Laurel's different, and her giving me devotion I haven't earned helps me believe that, but she's so young. How does she know how she'll feel in a few years?

"Tell me something," I say, bringing her big blue eyes back to my face.

"Okay," she says, easily. Too easily. Too trusting, considering what I've done to her.

"If you're willing to cheat on him with me, why shouldn't I think you'd do the same thing if we were together?"

Laurel rears back as if insulted. "I am not *cheating* on him. I've never cheated on anybody. I don't *belong* to Rafe. How many times do I have to say that?"

"Maybe you didn't," I allow. "But as soon as you let him fuck you again, you changed that."

Her face relaxes instantly, like my annoying her was a false alarm. Then she brings her free hand up to caress my jaw. "I didn't sleep with him, Sin. I'm not going to. I don't want to. I'm yours, not his. Can't you tell?" With a little smile, she adds, "And what kind of crazy woman would cheat on *you*? You kill men for a living, and you're hotter than anyone else alive."

My lips tug upward. "You might be a little biased right now, seeing as you're nearly naked and pinned beneath my body."

"No, I did a study of the world's men. You're the hottest. I was the only subject polled, so it was pretty exclusive, but in this instance, mine is the only relevant opinion."

I shake my head at my little nerd and lean in to kiss her on the forehead again. When I pull back, she purses her lips at me, prettily displeased.

"Still no kisses? Really?"

I feel shittier about it now than I did before, but I brush her hair back tenderly and tell her, "You're not mine to kiss."

"I'll tell Rafe this isn't working tonight. As soon as he gets home. Hell, I'll text it to him. That's about all he deserves since he can't even be bothered to come help me with Skylar. I'll text him as soon as Gio and Lydia pick her up. I'll grab my stuff and we can be gone before he even gets home to try to talk me out of it—*if* he even tries to talk me out of it, which he might not at this point. This thing between us is not working. He wants someone who isn't me, and I want someone who isn't him. It's no one's fault, but he and I don't have a future together."

I think she's being naïve, but it'll only piss her off to tell her that. She doesn't know Rafe the way I do, hasn't known him as long as I have. In her mind, it's as simple as breaking it off and walking away, but it won't be. It can't be. Not with who he is. Not with the family he hails from. Laurel might object to being referred to as Rafe's property, but she is. Right now I am begging for a bullet to the back of the skull, just being here with her like this.

Laurel continues trying to convince me. "This isn't wrong, you and me. It's right."

As if the motherfucker has some secret sense and he knows he needs to make his presence known right now, her phone vibrates between us. I know it's Rafe. It fucking has to be.

"Guess who," I murmur.

Laurel frowns, fishing around for the phone but apparently not finding it. It vibrated against my hip and I'm flush against her, so it's gotta be in her pocket.

"I can't find it," she mutters, then it vibrates a second time and her hand stops moving. Suddenly it moves again, too quickly for me to realize she pulled the phone out of *my* pocket. Flashing me a mischievous smile as she takes a peek, she says, "Ha, my turn."

"Give me that," I say, grabbing the damn thing away from her, but I'm confused by the couple shades of color her face loses. Fuck, she shouldn't be reading my work messages. I turn the phone around to see what the hell she just read—not that anyone should be explicit enough in a text message that she would know what they were saying anyway—but then I see something far fucking worse.

Two messages in a row from Marlena.

Coming back soon?

I thought you said this was gonna be quick ;)

Laurel has the same look she had when she saw us out

together, like I just took a sledgehammer to her rib cage. Like her heart can't beat right and her lungs can't draw in air.

"You were with her," she says, softly. I wait for the feeling of being socked in the gut when I see betrayal in her blue eyes, but it doesn't happen because she can't even fucking look at me.

I wanna explain, but I can't. More than that, I shouldn't. I didn't want to go the route of making her despise me to get her over me, but it's clear as day we can't be friends. Not now, at least. Maybe someday down the road, once she's settled, but right now it's too hard.

"Get off me," she says, shoving at my chest, moving her legs to dislodge me.

For all that she couldn't get me close enough a minute ago, now I'm clearly not moving fast enough, so she keeps shoving me. Once I climb off her, she springs up off the couch and turns around, glaring down at me.

"You have some fucking nerve, you know that? Accusing *me* of cheating when you left your fucking date to come rescue me. Tell your little girlfriend about that, why don't you?"

I debate saying something to make it worse, but I can't. I hate hurting her. I feel guilty for every second she struggles to breathe and I know it's because of me. As much as I miss her, I wish she'd never met me. Her life would be better for it.

When I look back up at her again, tears are shining in her big blue eyes. Pools of hurt, and I'm the one responsible.

Fuck me.

Before I can make things worse, I reach forward and grab my shirt off the floor, dragging it over my head and standing.

"I'm sorry," I say, simply.

"Just go," she says, turning away and walking over to check on Skylar.

I want to tell her I won't come around again so she knows to stop waiting on me, but it feels too much like she'll take it as a punishment. Selfishly, I want to tell her I wasn't faking any of it, and yeah, I'm a bastard, but maybe not as big a bastard as she thinks I am. That's the last thing I can say to her, so I keep my mouth shut, keep my head down, and with one last glimpse of her reaching into the baby's bassinet, I'm gone.

24

LAUREL

I am snuggled up in bed when Rafe gets home.

Actually, I went to bed as soon as Gio and Lydia packed up all of Skylar's belongings and left. Probably before they even made it out of Rafe's long-ass driveway, I was upstairs peeling off my bra, slipping on pajamas, and climbing into bed alone.

Las Vegas is a lonely town. Who would have ever thought?

After Sin left, I felt lonelier than ever. I curled up in bed and looked at my phone, but there was no one to call. I couldn't call Carly and tell her what has me upset, because she doesn't even know about Sin. Even though I want to rip his dick off right now, I'm still protective enough of him that I don't want *this* to be the first she hears of him, either.

That just pisses me off more.

I thought about calling Mia, but she's too connected to Rafe. I do believe completely that she meant what she said and she'll take me in if I come back, but I can't tell her what just happened between me and Sin. Rafe is her family more than I am, and I don't think she's given up her idea of me and Rafe having our fairy tale ending. It just seems like telling her I nearly fucked Sin on Rafe's couch may be a conflict of interest.

I'm going to rip Marlena's eyeballs out. I'm going to strap her to a chair, light cigars and burn her arms with them, take a knife and cut open her abdomen so her stupid innards spill out all over the floor.

I just want to murder her, that's all.

It's probably Sin I should want to murder, but I would miss that monster too much if he died. As mad as I am at him, I still wish he were here instead of with her.

I'm so fucked.

My eyes are adjusted to the dark, but Rafe's aren't yet, so I see his hand go to the light switch when he comes in, but he pauses when he realizes I'm in bed. He decides to leave the light off so as not to disturb me and steps inside. He moves slowly, peeling off his jacket, then starting on the buttons of his dress shirt. I wait to see if he's drunk, but if he is, I can't tell. He's too graceful to stumble. It's odd to think of a man like him as graceful, but it seems like everything comes easily to Rafe Morelli, even walking while drunk.

Well, everything but me, I guess.

Bet he didn't see *that* coming when I fucked him the first day I met him.

My lips curve up in mild amusement, but it's too much effort. Rafe peels off his shirt and I see his muscular back in the moonlight. I watch as he unbuckles his black belt and draws it off.

Ever since Sin made taking off belts so sexy, I can't not respond to them. Seeing Rafe's hand wrapped around that belt makes me yearn for things, but I think it's rooted in sadness more than real sexual desire. It's the horrible thoughts that have been replaying over and over in my head that Sin was with Marlena, that he was going back to her. Especially after I turned him on and left him unsatisfied, he undoubtedly did *something* with her. Even if he didn't fuck her, he probably let her suck him off, and the thought of someone else's mouth wrapped around him makes me feel like I'm dying.

I should fuck Rafe.

Rafe is undeniably beautiful. I'm not in love with him, but he could give me an escape, even if only for tonight. At least, I think he could. I would hate to be a cocktease again, like in the bathtub. I don't want to get him going if I can't finish the job. It's not nice, and I don't mean to, it's just I lose my nerve and get cold feet when it comes down to it.

Rafe just isn't Sin, and even though I once thought Rafe the hottest man I had ever seen, that was before I met that ruthless asshole. Before he chained my wrists to his bed and stole my stupid, fool heart.

Everything aches, and I just want it to stop. Love isn't supposed to hurt this much. The only way it should hurt is maybe the enormity of it weighing on you, the feeling of loving someone too much to handle—fleeting moments, but not this. Not searing pain. Not a tortured mind and endless misery. I should never have to think about someone else physically possessing what belongs to me. I feel like Sin belongs to me, but if he's spending the night with another woman, he clearly doesn't feel the same way.

Then again, if I fuck Rafe because I'm sad, I'm letting someone else physically possess me. But fuck, why should I be loyal to Sin if he doesn't have to be loyal to me?

Maybe he didn't do anything with her.

I feel pathetic holding onto that. It's a stupid thing to think. Sin had reasons for not fucking me, reasons he *doesn't* have for not fucking her. I felt how hard he was on the couch; I know he was turned on. He certainly didn't get relief from me, and I know he went back to her, with her skanky winking smiley face bullshit.

She won't be able to wink after I cut out her goddamned eyes, now, will she?

See if Sin still wants to fuck her then.

"Hypothetically, if I wanted to maim someone, would you help me cover it up? And clean up the mess? I want to do the harming, not so much the cleaning."

Rafe spins around, surprised, since he must have assumed I was asleep. "Sure," he says, off-handedly. "I've got a whole team for that kind of thing. You think I get these hands dirty mopping up blood?" He shakes his head, dismissing the idea.

Cracking a smile, I ask, "You never have?"

"Well, sure, back when I was a baby gangster," he allows. "Not recently. I'm too high up for that kind of thing now. You only get your hands dirty on my level if you want to. You get my perks by association, though. If you want someone dead, you don't have to do the dirty work. Give me a name and I'll get it done."

"No, I *want* to do the dirty work. At least, I think I do. I've never carved out someone's eyes with busted sticks before, but that's what I'm leaning toward right now."

"Ouch," he replies, stepping out of his pants and kicking them into the corner. "Who pissed you off? I hope it wasn't me. I like having eyes."

Rolling mine, I tell him, "Yeah, I bet you do, that way they can wander all over the place. How many chicks draped themselves around your table tonight while I was away? Maybe carving out the eyeballs of whorebags is going to be my new hobby. That's a pity. I would have preferred painting."

Smiling without concern for my bloodthirst, he walks over

to his side of the bed and pulls back the blanket so he can climb in. "Someone's grumpy tonight. Do you need another massage?"

"Why does Gio cheat on his wife?"

That clearly was not the response Rafe expected. "Uh... I guess for the same reason most unfaithful men do. Boredom. Dissatisfaction. The desire for something different. He's been fucking the same woman for over a decade."

"Yes, because he *married* her. He chose her. He agreed to that. Does she cheat on him, too?"

"Of course not."

"How is that 'of course not'? If he's fucking around, she should get to. Maybe she's bored, too. Taking the same dick for a decade, then he decides to fuck around on her after they have a baby? Gio is an asshole."

"Uh huh," Rafe murmurs, knowingly. "We're not talking about Gio, are we? I'm not fucking anyone else, Laurel. I'm not even fucking *you*. I'm more celibate than I have been since my teen years," he states dryly, clearly not happy about it.

"Well, if you think refusing to come help me with an angry baby is a step toward ending that dry spell, boy, have you got some learning to do."

Smiling faintly, he drapes his strong arm around my waist and easily yanks me over into his space. "Is that why you're so fired up tonight? I can handle babies when they're calm and cute, but I'm not experienced enough with them to be any help in a crisis. I'm sure I would have made it worse somehow."

"I don't care if you're inexperienced with babies. How do you expect to learn if you don't try? In your idea of us as a couple, is that how it goes? I do 100 percent of the parenting and you just... what, show up at home before bed time once or twice a week and pat it on the head? I'm not sure what gave you the impression I would ever be happy with that sort of life, but I am not remotely interested in an arrangement like that."

"Skylar isn't our baby," he points out.

"It doesn't matter. If that's how you react when I'm in a jam, then I'm alone in this. I don't want to be a single mother with financing. I want a partner. I want a co-parent. I want someone who is going to have a *relationship* with this baby, an emotional investment. I want someone who shows up and does the work."

There is no longer amusement on his face, but he keeps his tone perfectly even, deceptively casual as he asks, "Why do you refer to this position like a job any applicant can fill? I'm the father. That's not really optional. Or did you have a back-up in mind?"

I know he means Sin, and I am *not* in the mood to talk about that with him right now. "You're the father, sure. But if you have no interest in being a *dad*, then I have no interest in even attempting to pursue this."

I don't know what I expect him to say to that, but he doesn't say a damn thing. He watches me, his face inscrutable, then pulls me closer and tucks me into his chest. Files me away, like a problem he doesn't feel like dealing with tonight.

I want to object on the basis of that being bullshit, but the physical comfort of being wrapped up in his strong embrace and snuggled up against his chest is too appealing. Too much what I needed tonight. If we fight, I'll want to roll away from him, and snuggling a pillow isn't quite as nice.

So, at least for now, I let it go.

R afe doesn't normally wake me up for no apparent reason, especially when I've had trouble sleeping all night long, but when I feel someone shaking my arm and I open my eyes, Rafe is standing above me, completely dressed for the day in a sharp blue suit.

"Time to get up, sleepyhead."

Grumbling, I bury my face in my pillow, intent on ignoring him.

Rafe snatches my pillow and tosses it over on his side of the bed.

"Hey!" I object, shooting him a dirty look.

"Time to get up," he tells me again.

"I'm sleepy. I have nothing to do. Let me sleep."

"You *do* have things to do, actually. First, you need to get your cute little ass out of bed and come downstairs so you can make breakfast."

"You have a *maid*," I remind him.

"It tastes better when it's cooked with love," he jokes.

"Then you should *definitely* have Juanita cook it," I deadpan.

Ignoring my sour mood, he adds, "Secondly, you have an appointment to get manicures and lunch with Lydia today. I guess she really appreciated you babysitting last night, and now she wants to thank you with pretty nails and female bonding time."

That all sounds completely terrible. He knows I don't like Lydia, so why would I want to have lunch with her? "I want absolutely no part of anything you just said. Tell Lydia I have morning sickness. I'm staying in bed."

"Sin's downstairs," he states.

My heart stops beating and I freeze.

252 | SINNING IN VEGAS

"Also waiting for breakfast," he adds, mildly. Then with an equally mild smile, he adds, "You know how we both like to be served."

This is a trap. It has to be. He couldn't *know* Sin was here last night, could he? I suppose he could. The first day I arrived in Vegas, he said something about a security set-up of some kind. Maybe he has some kind of camera system outside to keep an eye on who comes and goes, for safety reasons. Does he check it? I certainly didn't tell him Sin was here last night, but it's not like he asked. Granted, he probably wouldn't think to ask, "Did Sin come over to help you with the angry baby last night?"

Maybe I should confess. It's not like I did anything wrong. Well, okay, the mauling on the couch he probably wouldn't approve of, but calling Sin for help wasn't wrong, and Rafe and I aren't involved exclusively.

"Why is he here?" I ask, keeping my tone as level as possible.

"Business. Why else?"

Sighing, I throw back the blanket and push my legs over the side of the bed. "Fine. Give me like ten minutes."

25

SIN

This is the last place in the universe I want to be this morning.

I think Rafe may have checked his security footage when he got home last night and he knows I was here. Or maybe Laurel was pissed enough that she told him, I don't know. Maybe it's just his fucking sixth sense for people, and he smells me doing sneaky shit.

I don't like being the man who does sneaky shit—not this type of sneaky shit, anyway. Doing dirty work is one thing, but being an untrustworthy asshole you can't trust around your woman is not for me.

When I told Rafe I would rather meet away from the house like we talked about, he declined. Insisted I come to his house instead. Normally that would be fine, but after a sleepless night spent reliving last night with Laurel, and the way all that ended, I wanted to stay away. Attempting to steer us away from his house, I told him I was hungry, we should meet for breakfast somewhere.

I regret every last syllable when Laurel struts into the

kitchen, not even sparing me a glance. She's wearing the same thing she wore last night when I left, and I can still feel the soft fabric beneath my fingertips. Her skimpy robe is secured around her small waist, a little swatch of fabric from her bra visible underneath. Without shyness—and without words—she walks over to the cupboard with her back to us and bends over.

I turn my head swiftly, too tempted to look at the sight of her ass displayed right in front of me. Motherfucker. My gaze flickers to Rafe and of course he's watching me. He should be looking at Laurel's ass like I would be, but no, she's bait and he wants to see if I get a hook through my lip.

Sighing, I grab the black coffee cup in front of me and go to take a drink, forgetting I emptied it while I was waiting for him to come back downstairs. I want to get some more, but not enough to walk over and stand close to Laurel while I pour it. Definitely not enough to tell her to pour me some. Not after last night.

Only I don't have to, because Rafe says, "Sin needs coffee."

"Then he should go to Starbucks," Laurel states, dumping some olive oil into the pan she just put on the stove. "It's not my job to make him breakfast and I'm doing that. If he wants full service, maybe he should get a *waitress*," she snaps, turning up the heat with relish.

Despite her words, as soon as she finishes dumping the olive oil, she grabs the coffee pot and comes over to wordlessly fill my mug.

"Thank you," I murmur.

"I hope it's not too hot," she says, with enough bite that I know she hopes the opposite.

I ignore her attitude and take a sip, looking right at her. "Nope. It's perfect."

"Wonderful." She turns around and goes back to put the

coffee pot down, then returns to... brandishing a knife. Not sure I want her to be handling a knife when she wants to kill me.

"Uh, what are you doing over there?" I ask, eyeing the huge blade she selected.

"Cooking," she replies.

"No shit. Why do you need a knife to make eggs?"

Flashing me a smile over her shoulder, she says, "Why? Are you worried?"

"Little bit."

"Good," she says cheerfully, grabbing a cutting board out of the cupboard. I don't like the way she navigates Rafe's kitchen. She knows her way around it already, and as dumb a thing as it is to get annoyed about, I hate the idea of her cooking for him. Taking care of him. She shouldn't be doing that. Not for him.

Rafe's voice pulls me out of my thoughts. "Are we gonna get back to work?"

"It's hard to focus when I'm worried about getting stabbed," I inform him.

Smiling faintly, Rafe nods his head at Laurel, even though she can't see him. "You were just asking if I'd clean up a murder scene for you last night in bed. Were you talking about Sin?"

"Not specifically," Laurel replies as she chops her tomatoes.

"If you do murder him, I'd prefer it not happen in my kitchen," Rafe tells her. "I have a thing about eating meals in a room that was once covered in blood. Plus, I would have to buy new knives. It would be a lot of trouble for me, all things considered."

Laurel lifts the board and scrapes the tomatoes into the

pan. "Well, I would never want to make your life harder," she says, with exaggerated sweetness.

Rafe takes a sip from his coffee mug, then tells her, "Now *I* need more coffee."

Laurel shakes her head, but grabs the coffee pot and heads over to refill his. "I'm starting to see why you lazy bastards are so fond of waitresses."

"I'm not fond of waitresses," Rafe replies, looping his arm around her waist and pulling her flush against his side.

My whole body tenses. I tell myself not to look, but I can't look *away* as he presses his lips to Laurel's in a very slow, very deliberate kiss. Fury ravages my insides, surging through me like a livewire. Laurel is too surprised to respond too enthusiastically, but it's not like she pulls away. It's not like I should expect her to after last night, but flashes of me on top of her come back, my lips leaving a trail down her neck. Someone else shouldn't be fucking kissing her when 12 hours ago I was doing all that.

My gaze drifts to her neck now, and I see it. I feel fucking triumphant when I see it, even though I shouldn't. It's not a dark bruise. I caught myself quick, but not quickly enough. There's a faint mark on her neck, and I'm the one who put it there.

Clearly she didn't notice, or I would think she would have covered it up. Fuck. I'm not sure if I hope Rafe sees it—fucking asshole deserves it—or I hope he doesn't, because he might fucking kill me. In addition to killing me, he just might be pissed off enough to take off the kid gloves and stop waiting around for Laurel's feelings to fall in line. Nothing makes a man fuck his woman more brutally than the knowledge that she let another man leave his mark on her.

When he stops kissing her, he smiles at her tenderly and says, "I'm fond of science nerds."

Her gaze drops, some of the spunk going out of her. I take it to mean she's still uncomfortable being affectionate with him in front of me, but after last night I would expect her to want to throw it in my face. She doesn't have enough meanness in her, I guess. She's mad at me, but she doesn't want to cut me to the quick. Her strong sense of loyalty still tells her since she had me all over her last night, she shouldn't be kissing someone else in front of me this morning. She's fucking right, too. I know I deserve it for giving her up in the first place, but I don't want to see this shit.

Once Rafe releases Laurel, she goes back to the counter to resume making our food, this time without mild death threats or barbed comments.

When everything is finished, she splits the food between two plates. She brings them over, hesitating briefly before putting either plate down, then she reaches both arms forward and puts down both plates at the same time. She walks away muttering something about "sexist bullshit" but then she turns her little ass right back around and brings a plate of cut up orange slices and strawberries for us to share, I guess.

"Eat up, boys," she tells us.

"You didn't save any for yourself?" I question.

"It's probably poisoned," Rafe states, grabbing a fork and digging in regardless.

Laurel smiles to herself, then she does the most evil thing she has ever done. She holds up a banana and cracks the top, then slowly begins peeling it. "Oh, I have my breakfast right here."

Goddammit. I ignore her, stabbing the center of my egg so the yolk spills out. I will ignore Laurel eating the phallic-shaped fruit. I will not think about her lips around my dick. I will not wonder if her lips have been around *his* dick. I will not take my gun out, shoot Rafe mid-bite, and haul Laurel's little ass right out the front door.

Focus on the fucking eggs.

I can't focus on the eggs. My gaze darts to her just in time to see the tip of the banana disappear into that perfect fucking mouth of hers. My dick responds immediately, and then it only gets worse when I look at her neck and see the mark I left there last night, then my eyes drop to her tits and I see them begging to be let out of that white bra.

My heart beats in my throat and all the blood in my body rushes straight to my cock. In an attempt to behave like a man who isn't aroused to the point of fucking pain, I cut into the egg, shovel some herb-sprinkled tomato onto my fork, and bring it to my mouth. I'm sure it tastes good—it sure looks and smells good—but it may as well be cardboard for all the enjoyment I'm able to get out of it.

My whole body is so fucking tense, I feel like I might explode. I want to do things I can't do. I want to shove this plate away from me, walk around the counter, grab a fistful of Laurel's brown hair, and tell her to drop to her knees. I want to see unquestioning obedience in her eyes as she drops right in front of Rafe, like she did the day he brought her back from the Grand Canyon. I want to free my cock and shove it into her pretty little mouth, to see her big blue eyes looking up at me as she takes every inch. I definitely want that talented little tongue of hers running along my length until my cock hits the back of her throat. With Rafe sitting there, too fucking stunned to do a goddamned thing about it, I want to fuck Laurel's face and see the desire in her eyes, like letting me use her is the single greatest experience of her life.

Then I want her on her hands and knees, legs spread, this skimpy fucking robe bunched up around her waist while I give her pussy a good pounding and remind her that good girls get treats. I want to fuck her good and hard until her heart races in her chest and she struggles to breathe—but for a good reason, this time. Only for good reasons from here on out.

Only I can't, because of the asshole sitting on my left. Because he had the dumb luck of knocking her up on a one-night-stand, and now everything is a tangled fucking mess.

Why couldn't it have been me? Why couldn't I be the lucky bastard who knocked her up? Then she'd be mine and no one could say shit about it.

I shove back from the counter and stand, carefully angling my body to try to hide the hard-on as I do.

"What are you doing?" Rafe asks, watching me.

I need to get the fuck out of here, that's what I need to be doing. Before I do something I'll undoubtedly regret, before I alter the course of all our fucking lives because Laurel decided to have a banana for breakfast, I need to get the fuck out of this house.

Only I can't, because Rafe will know exactly why.

"Forgot to wash my hands," I mutter, as I head for the bathroom to jerk off to the mental image of Laurel choking on my cock.

Most days I have enough on my plate that I don't have time to think much about Laurel, unless it's her safety I'm worrying about. When I'm done doing the work Rafe knows about, I spend the rest of my downtime keeping an eye on all the fucking trouble-making women he has unwittingly invited into Laurel's life.

The southern belle was simple. Let the club manager know I need security tapes, slip a little money to one of the other waitresses to get the dirt on her, chat with a bartender I noticed she spent extra time with, keep an eye on everybody for a couple of days. The preliminary round of research on her tells me she's probably not the one who tampered with Laurel's glass—if anyone did. It could be I'm chasing my own tail here, but I'd rather find out I wasted my time than find out too late someone really is out to hurt Laurel and I didn't do a damn thing to stop it.

Marlena is easy to keep an eye on now that I got access to her apartment. I could break in and plant bugs, only problem is Rafe has that whole apartment community gated with a guard, and every license plate coming or going gets recorded. My original plan was to boost a car just long enough to get that particular job done—didn't want to take one from the shop, just on the off chance Rafe cared enough to trace it back to that—but then Rafe gave me a much easier in with his fake date. I'd like to stroke my own ego a little and say Rafe's cast-offs keep taking to me because I'm something special, but while Laurel and I really did have an attraction, I feel not a damn thing for Marlena, and she was ready to make the fake date real.

I haven't quite put my finger on what Marlena is, but there's something about her I don't fucking like. It could just be that Laurel hates her. I'm too close to it to see straight. Anyway, it doesn't matter. Whether her interest goes where the wind blows it or there's some other reason, Marlena was all too happy to invite me back to her place, and I was all too happy to plant bugs when she went to the bathroom so I could keep an eye on her comings, goings, and visitors from the comfort of my home.

Or my car, as the case has been, because I'm also keeping an eye on Cassandra Carmichael. That has been a lot harder. She goes out all the time, and in order to know what she's up to, I need to be following her. I put a tracker on her car to see where she goes when I can't be there, but all I have is unattached locations. I can't know who she is meeting with from a tracker on her car.

Today my life is a little harder, because something from this morning keeps sticking with me. Not just Laurel in the robe, my mental images of fucking her in Rafe's kitchen, or the smell of her when I brushed too closely on my way back to my place at the counter after my trip to the bathroom, but something she said before she went upstairs.

She's meeting Lydia for manicures?

I didn't get the impression Lydia especially liked Laurel, and seeing as how she's Gio's wife, it has been significantly harder to get a peek at her dealings. She stays at home with the baby, and I sure as shit can't get inside Gio's house without being noticed, let alone hide a bug anywhere. The Morellis are a paranoid fucking people, and Gio's house has a more advanced security set-up than Rafe does. Being a bachelor (and more easygoing than most of the Morelli men of my acquaintance) Rafe doesn't have as much to lose. He doesn't have as much to protect. Or he didn't. Now he does, but he hasn't caught up yet.

Now that he has Laurel and a baby on the way, he really needs to step up his security. It's not just him in the world anymore. It's not just himself he needs to keep safe, so he needs to lock that fucking place down like Fort Knox. He needs to pack go-bags for Laurel and the baby, walk her through what to do if anyone ever breaches the security measures he puts in place, and frankly, he needs to put in a panic room. He needs to make sure Laurel and the baby will be safe no matter what, and instead, his shit is so lax that I mauled the mother of his child on his couch last night, and he has no way of even knowing for sure, short of putting both of us in a room and trying to read our body language.

I know he gets a kick out reading people his way, but this is too important for that shit. Protecting your family isn't something you can afford to take chances with. There's no second chance when it comes to that.

Sitting here outside a fucking nail salon, of all places, I reach over and pop open the glove compartment. I go to reach for my sunglasses, and the Twix bar Laurel gave me catches my eye. The candy sealed inside is mushy and melted, of course, but I couldn't bring myself to throw the damn thing away. I shove it back inside and grab my sunglasses, sliding them on. Then I draw out my phone to check the time. I don't know how long manicures are supposed to take, but I know they're heading to lunch after this. I need to remind Laurel to be safe, but I don't want to text it, because I don't want there to be a chance Gio ever finds out I don't trust his wife around Laurel's food and drink.

I see Laurel and Lydia stand and head to the counter to pay, so it's time. I already scoped the place out before her appointment—the most ridiculous place I've ever had to check out, hands down—so I know the bathroom is in the door and to the right, while they're paying at a counter to the left.

I text Laurel a brief, to-the-point message. "Go to the bathroom."

Then I push open my door and head inside, hanging right

and going to the restroom area. It's single stall, not multi, but I slip inside and leave the door unlocked.

A moment later, Laurel shoves open the door and walks inside the bathroom, but she's frowning down at her phone, not looking up.

She jumps when she realizes she's not alone in the room, gasping and grabbing her chest. "Jesus Christ!"

I gently move her aside, reaching behind her and locking the door.

"What the hell, Sin?" she demands, eyes wide.

"Why are you going to lunch with Lydia?"

Laurel blinks at me, then shakes her head. "I don't know. Because Rafe told me to?"

That sours my mood, fast. "Oh, okay. I forgot you do everything Rafe tells you to do."

Narrowing her eyes at me, she says, "Yes, I do; I'm a *good girl*. Have you forgotten already?"

"Oh, I remember how good you are," I murmur, taking a couple steps closer.

Laurel swallows, backing up against the bathroom door. I should hang back, but she's being mouthy, and I want to crowd her. I like closing her in like this. I like the wariness that jumps in her eyes as she looks up at me. I can practically see memories of how good she was for me replaying in that dirty mind of hers, feel it in the way she loses steam now that I'm standing right on top of her, staring down at her.

Her voice has a faint bite to it, but more hurt than anger when she mutters, "Marlena probably wouldn't approve of you standing so close to me in a locked bathroom."

Ignoring her misplaced jealousy, I reach down and take one of her hands, lifting it so I can see what color she had her nails painted. They're a muted color, barely tinted with pigment at all. "Not what I thought you'd pick out."

Laurel wrinkles her nose up, looking at her nails disapprovingly. "It's not. I wanted the sparkly purple, but Lydia told me it was whorish."

Cracking a smile, I tell her, "Should've told Lydia you're a whore. Next time do that and send me a picture of what her face looks like."

Biting back a smile, she smacks me on the arm. "Stop it."

"Stop what?"

"Stop making it so hard to dislike you. You're the worst. Remind me that you're the worst."

I cock an eyebrow. "*I'm* the worst? Lydia is offended by nail polish. I think *she's* the worst."

Laurel nods and lifts her eyebrows, like she can't argue with me there.

That gets me back on track. "So what are you doing, going to lunch with her? I told you not to eat or drink anything she has access to."

"Yeah, but Rafe told me to go to lunch with her. I figured you guys would be on the same page if there was something to worry about."

Barely stifling a sigh, I murmur, "We're not on the same page about much lately."

Laurel's plump lips turn down in a pout. "I hate that. I don't want to come between you two."

"It's not your fault, it's his. It's mine. It's..." I shake my head. "Don't worry about it. I need to get out of here before she comes down the hall and catches me slipping out of here, though. I might have a hard time explaining why I was locked in a bathroom stall with you, and what with your on-the-spot lying skills, I don't think you could pick up my slack."

"You could have just texted me, you know," she states.

"Didn't want to leave tracks. Just in case things with Rafe..." I shake my head, since that will only worry her more. "It's just a precaution. I don't want to give anyone I work for any new reasons not to trust me right now."

Worry consumes her big, blue eyes as she looks up at me. "Is everything all right?"

"Everything is fine. Go to the bathroom while you're in here, and once you get to the restaurant, whatever you do, do not leave the table. Do not get up to use the bathroom. Do not turn around and look away from your plate or your drink for even a few seconds—and order something sealed in a bottle. I don't care if it's not cold."

"Sin, why are you so worried about this? Is there something I should know?"

"I don't know yet, okay? I'm trying to figure it out. But until I do, I need to know you're going to listen to me and be extra cautious. Guard your food and drink like a drunk girl at a frat party watching for some asshole with roofies."

"That is terrible."

"People are terrible," I inform her. "If anything goes wrong, if Lydia starts acting weird and you get a bad feeling, or she asks you to go somewhere off-plan or in her car, if she tries to get you alone for any reason, bail immediately. At that point, get yourself away from her, but calmly. Make an excuse. Go to the bathroom if it's somewhere like this where you have privacy, and call me or Rafe."

Eyes wide, she tells me, "You're scaring me. Should I not be out with her? I can just bail on lunch altogether."

"I'm sure you will be fine. Like I said, I'm just being cautious. It's my job to keep Rafe and his interests protected. You are obviously one of his interests." Her gaze darkens when

I add that, which is my intention. "I just want to run through your options now. People don't always think so clearly in a crisis. I didn't want you to be in a situation where you didn't know what to do, and Rafe with his fucking disposition, I'm sure he didn't prepare you."

"Great. Thanks for securing Rafe's property. I won't eat or drink anything I've left unattended. You can go take care of the next item on your to-do list now."

I hate the feelings I know lie beneath her snide tone. I hate hurting her on purpose, but I'm too tempted to stay. I'm too tempted by too many things I can't have, too many things I can't do, so instead of sticking around, that's exactly what I do.

26

LAUREL

I can't sleep again.

Extensive insomnia-induced Googling led me to the conclusion that it's probably from the pregnancy. I tell my body to let me sleep as I lie in Rafe's bed, staring at the high ceiling, but it's no use. The longer I lie here awake, the more frustrated I get. I can't seem to get comfortable, so I'm tossing and turning. Not wanting to wake Rafe up, I finally creep out of bed and head downstairs. Maybe a nice, hot cup of lemon tea will soothe my soul and help me sleep.

I brought my phone with me out of habit, but it's too late to call anyone. Carly is asleep, Mia is asleep, my roommate is... well, if not asleep, then she's doing other things I would feel icky interrupting.

Sin is probably asleep. Probably with that fucking waitress. If she makes him happy, I guess I can't kill her, but if she doesn't, I'm going to grind her up into dog meat. Dumb whore. I hate her face.

I roll out my shoulders, trying to shake off the blanket of sadness those thoughts bring with me. It's selfish not to want

Sin to be happy with anyone but me, but dammit, that's how I feel. I don't believe she could make him as happy as I could. He's just some man to her. He's more than that to me. Even though I have no basis on which to decide this, I don't think she deserves him. I think he would be much better off with me.

Sure, the pregnant baby mama of his boss—how could he score higher than that?

In an attempt to take my mind off Sin, I mess around on every app on my phone that stands a chance at holding my attention. They all fail within a few minutes, and I find myself opening up my text messages. His message from a few days ago is still there, telling me to go to the bathroom. There are too many things to get lost thinking about—his concern for my safety, regardless of his insistence that he only cares because it's his job to. The way he held my hand and looked at my nail polish disproves that bullshit claim. Why would he care what color nail polish I picked out if he didn't inherently care about everything related to me? He wouldn't. I reject that logic. Marlena is just a stand-in, a placeholder, what he's rebounding with since he can't have me.

Or, since he thinks he can't have me. The fact that I want him and he wants me should be all that's required for this to happen, but this family is so fucking weird. I want to take matters into my own hands and tell Rafe I want to leave his house and go stay with Sin, but every time I tell myself I'm going to have that conversation, I get scared. What if I'm wrong? What if Sin's right? It's not like Rafe has never tricked me before. No, he hasn't made any new threats about me getting over Sin, hasn't pushed for sex even though we're sleeping in the same bed. I don't know exactly where Rafe stands, and the thought of asking is nerve-racking because the stakes are so high. If I strut into this conversation, certain I can pull it off and everything will be fine, and then Sin ends up dead and Rafe casually reminds me he warned me, I will be destroyed. That guilt will follow me for the rest of my life, and just the thought of a Sin-less world makes me unfathomably sad.

Just thinking about it now makes me softer on him. What if something happened to Sin and the last thing I ever said to him was to basically get out of the bathroom and leave me alone? It's too hard to stay mad at him. I've never encountered that before—an absolute inability to stay mad at someone, no matter how much he pisses me off or hurts my feelings. Even when I try to hold it against him, it wears off. Being mad at him only lasts so long, and then it evaporates, and trying to prolong the grudge feels unnatural. That has never, ever happened to me before Sin, and I find it intriguing.

Sin seems like the sort of man who rubs people the wrong way more than the kind you can't stay mad at. He doesn't have Rafe's easy charisma. He's no one's definition of a charmer. I can't imagine anyone else who knows him struggling to stay mad at him—in theory, he makes it so damn easy—but I can't. I realized in that bathroom, when I felt myself giving just because we were in the same room, that I lied to Rafe. Finding out Sin slept with Marlena should be enough to turn me off him, but I don't think it would be. When he inevitably throws *that* in my face, it's going to hurt like hell, and I'm going to be pissed off and hurt, but somehow it won't last. I think the mean bastard could *marry* Marlena, and I would be mad at him for a week, sad at him for a couple more, and then like a rubber band snapping back, I would go right back to wanting him.

I don't know if there's something that *wrong* with me, or something that *right* with us. A new attachment shouldn't be so unbreakable. I've had relationships much more serious than

270 | SINNING IN VEGAS

this one, I've had my heart broken before by people I invested much more time in, but I have never encountered whatever this is. It's like we're connected by something deeper, something I could study for the rest of my life and never understand. Maybe from the first moment Sin walked through Rafe's front door, my soul recognized its other half, and now it won't let go for anything. Every little hurt, every major offense, somehow all of it feels insignificant by comparison. Like teardrops of pain falling into an ocean of love. There's so much of the good stuff, you can't feel the bad stuff for long.

I hate pining in theory and in practice, but the rules of ordinary relationships don't apply to my thoughts of Sin. I tap the message box on my phone and the straight line begins blinking, preparing to receive my message. Only it's 4 in the morning and I don't have anything to say. I just want to connect.

So, I open my recently used emojis, select the dolphin, and push send.

Since it's the middle of the night, I don't expect him to be awake. I don't even want him to be awake. If he's awake, that probably means he is with her, or he was with her, and I don't need to feel angry right now. I don't need more reasons to want to murder this cotton candy bitch.

I need to get Virginia's number. She may be one of Rafe's minions, but I think I could be friends with her.

My phone grabs my attention, vibrating on the surface of Rafe's island countertop.

"Why are you awake?" Sin typed back.

Lifting an eyebrow, I reply, "I'm pregnant. What's your excuse?"

"Some crazy person just sent me a dolphin in the middle of the night."

"Well, you better hurry up and get it in some water. Dolphins like water," I reply.

"Great, now I have a to-do list. I'm gonna have to find out what they eat too. I didn't ask for this."

Grinning, I type back, "Dolphins eat fish. Haven't you ever taken a science class? I need to take you to an aquarium or something and fill in the gaps of your aquatic education."

Less than a minute later, he sends back, "I just looked it up. Some dolphins eat squids and whatever the fuck a cephalopod is. Take that, know-it-all."

"Well, the one I sent you is named Wilbur and he eats fish. I asked him. Cod is his favorite."

"Great, so you sent me a high-maintenance fucking fish."

Grinning again, I send an emoji of a monkey hiding its eyes and tell him, "Dolphins aren't fish!"

"I know, they're mammals. I wanted to see if you'd correct me. See, I did take a science class." The trio of gray bubbles moves for a few seconds, then he sends back, "I could quiz you on shit you wouldn't know about too, you know."

"Oh, I know you could. Someone just asked me, where is Sin right now and is anyone with him? And I had no idea what the answer was."

The gray bubbles move for an eternity. Definitely long enough for me to imagine him either lecturing me for asking about his sex life when I do not want to know, or telling me horrible things about said sex life in an attempt to make me hate him. I'm braced for the worst when a large, dark rectangle that is clearly a picture shows up on my screen. Do I want to look? I don't, but I have to. If it's the waitress, I'm gonna throw up.

It's Sin's bed. More specifically, the empty spot beside him where I used to sleep. My entire being lightens and I breathe a sigh of relief.

His accompanying message reads simply, "Mystery solved."

"Thank you," I reply.

I click on the picture to make it bigger. The picture is dark given the time of night and Sin's blackout curtains. There's not even any moonlight spilling in. I can still see the empty space where I should be, though. I long to pour out my feelings, to tell him I wish I could be there with him, but I don't have the heart to be rejected again, and I know I will be.

"You're welcome," he sends back. "Now get some sleep."

"I will. You too. Sorry I woke you."

"Nah, I was awake. Goodnight Laurel."

"Why were you awake?" I ask.

"Goodnight Laurel," he sends again.

I sigh. "Fine. Goodnight, Sin."

I leave the messages open while I finish drinking my tea, just on the off chance he decides to tell me why he's awake, but he doesn't. I wonder how many of the other nights I've spent sleepless and alone I could have spent talking to him instead. I'm not sleeping because my hormones are all out of whack, but why isn't he sleeping? I try not to think about it as I head upstairs. I try not to entertain the lamest, most mundane fantasy ever—the simple ability to be lying in bed next to Sin if we are both unable to sleep. We could fill that time much more pleasurably. I could relax him and at least help *him* get some sleep if the baby doesn't want *me* to sleep. We could cuddle and talk—or I could talk, and he could listen to me until he drifted off. I would look up when I noticed him no longer responding. I would snuggle up against him, and even if I couldn't sleep, it wouldn't matter, because I love the feeling of his arms wrapped around me. It's worth staying awake for. Then the next morning when he has to get up and go to work, I could catch up on my sleep in the bedroom with the blackout curtains. Rafe's room lets in too much light to sleep peacefully during the day.

It's crazy that my most unattainable fantasy involving the dark, dominant murderer is just the ability to have a normal life with him.

I sigh at the sight of Rafe in bed, sleeping. I don't know why it annoys me that he can sleep. I don't want him to be awake, because I'm always worried he'll start pawing at me when we're both awake in the same bed. Still, he's ultimately the reason I can't sleep since he's the one who fucked up with the condom and put a baby in me.

Now that I think about it, I wonder *why* he isn't pushing for sex. I don't *want* him to, but the night at the hotel he was relieved when I told him as soon as I found out Sin slept with Marlena, I would be good to go, but it hasn't really come up again. I haven't seen him with Sin outside of the morning I made them both breakfast, and Rafe is overall calmer about everything than he probably should be.

Climbing into bed and pulling the covers up over me, I look over at him. Should he be so calm? Where is this sudden well of patience coming from? He never even addressed that bizarre morning when he made me *cook for Sin*.

Why haven't I questioned any of this before now? This is not the behavior I have come to expect from him. Things have been pleasant and friendly between us at the house over the past few days, but sexless and unromantic, and he hasn't once attempted to turn the tides in a different direction.

I turn over on my left side, yanking my pillow and blanket,

attempting to get comfortable. I'm facing Rafe, so I notice his eyes open as soon as they do.

"Sorry," I whisper. "Didn't mean to wake you."

He smiles faintly, closing his eyes. "Don't worry about it."

I should let him go back to sleep, but now this is weighing on my mind. I try to think of what I could ask him without coming off as guilty and suspicious. The night I think things shifted was the night Sin came over to help me with Skylar. The night Sin took his shirt off and mauled me on the couch. When Sin was there the next morning, Rafe made a point of being affectionate and kissing me in front of him, but I think it was only to piss Sin off, because he stopped once he was gone and hasn't really done it again since. I've been so relieved, I forgot to wonder why.

"Hey," I whisper.

Rafe's eyes open again. "Yes?"

"Can I ask you a question?"

He shifts, readjusting his head on his own pillow. "Sure. What's on your mind?"

"How come you haven't been..." I stop, trying to figure out how to finish this question. I'm thankful for the darkness in the room, because I can feel my face flushing as the words find their way out of my mouth. "How come you've stopped trying to kiss me?"

A faint burst of masculine laughter shoots out of him. "Listen to the way you framed that question, Laurel. How come I've stopped *trying* to kiss you," he repeats. "Do you *want* me to kiss you?"

My stomach sinks. Of course that question plunges me into an icy pool of awkwardness, because the answer is an apologetic no, but I don't want to say it.

He doesn't make me. He simply nods, his gaze dropping

briefly to my neck, then back to my face. "There you go. Why should I keep trying to kiss you if you don't want me to?"

"Are you kissing anyone else?" I ask.

"Are you?" he shoots back.

My face freezes. I shake my head no, but flashes of Sin on top of me on Rafe's couch flood my brain. He asked present tense, so I'm not technically lying. I am not *currently* kissing Sin. Hell, I didn't even get to kiss him that night, because apparently the man doesn't believe in kissing on the lips. It would definitely fall under the umbrella of what I mean to ask with this question, though. If Rafe is getting his needs met elsewhere, I'd like to know about it. Then we could end this whole charade of giving each other a shot, and each have the relationships we're actually interested in pursuing.

Since it's the most honest thing I can think to say in this moment, the most vulnerability I can offer him right now, I tell Rafe, "I don't ever want us to hate each other."

He watches me for a moment, but doesn't say anything. I've been overlooking him for days, distracted by my feelings for Sin and my relief that Rafe was staying more or less out of the way, but now it's all I can think about. Now it's twisting up my nerves that Rafe Morelli, a man dangerous enough to steal a criminal empire from at least two men who should have inherited it before him, is sitting back passively, not making any visible moves in regards to this situation. That doesn't seem like his style. Is he making moves I just can't see yet?

After a long pause, he finally asks, "What would make you hate me?"

"I'm too afraid to say," I admit, honestly.

He nods faintly, like that was more or less the answer he expected. "Your hatred might be more enjoyable than your indifference, kitten," he says, simply.

My heart stalls. That could mean so many different things, but given the line of my current thoughts, it only leads me to one thing. The thought that he *is* doing or planning something that will make me hate him. It may be my fear talking, leading me to jump to that conclusion, but what if it isn't?

"What does that mean?" I ask, flushing with even more embarrassment when I hear the unsteadiness of my own voice.

"Why don't you just go back to sleep?" he suggests. "You're safe. There's nothing for you to worry about."

"No. Tell me what that means. Am I going to hate you, Rafe?"

His lips curve up in a faint smile, but his eyes aren't smiling. His amber eyes are sharp, almost predatory, glistening with something unpleasant. Something angry. He reaches a hand out and runs it along the curve of my jaw. "It doesn't matter, does it?"

"You don't care if I hate you?" I ask sharply.

"I didn't say that. But it won't change anything for us, will it? Look where we are now, essentially locked into a marriage of convenience. Hell, maybe making you hate me will wake you up. If you show me your fire, I'll show you mine. That would be much better than this polite bullshit we've been doing."

I can feel the thundering of my pulse in my neck. "I don't know what that means. If you're going to threaten me, can you be more explicit?"

His hand drops and he rolls over, turning his back to me. "Go to sleep, kitten."

27

LAUREL

I lie there for a moment, processing his words and staring at the muscular expanse of his back. I can't let him go to sleep like that.

"Rafe."

I scoot closer, my nerves twisting up inside me. Reaching out a tentative hand, I wrap an around him until my fingers are skating down the muscles of his abdomen and I'm tucked snugly against his back. I'm not sure what the threat is, but I know there is one, and I've been too distracted to see it. I need to disarm him. I need to dissolve the need for the threat.

"Do you want to kiss me?" I whisper, my voice as tentative as my touch.

He's silent for so long, it makes my stomach hurt. Then he says simply, "If I didn't, you wouldn't be here."

Swallowing down the lump of nerves lodged in my throat, I pull him until he rolls over onto his back. He watches me, but doesn't move another inch. I shift my weight, moving half of my body on top of him. My fingers move through his hair and I bend down to brush my lips against his, but it feels so hollow.

Everything I feel right now is rooted in fear, not desire. Surely he can feel the difference. Surely it doesn't feel the same when a woman kisses you because she wants you, and when she kisses you out of sheer desperation.

If there's a difference to him, I can't tell. He deepens the kiss, his big hand moving behind my head to cradle it and guide me closer. My heart seems to flip over in my chest. Rafe shifts my body until I'm fully on top of him. I close my eyes, but all I can see is the empty spot in Sin's bed. As if my lungs are shrinking, it becomes harder to breathe. I can't do this. I can't do this. I can't do this.

What happens if I don't?

How am I supposed to abandon Sin in Vegas and go to Chicago? I don't know if he's safe. I don't know if Rafe is vengeful. I don't *know* the man whose bed I sleep in every night, and I've been so busy missing someone else, I haven't made much of an effort to change that. I don't owe it to him to do that, but it could be a grave misstep. I've heard stories about the twisted men in this family—what if he *is* one of them? What if I just don't know that yet? What if I won't find out until it's too late to change anything, and my whole life becomes a nightmare?

What was it he said about Mateo's dad and the woman he loved who didn't love him back? That he became her monster.

Is there some version of a future where Rafe Morelli is my monster? Not because he loves me, but because I won't stop longing for someone else and his pride won't have it?

I pull back, pushing my fingers through my own hair to get it out of my face. Looking down at Rafe, I consider what I could ask to find out who he is. What he's capable of.

"Tell me something," I begin, watching his face. "You loved Ben, right? He was your hero? Your family, your boss..."

"Yes, I get the picture. Is that the whole question?" he asks, knowing it isn't.

"He was murdered, wasn't he? Did you know beforehand that it was going to happen?"

He watches me for a moment like he's capturing data. Like I'm a study he's working on, or perhaps an opponent he needs to understand in order to defeat. "Yes, I knew," he admits. "Sin knew, too, in case you've decided to start imposing moral filters on all your love interests."

"You made it clear Sin can't be my love interest," I state, since it's the boldest I can be right now. Any bolder than that and I would be afraid I'd be admitting to something, endangering Sin with my hastily spoken words.

"Yes, I did," he replies, reaching up a hand to cradle my neck. At least, I think he's going to cradle my neck, but instead he closes his fingers around it and in one swift motion, he throws me down and pins me to the bed. I gasp, not so much because he still has his fingers closed around my throat, but because this feels like verification that his peacefulness is equivalent to a slumbering lion, resting quietly before attacking his prey and ripping out its throat. I hold his gaze warily, my heart dropping when he cocks his head almost mockingly and asks, "And did you listen?"

"I haven't done anything wrong," I state. I keep my hands at my sides, refusing to even reach up and pry his hands off my neck. He isn't applying any pressure, so there's no urgent need to. I think he only wants to remind me of the power he could have over me, if only he deigned to reach out and grab it. How easily he could break me, if only he chose to.

Sin's words flash to my mind, telling me breath play isn't safe during pregnancy. It makes sense, but I'm not sure Rafe knows that. Now seems like both the right time and the worst possible time to mention it.

"Neither have I," he says casually, like we're two assholes accomplished at lying to one another. "But I'm much better at skirting that line than you are, kitten. See, I would never come home with lipstick rings around my dick because I have more respect for you than that. We'll chalk it up to your inexperience, say you *do* respect me, you just suck at covering your tracks because you haven't done much sketchy shit in your time, but allow me to critique your performance. Next time he gives you a hickey, make sure you put on some fucking concealer before you climb into my bed."

Now fear leaps up within me, because I know exactly what he's talking about. I didn't catch it until I got home from lunch with Lydia, but when I got out of the shower, I realized Sin left a mark on my neck. I realize now, looking up at the controlled anger in Rafe's eyes, I have to lie. I don't like to lie, I'm not good at it, but I *need* to lie, and I need to be damn good at it.

"You think... you think I...?"

"Don't play innocent, Laurel. Don't insult me more than you already have. When you get caught, at least have the balls to own it, otherwise you're just a fucking pussy."

"Rafe, he didn't—we didn't... Nothing happened."

His eyebrows rise at the gall of my lie, and my stomach pitches. "No? He didn't come to my house the other night to see you when I wasn't here?"

Narrowing my eyes at him with righteous indignation I certainly don't feel, I say, "Yes, he came over. Because I was swimming in a pool of tears and baby vomit, and I needed someone to help me. I asked you first, and you said no thanks."

Rafe frowns. "What are you talking about?"

Now it's the right time, so I reach up and pull his hands away from my throat. "I was babysitting Skylar."

"Yes, I know that. Am I supposed to believe *she* gave you a hickey?"

Inspired, I crack a smile and laugh. "She might have. She's a baby. They suck on things when they're hungry. Their fingers, their toes. She tried to nurse on my poor sore boobs. She might have nibbled on my neck, I don't remember. I was too overwhelmed. I was desperate. Sin came over and helped me clean up the mess; he took care of Skylar so I could go upstairs and take a shower. That's it. Then he left."

Frowning as if this information makes no sense, he says, "He came over and did all that, and left without fucking you?"

I nod my head. "Sure did. I don't know if you know this about Sin, but he's a man with a lot of self-control. Even being the sexy siren covered in baby vomit that I was, he managed to resist me."

Instead of taking my joke bait, his eyes narrow again. "Has he *ever* fucked you?"

Swallowing down the lump of unpleasantness suddenly in my throat, I shake my head. "No."

He frowns, like I've just confounded him. "How is that possible?"

I shrug, at least sincerely in that. "I don't know. He's a mystery." Seeing an opportunity to make Sin look good, I drop my gaze. "I think it had something to do with you. He said he didn't feel badly about being with me after the way you treated me the night I told you I was pregnant, but I'm not sure it proved true. I think maybe his loyalty to you got in the way. He couldn't be with me fully knowing you wanted me."

Rafe looks at the wall as he weighs this information. "That

could be true. Sin is loyal as hell. Or that was my belief, until I thought he fucked you behind my back."

"He didn't," I offer quickly, shaking my head. "He really didn't. I swear. I'd say you could ask Skylar, but... well, she can't talk yet."

Smiling faintly, he looks down at me and sighs. "I'm gonna have to embrace my crazier roots and get better security on my house."

"Or you could just trust me," I suggest, guilt piercing my soul even as I say it.

"Trust is for lovesick schoolgirls and mindless idiots, kitten. I'm neither."

"That's a sad thing to believe. I hope you don't mean that." I don't want to be the reason he feels that way, either. I know I'm not the one who planted that seed, but I have probably watered it. I don't know how to stop. If we were actually together, I would have to be faithful because I'm certainly no cheater; I wouldn't hurt someone that way, but I don't foresee a future where I can turn my feelings for Sin off, either. That means I can't see a future where I ever fully commit to Rafe. I can keep fighting my feelings, but I'm not doing a great job so far, and why bother? Even when Sin stays away for a while and I can focus on Rafe, as soon as Sin comes back, whatever progress was made washes away the second Sin's eyes meet mine.

I can't keep doing this. I don't want to keep doing this. I don't want to be the one who breaks up this non-relationship because I don't know how he'll react, but I don't want to actually hurt him. I didn't even think I could. Honestly, I didn't think I mattered to him enough for that.

"Tell me something," I begin. "If you feel this way, why are we doing this? If you have felt for days like you couldn't trust me, if you have spent all this time thinking I slept with someone else behind your back, why keep up the pretense? Why not just confront me and end whatever it is we're doing here?"

"There is no end to this, Laurel. This isn't a relationship. It's bigger than that. You're not some sub I got sick of, you're the woman I impregnated. I'm not just going to kick you out because we aren't making each other happy."

I blink at him. "If we're not making each other happy, then... maybe it's because we aren't *right* for each other. It doesn't mean there's anything wrong with either one of us, there's no villain here, we are just two people who had a really great hook-up, and maybe that's where it was supposed to end. Obviously I care about you and you care about me, and nothing will change that. We're bonded, but... that doesn't necessarily mean we have to be together. I don't want to be your Lydia. I don't want to be your domestic dumping ground, the thing you have to deal with at the end of the day because of some archaic bullshit. I don't *want* to make you unhappy, but I'm not going to spend the rest of my own life unhappy to stay in a lukewarm relationship, either. I'm no martyr. I'm some girl you knocked up by accident. I know we like each other, I know we're attracted to each other, but whatever the reason, this thing is not taking off. Maybe it's time we call it. We don't owe each other a relationship, Rafe. We're not doing anything wrong by giving up and moving on."

"Morelli men don't divorce, kitten. Especially bosses."

"Okay, but we aren't married. We aren't even boyfriend and girlfriend. We are that level of relationship where when you're forced to make an introduction to someone, you're like, 'this is Laurel, my—' And then you fake cough to keep from having to figure out what the hell to call me."

"That's not true; I introduced you in Chicago as my girl-friend. Or Mia did. Same difference."

"Not really, and that was without my agreement. Since then, we have taken no steps in the direction of boyfriend-girl-friend classification, let alone marriage."

"I didn't mean it like that, I meant..." Apparently no longer needing to pin me down, he rolls off me and back into his spot. "You know why the men in my family don't divorce?"

"Nope, but I bet it's a crazy reason. Your family is fucking nuts."

Rafe smiles. "It's not, actually, it's a sensible one. The idea is, if a man can't even run his own household, how the hell is he supposed to run this whole family? You can't have confidence a man is a good leader if he can't even keep his wife in hand."

Groaning, I cover my face with my hands. "How? How did I get mixed up in a family of such sexist caveman psychos?"

Ignoring me, he goes on. "Now, I'm not saying I would kill you before I'd let you leave, but there are multiple men in my family who have found that a more suitable alternative than being made to look like an asshole to the rest of the family. I'm new to this position. It's weird timing to have to deal with a budding relationship to begin with, but for me to finally knock someone up and not be able to hang onto her? To actively try, and to lose her to my enforcer? I can't have that, Laurel. I'm sorry if it makes me sound like a prick, but there's a way of doing things, and appearances do matter. At least for right now, I need you to stick it out. I'm not saying forever, but I can't let you out of this right now. You have no idea how hard it has been to hold onto this power, how many of my own men I've had to eliminate or start looking at twice, wondering if I'm right to trust them. And now, yeah,

Sin is one of them. He was my hammer when I took over. He was someone I knew had my back, and then you happened, and now I don't know anything anymore. He's willing to turn on me over some girl he didn't even fuck. What the hell is that?"

"He has *not* turned on you, Rafe. He hasn't. He didn't fuck me and he has not turned on you. Don't start looking at your friends and seeing enemies."

"This boss job is no joke. It changes everything. Nobody is the same now as they were before, not even me."

He clearly needs someone, and even though I know I am not the one for him, I'm the only one here right now. So, I snuggle up beside him and wrap my arm around him. "I'm sorry it's harder than you thought it would be. Don't let me come between you and Sin, though. Every time he talks to me, he makes sure to remind me he only cares because I'm one of your 'interests.' Sin has *not* turned on you. He would never do that. He is loyal to you, so don't fuck it up over me."

Wrapping his arm around me, he watches me. "Would you tell me if that changed?"

"What?" I ask, hesitantly.

"If he turns on me, you'll likely find out before I do."

"Rafe, he's not going to turn on you."

"Humor me," he says, apparently relentless in this. "If it comes down to picking sides, I need to know you'll be on mine."

This conversation is making my stomach hurt. "It won't come down to that. You two are on the same side."

With a faint smile, he nods. "It's his side, then. All right."

"No—I didn't say that."

"Sure you did," he answers. "It's fine. Go to sleep."

My stomach twists with anxiety as I imagine the possible

ramifications of him holding such a belief. "Rafe, come on... I don't like this."

Instead of pushing me away like Sin would, Rafe's arm tightens around me. "You're right. It won't come down to that. I appreciate your honesty."

"I did *not* say I would take Sin's side over yours."

Instead of wasting his breath arguing with me, Rafe leans over, gives me a kiss, and closes his eyes. "It doesn't matter. Our relationship isn't where it needs to be yet. I knew that, it was just a nice thought. Don't lose sleep over it. Goodnight, kitten."

28

SIN

I have irons in the fire all over town today. Making Rafe's
love life my pet project was a bad idea for my sleep
schedule. There are too many fucking girls to keep track
of. I've blown Marlena off enough times that she has stopped
texting me, so that's one less pain in the ass I have to deal with.
Much easier to just check in on her with the bugs. Eventually
she was going to pounce on me, and it would have been hard to
explain why I kept coming over if I didn't want to fuck her. I
can't keep an eye on her outside of the apartment, but that she
hasn't done anything sketchy while she's home alone—not one
phone call—makes me think maybe she isn't that kind of problem. I still think Rafe was attracted to her, but I can't put them
together, so at least he seems to be keeping his distance.

Since Rafe and I are taking a little break from one another
right now, I'm defaulting back to my old routine and checking
in with Gio rather than Rafe. I don't like what that could
mean. I'm going to have to make time to meet him out one of
these nights. I've been so busy keeping an eye on Cassandra

and Marlena, I haven't had a few hours to waste at the club with him in the evenings. He might start taking that person-ally, and I don't want that headache.

When I roll up to Gio's, Lydia is the one who answers the door. The baby is on her shoulder, dressed in a bright teal sweatshirt and pants.

Lydia lets me inside, yammering on about how I need to walk carefully because the maid just waxed the floors, and how she told the maid never to wax the floors in the morning—on and on about these fucking floors.

I'm not paying attention to her, so I am caught completely off guard when the baby is thrust into my hands.

"You're a lifesaver, Sin. Thank you. How you're single, I don't know."

"Wait, what?" What did I just agree to? The baby smiles like she remembers me and since I have her on my chest, in reach of my face, her tiny hand hooks my lower lip and she grins at me. "Oh, you caught me, did you? Better women than you have tried, shortcake, sorry to break the news." Detaching her hand from my mouth, I follow Lydia into the other room. "Why am I holding your baby?"

"I told you, it's just for a minute. I've been asking Gio to come out of that office and watch her, but you know how he is."

That's still not a reason, but she's already waving me off, rolling her eyes, and heading upstairs.

Skylar's little head bobs and she touches my face again, staring at me like she's inspecting my cheek. At least she's not covered in spit-up this time, I guess. "Well, shit," I tell her. "Now what? Should we go see your daddy?"

She can't talk yet, so she just makes a grunt-like noise and squeezes my nose.

I have the damndest urge to take a picture to send to Laurel, but that would be mean. Still, she'd get a kick out of this baby man-handling me.

My thoughts drift to what it'd be like to have lazy days with Laurel and her baby. All babies like me, so I know hers would. Plus I'd be around from the start, so he or she would see me like its father, even with Rafe around.

I don't know if Rafe has it in him to be a good dad. Or a good husband. When I initially decided to hand deliver Laurel to him, I didn't know her, didn't care about her happiness. She was a pregnant parcel that needed to be delivered to my thick-headed boss, and I was just going to keep an eye on it until he was ready for her. Whatever their relationship was like beyond that shouldn't have mattered to me.

But then Laurel was Laurel, and now here we are. Me, with two hours of sleep on baby duty, having fucking daydreams about this baby being ours. Hers. I don't know. Skylar is so fucking cute, she makes me hurt. I don't know how I, of all people, have ended up babysitting this kid twice now. I *like* being the guy no one bothers.

Skylar smacks me in the face.

I level an unimpressed look at her and she gives me a big gummy grin. "You've got spunk, shortcake. You should've picked better parents. These two are gonna ruin you."

Her response is just drool. A river of drool down her tiny little chin. At least she's happy. I wish she'd been in a mood like this when Laurel babysat her. The last thing she needs right now is anything that makes her *doubt* her parenting abilities.

"Yeah, I guess you can't pick your parents, huh?"

Since I'm not sure what I'm supposed to do with her or how long until Lydia comes back for her, I head to Gio's study.

I rap my knuckles on the door once and he calls for me to come in.

Gio is in his chair, but he rears back when he sees I have his child on my chest.

"Moonlighting as a nanny now?" he asks.

"Seems that way," I reply, shifting Skylar on my chest so I can reach into my jacket and draw out the envelopes I have for him. "I have to stop by Giordano's later and have a little chat with him, but everything else is there."

Gio reaches over to take the envelopes. "He giving you trouble again?"

"Not on purpose, but yeah. The business isn't doing much lately. Good pizza. Too bad. Anyway, I'll handle it, make sure he's not late again next month."

"I appreciate that," he says, placing the envelopes down on the desk and leaning back in his chair. "You always do good work for us, Sin. Always have. I don't want you to think no one notices. I notice everything."

Unnoticed is not the thing I've been feeling lately. Unappreciated, sure, but it's not like I don't know why.

Anyway, I don't thank him for appreciating me. It's my job and I do it, simple as that.

I nod, looking at Skylar. She was ready to play a minute ago, but now she's snuggled up on my chest, content as a kitten. "If that's all, I should probably go find Lydia and give her back your kid."

"No, no, stay," he says, gesturing with his hand for me to take a seat. "There's something else I want to talk to you about. Not unrelated, but... something else, still. How are you feeling about things lately? With the business? Are you happy?"

Shuttering myself off as suspicion creeps in, I give him a

blank look, but I take a seat anyway. "Happy as a fucking clam. Why? Someone say otherwise?"

"No, no, of course not." This is what Gio does when he's uncomfortable—repeating certain shit twice. It's always, "Yeah, yeah, I'll be there," or "No, no, sit down."

"Let's talk like adults," I tell him, not in the mood to waste time. "What's on your mind, Gio?"

Clasping his hands together, he ponders for a moment. "I want to ask you some things, but I'm worried you might not trust them, all right? And I want you to trust me, but I know you've been more Rafe's guy in the past, and I understand that. The problem is, I get the feeling that maybe Rafe isn't utilizing all your potential. I think you could do more for us than you do now, and I think maybe your personal issues with Laurel... I worry Rafe is letting his own personal issues get in the way of doing right by you when it comes to business matters, and that's not right. It crossed my mind you might not be too happy about that."

I don't say whether or not I'm happy. I don't trust shit like this—one of my bosses asking me if I'm unhappy with another of my bosses. Particularly when Rafe might be looking for a reason to get rid of me, so asking Gio to feel me out would be a good way to find a reason he could get by the whole family for taking me out. No, of course he didn't kill me for fucking around with Laurel—he killed me because I was turning on him, just ask Gio. Because that makes all the fucking sense in the world. I risk my position in this family, risk my whole life to get his ass on the throne, so why wouldn't I turn on him? Makes perfect fucking sense.

Then there's the flipside of the coin, that Gio is older than Rafe and the rightful boss after Vince, only Rafe decided to skip the line. We let Gio live because he rolled right over—didn't even roll over, exactly, just made like he was never interested in the boss position to start with, and he'd be happy for Rafe to have it in his place. Some of the best snakes pretend to be on your side though, that's one of the first things you learn in any kind of business. The true betrayals come from the people closest to you.

Since I'm not saying shit, Gio nods and takes a few seconds to modify his approach. Clearing his throat like he's about to say something delicate, he tells me, "Sin, in the interest of treating you with all the respect I think you're owed, I want to put my cards down on the table. I want to be straight with you. I know about you and Laurel. I know you two had some kind of..." He waves a hand, not giving a fuck about my romantic dealings. "I know you still want her, that's the point I'm trying to make. I don't want you to get angry, and I don't want you to think this was intentional because it wasn't—I had no way of even guessing you would be at Rafe's house that night—but..." He pauses to clear his throat again. "I do have footage of you and Laurel together on Rafe's couch the night she watched Skylar."

My heart stops beating, then roars back to life, so loud I hear it pounding in my ears. I still have one hand on Skylar to keep her supported on my chest, but my free hand clenches into a fist. My knuckles are already fucking sore, and now I want to jam them into this motherfucker's face. Holding his baby right now is about to get inconvenient.

"Footage?" I ask, my voice carefully controlled. It's so fucking hard not to fly off the handle. Not only is this asshole spying on me—or Laurel?—but what is this now? A fucking threat? He thinks he can blackmail me with some fucking footage of...

Well, depending on what he has footage of, he *can*. There's no way in hell Rafe can ever see me and Laurel on that couch together. Fuck, why did I let that happen? I always get carried away with her and lose my damn head.

"Now, now, Sin, let's not get ahead of ourselves," Gio says, eyebrows rising as he holds a hand to try to placate me. "This is not me threatening you. I am not trying to disrespect you. I told you about this in the interest of being forthright, so you understand where I'm coming from. Why I know the things I know. It was purely by accident. Lydia has a nanny cam in the teddy bear. She likes to make sure the babysitters aren't up to anything—it's dumb, but it's just one of those things, you know? Your wife wants to spend hundreds of fucking dollars on a teddy bear with a camera in its eyeball, you just say 'yes dear' and move on. Anyway, in this case, it worked out a lot better than expected because... well, obviously, you were there. The point is, you don't have to deny it, because that would be pointless. I was not intentionally spying on you, but I did end up with this information falling into my lap."

"And of course you had to watch it. Despite all this trust you supposedly have in me, all this respect, when you saw what you saw, instead of turning the damn thing off, you kept watching."

He starts to smirk and I can almost see Laurel in her flimsy robe, her bra and panties. New rage surges through me at this philandering motherfucker even thinking about Laurel that way. He must see it on my face, because he pulls himself out of it, clearing his stray thoughts off his face and holds up his hand again. "I know, and I'm sorry about that. My curiosity got the better of me. I should have respected your privacy, and I apologize. The point is, I know you want her, I know she wants you, and I know there's only one thing standing in the way of you having her."

Aw, fuck.

I was hoping this wasn't where this was going.

Then again, if it went the other way, that would also be bad. Basically, I've been fucked from the moment I sat down in this goddamned seat.

"I want you to have her," Gio tells me. "I think you *deserve* to have her. And she *definitely* wants you—I don't have to tell you that."

"Don't," I say, not liking the way his tone is relapsing back into making it sleazy. There's nothing sleazy about what's between me and Laurel, and a guy like him could never understand it.

He holds up a hand and nods one more apology. "I'll be blunt, Sin. I know you're loyal. But I know something Rafe has let himself forget. Hungry dogs can't afford to be loyal. I think you're hungry, Sin. I think under Rafe's leadership, you're left wanting, and I don't see that changing now that what you want is Laurel. Here's what you deserve." He ticks off fingers. "You deserve to be treated with respect by the man you're working for. You deserve a seat at the table, not a spot guarding the door outside while everybody else gets rich. And you deserve to have the girl, if that's what you want. I want to give you more respect, a better position, a seat at the table, more money... and I want to give you Laurel. I want to make you whole again, Sin. I want you to have your girl, your family, your job—I want to do right by you in all areas. I think Rafe's a fool for not giving you what you need, after everything you've done for him. He doesn't even fucking like that girl. You know he's fucking around with that waitress he hired."

Rage explodes in my chest, pours through my veins like

molten lava from an erupting volcano. Breath rushes in and out
of my body, so fucking overcome with adrenaline and heat, I
feel like I might actually combust. Suddenly this baby on my
chest is like a space heater; my suit may as well be a garbage
bag, keeping in all the heat. I'm burning with rage.

Consequences be damned, I want to find that motherfucker and plant my fist in his face. That's not even good
enough. I want to beat the shit out of him in his driveway, the
same one where he first made Laurel cry, and then I want to
bash his fucking head in with the nearest blunt object.

That stupid fucking asshole has *Laurel* at home, keeps
Laurel from *me*, and he's out fucking some worthless whore
who doesn't hold a candle to her?

I am so fucking livid, I can't see straight. Thoughts of all
the nights I could've had with her that she's spent with him
instead run through my head, along with a sleazy imagining of
Rafe showing up on Marlena's fucking doorstep, sneaking
around behind Laurel's back. Maybe he wasn't even at the
club that night. Maybe he left her home alone with a baby to
go spend time with that skank. Maybe that's the future he
plans to give her. He keeps everything I want for himself, and
the fucker doesn't even appreciate what he has.

My jaw is clenched so tightly my fucking teeth hurt. Gio is
quiet, letting me simmer in my rage. It takes a while before it
occurs to me—looking up at the Morelli sitting on the other
side of his desk right now—that he strongly suspected this
would be my reaction.

If I wanted to piss off someone like me, it wouldn't take a
whole hell of a lot of brain power to guess lying about something like this would get the desired response. Gio knows I
have feelings for Laurel, he knows I'm currently coveting what
Rafe has, but he does not know I've been keeping an eye on

296 | SINNING IN VEGAS

Marlena myself. If Rafe *is* fucking her, why not do it at the apartment he is paying for her to stay in? I've reviewed the goings-on at her apartment every single night, and I haven't heard her even talking to Rafe on the phone, let alone fucking him—and I planted a bug in her bedroom specifically for that reason.

I don't like being lied to. I don't like being manipulated. If Gio is manipulating me, he's making a big-ass mistake.

Then again, Gio comes with Laurel. If I'm being honest, even without the family to back it up, I've had fantasies about turning on Rafe so I could have Laurel. If this is going down with or without me, if all I have to give up is Rafe to get Laurel... well, shit, that's tempting.

I don't know if I want to work for Gio, but that he's calling me in like this means he is planning a coup either way, and he's planning to clean house when he does it—but he doesn't want me swept up with the rest of them. He wants me on his side. He wants me to be *his* guy instead of Rafe's.

"How solid is this?" I ask him.

"Rock solid," he tells me, with confidence.

"Who have we got?"

Smiling faintly, he says, "You know I can't tell you that unless you've made a decision, Sin." Holding up that goddamn hand again, he adds, "There is something more. I wasn't planning to make a move just yet, but when I discovered Rafe's plans, I pushed up my own. You're an integral part of my operations—or, I want you to be—and much as I hate to be the one to tell you this, Rafe's been talking to Theo about taking your spot. Naturally he has kept this quiet, it's strictly need to know, but..."

I nod my understanding. I know exactly what that means. If Rafe's talking to my replacement—the only guy half as good as me—that means my time's up. Rafe's planning to take me out. If Gio is to be believed, anyway.

I wait to feel surprised, but I don't. I guess in the back of my head I knew this was coming. It had to. The first time I fisted my hand in Laurel's hair and guided her mouth toward my cock, I opened the door to this eventuality.

"Who all knows?" I ask, calmly.

"Rafe, me, and Theo. That's it. For obvious reasons, he didn't want this getting around."

Oh, the reasons are obvious, all right. It's not good business to kill the man who helped you get to the top. Conveniently, the only people who can verify this story are the one telling it, the one who might want to kill me, and the one who would replace me.

Well, now I have one more fucking thing on my to-do list today.

"Who is he sending? Freelancer?"

"Theo. It's his tryout."

"Huh." That's a little more convincing. Theo does good work. If Gio is sitting here telling me this, he knows I have to kill him now before he kills me. Why feed me one of our better guys when he could have easily convinced me he was hiring a freelancer? It's not the way things are always done, but Mateo sent a freelancer to kill Ben, and now that he and Rafe are chummy, I would have believed he decided to go the same route. It's cleaner, and this is personal, not business. You send your own guys when it's business, but when it's personal and you have as much money as these fuckers have, you can afford to hire your own cleaning service.

Since I've heard all I need to hear, I brace my other hand on Skylar's back and stand. She coos at me like a little fucking angel, and I wish I didn't have to give her back.

Of course, if I take Gio up on this offer, I'll have Laurel and a baby I won't have to give back. I won't even have to share. Rafe will be dead, Laurel will be mine, and there will be zero threats to my happiness. After we have that baby, I'll put another one in her. I'll have her in my bed every single night. I can have it all.

All I have to do is turn on Rafe, and since he turned on me first... well, it's worth considering.

Eyeing me as he takes the baby, Gio asks, "So, what do you say?"

"I need a day or so to think on it. Run through it. I need to know who's on board and who I'll have to deal with. I'm gonna have to replace Theo. There's a lot of work to do. I've done it once, but it wasn't easy. We do it this time, we need to do it better. We need to clean house so shit like this doesn't happen again."

"I think you'll be surprised how many men are on our side," he tells me, with confidence. "It won't be as big a job as you're imagining."

I straighten, glancing down at the baby on his chest. He doesn't hold her right. She's still little, but he should know how to hold her by now.

"Let me tell you, Gio, I appreciate everything you've said to me today, but you need to know, I don't go for the Morelli bag of tricks. I don't like being lied to and manipulated. Me and Rafe have never had a problem before Laurel because he didn't pull shit like that with me, and I would hate for you and me to start out on that foot. If anything you've said to me today wasn't exactly the truth, just a little bending of the facts to piss me off at Rafe, now is the time to tell me. Once I walk out that door, it's too late."

Gio shakes his head firmly. "No lies, Sinclair. I know how

you like to be treated. When you're working for me, you'll know you're working for someone who respects what you bring to the table, and you'll damn sure be treated as such. There are no hungry dogs on my crew, and you? You'll be leading the pack."

29

SIN

I'm pretty fucking tired by the time I load the last trash bag full of Theo into my trunk. I don't like to leave bodies back there longer than necessary, but damn, I'm considering parking the car in the garage tonight and dealing with this shit tomorrow. Not sure it's worth the smell though. I'm probably gonna have to deal with it and just get by tomorrow on two hours of sleep again.

He put up a hell of a fucking fight, that Theo. Made me feel even worse about having to kill him. Thankfully, he was young and single, so at least he won't have a family mourning him. Probably a mom out there somewhere, but she should have raised him to have better judgment.

Nah, I'm not being fair. This isn't Theo's fault, it's Rafe's. I'm misplacing blame, getting pissed off about shit that isn't worth getting pissed off over. The problem is, Theo verified what Gio said, and that means a man I considered a friend a couple weeks ago really was planning to have me killed. If he knew about the night I mauled Laurel on his couch, I'd probably understand, but since he doesn't, I'm pretty fucking salty about it.

It also probably means Rafe is fucking Marlena, and I don't know how I missed that. I'm tempted to follow him tonight and check, but I have bigger fish to fry.

Tonight, I follow Gio. He's more watchful about that shit, more paranoid, but if I'm going to jump ship and turn my back on Rafe, I need to make sure the ship I'm transferring over to is solid, especially if I'm bringing Laurel and a baby with me. Laurel might be pissed at me for killing Rafe, too, and that's going to be annoying to deal with. I can already hear her bitching at me that I didn't have to do it, that I could have just moved to Chicago with her. She's so fucking sure Mateo's wife is the Underground Railroad that would bring us to fucking sanctuary, like Mateo and Rafe aren't cousins, like they aren't friends, like he'd ever take my side against his own family. I don't know much about Mateo's wife, but I do know Mateo, and I have a hard time believing any woman has that ruthless asshole under her thumb. Especially some tiny blonde who looks like she popped out of a fucking Disney movie.

Sorry, Laurel, Chicago isn't a solid plan.

Gio might be, though.

I'm not going to have long to make a decision. Now that Gio has shown me his hand, there's only a brief window before I can get on board with any kind of credibility.

I'm in fucking luck though, because Gio heads to Rafe's restaurant for a meeting with a few men. I text Virginia to let her know I need her to pay extra attention to Gio's table tonight, tell me what they talk about. While I wait for her to text back, I set up my little mobile surveillance center. An iPad with Marlena's apartment pulled up on the screen, a second one with the map open, my tracker on Cassandra's car moving across the screen as she heads to wherever she's heading tonight.

Virginia texts back a brief, "Got it."

I alternate between screens until Cassandra makes her first stop. I zoom in to get the location, then open up the browser app on my phone to type in the address and see where she's at. Just a gas station. She's only there long enough to fill up, so that's nothing to worry about.

I shoot Virginia another text. "Hey, why don't you bring me out a snack?"

A few minutes pass before she sends back, "Seriously? Do you know how busy it is in here?"

"The better question is, do I care?"

"Give me a few minutes," she tells me.

A short time later, Virginia shows up outside my window with a to-go container and a sealed bottle of water. After handing them over, she leans in and frowns at the screen. "Who are you watching?"

"Nobody important."

Frowning, she asks, "Carla?"

I frown right back. "What? No. Who cares about Carla?"

Virginia shrugs. "Well, it's her address in the bottom corner there; forgive me for drawing a logical conclusion."

What the fuck is she talking about? I point to Cassandra's home address in the corner. "This address, right here? This is not Carla's address."

"Yes, it is. I had to give Gio a ride home one night when he was too drunk to drive—well, not *his* home, he wanted to go bang his girlfriend first. I didn't stick around for all that, but that's where I dropped him off."

No. No, no, no. Please no. That crafty fucking whore could not have done this to him again. Leaning my head back against the headrest, I ask a pointless question. "You sure?"

Virginia nods once. "You know I don't forget addresses."

She doesn't forget anything, that's why I like to have her keep an ear to the ground for me, see if there are any signs of trouble. She's not an effective all-around informant though. She's completely loyal to Rafe; if she caught wind of him turning on me, she'd stop talking to me, but since she doesn't know about that yet...

I need her to be wrong. She has never been wrong before, but I need this to be the first time. "You're *positive* this is the address you took him to?"

"You can keep asking if the world is round, Sin; the answer won't change."

"God-fucking-dammit."

Cringing, she says, "Why is this such bad news?"

Because if Gio is fucking Cassandra Carmichael, that changes everything. There's not a snowball's chance in Hell I'm going to find myself working for Cassandra Carmichael, and if she's the one behind this, if she's grooming for Gio to take over, it's not so she can be his side dish. Does Gio not realize how ambitious she is, or does he not care? What about Lydia? What about Skylar?

All that aside, Rafe would be fucking crushed. Seeing as he tried to have my ass killed, I probably shouldn't care, but loyalty doesn't just drain out of you in a couple hours. I'm mad as hell on his behalf. If someone is going to take him down, Cassandra Carmichael shouldn't have a hand in it. That's not right.

Maybe she's not a dealbreaker. Maybe Gio hasn't been caught up in her web the way Rafe was. Maybe he only likes fucking her and the takeover has nothing to do with her.

Maybe I can push her out of the picture. If I'm going to work for Gio, I have to have to make sure she doesn't come bundled together in that deal, because fuck no. I'd rather be hungry than work for a snake like her, and if she's involved, no matter how much Gio thinks he's the one in charge, I'll know differently.

"Sin?"

I look over at Virginia and she's frowning at me again. "I don't know yet. I'm gonna have to look into it."

"This is not a commensurate response. If that's not Carla's house, who is Gio sleeping with that it would bother you?"

"Don't do that. Don't try to puzzle it out. You know too much already. Go give people breadsticks and keep an ear out for anything Gio says about anything."

"It's not Laurel," she says, ignoring me. "She's staying with Rafe. I did notice Gio giving Marlena looks. Is it Marlena's address? I'm going to check her employee file," she says, more to herself than me as she pushes off the car.

"Wait, back up. When was he giving Marlena looks?"

"The other night they were eye-fucking on the sly. Well, on the sly for normal people, obviously *I* noticed. I hope you didn't bang her, and if you did, I hope you wrapped it up. She's not very discriminating. I'm gonna fish and see if I can get an admission out of her."

Nodding my head, I tell her, "If you get anything, let me know."

"Got it, boss." With a mock salute, she turns and heads back inside the restaurant.

It's basically morning by the time I crawl into bed. Between spying on everyone, disposing of Theo, and running through a fuck ton of nightmare scenarios, I'm fucking beat. It'd be nice if that meant I'd fall right to sleep, but that's never the case anymore. Too much on my mind. Now I have even more weight on my shoulders than I did when I got out of bed this morning, and I thought I had a lot then.

I grab my phone off the night stand, opening my messages and looking at the ones Laurel sent me last. Her fucking dolphin emoji. I wonder if she's awake? I wouldn't text her first, not in the middle of the night like this anyway. Too great a chance Rafe would see it.

I close the messages and tap my saved pictures, pulling up the picture of Laurel by the water. The one Rafe sent me from their date—fucking asshole. I always warn his ass, and he never fucking listens to me. Don't let Laurel get away if you want her, don't test my fucking patience, don't forget who brought your ass up to the level you're on now, don't fuck the waitress.

Trying to put Rafe and Laurel out of my mind, I plug the charger into my phone and roll over, hitting my pillow and closing my eyes, hoping I fall asleep before the sun comes up.

The next day is more of the same shit, but now that Gio has made me an offer, I'm on borrowed time, and I don't know how much of it I have left.

I don't know how I'm going to get all this shit done, and on top of all that, Virginia texts me from the restaurant. "I need to talk to you."

"Is it important? Kinda busy," I tell her.

"Yep. Meet me for dinner? I'm off in a half hour."

Scowling at the phone, I send back, "I have to wine and dine you for information now?"

306 | SINNING IN VEGAS

"I'll buy, cheapskate. Let's share a pizza though. I'm poor."

The last thing I have time for is going out to eat, but I tell her to meet me at Giordano's. I was supposed to talk to him last night anyway and I didn't, so at least this way I can knock something off my to-do list.

When I get to Giordano's and Virginia flashes me a smile and waves me over, I feel overwhelmingly uncomfortable—and not for any sane reason, like I have to be an asshole to a nice old man who makes good fucking pizza, or I don't know what kind of information she has for me, but because I have the feeling Laurel would be pissed off if she knew I met another woman for something like dinner.

"What's funny?" Virginia asks as I drop into the seat across from her.

"I'm fucked."

Cocking a skeptical eyebrow, she asks, "That's funny?"

"It'll be all right." I meet her gaze. "What have you got for me?"

"All right, so, bear with me because this is going to get weird. Last night you piqued my curiosity with my mission."

"Occasionally a good thing," I remark, though since I'm straddling the line of loyalty right now, I wonder if this is one of them.

Virginia is like a dog with a bone when I give her anything to do, so I try to only use her sporadically. She doesn't work for us in any official capacity outside of being Rafe's waitress. Literally Rafe's waitress—he only goes to the restaurant on days she's working—says he likes the way she takes care of him. Rafe is the least habitual person I have ever met in my life, so that he is so set in his routine with Virginia is an oddity, but I get it. I don't like people, and I like Virginia. Of course, I like her because she's not just free labor; she's a sure fucking thing.

I don't think he's ever fucked her, so I don't think he likes her for the same reason.

When I wanted to collapse Ben's empire and weed out the unshakably loyal, I couldn't use my men in every situation. I used Virginia to fill in the blanks. I think she's some kind of genius—not the stuffy sort Laurel probably reads books by, but anything I tell her to do, if she doesn't know how, she can figure out and master like she wrote the manual herself.

Rafe would be pissed if he knew how many times I've used his waitress to do illegal shit—and her law school probably wouldn't be too psyched, either—but sometimes you've gotta do what you gotta do. Virginia would do anything for Rafe—not because she has some lame crush like all these other girls, but because she actually cares about the guy. I don't know why, she never gave me the story and I didn't ask, but her actions over the years—while simultaneously serving an endless string of disposable women who go home with him afterward—have made that pretty clear. I don't think she's waiting around on him to notice her, I think she's just his loyal subject, and she doesn't ask for anything in return.

Resourceful, smart, and loyal—yes, I'll take her help. Well, usually. Right now I'm switching sides, and I might actually have to worry about Virginia. She doesn't know how to fire a gun right now, but give her a weekend and the knowledge that I plan to hurt Rafe, not only will she be able to fire one, she'll be able to *build* one from paperclips or some crazy shit.

So, if she already started looking into this on her own, it's possible she brought me here to ferret out whether or not I'm planning to turn on Rafe, and if I am, she'll kill me with some kind of lethal weapon she forged from bobby pins on her lunch break. Then later she'll feign horror and sympathy for Laurel while she's feeding her and Rafe dinner tonight.

Why do all the women in Rafe's life have to be some kind of crazy?

"Okay, so, I decided to investigate Marlena today, poke at her while I trained her hopeless ass." Switching to a ridiculous old timey detective accent, she plucks an imaginary cigar off the table and holds it between her fingers. "I put the screws to her, see."

"No." I shake my head. "Don't do what you're doing. Not in my presence."

"God, you're no fun. I don't know why Laurel likes you."

I give her a dead look, but she doesn't linger. At least it's unlikely she's onto me if she's being a giant nerd.

Rolling her eyes at me, she says, "Anyway, I'll skip the fun stuff since you hate fun. Gio is fucking Marlena. And Cassandra. And I think Carla, though that doesn't seem to be relevant. He has curated a harem of troublemakers, and he's using them to his advantage. I don't know exactly how or why, didn't have enough time to get my Veronica Mars all the way on, but I will if you want me to. I have tonight off, so I could use a project."

I stare, mildly horrified, at the energetic brunette across from me. Deciding to fill the silence with activity, she flips open the pizza box and plates pizza for me, slides it over, then plates some for herself. She does all this casually, like she didn't just deliver me a fuck ton of bad news. Closing the lid so the pizza stays hot, she asks, "Any questions, or still processing?"

I have a lot of questions, but since she's never given me bad information before, the one I go with is, "You're sure?"

Virginia nods her head, lifting a piece of pizza to her mouth. "Positive." Before I can think of what to do next, who to confront first, what to ask Virginia, she finishes her bite and says, "Sweet baby Jesus, why is this pizza so good?"

"No one knows," I murmur.

Looking at the basic menu board with blue block letters over the register with faint astonishment, she says, "I never even knew this place existed."

"You and everyone else. He's about two months from shutting down. After I finish eating, I have to go have a little talk with him."

Scowling at me, she says, "A talk? That's Sin speak for hand-breaking, isn't it? If you break his pizza-making hand, you're a legitimate monster. Also, please don't, because I want to come here more."

"Hey, you think you can convince him to pay his bills in a more timely fashion, be my guest," I mutter, grabbing my own piece of pizza and taking a bite. Fuck, it is good. Maybe I can avoid hurting the hands so I can keep buying until he's out of business.

I was joking, but Virginia doesn't appear to understand that. Nodding once, she says, "Deal."

"That wasn't a serious suggestion," I inform her.

"I'm gonna take care of it," she assures me. "Rafe only cares that he gets paid, not that the pizza maker gets hurt. Violence isn't the answer here. There's no reason this man shouldn't be making money. That doesn't even make sense. I'm going to volunteer my services and straighten out his books for him. With great marketing, you can move a large quantity of shitty product, and this is *delicious* product, so this guy should be spending his summers on a beach. From the look of this place, he probably needs help marketing."

"What do you know about marketing?"

"Well, not a whole lot, but I'm gonna talk with—is his name Giordano?" I nod. So does she. "Giordano. I'm going to get the scoop on his financial situation, then I'll do some research over the next few days. Rafe will get paid next month on time, you have my word. If he doesn't, he can take it up with me."

Cocking an eyebrow in amusement, I ask, "You're going to vouch for a perfect stranger to the *mob*? You must really like that pizza."

"I'm exceedingly confident in my abilities. Call me cocky, but I'm not worried. Also, perfect cheese to sauce ratio is worth risking my ass for," she tells me, closing her eyes in exaggerated ecstasy as she takes another bite.

Shaking my head, I tell her, "You're crazy."

With a cheeky smile, she winks at me. "All the best people are."

30

SIN

After making sure Virginia would be kept busy fixing Giordano's pizza place, I have a few decisions to make.

One: do I waste more time investigating Gio's harem of troublemaking mistresses, or do I just go to Marlena's apartment and confront her? Cassandra's a psychopath; she's not going to crack. Carla is useless. Marlena seems like a somewhat normal woman who just got mixed up with the Morelli charm. I don't see Gio having much of it myself, but women eat their crazy shit right up. He's never tried to fuck me, so I guess I just don't get to see that side of him.

Two: do I put some trust in Gio and call him out on his association with Cassandra to see how deeply she has rooted herself in him? She got her hooks deep into Rafe and gutted the guy, so while I don't understand her appeal, clearly she has some. Then again, I don't like crazy bitches. Weird and nerdy? Sure, okay. A psycho bitch that's only out for herself? No fucking thank you. Call me crazy, but I'd rather wake up to a surprise blow job than some bitch with a knife she's about to plunge into my back.

Three: if Cassandra *is* part of the deal, is there any way I can handle that? My initial response was an enthusiastic fuck no, but Gio offers Laurel. I really want Laurel. I could arrange an accident for Cassandra down the road and get her out of the way, so she's not necessarily a permanent problem. As long as Gio can't trace it back to me, we're fine.

Four: do I give in to the overwhelming temptation I have right now to go see Laurel? Since my life is in such fucking chaos all because I'm trying to figure out how to get her and also stay alive, it would be really nice if I could see her face. Pulling out the spite photo Rafe sent me isn't good enough. I want the feeling she gives me when we're together in the same room. I want her kneeling on the ground at my feet, looking up at me like I'm her sun and she'll beg for the chance to revolve around me.

I want her mouth around my cock, her pretty blue eyes looking up at me when she's already so fucking full of me and I can see how much she craves more. Before I had to stay away because of Rafe, but right now, Rafe is a temporary problem. If I go with Gio, fucking the face of his baby mama is not the worst thing I'm going to do to Rafe, not by a long shot.

Plus, Laurel's as good as mine, so I'm not stepping on his fucking toes anymore. He's had more chances with her than he's earned, and he's clearly failed to capture her interest or she wouldn't still want me.

The problem is his security. He must have checked it when I was alone with her last time, so I have to assume he's checking tapes now every time Laurel is left alone. I could technically sneak in though, because I know where the blind spots are. All I have to do is park my car somewhere else and walk up to the house.

I don't want to get Laurel involved, though. If I show up there wanting things I walked away from the other day, I'll have to explain why. Won't I? I suppose I could confuse her. It's not like she's going to tell Rafe on me. I could show up at her door with a gun and she wouldn't tell Rafe about it, provided I told her not to.

Hey, that's not half bad. Laurel would have no fucking idea what's happening, but at least if something happens and shit goes sideways, I got to feel myself in Laurel's mouth one last time. Even if Rafe catches on that something happened, Laurel can't be blamed for it under those circumstances. Anyone would tell her to cooperate under threat of duress, and while Rafe wouldn't believe I would hurt Laurel, if I jump ship, he *would* believe I would trick her into *believing* I'd hurt her. I'm a crafty bastard when I want to be.

Confronting Marlena is probably more urgent than getting my dick sucked.

It's the easiest out of all my decisions, so I head over to the apartment complex Rafe owns to pay her a visit.

Her greenish eyes register no small amount of surprise when she sees me on the other side of the door. "Hey, Sin."

I smile. "Marlena. Can I come in?"

"Um..." She must sense that I'm onto her, because last time I stood on this doorstop, she *wanted* me to come inside. Now she's glancing back in the apartment like she's searching for an excuse to tell me no.

I save her the trouble, taking a step forward and pushing on the door. "I'm gonna come in."

God, her eyes are expressive. She's nervous, but she forces

314 | SINNING IN VEGAS

a smile and attempts to pick up where she left off. "I like it when you're bossy."

"That's not gonna last long," I tell her, shoving the door shut and turning to face her, my eyes hard. "Tell me why I'm here, Marlena."

Fear jumps in her eyes and she backs up. Her gaze flits across the room briefly to a little table. I wanna know what's over there, so I walk backward, keeping an eye on her.

Taking a few nervous steps forward, she says, "We could go to my bedroom and talk there."

I check behind the table. I'm more than a little surprised to find a gun stashed back there.

Well, shit.

Just in case she's more dangerous than I expected her to be, I straighten and stare at her. Then I pull out my own gun, because while I like to be cocky sometimes, I don't like to be so cocky I get my ass shot.

Marlena gasps, backing up against the wall. Her hand shoots out and she reaches for the doorknob, but before she can throw the door open and run, I'm there, shoving it closed.

"Help!" she screams, before I get the door all the way shut.

Glaring at her, I say, "Now that wasn't too fucking smart, was it?" Grabbing her by the hair, I yank her back, ignoring her yelp, and lock my arm around her neck.

"Sin, please," she begs, her hands coming to my arm, trying to claw it away from her neck. I ignore her, leaning over to look out the window, make sure there was no one around to hear her. She continues to waste her breath. "I really liked you, Sin. I really do. Please don't hurt me. I didn't want to do it. She made me. I tried to talk her out of it. I told her it was too far. I swear to God, I never wanted to hurt Laurel."

My blood runs cold, but she can't see my face. Even if she

could, I doubt she'd know I'm surprised, but I'm doubly glad anyway. "No?"

Her breath hitches and she shakes her head, still struggling pointlessly against my hold. "I didn't. I swear to God."

"Then why the fuck did you do it?" I'm vague, since I'm not entirely sure what she's talking about, but angry, because she needs to think I do.

"I don't know," she wails. "Cassandra was so angry that Rafe got her pregnant. It ruined everything and she had to go with plan B. It's over now, I swear. That was only when they thought Laurel came with Rafe. Now that Gio knows you like her, he'd never hurt her. I'm so sorry. We hoped you wouldn't find out."

"Cassandra's fucking Gio, why the fuck did she care if Rafe knocked up Laurel?"

"Gio was just her insurance plan," Marlena says, somewhat defensive. "She started fucking him so she had a back-up, but she doesn't really care about him. She wanted to marry Rafe, but she doesn't love him either."

I'm starting to get a weird feeling here. "Who does she love?"

"Me."

Oh, Christ.

Sighing, I tell her, "I've got some bad news for you, dipshit. Cassandra only loves Cassandra. Far as I know, she's not even into girls. She's using your dumb ass, just like she's using them."

"No, she isn't," she objects, spirited rather than afraid now, in the kind of brave burst that only afflicts the truly devoted as they defend their hero. Her hero sucks, unfortunately for her. "Cassandra only uses people because she has to. They both deserved it. They don't even deserve to touch her, and they get to. She's wonderful. She's so smart and strong and.... Sure, sometimes she does bad things, but everyone does. She's the most fascinating person I've ever met, Sin. I think you've misjudged her."

I'm gonna throw up if she keeps talking about this game-playing little cunt like she's the next Messiah, I swear to Christ. "Just so I have your official confession, that night at the club when you showed up in the dress, you tampered with Laurel's drinking glass, correct?"

Marlena hesitates. She hesitates for-fucking-ever. At this rate, Cassandra's going to have a dozen new lovers to manipulate by the time this chick opens her fucking mouth and tells me what I need to hear.

"It's okay," I assure her, affecting a more soothing tone. "I don't blame you. I know how this works, I've seen it before. You got mixed up with the wrong people. I get it. They told you to poison some fucking girl, you did what you were told. I just need to hear you say it."

Since I have my arm wrapped so tightly around her neck, I feel it when she swallows. I know she's afraid to trust me, but Marlena isn't versed in this life. She has no idea who to trust and who not to. She can't tell the bad guys she can trust from the worse ones she can't. She might be Cassandra's star pawn right now, but that's because of her doe eyes and the nice ass she admittedly possesses. Once she has what she wants from her, Cassandra would throw this poor girl to the wolves. Meanwhile, this lovesick little fool would die defending Cassandra's make-believe honor.

Jesus, I hate that woman.

More than any other woman I'm currently thinking about, until the pawn finally decides she can trust me. Thickly, she says, "I did. I'm so sorry."

Nodding grimly, I bring my other arm around her body to support her weight, then I snap her neck.

"I appreciate your honesty," I murmur, as her limp body falls to the ground. Sighing as I look down at her and debate how to get her body out of here without being seen, I tell her, "Unfortunately for you, Laurel wasn't just some fucking girl."

She's *my* fucking girl, and as long as I'm breathing, nobody goes after her and lives to tell the story.

Nobody.

31

LAUREL

I'm getting used to Rafe going to his clubs without me.

Juanita made me some dinner before she left earlier, but now I have peace and quiet. Since I've had such difficulty sleeping at night, I do everything I can to establish a peaceful nighttime routine. I've put my cell phone on charge already. I read that the screen makes it difficult to fall asleep if you're playing on your phone right up to bed time, so tonight I'm screen-free for an hour before bedtime.

I make myself some sleepy time tea and bring the novel I picked out for tonight—*Dreamcatcher* by Nikki Reid. Rafe and I were supposed to go to the bookstore to pick out a baby book every week, but he never mentioned it this week and we definitely never stepped foot inside a bookstore. Since things have been a little weird between us but I wanted to make sure the baby got a new book, I took matters into my own hands and ordered online. While I was shopping, I decided I deserved a few new books to keep me company on these quiet nights, too.

While I drink my tea at the island counter, I decide to start reading. I run my hand over the lovely cover and caress the spine. The cover photo is a shot from behind of a blue-haired bride with a dreamcatcher tattoo on her shoulder—super pretty. Carly tells me I'm creepy with books. She's always on me about switching to a Kindle, but I can't fondle the cover of my book if it's trapped inside an e-reader. I love the feel of books, the smell of them, the ability to fan the pages and see the entire story yet to come. I'll never give them up, no matter how creepy Carly accuses me of being.

Opening the front cover, I flip past the title and dedication pages and settle in to start chapter one. I get sucked in right away and forget about the tea. I only planned to read for an hour while I relaxed myself for bed, but before long I realize reading may have been a bad idea. Instead of wanting to sleep, I'm thinking I may end up staying awake even longer so I can figure out why the bride just abandoned the groom she's crazy about at the altar!

I turn the page to start the next chapter, but freeze when I feel a disturbance in the room. The hairs on the back of my neck stand up and I swallow.

"Rafe?" I ask hopefully.

I hear a metallic click, then a hard, "Try again."

My heart tumbles right out of its cavity. "Sin."

"There you go. Sorry to disappoint," he murmurs, an edge of attitude in his tone.

I can't help the faint smile that steals across my lips as I mark my page and close my book. "I'm not disappointed. What are you doing here?" I start to turn so I can face him, but before I can, he moves closer, his chest pressing against my back. Then he places one hand on my shoulder to anchor me, and brings the other one up near my head.

I gasp as the hard, unforgiving barrel of Sin's gun presses against my temple and I go still.

What the fuck is happening?

Even though I know this is Sin, and I know he would never hurt me, fear slices through me.

It's Sin, I tell myself. My heart knows that, but my brain and my body respond to the threat—to the dangerous, loaded weapon of a hardened killer currently pressed against the side of my fucking head.

"Sin, what are you doing?" I ask shakily.

I can feel his breath on the back of my neck, the heat from his chest rolling off his body. His lips brush the shell of my ear and I jerk.

"Get off the stool, Laurel."

"This isn't funny," I tell him, forcing a nervous laugh. "This isn't funny. Please put the gun away. I don't know what this is, but I don't... I don't get the joke."

His voice is low in my ear as he drags the barrel of his gun down the side of my face. I shudder at the cool feel of the metal, such a contrast to his heat at my back. "Does it feel like I'm joking, Laurel?"

It doesn't, but he has to be. Maybe it's foolish to trust this man who burned me once before, but I trust him enough to know he wouldn't do something like this. This has to be some kind of game I just don't understand.

Whether it is or not, his fingers dig into my arm as he drags me off the stool, keeping the gun trained on me. I don't want to fall, so I force my shaky legs to work and I let him escort me out of the kitchen.

"Can we please talk about this?" I ask as we walk. Swallowing again, I try to look back at him. "Why are you... why are you doing this?"

"You wanna know why, Laurel? I'll tell you why." He abruptly stops walking and yanks me back against his hard body. *My* stupid body melts against him like it can't decide if this is more scary or hot. The only hand that's not keeping me captive is the one with the gun, so he uses that instead of his finger to fondle me. The way he drags the barrel over my breasts is already borderline erotic, then he uses it to nudge open my robe and a tickle of lust hits me. It only ratchets up at the gruff impatience in his voice as he tells me, "First, take off this flimsy fucking thing."

God, I love his voice. I don't know what's going on, but I know Sin wouldn't hurt me. If I'm wrong, then I'll die believing that until the very last moment.

We're in the family room at the back of the house—the one we never use. There are elegant, untouched furnishings—a black couch with silver pillows that are only touched when Juanita periodically fluffs them. A big, soft-looking rug in front of it.

I want to ask a million questions, but I'm afraid to. My back is still to him so I can't see his face—does it look the way it did the night I knelt for him? I didn't know what to think that night, either, but this time there's a gun. That sort of intensifies things.

"Now," he says.

My mind races as I reach for the belt of my robe to untie it.

"Slowly," he snaps.

I gasp at the sharpness of his command and take a deep breath, nodding my head. My nerves are shot, but I work the soft, knotted belt loose and slowly let each end drop in front of me.

Keeping my tone low and as even as possible, so as not to startle the man with the gun, I ask, "Why are you doing this? Is this some kind of test? Or game? Are we roleplaying?"

"Don't ask again," he says, simply. "Turn around and look at me while you take the robe off."

He lets me step away from him slowly. I turn just as slowly, no sudden movements, and meet his dark gaze. My heart gives for a split second, forgetting the weapon and the circumstances, seeing only the eyes of the man I'm meant to kneel for. My heart squeezes and my gaze drops to the gun. He still has it trained on me, and I still don't understand why.

He told me to take the robe off, so I push the robe over my shoulders and let it slide off my body. The room is so quiet, I can hear the soft material hit the floor. Hear the roar of blood raging through my veins, the pounding of my heart.

Using the gun to gesture to the couch, Sin says, "Grab that pillow."

My gaze darts to the couch and I see the silver pillow. I step sideways and grab it, then look to Sin for direction.

"Put it on the ground."

"Where?"

"Just on the fucking ground."

I don't know what he wants, so I just drop it right there on the ground by the couch.

Now Sin steps closer. My skin burns as his gaze drops, raking across my uncovered breasts. I already took my bra off for the night, so the only thing that stops me from being completely naked is a pair of panties.

I *feel* completely naked as Sin moves closer, so close he towers over me. I feel small and fragile—he's the one I'm supposed to turn to for protection, but right now he's what I need protecting from. He stops in front of me, but he's so close, I can feel his heat—this time on the front of my body.

"Now, listen to me very carefully, Laurel. You don't want anyone to get hurt, right?"

I shake my head, unable to formulate words. There's a lump in my throat, and I'm torn between fear and sadness. This can't really be happening. Sin can't be bad.

I mean, not worse than I already know he is.

His tone is briefly comforting as he says, "No. I don't either. So it's very important that you listen to what I'm about to say to you, and fucking remember it. Something is going to happen right now that you don't want." I stare at the ground, because I can't look up at him. "You can fight me, but it won't stop me. I can do whatever I want to you, and do you know why?"

I swallow, refusing to answer.

His tone hardens and he nudges under my chin with the gun. "I'm fucking talking to you."

"No," I blurt, meeting his gaze. "I don't know why."

Lifting his eyebrows, he says, "Because I'm the asshole with the gun. Now, if you play by my rules, nobody has to get to hurt. Here's what's gonna happen. You wanna hear?"

I nod.

"You're gonna do whatever I tell you to do, and you're gonna do it nicely. You're gonna do it with enthusiasm. You're going to convince me you want it—even though you don't."

My pulse quickens and I meet his gaze, a sudden feeling of understanding sweeping over me. I know what he's here for now, and while so much of me would love to give it to him, Rafe's shadowy threats ring in my ears every time I even *fantasize* about doing anything naughty with Sin. "Sin, I want to, but I can't. We can't—"

He grabs a fistful of my hair and shoves my head down, pressing the barrel of his gun against my forehead as I cry out. "It's time for you to listen, Laurel. No talking. I know how fucking hard it is for you to keep your mouth shut, but just give me a minute."

I draw in a hitching gasp, on instinct reaching for his side and holding on. As my fingers dig into his side, alerting him to real fear, he eases the gun away from my forehead.

Coincidence? I have an awful feeling that I know what he's doing, but he doesn't want me to talk, so I keep quiet.

"You're going to do everything I tell you to do. You're going to let me take whatever I want. You don't want this, and you can beg me to stop, but I won't listen. If anyone ever finds out about this, if anyone ever asks, you *did* beg me to stop and I ignored you. Understand? Open that pretty little mouth right now and tell me you don't want this."

I swallow audibly before forcing that lie past my lips. "I don't want this."

"Good girl." Everything inside me goes soft at those words from his mouth, at the tender reassurance in his tone.

As much as I *do* want this, I don't want to put him in danger. I want to play scary, sexy games with him, but more than that, I want to protect him.

"Sin..."

"No. We're back to no talking, Laurel. Keep that pretty mouth shut until I tell you to open it again. Nod once if you understand."

I nod once.

"Okay. When all this is over with, after I've taken what I want from you, you're going to put your skimpy little robe back on and go about the rest of your night. You are *not* going to tell anybody what I did here, do you know why? Because then someone *will* get hurt. I don't mean someone's feelings, either. If you care about Rafe, if you want to keep him safe, you keep your fucking mouth shut. He comes after me, he won't come back."

My heart drops at the threat. I don't think he means it, but I do know he's capable, so it's actually not impossible.

I know that Sin knows my safe word, and I'm tempted to use it, but I can't get it out of my mouth. I'm not sure if I'm more afraid to utter it because he might stop, or because he might not. I'm 90% sure this isn't real, but what if I'm wrong? I do remember him asking me if I'd fight him if he fucked me, so I was mentally prepared for him to be into some kinky shit. I haven't explored that kind of play, but I would try it out with him. I didn't think a gun would be involved, I just imagined him pinning me down, making me helpless with his body...

I sigh, my stupid body responding to my own damned thoughts. Fuck, I like when he's dangerous.

I should try to stop him, though. Even if my heart feels like it belongs to him, even if my body is fully on board, I'm not his to play with and this should not happen. If Rafe ever found out about this... God, it makes me sick thinking about it.

This is a dangerous fucking game Sin is playing, if that's what this is. High stakes doesn't even begin to cover it.

"Now, get on your knees, Laurel."

32

LAUREL

I look down at the pillow, then lower myself until I'm on
the floor in front of him. It's been so long—too long—
since I've been down here, but I take a moment and close
my eyes, keeping my head bowed.

"What do you want, Laurel?" he asks me.

I don't know the right answer. This position fucks with my
head, and I don't know what's going to happen when I open
my eyes and look up at him. I remember what happened
before. I also remember his instructions though, so with my
head down and my voice low, I tell him, "I don't want this."

There's light approval in his tone. "That's right, you don't.
But I want you to pretend you do. I want you to put on a good
fucking performance, Laurel. I want to feel like you're my little
whore, hungry for my cock. I want to feel like you crave me.
Like you want to fucking devour me." Reaching a hand down
and running it along my jaw, he ignores the way I lean into it.
"You convince me and I won't hurt you. Got it?"

I nod my head one more time.

I shouldn't. I should say "plutonium" and see what

happens. I'm fairly certain this would stop. I'm fairly certain he would leave. He would know I really do want this to stop, so he would leave me here kneeling for no one, and we would never have to talk about this again.

But there's that sliver of a chance he wouldn't stop, and then this would turn into something scarier than what it is right now.

Right now it's just a blow job. I can handle a blow job. Never given one at gunpoint before, but hell, there's a first time for everything.

I adjust my position on the pillow and take a calming breath before I tilt my head back to look up at Sin.

Subservience washes over me. It's the most natural feeling in the world, and when I look up at him like this, it flows through me in the most harmonious wave. It feels right, even though this is wrong on so many levels. My brain hides under the shelter of his words, of the violent threats, the cold steel he *actually* pressed against my forehead. He beats people bloody and kills those who don't cooperate for a living; it's not outside the realm of possibility that he's being real with me right now. I don't think he is, but it can't be ruled out entirely.

"Unbuckle my belt," he commands.

I don't hesitate. I reach for the black belt around his hips, remembering how he used to watch me as he took it off every night before bed. Remembering the little hook in our room where he hung them, on the wall he backed me up against the night he broke my heart. That mended heart aches now, as I draw the leather through the frame and start on his button. I miss this man and he's standing right here. I always miss him when he's standing right here. If he's doing what I think he's doing, this isn't enough. A taste of him, a single hit, that will only leave me wanting more. Bringing to life such a dangerous fantasy will only spawn more and lead to more emotional torture as I long for things I can't have.

I swallow as I drag his zipper down and look up at him. He's watching my every move, so his attentive gaze meets mine.

"Why are you doing this, Sin?"

He drags his thumb across my lower lip. "Because I need a pair of plump lips wrapped around my dick, and only yours will do."

I anchor my hands on his hips and lean my head against his pelvis, hugging him, even while his hardness nudges my cheek. "This is so dangerous," I whisper.

"Then make it worth the risk," he says, simply.

I draw in a breath and try not to think. There are so many horrible things I could think about right now, but I shove all of them down inside myself as I drag down Sin's slacks and underwear. His cock springs free and I sigh, gripping it in my hand and nuzzling the side of it with my face.

God, I've missed you.

If this is real and not the performance I expect it is, I'm going to look back on this moment and feel pretty fucking stupid, but if this is the last moment I ever get to look at Sin and feel like there's still even a sliver of a chance that he's not my enemy, I'm going to take it.

Peace settles over me as I drag my tongue along the underside of his dick. I lick it all the way to the tip, dart my tongue into the little valley there, then use my lips to kiss my way down the side, back toward the base. I want to taste and touch and please every part of him, so I duck my head and catch his balls in my mouth, using one hand to massage them, and my lips to suck.

"Oh, fuck, Laurel."

His fingers glide through the silky strands of my hair. Like old times, he gathers some in his fist.

"Do you like that?" I ask, before taking them into my mouth again.

"I do," he murmurs.

Since he gave me license to make this convincing, I don't hold back. "I love your cock, Sin." I place a kiss to the underside of it, then make a circle with my fingers near the base and pump back and forth. "When I go to sleep at night, I dream about it. I touch myself in the shower. I close my eyes and imagine you're there behind me."

My heart sinks with the truth of that confession, then sinks deeper at the sound of his sigh. That's not a sound of pleasure. I should stop talking. I don't want to make him sad. It's just that he's given me such a perfect excuse to tell him my deepest, darkest secrets. He's given me the perfect lie to hide behind so I can tell the truest of truths.

Since my words are making him sad, I put my mouth to better use. I slide my lips over the tip of him and suck while my fingers keep working him closer to the base. His cock is so long, I have plenty of space to work with. I continue to stroke him as I take more of him into my mouth, moaning with pleasure when his smooth tip brushes the back of my throat.

"Mm, yes," he murmurs, running his fingers through my hair.

I've missed you so much. The words I can't speak seep out of me as I suck him like the air I need to breathe. Blow job is a misnomer when Sin's is the dick in question; this isn't a *job*. This isn't menial labor. This is a privilege. This beautiful, perfect cock needed attention, and he wanted it from me. Gratitude flows out of me, this feeling I've only ever felt when I'm serving *this* man. I'd forgotten how it felt, forgotten how *good* this felt. This is the worst kind of torture, because I never want to stop, but it will. When it's over he's going to leave me here by myself, and I'm going to miss him more than ever.

I hear the sound of him placing the gun down gently on the end table, but I don't care. The gun doesn't matter anymore. I keep one hand anchored on his hip and keep laboring over his cock, striving to make him feel my hunger for him. It's like I'm a dying woman, and he's my life support. Like the world has been rotating without sights or sounds or feelings, and suddenly it's back all at once.

I know I'm where I belong, and it kills me because I know I can't stay here.

I close my eyes and savor his taste, his feel. I try to commit his noises to memory, so I can replay them again when I'm all alone. Even before this began, I knew it would end. He told me so, when he slyly gave me permission to enjoy this. When he took all the blame onto his shoulders by pulling his gun out and pushing it against my head.

More gratitude wells up, because while he scared me for a few minutes, he's the one who's going to have to watch his back. If Rafe finds out about this, he'll do more than inflict an uncomfortable breakfast on us—he'll kill him. He'll be right to. Sin is supposed to be loyal to Rafe, and maybe I am too, but I have an excuse. Sin gave me one, at the expense of himself. This man is willing to risk his life just to have me one more time.

I love you.

Tears spring to my eyes. I try to ignore them, but they well up and spill down my cheeks. I don't expect Sin to even notice, but the rough pad of his thumb catches the very first tear in its track.

"Stop," he says suddenly, pulling my hair to tug me off his dick.

"No," I say, looking up at him quickly and shaking my head.

His brow furrows as he searches my face, trying to decipher what's wrong with me. Am I crying because of what he's "making" me do, or is this something else?

This is definitely something else. I stroke his cock with my hand and lean my face against his toned stomach, kissing every inch I can get my lips on. My face still feels a little wet and cold from the tears, but it doesn't matter. This is very likely the only chance I'm ever going to get to do this. It can't be a regular thing, or I won't have even the flimsy excuse of being afraid if I told him no. Plus, the more this happens, the greater the chances of Rafe finding out. I was already worried Rafe had something horrible planned for Sin; we can't afford to give him more incentive.

Sin's hand moves to the back of my head and he holds my head against him tenderly.

I stay like that for a moment, just enjoying this half-assed embrace, then I pull back and get back to adoring his cock. I slide my lips over him, then ease him bit by bit until my lips reach his base and I have his whole cock in my throat. Then I look up at him.

"Fuck," he says, meeting my gaze.

I moan around his cock and pleasure fills me as he throws his head back and growls.

Make me yours.

He does. He grabs my hair on both sides of my head and holds on like handles while he fucks my mouth. His thrusts are brutal and they make me ache with arousal. I lick up every salty drop of him like it's the sweetest thing I'll ever taste. It *is;*

Sin's pleasure is without question the sweetest thing I'll ever taste.

I wish it could last forever, but it can't. I'm too enthusiastic and it's been too long.

At least, I *hope* it's been too long. The thought of another woman on her knees for Sin makes me want to die. When he comes down my throat and groans with pleasure, holding my face in place and making sure I get every last drop, it feels like reassurance. Who else could do this for him? Any mouth could take his cum, but no one else would be this grateful for it.

He pulls out of my mouth and I sit back on my heels.

"Fuck," Sin murmurs, pulling his pants back up and zipping them.

I swallow and look up at him, licking my lips.

"Fuck," he mutters again, dropping my gaze.

I wait for him to get himself together, but as soon as he retrieves his gun, my mind snaps back. Gazing up at him from my spot on the floor, I ask, "Was this real?"

His tone is detached, like this moment is already a memory for him. "Did it feel real?"

My tone is quiet and I look down as I admit, "Everything with you feels real."

Even if he's the biggest lie I've ever known, that's the truth. Sin feels like the only real thing in a world full of make believe. He did before and he does now, and if at any point in between I've imagined otherwise, I was only fooling myself.

"No one gets hurt as long as you don't say anything," he reminds me. Glancing back down at me, he says, "I didn't give you a choice in the matter. You have nothing to feel guilty for."

Biting down on my bottom lip, I mull it over for a moment before asking, "What if I had said my safe word?"

"We don't have a safe word," he says, simply.

That's bullshit. He knows my safe word. He doesn't want to admit I had an out though, and that answers my question. This wasn't real. He wanted a blow job, he wanted one from me, and he knew a way to get one.

I should leave it at that. I can only pretend to be blameless if I leave it at that, but I can't. I'd rather be the guiltiest whore in all the world than let him walk out of here and stick his dick in someone else.

"Sin."

He looks down at me and cocks an eyebrow expectantly.

"Please don't fuck the waitress."

He looks down at me for a moment, caught somewhere between tense and tender. His big hand comes close and I lean in once more as he caresses the side of my face. "Don't worry, Laurel. I won't fuck the waitress."

I wait for him to say more, but he doesn't. He leaves me here kneeling on the floor and strides away without looking back.

33

LAUREL

Sin is at breakfast again the following morning, and I'm so tense, I think I might throw up. I wasn't suspicious enough last time Rafe made Sin come to breakfast, but afterward it turned out Rafe was watching us.

Does that mean he's watching us again?

Does that mean he knows Sin was here last night?

He said he was going to up his security, but no one has been here to install anything. I'm here all the time; I would know. Plus, I assume Sin would be smart enough not to come here if he knew Rafe would find out.

I don't know, but I can feel guilt all over me. The worst thing is, I shouldn't have to feel guilty. I shouldn't be held prisoner by Rafe's vague threats. If I want to be with Sin, I should be able to. I am not in a relationship with Rafe, I'm just shackled by the genes he contributed to my little wiggle worm. Personally, I could not give less fucks about Rafe's weird family's view of how things should be.

I want to rebel. I want to fight back. I want to be reckless and tell him where he can shove his threats. The problem is, he's the head of a criminal organization, so it's safe to assume they are not just threats. It's safe to assume they are real, and if I piss him off, he may act on them.

I literally can't believe I'm in this situation, but since Rafe has me and Sin in the same room together, I'm feeling fearful about how tonight's going to go. I don't know if I'm more afraid Rafe will figure out what happened and kill Sin for it, or more afraid Rafe will figure out if he *clearly* threatens me, gives me a straight ultimatum, I would stay with him indefinitely to ensure Sin's safety.

Never thought we'd be here, that's for sure.

I'm doing my best to ignore Sin completely, but it's really hard to ignore him when he's in the room, and I'm worried ignoring him is too obvious. Thank God he didn't give me a hickey this time.

"That's too bad," Sin murmurs, his voice catching my ear as I turn to bring their plates to the counter.

I look up, briefly catching Sin's eye as I put his plate down in front of him. My heart burns with the memory of last night, looking up at him again, tasting him again. I'm afraid it's all plain to see in my eyes, so I look away just as quickly and move to put Rafe's food down in front of him.

As Rafe cocks his head at me, I realize I've already fucked up. Without thinking about it, I gave Sin his food first. I served Rafe second. Dammit, these fucking Morelli customs.

I decide to go for oblivious and pretend I forgot about all that, flashing Rafe a smile and going to turn away. Before I can, his hand locks around my wrist. I swallow down dread as he pulls me around the counter closer to him.

"Where's my kiss?" he asks.

Oh, God, this is going to be so much worse after last night. Dread forms like a physical lump in my throat, but I can't say no. He knows it, too, the evil bastard. His dark eyes dance with amusement, like he's enjoying this.

Twisted motherfuckers, every last one of them.

Since there's no getting out of it, I decide to deprive him of his joy in scaring me. I loop my arms around his neck, sigh happily, and plant one on him.

He's too surprised to respond, so I'm able to pull back and dart away before he can stop me.

I hope it didn't hurt Sin's feelings, but if it did, he's in for a lifetime of hurt feelings. Rafe clearly likes torturing us both. Refusing to let him see my agony, I make myself some oatmeal with strawberries and pull up a seat at the island, immersing myself in my book from last night while the men discuss the disappearance of someone named Theo.

I get lost in someone else's world for a while until Sin's voice pulls me out of my book.

"I want more."

Given his tone, it sounds like he's talking to me. I look up, blinking in confusion. He cocks an eyebrow and shakes his empty mug expectantly.

Arrogant prick. I roll my eyes, but it makes my indulgent heart happy. I'm so fond of this lazy bastard, I can't even handle it. I slide my bookmark between the pages and stand, grabbing his mug and taking it over to the coffee pot so I can get him a refill.

Rafe gets up and follows me. I stiffen as he encircles my waist from behind, holding my body against his. "You're so attentive to his needs," he murmurs with deceptive pleas-antness.

My heart skips a couple beats, but I try to keep my breathing steady. Chances are, holding me like this, he'll be able to feel my body's response if it's not subtle enough. "Are you trying to embarrass me?" I murmur, preferring Sin doesn't hear, but knowing he might anyway. We aren't far enough away from the island that I can be sure he won't.

"Do you like being embarrassed?" Rafe asks, bending his head to kiss my neck. I'm sure it's no coincidence that the spot he kisses now is exactly the same spot where Sin left the hickey.

This is so fucking mean. It's torture knowing Sin is back there watching this. I wish I could convey a silent apology, but I'm sure he knows I'm not doing this on purpose.

"No, I don't," I tell Rafe firmly.

"Neither do I," he responds smoothly. "Don't ever give him his fucking food before you give me mine again." His hand grips my jaw and he tilts it up firmly as he murmurs into my ear, "Understand?"

I'm vibrating with fury, but I nod my head as he leans in and kisses my jaw. "I didn't think about it. I forgot."

"It's not that hard to remember. You serve your man first. Unless you were having trouble remembering which one of us you belong to?"

I glare, but he can't see it since he's behind me. Still, I'm sure he can hear the hostility in my voice when I assure him, "Oh, no, I know exactly who I belong to."

Sin's voice startles me as he snaps, "Hey, are we gonna work, or what?"

"Keep your pants on," Rafe tells him.

My blood runs cold, since I don't know if that's pointed. Since I just pulled Sin's pants down and sucked him off last night, I'm paranoid. I'm convinced that means he knows.

Concern for Sin helps me put a leash on my temper and I turn back to Rafe, looking up at him with a little remorse. "I wasn't trying to embarrass you. I really just forgot. There's no one here to see, anyway. It's just us."

"Just don't do it again," he tells me, holding my gaze.

Do *what* again? Serving Sin breakfast, or what I did last night? I'm so confused. I wish he would just say what he means. That's all I want from Rafe—clear communication. If he's going to go full on villain and blackmail me into this relationship, I wish he'd just tell me that. The guess work and reading into every little thing is so stressful.

I'm terrified he'll do something that can't be undone. I'm terrified of what he's capable of. With Sin, it's sexy. With Rafe, it's scary. I don't know why.

Well, I guess I do know why. I'm never *really* worried Sin would hurt Rafe, but I *am* worried Rafe would hurt Sin. Rafe doesn't have the same kind of loyalty Sin has, and that makes him a bigger threat right now.

At least for the moment, I get a breather. Rafe goes back to his seat and starts eating the breakfast I made him, and I take Sin his coffee, sliding it across the island without meeting his gaze this time. As much as I enjoy his presence, I just want him to leave. I'm too anxious about Rafe watching us to be in the same room with him.

I open my book, planning to hide between its pages until Sin is gone, but what I see makes my heart stop. Scrawled in the margin of my paperback is a note that was not there when I last closed the book.

Go for a walk at 2pm.

My chest feels tight, like I can't breathe properly. Did Sin *really* just jot this note in my book while I got him coffee? I peek at Rafe first to make sure he's not looking at me, then I steal a glance at Sin.

As he sips the coffee I just gave him, he meets my gaze over the brim.

It's all the verification I need.

My heart speeds up because I don't know what this means. It can't mean anything good. Whatever we're doing here, it was a lot easier to ignore the magnitude of it when Sin was resisting. I don't know what it means if he's not now, all I know is it has to be bad.

I want him, I do. This isn't a game to me; I'm not in it for the thrill of the chase or the "fun" of sneaking around. I legitimately want him, but I know I can't have him unless Rafe says it's okay. Sin and Rafe are clearly not on friendly ground right now, so it can't be that. As much as I want the experiences, I don't want Sin to be risking his ass to steal these moments with me.

And as big a dick as Rafe is being, I don't want him hurt, either.

I have no idea what it all means, but I do know one thing: I will be going for a walk at 2pm, because wherever I live, whomever I sleep next to, I am now and will forever be Sin's good girl.

I feel weird about leaving the house to go for a walk, mostly because it's nothing I've done before. Rafe left two hours ago and Juanita is at the house cleaning, but I slipped out without telling anyone. I brought the book with me in my purse. On one hand, I can't believe Sin vandalized my damn book. The bookworm in me is outraged. On the other, as much as I was enjoying all the words the author put on the page, having Sin's words there makes it so much better. It's my new favorite book now, just because it has Sin between the pages.

But on a less sentimental note, there's the fact that he left a paper trail, and I'm reading that book while staying at Rafe's house. I can't imagine he would ever think to fan the pages of my books, looking for illicit notes, but now I can never leave the book lying around, just in case.

I get to the end of the driveway and look left, then right. I don't know which way I'm supposed to go. I head to the right, toward Vince's dad's old house. It takes forever to get over there. Rafe's house is in sort of a development, a cluster of expensive homes, but there is so much space between each one. It's a nice walk, probably a safe walk. I imagine the future, pushing a stroller down this street with a babbling baby inside. Even if I might potentially be trapped in a loveless relationship with a mob boss while quietly yearning for his hired muscle, at least there's a pretty big bright side. Thoughts of my little wiggle worm warm me all over and I place a hand on my belly.

I know *I'm* safe, I know the baby is safe, but I need to know the people I care about are safe, too. If Sin is going to accost me while I'm on this walk, he better give me some goddamn answers, because I am drowning in questions.

I hear the purr of his car just before he coasts to a stop beside me. I bite down on my bottom lip, barely able to contain the burst of happiness I feel when I look in the rolled down passenger window and see Sin in the driver's seat.

"Get in," he tells me.

I open the door and slide in without delay. "What's going on?"

Putting his hand on the gear shift, he pushes it into drive and speeds up. "We're going to my house."

That wasn't at all what I expected. "What? Why?"

Nodding toward the door, he says, "Put your damn seat belt on."

I huff, grabbing the seat belt and stretching it across my body. When it clicks into place, I demand, "Fine. Now can you tell me what's going on?"

"I've got a long night ahead of me. Some long days after that. These are my last few hours of peace. I want to spend 'em with you."

The raw honesty of those words knocks the words right out of me. I can only stare at him for a long moment, then eventually I find just enough of my voice to murmur, "Good answer."

34

SIN

This was not the plan.

Last night when I left Laurel, I had no intention of seeing her again until it was all over, but then Rafe invited me to breakfast this morning. Each of us sat there, going through the motions of a liar's dance, and I know that he knows. I'm not sure how much he knows, but whatever he knows, it's too much.

He definitely knows I killed Theo, which means he knows why.

He might know I was with Laurel last night.

He doesn't know Marlena is dead, and he must not know beyond a shadow of a doubt that I've turned on him, because if he did, I would not have left breakfast. He would have splattered my brains all over the tile floor, and depending on if he knew Laurel and I were together last night, maybe he would have made her clean it up as punishment.

The time for debating my options is over. I debate much longer, I won't have any options left. I know what I have to do, but as with any war, there's no guarantee my side wins.

There's no money-back guarantee I even have a side. I think Gio is being real with me, but it's not impossible he and Rafe are in cahoots and Rafe just wants me gone. If I'm wrong about all this, I won't be wrong for more than a few seconds, then I'll be nothing.

Either way, whether it's my last day or just my last day of peace, I want to spend it with Laurel. I don't even care if Rafe finds out at this point. Let him find out. He'll know soon enough. Laurel is mine, not his, and if he doesn't have the fucking sense to figure that out by now, that's on him.

I look over at her now and she looks peaceful. I stopped and bought her a milkshake, so she's sipping on it, watching out the window as the wind blows her long dark hair. She seems content, even though she doesn't know where we're headed. I mean, sure, she knows we're going to my house, but in the larger sense she has to know something is up.

I get the impression she'd follow me anywhere, and I fucking like it.

I'd follow her anywhere, too.

I sort of wish I'd said yes the first time she asked me about Chicago. I don't want any part of the war I'm about to start. I don't want to lose men I've worked beside for years, I don't want to upend this whole damn family *again*. We can't keep doing this. Shit like this needs to be handled and then not repeated again for a long time so people have enough time to forget, otherwise you start looking like you have instability, and instability brings out the predators. Other crews sense weakness, they'll pounce on it and try to take more power for themselves. You lose enough of your guys, you're asking for an ambitious up-and-comer to come at you with all they've got.

Especially now, that's the last thing any of us needs.

I can't think about what comes after, though. First things first, and the first thing is dealing with Rafe.

Well, the first thing after I make sure this is what Laurel wants. I'm tempted to keep her in the dark about some things—I know she'd let me get away with it—but before I make her mine permanently, I need to make sure she knows what she's in for. I already see things going sour with her and Rafe, and I couldn't bear to have that happen to us. I've lived through that hell before. I won't do it again.

"Good milkshake?"

Laurel looks over at me, smiling brightly and nodding her head. "Very good. Thank you."

"You don't have to thank me," I tell her, reaching over and taking her free hand, twining our fingers together.

"I'll thank you more vehemently when we get back to your house," she offers, her smile turning suggestive.

"Damn right you will," I tell her.

This makes her grin, and her happiness makes all this bullshit feel worth it. She wants me as much as I want her, and there's not a single fucking reason we shouldn't have each other if that's the case. Rafe can fuck right off with his bullshit.

When we pull into my driveway, I'm struck by a memory of the first time I stole her, how pretty she looked sleeping in the passenger's seat, how unaware she was of the shit she was about to go through.

She took it in stride, though. I'm not sure anything can keep Laurel down, and I love that about her. As much as it pissed me off when she kissed Rafe at breakfast this morning, I couldn't help cheering for her a little, too—he clearly wanted to intimidate and bully her a little bit, and she wasn't having that shit.

She's so fucking great. I squeeze her hand again before releasing it altogether so we can get out of the car.

Laurel pauses in front of the car and looks up at the house, sighing. "I missed this place."

I smile faintly, heading for the front door. "Missed your cage, did you?"

"I did," she says, following me. "Lock me up inside and don't let me out again, I won't complain. My sister will. She'll definitely show up on your doorstep with something to say about it. But personally, I'll be fine until fall semester starts."

"I have to let you out then, huh?"

"I'll probably want to go out to eat, too. I'll need field trips. But I'm down to spend most of my time cuffed to your bed."

"I can't believe I forgot to buy you a ball gag," I murmur, twisting the key in the last lock and opening the door.

"Oh, you love listening to all my nonsense," she tells me, following me in the house.

Once we're inside, I feel edgy. I know there's no chance anyone is inside because I had the place locked down, but knowing what's coming, I can't help feeling a little tense. I put an arm out in front of Laurel, backing her up against the wall. I secure each lock on the door, then make my way up the stairs and take care of the alarm. Even though we're inside, I lock up like we're going to sleep.

I'm hoping I can have these last few peaceful hours, but I'm a little cagey as I stalk through the house with my gun at the ready, double checking every potential place to make sure we are, in fact, alone.

Laurel's good mood ebbs as she realizes what I'm doing. She doesn't say anything, but I see it in her face. Before we were just taking a ride while she had her milkshake and she could believe everything might be fine, but now I'm checking every crevice of my own house like there might be danger around the corner.

Then there's the fact that after telling her she can't have me over and over again, I just showed up at Rafe's house and shoved my dick in her mouth last night. Clearly something has changed, and it doesn't take a genius to figure out it can't be all good news.

I check my bedroom last. Since she's following me, we both end up there. Once I know the place is secure, I sigh and put my gun down on the bedside table.

Laurel attempts a smile, but I can still see the worry weighing her down. "No gun foreplay today, huh?"

"Nah, not today."

She looks down, causing her hair to fall in her face. As she tucks it back behind her ear, she looks up at me. "Are you going to tell me what's going on now?"

I shake my head, advancing toward her. "Not just yet."

Her gaze remains on me, but she backs up against the wall. I don't mind; that's right where I want her. Right against the wall where she stood last time she was in this bedroom, when I fucked it all up.

I can see the memory replaying in her mind as she stands with her back against the wall, looking up at me. The room is so silent I can hear her swallow. "I'm sorry I ever let you leave," I tell her.

A mess of emotions shine in her eyes, but she doesn't speak. That's all right. She's done plenty of talking; now it's my turn.

Since I'm more effective at communicating things to her with my body than my words, I start there. I grab her hands and push them over her head. She looks perfect here—part masterpiece, part sacrifice. I'm not much for art, but I know awe-inspiring beauty when I see it, and it shines right out of her. Not just her face or her body, but her heart. She's got a gorgeous heart, and she's opened it up to me right from the start. I don't know why, but I won't question my luck.

As my gaze rakes over her, hers warms. The worry falls off her shoulders, the conflicted feelings drain out of her eyes. There's nothing in her eyes right now I don't want to see.

I run my fingers lightly down the backs of her arms, my blood heating as she sighs and closes her eyes, relishing the pleasure of my touch. Settling my hands around her waist, I lean into her, pressing close and bending my head to kiss her neck. She sighs again, lowering her arms so she can wrap them around my body and tug me closer.

When I finish kissing her neck, I kiss my way along her jaw, but stop just before I get to her mouth. Force of habit. She doesn't even complain now, she just leans into my hand as I cup her face.

I watch her, trying to read her face like she tried to read her book this morning.

"I don't want him to kiss you again," I tell her.

She meets my gaze with surprised blue eyes, but she nods her agreement. "Okay."

"Can you make that promise?" I ask, out of curiosity, caressing her face. "Does he make you kiss him?"

Now her gaze drops briefly, but it rises to meet mine again after only a second. "I should be able to. I mean, unless you're around, he hasn't wanted to kiss me much lately anyway."

That draws a frown out of me. "Why not?"

Amusement flits across her face. "Are you offended on my behalf? You've never kissed me once, so you don't have room to talk."

"It's been a very long time since I've kissed someone," I admit.

The amusement on her face dies, like she knows there's a reason behind that, and it's not going to be a bit funny.

There is, but I'm not ready to get into that yet.

Pulling back, I tell her, "Take your shirt off."

She does, without hesitation. While she draws her shirt off, I draw mine off, too. I see the desire blossom in her eyes as soon as she sees my bare skin. I don't plan to give up control of this moment, but she must need to kiss me, because instead of pressing me for my story—or even just waiting for it and not distracting me—she bends her head and starts kissing me all over. My neck, my shoulders, my chest. Her plump lips are everywhere, covering as much of me as she can. Her kisses get hotter and slower when she makes it to my hands. I don't know why she loves my hands so much, but she fixates on them, kissing my fingers and holding my gaze.

"Can I taste you?" she asks, her hands dropping to my belt.

"You like to taste me, don't you?"

"I love it." She leans in and kisses my neck again, like I might need to be sweetened up before I let her suck my dick. "Will you fuck my face like before? On the bed, with me under you?"

Christ, she's making it hard to remember why we need to talk. Fisting a hand in her hair, I pull her close, kissing the side of her face. "I'll fuck your face, but I want you in the shower. I want you naked and wet. I want you cuffed and helpless."

The breath goes out of her and she bites down on her bottom lip, nodding her head. "Yes. Yes to all of that."

35

LAUREL

I t feels like Christmas and my birthday all at once when Sin takes my hand and drags me down the hall, toward his bathroom. I can't believe this is happening. I don't know *why* it's happening, but I'm not going to worry about that right now. I've fantasized about Sin on top of me so many nights, craving the way he dominated my body, the way he made me his treasured toy. I've never been as into oral as I am with him, but I've never felt the way I feel when he shoves his dick into my throat, either.

I want it so badly.

I want *him* so badly.

As soon as we get to the bathroom, he spins me around, pushes me against the door, and starts unbuttoning my shorts. My pulse pounds. Like he can't wait another second to touch me, instead of shoving my shorts down, he shoves his hand down the front and cups my pussy in his palm, pressing me against the door with his body and kissing my forehead.

"This is mine now," he tells me.

"God, yes." I tip my head back, feeling my pulse in my neck.

"Nobody else touches it," he informs me.

"Never," I promise.

He fists his free hand in my hair again and pulls my face close to his mouth so he can kiss my forehead again. "I'm glad we understand each other."

I'm so happy, I could die. I need him closer, so I wrap my arms around his neck and tug him close. I need him to kiss me. Really kiss me, on my mouth. I don't want to ask, because it seems like a kiss from Sin might require a few signed documents and a blood oath, and all I want to do is get in that shower. I want the man who just told me he owns my pussy now to fuck my face, because it's pretty much my favorite thing now that I've been on the receiving end.

From him, anyway.

I feel icky that Rafe ever touched me, even before Sin. I wonder if I should tell Sin that while I didn't have sex with Rafe since I got involved with him, that doesn't mean I didn't do *anything* with him.

Then again, this is probably not the time.

Reaffirming that supposition, Sin keeps one hand tightly fisted in my hair and spins me around, planting my hands against the wall with the other one. I close my eyes as he drags his lips along my neck and across my shoulder. A horrible thought leaps to mind, that awful waitress and that horrifying date I saw them on.

Reaching back to loop my arm around his neck, I stop his kisses so I can have his attention.

"Sin."

"Hmm?" he murmurs, nuzzling his face into my neck.

"Did anything happen with Marlena?"

The nuzzling stops, and my stomach sinks. Oh, no, that can't be good. "What?" he asks, faintly guarded or surprised or... something.

"I don't know why I need to know," I say quickly. "I'm not even sure it's fair, all things considered. I just feel like if we don't address it now, I'll always wonder, and maybe that's worse than knowing."

"You mean sexually?"

I frown, confused. "Of course I mean sexually. How else would I mean?"

Now the kisses start up again, his lips moving up and down my neck. "No, nothing sexual."

That should make me feel better, but it doesn't. Does that mean he maybe had an emotional draw to her? Did he actually like her? I desperately wanted to believe he was covering for Rafe, but then those awful text messages come to mind. I would hate for him to like her, too. "Did you like her? What does that mean, not sexually?"

Sighing, Sin gives up kissing me for the moment. "I had no interest whatsoever in Marlena. I was keeping tabs on her to see if Rafe was fucking around on you, that's it."

"Was he?" I ask, out of curiosity.

"I'm not positive. Gio says he was. I forgot to ask Marlena. Didn't really care at that point."

"What do you mean?"

"She's dead," he says, gathering my hair and pushing it over my shoulder so he can kiss the other side of my neck.

The news that someone I vaguely knew is dead lands like a rock in my gut. "Wait, what? When did that happen?"

Barely pausing in his neck kisses, he murmurs, "When I got verification that she tried to poison you."

My blood freezes and I push back against him, but he

doesn't budge, so I remain plastered against the door. "Wait, *what?* Does that mean *you* killed her?"

"She tried to hurt you," he states, like this is all the explanation he owes me or anyone else.

I can't breathe properly. My face feels stuck in a permanent gape. Not similarly afflicted, Sin spins me around so he can look into my eyes.

"Is that a problem?" he asks levelly.

"You killed for me?" I ask, a little breathless.

He takes my hand, bows his head, and kisses my knuckles like a soldier swearing his fealty. I guess in a way, he is. Only Sin's fealty is supposed to be to Rafe, not me. I have a feeling maybe he has changed allegiances.

I have a feeling Rafe isn't his king anymore.

I have a feeling now he serves his queen.

And *I'm* his queen.

Jesus, that is so hot.

Taking a deep breath and letting it out, I wrap my arms around him and attack his face. Maybe he won't kiss me, but goddammit, I will kiss him. Out of respect for whatever issues he has, I don't kiss him directly on the mouth, but I kiss him everywhere else. I hold him close, let my eyes drift shut, and kiss his scruff-covered jaw. I want his lips so damn bad, but when I get close, I lower myself slightly, kissing his chin, then along his other jaw.

I feel his fingers tighten in my hair and he yanks my head back against the door. I try to pull forward, but he holds me in place, so I stare at him, breathing hard.

He stares back, his face inscrutable. Then he leans in, and finally his lips brush mine. My heart nearly gives out, just at the gesture. I could weep, I'm so happy. My arms tighten around him, my fingers digging into his muscular back. It's such a sweet kiss, so slow, almost tentative. Like it's been so long, he wants to savor this one. He can savor it forever. I'll stay against this door with my pounding heart in his scarred hands for as long as he wants to kiss me. I'll stay here forever, if I'm that lucky.

After a few soft tastes of my lips, he unclenches his fist and cups my head in his hand instead. His lips continue their tender exploration of mine, but his tongue darts out, wanting more. I open eagerly, grasping his muscular shoulders, sensing I'll need to hold onto something. Touching him backfires, making me drunker. The hard, hot feel of him causes lust to twist in my gut, and in a perfectly timed assault, his tongue sweeps mine and I can't breathe any longer. I don't know how I'm still standing, because my legs feel like they're made of jelly. I've never felt this incapacitated by a kiss before, but Sin doesn't just kiss me—he moves into my mouth. It's his now, just like my pussy. He doesn't even have to verbalize it for me to know. I'm not sure I'll possess any part of myself when he's done with me, but that's all right. More than all right. I feel high on his kisses, breathless with every taste he takes. Even while he's kissing me, he tastes me, like I'm the sweetest flavor he has ever encountered.

As good as he was with his mouth between my legs, I really should have known he would be an amazing kisser.

I grab onto the door handle for purchase, my vision wobbly. I literally feel dizzy from the explosion of pleasure just being kissed by him triggered inside me. It occurs to me in this moment I am *not* ready to be fucked by him, no matter how much I want him inside me. He's too much of everything. I don't know how I'll take it all.

Breaking away from my mouth, he yanks down my shorts, then my panties, pushing all my clothes off like a man

354 | SINNING IN VEGAS

possessed. Now that he's had a taste, he's unleashing a new level on me. He can't get me naked fast enough, then he's pulling me against his hard body, claiming my mouth again. There's nothing tentative in his kiss now—it's hard and hot and fast, and it leaves me just as dizzy.

He releases me just long enough to get out of his pants, and I brace my weight on the wall, trying to give my equilibrium a chance to catch up. I get distracted by the sight of his ass. My heart aches, recalling lying in his bed and seeing that perfect ass. I want more nights like that. Will he take me back to Rafe's after this, or can I be done with all that? In this bathroom, it feels like no time has passed, like I didn't go back to Rafe, like I've always been right here, since the first night he cuffed me to his bed.

Sin doesn't give me time to worry about the reality that comes after all this. He bends and turns the faucet on, moving his hand under the explosion of water to check the temperature. Once he's satisfied, he pulls the silver valve on top of the faucet to turn on the shower.

A peculiar wave of nerves hits me, followed by excitement.

When Sin turns back to me, he must see it on my face. "What?" he asks.

"I've never taken a shower with a guy before."

Making a dismissive noise, he snakes his arm around my waist and pulls me close. "You're never gonna. Right now you'll take one with a man, though."

"Mm," I murmur, pecking him on the lips again. "I'm so happy."

I start as he smacks me hard on the ass, a little jolt of arousal shooting through me. "In the shower," he commands.

"Yes, sir," I murmur, lifting my leg and stepping over the side of the tub and under the spray.

Sin follows me in, pulling the curtain shut behind him. I love how little space there is—it forces closeness. Sin takes up quite a bit of space on his own, but I'm in here, too. I'm a little dazed by how incredibly hot he looks at soon as the water hits him. I get short of breath, recalling that first night I saw him naked, standing bedside with wet hair. Holy Christ, he is a beautiful man. I want to worship at his altar. I want to kneel and kiss every hard inch of his body.

Before I can, he catches me around the waist with one arm and cradles my head with the other, pulling me into the most intimate embrace ever and kissing me. It's not a demanding kiss, but it melts me. The way he holds me, I've never felt so cherished in my life. I'd give him anything he asked for right now. My heart? It's yours. Need a kidney?

If I've ever doubted my connection to him, if I ever doubt it again, I will only ever need to recall this memory right here and all those doubts will be flushed away. It doesn't matter what he does. It doesn't matter who gets hurt. This man is mine, and I am his, and that's the way it's supposed to be.

I feel the jut of his cock against my belly, and though I want him to take my mouth again, right now I'm wondering if I should just go all in and beg him to fuck me. I've never felt so close to him, and I want to know how I could possibly feel closer.

Reaching down, I grasp him in my hand and begin stroking him. He growls against my mouth and that light-headed feeling hits me again, then intensifies as he backs me up, slamming me against the tile wall. Excitement courses through my body and I feel myself sinking down the wall. I look up at him, feeling more and more intoxicated by the hard look in his eyes as I lower myself. His dark eyes are laser-focused on me, so intense.

My heart pounds wildly in my chest as I look up at him, finally on my knees. I break eye contact to lean forward, kissing the length of his dick as I stroke it. I'm so in love with every inch of him. I want to savor every moment, every taste, but I also want to swallow him whole. Lust twists me up, but I try to pace myself, running my tongue along his length the way I know he likes. When I finally take the tip into my mouth and suck on it, it feels like a decadent dessert I've been waiting for half my life. I know I just tasted him yesterday, but I'm so desperate for him, it seems like it's been decades.

As I lavish attention on his dick with my mouth and my hand, I steal a peek up at him. Pleasure swirls through me at the sight of his head thrown back, his eyes closed. The evidence of his pleasure makes me hungrier for him and I lean forward, taking him deeper.

"Oh, fuck," he murmurs, fisting his hand in my wet hair and pulling my mouth back and forth over his cock. I anchor a hand on his hip and let him use my mouth, let him guide me to do just what he wants. Desire rests heavily in my gut, need growing with every forceful thrust of his dick into my mouth.

He lets up so I can take a few deep breaths, and I look up at him, heat coursing through my whole body when his gaze meets mine.

I can scarcely breathe, but it's more from need than his rigorous use of my mouth. "Please fuck me," I beg him, holding his gaze. "Please."

He reaches down to caress my face reassuringly, but the first glimpse of something guarded flits across his features. "Not yet," he tells me.

Then, before I can ask again, he backs up, pulls back a small corner of the shower curtain, and grabs something.

When he comes back, he has black cuffs. Not the same

ones from the bedroom, different cuffs, but I know the drill. Anticipation fills me as he moves me back against the wall and secures each of my wrists in the flexible cuffs, then latches them to the bar installed on the wall. He gives them a tug to make sure they're secure, then looks down at me, smug satisfaction crossing his features.

"You're at my mercy now, pretty girl."

"Use me however you like," I tell him, relishing my complete vulnerability.

"I will," he assures me, grasping his dick in his hand and moving closer.

I open my mouth for him, but instead of putting it in my mouth, he smacks it against my face. I gasp, surprised, then he does it again.

Oh, God, why do I like that? I don't know, but I do. I close my eyes, then open my mouth wider, pushing my tongue out, trying to invite him inside.

"You want my cock, Laurel?" he asks, rubbing his dick near my mouth, but not giving it to me.

"Yes. Please let me suck you, Sin. Please."

"You need it?"

"Oh, God, yes," I tell him. "I want to pleasure you. Please let me have you in my mouth."

Deciding to give me my wish, he brings his cock close and lets me taste it. I sigh with relief as soon as his tip is in my mouth, then I suck on him to say thank you. I can't use my hands since they're cuffed to the wall, so I can only use my mouth to please him. After a minute, I feel his big hand behind my head, providing a cushion between my head and the tile wall. That's the only warning I get, then he thrusts his cock deep, pushing my face back with the force. This is the greatest position man has ever discovered, because as he holds onto my head and fucks my face, I get to look up at him, see the beautiful lines of his well-muscled body, feel his power in his thrusts. He's purely male, so beautifully masculine, and entirely mine. He tells me over and over again as his cock moves in and out my throat. He owns this territory, and my ass could not be happier about it. He pulls out to let me catch my breath, his reassuring hand caressing my jaw again, comforting me in case I need it before he takes hold of my face and fucks it hard again.

I'm so fucking turned on, I can scarcely function, and then he pulls out of my mouth and starts pumping his cock. I open my mouth like a bird, wanting every drop of cum he'll give me. His lips curve up with amusement.

"You're still hungry for me, aren't you, baby?"

"So fucking hungry," I tell him.

I don't just want him in my mouth, I want him in my pussy. I don't know why I can't have him there.

"I'm going to come on your tits," he decides.

I wish I could touch them. Everything aches. My breasts feel so heavy, my nipples are so hard, and I've been throbbing nonstop between the thighs. I need relief, but I need him to get his first. I wish he'd impale me with his cock, but I'll take whatever he'll give me. "I want you all over me."

It should feel dirty, but it feels just the opposite. I wait on my knees with my arms restrained, my breasts pushed out, craving the first drop of his cum on my body like a sinner at baptism. I want to smear it everywhere until it covers every inch of my skin. I want to bathe in everything Sin. I want him to cleanse me and make me his. I never want anyone else to touch me ever again. Hell, I never want to see anyone else ever again, I just want to live in this bubble with him and never let it burst.

I'm already consumed by him, then he groans and braces a hand against the shower wall, pumping his cock and raining his cum down on me. Aside from the nearly painful level of arousal I'm currently experiencing, I feel so peaceful. When he groans with the last of his orgasm, he gathers me close, pulling my face against his pelvis.

I'm shameless, so I take the opportunity to lick his dick clean.

Rough laughter escapes him as he leans against his arm on the shower wall. "You're something else."

I beam up at him. "I'm addicted to you, what can I say?"

"I wasn't complaining," he assures me.

Once he recovers enough, he moves to unfasten my cuffs. He offers me a strong hand, helping me up, then he snatches the back of my neck and yanks me in for a kiss. My eyes drift closed and I kiss him back. Then my body arches closer to his as he pins me against the shower wall and kisses the fuck out of me.

"Spread your legs," he tells me.

Oh, thank God. I inch my legs apart until he reaches down and touches me. Just the touch of his hand knocks my heart out of my chest. I have to grab onto his shoulders, my breath hitching as the pad of his thumb brushes my clit. I'm hypersensitive, so turned on that my stomach is a mess of desire. My whole body is so twisted up, strung so tightly, needing relief so badly, it won't take much to get me there. I swear, the man could just *tell* me to come and I would.

He doesn't, but I think it would work. I'm swept away as he rubs me with his rough fingers, sending jolts of electricity coursing through my body. The tension in my tummy tightens and tightens. I'm grasping for purchase against the slippery tile wall, panting and whimpering as he works me into a frenzy. I need it so badly.

Pleasure attacks me, bursts open inside of me, consumes me. I cry out and Sin covers my lips with his, catching the sounds of my orgasm and trapping them in his beautiful mouth.

Weak and breathless, I cling to his powerful body, resting my head against his shoulder. I could stay like this forever, but I only stay until it feels like I can breathe again. Until the strength returns to my limbs and I'm confident I can stand without falling.

God, I love this man. I love every feeling he ignites inside me, things no one else has ever had access to. It's like my heart, body, and soul knew to wait for him.

I would wait forever for Sin, but I'm glad I won't have to.

36

LAUREL

I'm in heaven as Sin stands behind me in the shower, my body fitted snugly against his, one strong arm wrapped around my upper body to keep me close while he uses the other one to soap me up. Now that he's covered me in the evidence of his pleasure, he cleans it off, holding me in his arms all the while.

I'm sleepy and happy and all I want to do is live in this moment for the rest of my life.

Once we're both clean, it's time to leave the shower. I've never been sad to leave a shower before, but I should probably be relieved his hot water tank didn't chase us off before now.

The casual intimacy of standing in such close quarters and drying off after the shower gets me, too. I wouldn't have said I was holding back if asked, but the way I feel now, I must have been. My feelings for Sin haven't just been unleashed, they've intensified. Two days ago I could have convinced myself I could go to Chicago and lead a happy life without him, but right now, I don't know why I would ever want to.

I'm exactly where I belong, and I never want to leave.

As if reciprocating the thoughts I didn't give voice to, Sin appears in the mirror behind me, wrapping his arm around my waist and kissing the ball of my shoulder.

"Every shower I take alone now for the rest of my life will be an immense disappointment."

Smirking and placing my hand over his around my waist, I say, "No kidding."

We go to his bedroom, still with damp hair, wearing nothing more than towels. I don't even want something as flimsy as material between us, so I drop my towel and climb on his bed naked.

Sin slows in front of the bed, but doesn't move to follow me. His eyes rake over me, a gleam of interest on the surface. I wait to see what he'll do. I really want him to fuck me. I can feel him opening up more to me today than he has before, so I don't know what we're waiting for.

"Spread your legs," he tells me.

A faint flush crawls up my neck, heating my cheeks, but I do as I'm told. I watch him as I part my legs, baring myself for him. Even though he just got me off, I feel the stirring of arousal as his hot gaze lingers on me, like he's looking at something beautiful. Something he likes a whole hell of a lot. I've never had someone *look* at me there the way he does.

After a moment, I finally break in to tease him a little. "See anything you like?"

His gaze drifts to my face and he smirks. "Oh, yeah."

I smile, but then he drops his towel and my smile melts as my gaze drops. I realize when I have the chance, I'm admiring his dick just as much. My love for his dick is intensely irrational and I've never experienced it before. If I could look at it, hold it, or taste it endlessly, I would.

Sin places his palms down on the bed, narrowing his eyes

in a predatory fashion, then he pounces on me. I grin as he climbs on top of my body, bringing my hands to his sides and tugging him down for a kiss. Now that I can have those, we have a lot of lost kisses to make up for.

He leans down in his own time despite my tugging. Then his lips brush mine and I sigh with pleasure. I love all of this so much. I want to ask if I get to stay here after this, but I'm too afraid the answer will be no, and I don't want to ruin it.

When his lips leave mine, I decide to ask about something else I noticed the night he took his shirt off at Rafe's. I intended to ask that night, but then that stupid whore texted him.

Well, I guess now she's dead, so I shouldn't call her a whore anymore. Not altogether sure how I feel about that, but hey, if she tried to poison me, the bitch had it coming.

I reach a hand up and rest it on the inside of his left bicep. There was no tattoo there when I was in his bed before, but now there are a pair of handcuffs inked into his skin.

"This is new," I say.

"It is."

"Why did you get this one?"

He glances at the tattoo, casually flexing his bicep as he does. "Same reason I got the others. I hurt a woman I cared about. If I leave a mark on them, they should get a mark on me."

My stomach drops. I'm not sure if it's because I must be the woman he's talking about—that must be *my* mark on his body—or because when I met him, he already had two other tattoos. That means he hurt two other women who matter to him—or mattered.

"You got it for me?" I question, since that's the safest question.

He nods his head, his lips curving up faintly. "It seemed fitting."

Despite my anxiety, I offer a little smile back and roll my eyes. "Because you held me captive, you big brute."

Sin shakes his head. "Nah. I may have kidnapped you, but you're the one who's held me captive."

My stomach sinks again. I reach up and grab his shoulders, yanking him down until his perfect lips are on mine again. He gets so many kisses for saying that. I never want to stop kissing him. I lock my legs around his hips, pulling him against me. I want him inside me, but I'll settle for as close as I can get him. As I kiss him, I push my fingers through his hair, overcome with tenderness, bursting with affection. There's nothing better than his naked body pressed against mine.

I feel him getting hard again and it triggers arousal in my core. Before I can get too excited and think he might *actually* fuck me now, he breaks our kiss and pulls back to look at me.

"Don't you want to know who the others ones are for?" he asks, like he was waiting for me to ask.

"Sorta." I cock my head in consideration. "But I also really want you to fuck me, and I feel like that's close to being on the table."

"I'm not going to fuck you before I tell this story. If you distract me you will get an orgasm out of it, but I'm not going to fuck you."

Sighing heavily, I relent. "Fine. Let's do this. Tell me whatever dark secret is lurking in your past. It's not going to change anything for me."

"Well, I hope not, but I have to be sure. Things with you have gone way too far beyond casual for me. I fuck you, that's it. That changes things between us, things that can't be changed back again."

I remember him saying something similar when he thought I'd slept with Rafe again after the night I saw Sin with Marlena, how I might not have been Rafe's before, but I changed that when I slept with him. "Sex is permanent for you," I say. It's not a question. I don't entirely understand, but the evidence points to that conclusion.

"Sex with someone I love is."

My eyes go wide and his gaze drops.

"Ah, Christ," he mutters, raking a hand through his hair.

"No." I reach up, my heart pounding in my chest, by tummy filling up with butterflies. "It's okay. I love you, too, Sin."

"I've never fallen for someone this fast before," he says, like he's trying to explain. I don't know why he thinks he needs to, given I suffer from the same affliction.

"I have a theory," I tell him. "Sometimes people in... I don't even know how to describe our situation and circumstances, but... Sometimes when two people go through something together, they form an attachment to each other. My sister could probably explain it better, but the point is, I don't think there's anything wrong with us. I think our circumstances opened a door, and our compatibility with one another lured us through it."

"Does it last?"

He asks so earnestly, it makes my heart ache. Reaching a hand up to caress his face, I nod my head. "Sure, it can. It's like any other kind of connection. What happens next is up to the two people involved. It could amount to nothing, or you could choose to build something that endures. The connection is just the beginning, Sin. We decide if it lasts."

"I want it to last," he tells me.

"So do I," I assure him.

His gaze drifts past me at the bed for a moment, like he's lost in thought. All of a sudden he climbs off me, moving over to his side of the bed. I climb into my spot, preparing to lie down and cuddle with him, but he doesn't lie down; he reaches into his nightstand drawer.

A moment later he turns around with something in his hand, something so small that I have no idea what it might be with his hand closed. He hesitates another moment, then unclenches his fist.

My eyes widen as the light in his room catches on a golden band nestled in the palm of his hand—a wedding ring. I don't know what I'm supposed to do with it, so after staring at it for a moment, I look up at him.

"I used to be married."

That's the logical assumption to draw from him presenting a wedding band, so I don't know why his words cause my stomach to drop, but they do. "Okay," I say with forced calm.

Nodding at the kneeling angel on his right arm, he says, "That one is for my wife."

I cringe, hearing him say those words. Shit, that shouldn't sting. Clearly she isn't his wife anymore. I wish he would call her his *ex-wife,* but this isn't the time to be territorial, so I shake it off.

"Paula," he adds. "Her name was Paula."

I don't know if I should keep urging him, or just wait for him to tell me everything, but it seems like he's trying to get the words out. Or maybe trying to get them right? For now, I remain silent and let him talk in his own time.

Looking down at the band in his hand, he says, "We got married young. You may have picked this up, but I tend to be a one and done kind of man. I don't piss around looking at what else is out there once I have something worth hanging onto. I lock it down and that's it."

Smiling faintly, I nod my head. "I like that about you."

"Yeah, she did too, back then." He says it absently, maybe a little dismissively. He says it the way you talk about something you don't believe anymore—just a review of what you thought then, before you knew you were wrong. "Thing is, it *didn't* last. I liked our life. Even when it got harder, less exciting. Even when it wasn't perfect, I never wanted to leave it. To me, it was just something we needed to get around to fixing. She felt differently."

Even though a small, selfish part of me is glad this idiot threw him out so I could have him, the larger part of me feels bad for the pain this must have inflicted on him. "She left you?" I surmise.

He shakes his head, looking a little haunted. "No. That would have been one thing, I guess. Direct enough that I know there's a problem I clearly need to fix. No, that's not what she did. I felt her pull back, I started to notice distance, but I didn't want to see it. She stopped responding to things, even when I would try. If I'd surprise her with something I knew she liked, she could hardly muster a smile. It was like she was just so fucking tired of me, nothing I did could renew her interest."

I want to hug him. I *need* to hug him. I can hear leftover agony in his voice, and it hurts me—not in a jealous way, I just don't want him to relive this old pain. I don't need him to. He was married and now he's not—fine. I can accept that. Not a big deal. Let's put it behind us and never think about it again.

"This part's almost funny," he says, glancing at me, though there's no humor expressed in his features. "She came onto Rafe one night when we were all hanging out, when I was in the other room. He came and told me because, you know, we were friends. I told him he read too much into nothing. I didn't want to believe that, you know?"

I nod. "Sure, of course."

"I should have confronted her that night. We should have fought. There should have been a big fucking blowout where we just aired all our problems and dealt with it—I realized that later, but at the time, I just.... I convinced myself she would stop, she was just bored and acting out for some reason. I told myself the problem would fix itself, even though I know from professional experience, problems almost never fix themselves. I had my head in the sand. I was young, you know."

I remember him telling me I'm young that night he said all those awful things and chased me off. It seems like he has more faith in me now than he did then, but the way he uses youth as an excuse has me thinking we should touch on this base again later so I can remind him my age doesn't mean I'm an idiot.

Finally, he says, "She cheated on me."

Oh, God. "Not with Rafe?"

That startles him, and he finally looks at me. "No, no. Not with Rafe."

Sighing with relief, I nod my head. "Okay."

His mouth curves up faintly now. "You think I'd have stayed his friend after that? Fuck no. No, our relationship wasn't complicated until you came along. Before that, we were friends. Neither one of us would have ever worried about leaving our wives alone with the other."

That makes me feel kinda shitty. "Sorry," I murmur.

He transfers his old wedding ring to the other hand, freeing up the one closest to me so he can reach over and place his hand over mine. "None of this is your fault."

I don't want to drag him off track, so I tell him, "Anyway, sorry, I interrupted. What happened?"

"She got pregnant," he states, looking down at the bedding. Just in case there's any doubt, he adds, "Not by me."

"Oh, Sin." Now my heart isn't the only thing aching—my stomach joins in.

He doesn't look up. "When she told me, I think she expected that to be it. Most sane people would probably... they'd be done at that point, but I wasn't. I'd made a commitment, and I intended to see it through. I was so pissed and hurt and—" He trails off, shaking his head, like he can't find the right words. "My whole life was just ripped out from under me in an instant. I should have had the upper hand—she fucked up, everything was fucked up, but she'd be sorry and she would be desperate to fix things. It was too big for me to shove aside and ignore, too big to pretend it didn't happen. This wasn't flirting with my friend, this was fucking another man and getting pregnant by him. This was fucking huge. Insurmountable, some might say. But none of that happened. She wasn't sorry. She wasn't desperate to fix things. She was cold, detached. Told me there was nothing *I* could do to fix it—me, like I was the one who fucked up. Our marriage wasn't even over, and she had already moved on. She told me she was leaving me for that fucking asshole, and I saw red. Literally... just a red haze overtook me. I didn't even realize what I was doing until it was too late."

Oh, God. Oh, no, please not this. I want to stop him, I want to beg him not to tell me his deep dark secret is that he killed his pregnant wife. I swore to him nothing he said would change things for me, but I cannot stomach the idea of *that* being the skeleton in his closet.

I fight the urge to clamp my hands over my ears, but just barely.

Fuck. My mind is already trying to salvage this, reaching

for excuses—a crime of passion, temporary insanity, perhaps a legitimate mental break as his life shattered, an episode of psychosis. Things that would make this less his fault.

None of them make me feel less icky.

Why wouldn't Rafe have played that card? How could he leave me here alone with Sin after that helicopter date if he knew Sin had a history of snapping like that? I could have been killed!

Unaware of my nervous breakdown, Sin continues his story. "I drove to the guy's house. I knew who he was, but I don't know how she met him. I meant to ask her, but I forgot. It didn't matter anymore, all that mattered was making it go away. Making all of it go away. Getting control over my life, because it was spinning the fuck out of control."

"Was this after...?" I halt, not knowing how to phrase this. *After you killed your pregnant wife?*

Sin frowns slightly. "After she told me she was pregnant? Of course. So, anyway, I go over and get this guy and I bring him back to our house. Paula's here, but she doesn't know what's going on."

Wait, Paula is alive? I realize I got the story he's telling and the story in my head confused—he has *not* killed the wife, he just left his house in a hazy red fog and went to get the man she cheated with. Okay, I'm back on track. *Phew.*

"I bring him inside and she freaks out. I mean, I was pissed, so it wasn't pretty. His face was all busted up, I had already beat the living shit out of him. She was flipping the fuck out, calling me a psycho, telling me I was going to get us all killed."

"Get you all killed?" I question.

"He was connected. Ran with a rival crew."

I nod my understanding. "Got it."

"Now, I could hear her, but I couldn't find it within me to care. I hauled his ass upstairs to the bathroom, shoved him in the bathtub. I went back and got her, dragged her upstairs."

Oh shit, I hope he isn't getting to the "then murdered her" part. I won't jump to conclusions this time, but I'm struggling to see a way this story ends without someone being murdered.

"I cuffed her to the towel rack on the wall by the sink. I didn't have the house set up the way I do now, so I didn't have the bars. Towel rack had to suffice." He pauses, glancing at me briefly, but then turning his attention back to the bedding, like he can't look at me for this next part. "I chained her there and made her watch while I bludgeoned him to death in our bathtub. The whole time she's screaming bloody murder, begging me to stop, but I couldn't. I wouldn't. Not until he was dead."

Wow. This is pretty fucking intense.

"She knew what I did for a living, that I did dirty work for the Morelli family, but she had never seen it with her own two eyes. She'd never seen me like that. It horrified her, understandably. She was screaming and crying, telling me not to touch her, that I was a monster."

I flinch, remembering when I called him a monster before I fled Vegas.

"I knew she wasn't going to stay after that. She was terrified of me at first, then when she realized I wasn't going to kill her too, it all turned to hatred. She fucking hated me. The sane thing to do at this point, I realize, would have been to let her go. Let it end, let her get away from me."

Grimacing, I say, "I take it that's not what happened."

"That is not what happened," he verifies. "I convinced myself that with the other asshole gone, we could come back from what happened. The cheating, killing that motherfucker, the pregnancy. We had always planned to have a family one day. It wasn't the way I pictured it, obviously, but I still loved her even after all that. Or, I convinced myself I did, anyway. Looking back, I don't know if I can call that love. Anyway, I installed shit all over the house so I could keep her here, whether she wanted to be here or not. For a while, I had to keep her locked up a lot of the time."

Oh, God.

"I realize how this sounds," he says, glancing at me again.

"I'm still listening," I assure him.

He nods, dropping the wedding band on the blanket and looking at it. "Eventually, it got almost normal. Time passed. Her love didn't come back, she didn't even like me anymore, but the baby was growing in her belly and she was changing. I won't lie, I was pretty excited to be a father, regardless of how it all went down. The baby would still be half her, even if it wouldn't be half me. And then she was born. Ellie. My sunshine."

He looks sadder now than he ever has in my presence, and I can't help leaning over and wrapping my arms around him. Before, *I* needed a hug, but now I sense *he* needs one.

"She was perfect. As soon as I saw her little face..." Sin stops, shaking his head and clearing his throat. "She was mine. It didn't matter if she wasn't really mine, that was my daughter, and I loved her. More than anything. Once Ellie came, everything changed. I took care of her every minute I was home. I'm the one who put her to bed every night. We finally felt like a normal family—maybe not the happiest family, but hell, every marriage has its rough patches."

I lift my eyebrows, not entirely sure his situation falls under "rough patch," but sure, I guess we'll go with that.

"Paula was less hostile because she had a baby to love on, and I think seeing how much I loved Ellie finally softened her toward me a little. I could have still been an asshole to her about what she did, but I wasn't. I just wanted to give Ellie a happy life, I didn't want to fight over shit that couldn't be changed. I had this idea that maybe being a family would make her fall back in love with me. That didn't happen, but she did grow to tolerate me. By that time, I wasn't forcing her to stay anymore, she just... stayed."

Now he pauses to sigh and drag his hands over his face in such a way that it's impossible not to feel dread. A knot of it forms in my stomach, because I have a bad feeling I know where this is going, and while it's certainly not a dealbreaker, it is going to stress me out. If Paula left him and took that baby with her, I am going to have to accept that even if Sin is mine now, there will be a part of his heart out there in the world that I will never be able to touch. What if she came back? What would happen to us then?

Moving his body, he looks back toward the tattoo on his back. "Ellie's favorite song was *You Are My Sunshine*, so I got this one for her."

I examine the tattoo, running my finger over the symbol in the center of the sun. "Why is this in the middle?"

"It's a trinity knot."

"Like, the Holy Trinity? I thought you weren't religious."

He shakes his head. "That's not what it meant for me. It was three separate entities knotted together. It represented our family to me. Me, Paula, and Ellie. Bound to each other. It was an unbreakable bond."

At least, to *him* it was an unbreakable bond.

"So, anyway, we made it through Ellie's first year. Threw her a big birthday party in the backyard. Things were finally good again—not perfect, but good. When Ellie was opening her presents—she had a ton of presents, just so much stuff—we

374 | SINNING IN VEGAS

lost track of who some of them were from. Some had arrived in the mail that week from out of town. She got bored of opening them before she finished anyway, so I helped her. One of the unmarked boxes had three little coffins in it, nothing else."

Dread sinks into my gut again, but before I have time to let my imagination run wild, he starts talking again.

"About a month later I came home late from work one night and the house was dark. It was late enough that it was dark outside, but not so late that Paula should have been in bed. Her car was in the driveway, so she had to be home. The house should not have been dark. A sick feeling came over me. I knew something wasn't right."

"Oh, God," I murmur, covering my face with my hands.

"When I opened the door, I was hit by the smell. It wasn't a sickening stench, but it smelled off. The house was hot. The air had been turned off, and Paula never turned the air off. She liked it cold. The heat was why it already smelled, though. Someone wanted the house to smell when I walked in. They wanted me to know what I was going to find before I found it. I turned on the light and walked up the stairs, and right at the top, lying face-down on the hardwood floor... Paula. Her eyes were open. Cloudy. She was lying in a pool of her own blood. She'd been brutalized before they killed her."

"Oh, Sin..." I have no idea what to say, and I'm terrified to hear the rest. Terrified.

"I ran upstairs. Paula had obviously been dead for hours, but I didn't know... I didn't know if Ellie was okay, or if they took her. Then I opened her bedroom door..." He stops, bowing his head and massaging his temples. "They killed her, too."

I'm sick to my stomach, tears burning behind my eyes. I

need air, I need to get away from this horror, but I can't. He needs to finish.

"I lost my fucking mind. They left their calling card in her room for me to find. I guess they didn't know Ellie wasn't mine. It probably made more sense to them to think she was—that after Paula cheated, she stayed with me because she was pregnant." Shaking his head, he says, "Anyway, it was retaliation. Paula and Ellie were dead because I killed the asshole she cheated with. At first I thought they only left me alive because I wasn't home—the three coffins—but it didn't take long before I realized what they did to me was worse than death. They took everything I loved and made me survive it." He shakes his head, looking down. "I had to have retribution, but I couldn't take them on myself. I took it to the Morellis. Rafe helped, he convinced Ben we could squash them. We did. We took them all out. I got my revenge. Didn't matter though. Didn't bring my family back."

I can't hold back tears any longer. Burying myself in his side, I wrap my arms around him and hug him. "I'm so sorry, Sin. I don't... I have no words."

He pushes my hair back over my shoulder, tips my head up so I'm looking at him, and shakes his head as he brushes away my tears. "Don't cry for me. It was my fault."

"No, it was not. If it was anyone's fault, it was Paula's. She was your *wife*. She didn't have to cheat."

"And I didn't have to kill the bastard," he reasons. "But I did."

37

LAUREL

The idea of him taking responsibility for this atrocity, carrying that on his shoulders for all these years, hurts my heart. He said he hasn't kissed anyone in a long time—did he mean since Paula? Did he ever move on from this, or did he just stop living when they died? Maybe if he blames himself, he thinks he deserves that.

"Sin, you can't blame yourself. What happened was not your fault."

"My actions had consequences. Her actions had consequences. Before that, our inaction had consequences. We both knew we weren't happy, but we didn't fix it. It was a chain of consequences, it wasn't just one thing, but *mine* is the transgression that resulted in their deaths. Mine."

I shake my head, climbing on his lap and wrapping myself around him. "I'm so sorry that happened to you. That's horrifying. I literally don't know what to say. That's the worst thing I've ever heard. It literally breaks my heart that you had to go through that, especially alone. I wish I had known you then. I wish I could have been there for you."

"You were a kid," he points out. "That would've been weird."

"I don't care," I mutter. "I could have still been a shoulder to cry on."

"I would not have cried on your 15-year-old shoulder."

All I want to do is comfort him, and I can't find the words to do it. Instead, I press tender kisses along his jawline, caressing the other side of his face with my free hand. I want to wrap him up in my love and protect him from the pain of his past. I want to rewind to the times I may have said unknowingly hurtful things and shove all the words back inside my mouth.

There's one in particular I *need* to take back. Leaning back just enough to meet his gaze, I tell him, "You're not a monster. I'm so sorry I said that to you. I didn't know... but I shouldn't have said it anyway. My feelings were just hurt, and—"

Sin cuts me off with his finger against my lips, shaking his head at me. "You don't have to apologize. I was a dick. I deserved your wrath." Running his fingers through my hair and regarding me curiously, he says, "This is not the response I expected to that story."

"What did you expect?" I ask. "For me to run away from your house screaming?"

"I don't know, less affection, more caution. I just told you I cuffed my wife to the wall and made her watch me bludgeon her lover to death."

"In your defense, she shouldn't have *had* a lover for you to bludgeon to death," I point out.

He stares at me. "Laurel."

Sighing, I shrug my shoulders. "I don't know what to tell you. I know who you are, Sin. I know the violence you're capable of. I didn't expect you to be a big loving teddy bear 100% of the time."

Cocking an eyebrow, he says, "I hope your expectation there is closer to 0% of the time, because if not, it's wrong."

I want to crack a smile, but I can't. I'm still too sad from his story, and the fact that he's been suffering over it for so long. "I mean, it's not a nice story, but... it's yours. I would never make the decisions she made, so it isn't relevant to me. I would never put either one of us in that situation to begin with."

"Some people considered it an overreaction," he tells me.

I shrug. "I'm not your judge and jury. I'm not here to tell you what's right or wrong. You responded emotionally to someone ripping your heart out. I would too. I mean, I'd probably just slash tires instead of actually killing someone, but we're different people. It's weird, but that's your life. I get that. I sort of joked about wanting to kill Marlena when I thought you were hooking up with her, and you weren't even mine, as you pointed out. I can only imagine how crazy I would feel in your circumstances. But I would *never* put you in that position. Not ever."

His arms are wrapped around me, his hands caressing my lower back as I talk. Now that I'm done, he warns me, "This part won't last forever. The fascination. The excitement. You won't always feel addicted to me."

"I'm not sure about that," I tell him, resting my arms on his shoulders. "You're pretty addictive. I trust Paula's choice in shoes, but not men—not if she had you and she went looking elsewhere. Maybe it was her. Maybe she needed a lot of male attention. I don't. I'm happy to just have yours."

"Or maybe you just want to blame her and let me off the hook," he suggests.

"It's possible," I admit, leaning forward and catching his

lower lip between mine, sucking on it then releasing it and kissing the corner of his mouth. "Either way, this hasn't changed anything for me, so if this is what you were waiting for... We're good."

"You're sure?" he asks.

I nod my head. "Super sure. I was worried for a minute that story was heading in a different direction that would have made me more nervous, but as you told it, nothing I can't live with."

"Where were you afraid it was going?" he inquires.

Grimacing, I tell him, "I can't tell you that now. I don't want to offend you."

Drawing me close until my breasts are crushed against his chest, he demands, "Tell me."

I sigh, but as his hand moves up my back and his eyes bore into mine, insistent, demanding, I relent. It's too hard to deny him. "Don't be mad. When you were talking about how she had cheated and you went into a rage fog, I thought *maybe...* you might have killed her."

That's not exactly a nice thing to say to someone, but he doesn't get mad. "Makes sense. Definitely didn't do that, but I can see how you'd get there."

Reaching back and grabbing his wedding ring, I move it to the end table so it doesn't get lost. I'm not entirely sure where we're supposed to go from here, what should follow a story like that one. When I look around this empty house now, it looks a little bit different. I wonder what it looked like when he had a wife, a family, a whole life. I wonder if the sparseness now is intentional, if in some quiet corner of his mind he feels he deserves the emptiness.

He doesn't deserve emptiness. This may be the man who kidnapped me, but this is also a man capable of loving women

380 | SINNING IN VEGAS

who fuck everything up, fathering babies that aren't his. He's incredible, and I don't care how fucked up his moral compass is. I'm not here to play morality police. I got knocked up by a mob boss during a one night stand, for fuck's sake. So Sin murdered the dickhead who had sex with his wife—that's not so crazy, given what he does for work. That dumbass should have known better than to fuck with Sin.

There is nothing in his past I'm interested in holding against him. I want his present, I want his future. I want to fill the empty rooms in this house once more; I want to creep down the hall and stand in the doorway, spying on him while he puts my baby to bed in its crib.

My heart aches with how much I want all that.

I can't believe he thought I would greet any of this with anything less than tenderness and sympathy.

I catch his ruggedly handsome face between my hands again and just look at him. I admire the perfect amount of stubble dusting his strong jaw, his soft lips, his gorgeous eyes. I rub my cheek against his to feel the scratch, then—because I can now—I brush my lips against his.

When I pull back I catch his big hand in my smaller one and drag it down, placing his palm over my abdomen. "I know it's messy, and I know it would be nicer if you were the baby's actual father, but... this one needs a daddy."

He smiles, catching the back of my neck and tugging me in for a kiss. After a few soft kisses he murmurs, "Oh yeah?"

"Mm hmm," I murmur, resting my forehead against his. "And if your help the night I had Skylar was your tryout for the position, I have to tell you, you're a shoo-in."

"A shoo-in?" he repeats. "That implies I have competition. Didn't you hear that story I just told? I'm not a big fan of competition."

"Nah, just Rafe, and I wouldn't consider him competition. I think he'll be more of a fun uncle than dad material. Babies just aren't his jam."

"His loss," Sin tells me, rubbing my still-flat belly.

"I'm not sad about it," I assure him. "Can I stay here now, or do I have to go back there?"

Sighing, Sin says, "You'll have to go back to his house tonight. As long as everything goes according to plan, this is the last time though. Tomorrow you'll be coming home with me to stay."

"I like that a lot. I would like it better if I didn't have to go back, though. I don't want to sleep next to him another night, I'd rather be here with you."

"Trust me, I would like that better, too," he assures me. "It's just one more night."

The day slips away faster than I want it to. Sin and I spend most of the time in bed talking and cuddling. He drifts off at one point and I let him sleep, figuring he probably needs it. I'm content to lie in his arms, listening to the beat of his heart, the steady sound of his breathing.

He hasn't told me what the plan is, but it's impossible not to worry about it. Before, he said we couldn't be together, and now he says we will be starting tomorrow, so what changed?

I know there is probably nothing I can do about it and worrying won't help, so I try not to. I think about the nights I stayed here with him before and look forward to the nights we'll have after tomorrow. It's crazy that we have spent so few nights together. I've spent many more nights with guys I liked much less, but Sin is in a class of his own. I've never known anyone like him in all my life, and I know I never will again. He's one of a kind.

I don't know what my sister is going to say about this though. Actually, I think I do, and that's the problem. When I tell her I'm going to move to Las Vegas to be with a man she has never even heard of—and no, not because he knocked me up, he *works for* the guy who knocked me up—she is going to have a freaking heart attack.

Maybe I should take a picture of Sin's super sexy body to show her and help her understand. She's always joking that Vince gets away with more because of his six-pack, and Sin is way hotter than Vince. Or, I guess I should think that, given Vince is my brother-in-law.

But also, no, he just really is. No one is hotter than Sin. I know I'm biased, but I'm also pretty confident in this assertion.

Once I show her all he's got going on, I can add in the stuff that matters—when Rafe failed to impress, Sin stepped up and wanted to parent this baby with me, even though it's not his responsibility. He's so protective of me that he would literally kill anyone who tried to hurt me. Hell, I can even sell him as a gentleman, since we haven't had sex yet. He's waiting for me—even though I definitely don't want to wait. I won't tell her that, because then she'll get all suspicious about his issues, and those are none of her business.

I will definitely leave out the fine details of that situation, but a widower who lost his family? She should feel softer toward him after hearing that.

Yeah, I can totally make her like Sin. Hopefully they don't discuss any of the many things she would hate about him. Maybe I can prepare him before her visit. Then again, what can I say? Don't be yourself? Can't ask that. I doubt he would, anyway. He may protect me, but he's no pussycat; he's going to do whatever he damn well pleases. My sexy, stubborn cave-man. I don't know what I'm gonna do with him. Maybe I can introduce Carly from a distance and just have her wave at him, then hurry her out to go baby shopping.

I don't want her to be disappointed or think I've lost my mind again. I don't want her to think this is anything like that weekend with Rafe, because it's not. It's so much more than that, but I'm not sure she'll see it that way.

I run my hand along the V-shaped pelvic muscle on Sin's body that makes me forget all about the practical problems we may have. Looking at it now, I'm tempted to lick it. I don't want to wake him up, otherwise I would.

Then again... I grab my phone, checking the time. It is approaching dinner time. He's probably going to need to feed me soon. Maybe I could wake him up. It's not like he's bound to complain when he wakes up to my mouth hovering over his pelvic region. I'm no tease; he knows I'll happily follow through.

Yep, it's decided. I crawl down the bed, pulling my hair over my shoulder and dropping a soft kiss at the top of his V, then trailing kisses all the way down to his cock. I move across and run my tongue along the other side of his V, and when I make my way back down, his cock is hardening.

I bite back a grin, peeking up at him. Sure enough, he's looking down at me with sleepy, hooded eyes. "That's one way to get me up," he murmurs.

"I look forward to discovering all the others," I tell him.

"If this your method of figuring them all out, I approve of this plan."

"You know something?" I ask, taking his cock in my hand and stroking it. "If you wanted to fuck me a day early, I wouldn't object. It could be our little secret."

"Tomorrow," he tells me.

"Why not today?" I ask, before bending my head to lick the head of his cock like an ice cream cone. "You know I'll happily suck you, but I desperately want you inside me."

Reaching down and grabbing me, he tugs me up his body and settles me against his chest. "I said tomorrow. My terms, not yours, remember?"

"This seems unfair. I object. I'm going to collect signatures and file a petition."

Smiling faintly, he tells me, "By the time you do all that, it'll be well past tomorrow. You'll be so busy getting your signatures, you won't even have time to get fucked."

Nodding once in consideration, I admit, "It wasn't a well thought out plan." Then, because I'm honestly baffled, I ask, "Why am I more impatient about this than you are?"

"Because I know something you don't," he tells me.

Cocking an eyebrow, I say, "Go on."

His fingers tenderly trace the curve of my face, somewhat negating the brutishness of his next words. "Once you open those pretty little legs and let me fuck you, I'm the last man that ever will. I'll literally kill any bastard who thinks he can touch you once you're mine."

"Ever, huh?" I ask, casually. "That's kind of a long time."

"A very long time."

"Almost like a formal commitment," I add.

He nods his head. "Exactly like a formal commitment. Once I fuck you, we might as well be married, because that's it. You belong to me."

I smile, snuggling against his chest. "You're a sexy maniac. I like it. I don't object to any of this, though. What's the difference if it's today or tomorrow? I can get the paperwork ready and sign the Laurel deed over to you right now. No rush charge or anything."

Sin cracks a smile. "Tomorrow."

There's only one conclusion I can possibly draw from this, so I decide to ask. "You can't seriously think I would sleep with Rafe tonight. I already told you I wouldn't even kiss him."

"You can fuck without kissing. And no, I don't think you have any intention of sleeping with Rafe tonight, but just in case he picks up on your absence today and... I just want to wait until tomorrow."

"What am I supposed to do if he *does* pick up on my absence today?"

"Say you went shopping."

"And bought nothing?" I ask, skeptically. "You're asking for another Winnefer situation."

"You left the books you brought home after your date here. They're in the closet. Grab a book out of there, say you were at the bookstore."

As much as I hate to ask, I have to. "What's going to happen, Sin?"

"Don't worry about it," he tells me, pulling me more snugly against him.

"I understand you can't give me all the dirty details, I just want to know that everyone is going to be okay," I tell him. "Can you at least give me that?"

"I can't make any kind of guarantee, Laurel. I'm sorry, I know this involves you too, but I can't talk to you about this. I can't tell you things and then send you off to Rafe. If I want to make sure he stays in the dark, I have to keep you in the dark, too."

A chill runs down my spine at that. "Does that mean you're going to hurt Rafe?"

"Please stop asking me questions I can't answer."

My tummy roils in protest. Maybe I don't have the stomach for this. Placing a hand over my abdomen, I picture Rafe—not the Rafe I live with right now, but Rafe when he tries. Rafe when he's charming. Rafe when he's nice and not plotting against me. However much of an asshole he has been, I don't want anything to happen to him. Everyone is an asshole sometimes. I can forgive him for being a jerkface. None of us knew exactly what to do in this scenario.

Then again, he was vaguely threatening Sin the other night, and I am sort of stuck with him right now. We aren't even dating, and we're already in a loveless "marriage" of convenience.

I can feel Sin's eyes on me as I go quiet, thinking about all this. It's like he knows where my mind is and it irritates him.

"If it comes down to a choice between his side and mine, you're on mine," he says, though there's a hint of question there, like he needs verification.

"I don't want you guys to *be* on opposite sides," I tell him. "I want his side and yours to be the same. I only want to *be* with you, but..." I trail off, shaking my head.

"I understand that. But in the event that isn't possible. If only one of us is left standing at the end, I need to know you want it to be me. And if you *don't*, you need to tell me that now.

Don't worry about my feelings or a fight. If there is some sleeper cell within you that *does* want to be with Rafe, you need to tell me that right now. Tomorrow is too late."

"I don't," I swear, shaking my head. "It's not about being with him. It's nothing romantic. It's not like that. I just want a future where we all get along, and I don't see why we can't have that. Rafe isn't in love with me. This isn't going to break his heart. His major issue right now isn't how much he cares about me, it's that he's the boss, and it would look bad to his men if he lost the chick he knocked up to his enforcer." I roll my eyes. "It's incredibly stupid, and how many of his men even know that? His cousin Gio, Lydia, you—it's not like his whole crew even knows about me yet. It's really none of their business."

"He said that?" Sin questions. "He said his problem is what people will think if you're with me?"

I nod my head. "Some shit about how bosses don't divorce, how it looks bad if they can't even keep their own families together, how are they supposed to run things? It's dumb. It's literally all about his ego and his position, it has nothing to do with affection for me. If he'd stop being stubborn, he could even spin this like it was his idea. He didn't want to be shackled with a woman and a baby, so he was happy for you to take on the responsibility. I mean, I realize maybe *your* ego would get a ding that way, but it seems like a better solution than anyone having to die over this nonsense."

Sin frowns like he's pondering what I've just said, but before he can further comment, my phone vibrates on the bed beside me. I grab it and my stomach bottoms out when I see it's a text message from Rafe.

"Where are you?" he asks.

"It's him," I tell Sin, holding the screen up. "What should I say?"

Sin eases out from under me, throwing back the blanket and getting off the bed. "Tell him you're shopping. Tell him you're at the bookstore. Ask where he is."

"I don't like this," I tell Sin, shaking my head. "I don't know if I can do this. Why don't I just pretend I ran away again? I can say I'm going home, but I'll stay here. When the dust settles tomorrow—"

"We won't make it to tomorrow, because Rafe is not a moron, and he'll show up on my damn doorstep twenty minutes from now. Nobody wants that." Pulling up his pants, he turns back and shoots me a stern look. "Keep it together. You've got this."

I do not have this. He is super wrong. Swallowing down my nerves, I look down at my phone and try to remember how to type words.

I send him, "Bookstore. Where are you?"

He types back right away. "Came home for dinner. When did you leave?"

Instead of answering that, as my stomach knots up, I tell him, "I'm hungry too. Want to meet for food? I brought an Uber here, but I could walk over to that Italian restaurant we saw last time we were here. Remember? I told you I'd never been there. It's not a long walk and I could go for some pasta."

"We can go out," he sends back. "I don't want to go there though, we'll go to my restaurant. I'll pick you up."

My head snaps up. "Rafe is going to pick me up from the bookstore. How far are we from the bookstore? Dammit, I don't like lying."

"One day," Sin promises. "I don't like it either, but it's one day. Is he at his house? I can get you to the bookstore before he gets there. Get your clothes on, we have to leave now."

38

LAUREL

My fingers tremble as I flip open a brand new copy of *Jane Eyre*, moving slowly down the aisle as I wait to hear from Rafe. Sin just dropped me off after spending literally the whole ride here telling me over and over again that I *cannot* fuck this up, and I *cannot* try to help, and I *cannot* interfere in any way, because there *will* be hell to pay if I do.

I really want to interfere. It's extremely difficult not to. I'm not confident the men are handling this situation well, but Sin assures me I do not know the whole situation and I need to keep my nose out of it.

So, I'm burying my nose in this book and hoping against hope that Rafe isn't suspicious when he gets here. My stomach is already rioting with nerves, my brain is castigating me. Basically, I can't take much more right now. I didn't feel badly about sneaking off with Sin until Rafe texted me, then all of a sudden I felt like I'd done something wrong. The simplistic part of my conscience was like, "Listen, you need to dump Rafe. I know you aren't technically dating, but you're now actively sexually involved with someone else, and the right thing to do is let Rafe know you guys are never gonna happen."

Meanwhile Sin was like, "Don't you fucking dare. This will all be over tomorrow anyway, so it doesn't matter."

Sin makes more sense. I don't know why I'm worried about doing the "right thing" when Rafe may be in actual mortal danger. But I can't warn Rafe, because that puts *Sin* in actual mortal danger.

Caring about two dangerous, homicidal men totally sucks.

"Didn't I buy you that book already?"

My stomach drops at the sound of Rafe's voice. I look up and see him heading up the aisle toward me. I nod my head. "You did. I love this book. Listen to this."

He moves closer and peers at the page as I read.

"'If all the world hated you, and believed you wicked, while your own conscience approved you, and absolved you from guilt, you would not be without friends."

Rafe reads from the page, "'If others don't love me, I would rather die than live.'" Cocking an eyebrow, he meets my gaze. "Someone is rather dramatic."

I smile, closing the book. "You wouldn't die without the love and admiration of others?"

"Certainly not. Their bad taste isn't *my* problem."

My happiness dies a swift death as my thoughts drift away from this aisle in the bookstore, away from *Jane Eyre*, and toward tomorrow, and whatever darkness that's going to bring. I know Sin told me not to interfere, but dammit, I want to so badly. I want to talk to Rafe. I want to reason with him. I want a future where we can bring our baby to the bookstore together and get ice cream, and then afterward, I can go home to Sin and we're all happy. I don't understand why we can't have that. It's so doable.

"What about you?" he asks casually, shoving his hands into his pockets. "If everyone hated you and believed you to be wicked, how would you feel?"

"I imagine it would depend whether or not they're right. It's hard to be happy if your happiness comes at the expense of someone else."

Rafe smiles, like that answer pleases him. "Only if you're a good person, kitten."

"Can *you* be happy if your happiness comes at the expense of others?" I ask him.

"Yes," he answers easily.

"Oh."

Draping his arm over my shoulder, he says, "That's an interesting quote to gravitate toward. Are you experiencing a conflicted conscience?"

It's hard not to stiffen, but he can feel me now, so I try to keep my body relaxed even though his question puts me on edge. I should know better than to talk to him at all. I should have told him I had laryngitis. I don't want him reading me today. Sin is trusting me to keep my damn mouth shut, and I don't want to try to withstand Rafe's prying powers.

"I gravitate toward plenty of quotes from this book," I tell him, leaning forward to replace it on the shelf.

"Don't put it back," he tells me. "We'll buy it."

"I already have it."

"This edition?"

"Well, no," I say.

"Get this one. Highlight all your favorite passages and I'll read it afterward. Try to ferret out why you like them," he says, smiling faintly.

Goddammit, it's like he knows. It's like he's burrowing into my heart and making my stomach hurt on purpose.

"I like you so much when we're in bookstores," I inform him.

"Maybe we should move into one," he suggests lightly.

"Maybe we should only ever talk to each other when I'm holding a book. It seems to make a difference."

"I do like the sight of you holding books. Reminds me of my professor fantasies."

Ugh, another fucking hit. He needs to stop. He's going to kill me with guilt.

I need to see Sin again. I need to know what is happening tomorrow. I can't do this. I can't keep quiet and wake up tomorrow in a Rafe-less world.

"Maybe you and I are better friends than lovers," I suggest, even as my heart turns over in my chest. "If we weren't together, we could still do things like this. We could still be friends. We could still take trips to the bookstore and grab lunch or dinner. You're well-versed at spending time with women you're not in relationships with. It's second nature to you at this point. I think we might even get along *better* if we took the pressure of a relationship off the table. I know you think people would see it as you not being able to manage your personal life, but I actually think it could look exactly the opposite if you spun it the right way. It would be the easiest thing in the world to believe you don't want to be tied down, that you *want* to keep your freedom. How could anyone who knows you possibly question that? Commitment isn't for you—so what? It's not for everybody. That doesn't make you incapable of handling your shit. If anyone tries to say shit about it, make an example out of them. Show them your strength as a leader and after you've decimated them, ask if anyone else has a problem with the way you run your family." I nod my head, confident in this plan. "This is a good plan. I don't want to say

I should be in charge of all your decisions, but, I mean, maybe."

Rafe nods absently, pulling his wallet out as we approach the cash register. "Are you done now?"

"Come on, you can't dispute any of that," I tell him.

He nods at the cashier. "Give the nice lady your book so we can go to dinner."

I sigh heavily, laying my book down on the counter. "It's a good idea," I grumble.

Rafe ignores me, pays for my book, and then walks me out to his car so we can go to dinner. I hope to pick the conversation back up in the car, mainly with Rafe saying, "You know, Laurel, you're right. Why don't you and I just be friends, you can be with Sin and do the heavy lifting parentally, and I'll pop in to have fun from time to time while still maintaining the freedom to bang as many pieces of cotton candy as I want to bang? That actually sounds perfect for me. Good thinking."

Because Rafe despises logic, apparently, that does not happen.

When we get to Rafe's restaurant, we go to his usual curved booth with the beautiful city view. Virginia is our waitress, as usual. She pops over to get our drink order, then goes to get them. While she's away, I notice Rafe looking around, his eyes narrowed as if in confusion.

"Everything okay?" I ask him.

Glancing back at me, he nods. "Yeah." Rather than further commenting, he nods at the copy of *Jane Eyre* I brought in and put down on the table in front of me. "Planning to start reading while we eat?"

"No, I just didn't want the book to get lonely in the car," I inform him.

Virginia comes back, serving Rafe first, then putting my

drink down in front of me. "Ooh, *Jane Eyre*. Good pick. First time reading it?"

I rest my hand on the cover. "Oh, no, I've read it a bunch of times. You like it?"

"Love it. Not Rochester, he's a dickface, but Jane is a kick. Sometimes awesome chicks like dickfaces; it's a fact of life, can't be helped."

I grin. "I really like you. I want to be friends."

"I've never received an in-person friend request before. I like your style. I accept. What can I get you to eat?" she asks, without pause.

"You think Jane is *awesome?*" Rafe asks, his tone tinged with disbelief.

"You don't?" she questions.

Rafe shrugs. "She's prickly. I don't like prickly. And I like Rochester."

"What?" she demands, her eyes bugging out. It only lasts for a moment, then she cocks her head from side to side and relents. "Okay, never mind, I can see that. You *would* like Rochester."

Rafe cocks a golden eyebrow at her. "What is that supposed to mean? Is that some variation of 'dickfaces stick together'?"

"I didn't say it," she tells him sweetly, leaning forward and swiping his menu. "What do you want to eat? I have other tables, you know."

"None as important as mine," he tells her, with exaggerated arrogance.

Virginia grins, her eyes shining with affection as she looks at him. "We're busy, and you're an ass. Tell me what you want or I'll order for you—really shake up your routine."

"I'm the one who signs your paychecks," he states. "You'll stay here as long as I want you to."

"Keep thinking that," she tells him, looking over at me. "What do you want, Laurel?"

"Chicken alfredo. No onions on my salad."

"Gotcha." Lifting an eyebrow, she looks at Rafe. "Last chance."

Instead of answering her, he makes a show of crossing his hands behind his head and leaning back, relaxing. "Let me think about it."

"Fine. You get what you get," she says, turning away, menus tucked beneath her arm.

"Hey, get back here," he calls after her, sitting forward.

"Nope," she calls back before rounding the corner and heading to check on another table.

"That little shit," he murmurs, as if surprised she followed through.

I shrug, opening my book and fanning the pages. "She gave you adequate warning. Should've just told her what you wanted."

"I wanted to fuck with her. She's not normally impatient with me. I wonder if I did something to piss her off."

"Probably. You're good at pissing women off," I inform him.

Rafe sits back, glancing over at me as I fondle my book. "I'm better at *getting* them off, but all the ones in my life lately are giant pains in the ass."

"Hey, I am not the pain in the ass. You are the pain in the ass in this non-relationship. You're the one who would rather keep me trapped even though you barely like me than tell your goons you'd rather stay single. I am the one who logically presented a better plan."

"Not this again," he says. "I do not barely like you. I *like* you. I would like you a lot more if you didn't want to fuck my enforcer."

"And I would like you a lot more if you actually wanted to parent our kid with me, but here we are," I shoot back.

Rafe sighs and lets his head fall back, staring at the ceiling. "For the love of God, can't we just have a simple dinner? I came home to see you, and this is what I get."

"Don't do me any favors," I tell him. "So sorry if having dinner with me cuts into your mandatory 40 hours a week socializing with skanks at night clubs."

"Don't act like you care. You're never there to scare them off, are you?"

"And I never will be," I assure him. "I am not your babysitter. If I can't trust your ass, I don't want your ass."

"Yes, I'm aware," he mutters, his eyes darkening. Without a word, he pushes up from the table.

"Where are you going?" I ask, watching him.

"To find my damn waitress."

39

LAUREL

When Rafe stormed off, I assumed he meant he was going after Virginia. She was the one he had just been concerned he pissed off, and she is obviously our waitress tonight.

But when Virginia returns to our table, Rafe isn't with her. She puts a drink down where he should be sitting and shoots me a polite smile before turning to walk away.

"Did Rafe find you?" I inquire, before she can get too far.

She turns back, her dark eyebrows drawn closer together in confusion. "Did he find me?" she questions.

"He said he was going to find his waitress. He thought he might have pissed you off. Apparently, you normally tolerate more of his shit."

"When I have time to indulge him, I do. He's such a baby sometimes. They all are though," she says, waving it off. "No, he didn't find me. I'll keep an eye out."

Just as she turns to walk away, Rafe rounds the corner and she nearly collides with him.

"Whoa," she murmurs, holding her hands up against his

chest, then taking a quick, awkward step back and dropping her hands.

Casually touching her hip, he says, "Sorry, wasn't watching where I was going."

"Uh huh." Her face is flushed and she's looking down, shaking her head slightly. It strikes me as a 'shake it off' sort of thing, then she puts a smile on and looks back up at him. "Laurel said you were looking for me?"

"No, I was looking for—Yes, I was looking for you."

Her smile tightens as he lies poorly, but she doesn't say anything.

"Aren't you still training Marlena?" he inquires.

"She didn't show up for her shift. No call, no show."

He scowls. "What?"

Virginia shrugs. "We're all trying to go on without her. Not having her constantly in the way as she accomplishes absolutely nothing is trying, but we're managing somehow. Now, if you don't need me to locate anyone else for you, I have to get back to work."

Then she's off. Rafe glances after her, shaking his head, but he takes his seat. "She's moody tonight."

"You're an idiot," I inform him.

He lifts his eyebrows. "Excuse me?"

"How can you notice and read into subtle shit, but be so blind to what's right in front of your eyeballs?" I shake my head, drawing my ice water close and taking a sip. "She likes you."

Instead of offering a playboy grin and taking pride in the adoration of yet another woman, he shakes his head. "Nah, not like that. Not Virginia."

"Why not Virginia?" I ask.

"She's too smart to fall for me," he says dryly.

I don't bother arguing with him, even though he's clearly wrong. Having experienced Rafe myself, I wouldn't wish him on her anyway. She's probably better off if he resides in denial and never looks at her that way.

With everything else going on, I forgot all about Marlena. If Rafe still expected her to be here, then he doesn't know she's dead. Will he find out, or will she just turn up missing? I have no idea *how* Sin killed her, or what he does with a body after a kill.

Then again, Sin said everything changes tomorrow, so Rafe probably won't have time to find out that Miss Cotton Candy kicked the bucket unless it happens tonight. He hasn't said whether he's staying at the house tonight or going out, but he clearly likes to go out, and since I'm not the most pleasant company tonight, he probably won't stay in.

On one hand, that's good, but on the other... I still don't want anything to happen to Rafe. It's so hard to prepare for tomorrow when I have no idea what will happen. My hope was that Rafe would suddenly come around today, then tonight I could reach out to Sin and tell him a miracle happened, Rafe will let us be together, call off whatever horrible thing he has planned.

I only have tonight and I was told explicitly not to interfere.

We get through the meal without fighting about anything else, but it's not the friendliest meal we've ever had together. It brings to mind the people-watching date we were supposed to go on, but we never got around to it. Something is always in the way for us. Anytime either of us has a spark of interest in the other, something happens to douse it.

It's not that I think I would be utterly miserable with Rafe all the time, it's just that being with Rafe would be settling, and I shouldn't have to settle. It's crazy to even consider *Rafe* settling when I'm sure so many women he has been with would trade a kidney for a chance to keep him, but I don't want to spend the rest of my life sleeping with a friend, and that's all Rafe is to me. He doesn't ignite me the way Sin does. I could never greet him with the same genuine enthusiasm. Sin insists I won't feel this way about him forever, that the infatuation will wear off someday, the passions will cool, but even if he's right, that will be after I got to experience it. While I *am* infatuated with him, we'll be building a solid foundation. If the excitement ever wears off, the relationship we built will still be there.

That's what is missing with Rafe. I have never been in love with him, and he has never been in love with me. In order for the flame to catch, there needs to be a spark to ignite it, and we can't seem to spark at the same time. I only like him when we're in bookstores or I'm worried for his life, and he only likes me when I'm naked or effortless.

Rafe and I don't just lack the building blocks to form a strong foundation, we can't even find the building blocks store. Meanwhile, when I'm with Sin, building blocks rain down from the sky like colorful tiles in Tetris.

I'm not a quitter, but I'm not a settler, either. Why should I settle into a relationship with someone I have never loved, just because one night of fun went horribly wrong and resulted in the joining of our genetic materials?

I can't and I won't, but I'm really struggling with the possibility that Sin might be planning to hurt him. Like we just talked about at the bookstore, how can my happiness grow from the ashes of someone else's misfortune? Maybe Rafe is capable of being happy at the expense of someone else, but can I? I'm not like him. I haven't been raised to only look out for myself. I was raised by a loving, compassionate sister who sacrificed endlessly to make sure I had all the opportunity in the world. Carly would sacrifice her own happiness for a loved one if it came down to it. Can I be the kind of person she would be proud of if I let this happen?

At this point, is there anything I can even do to stop it?

I adore Sin, but I got the distinct feeling that he is going to do what he thinks needs to be done now, and my opinion on the matter is not pertinent. On one hand, I get it. It's not like this is the first time Sin has expressed such a stance, and this time he has much more validity than the others. This is his wheelhouse, not mine. He wouldn't trudge into my lab and tell me how to mix chemicals in my Erlenmeyer flask, so I shouldn't try to dictate how he handles conflict within his crime family. I *don't* know all the facts of the situation, and I don't want to do anything that could potentially endanger him. But on the other hand, I don't know how I'll live with this.

When Rafe gets up to go to the bathroom and leaves me alone at the table, I get out my phone. There's nothing from Sin—which I expected—but I open up a text to him and send him an emoji with a single tear dropping from its eye.

He immediately sends back, "What's wrong?"

"I'm sad," I inform him.

"Why are you sad?" he demands.

"Because I want us to all be here for the baby. I want us to all get along and be friends. I don't want our happiness to grow out of something ugly and horrible."

"This whole way of life is ugly and horrible, Laurel. It's a little late to have a crisis of conscience."

"I know that. I don't care about that. I just don't want the people I care about to pay the price for our happiness. I don't understand how that's impossible."

That time, he doesn't respond. It's just as well. I need to put my phone away before Rafe comes back anyway. Virginia brings the check to the table, and when Rafe comes back, he slides some cash into the black billfold and pushes it toward the edge of the table.

"Ready?" he asks me.

I nod and gather my things while he grabs the takeout boxes. I got so lost in sad thoughts that I lost my appetite, so I have leftovers for lunch tomorrow. If I even get to have lunch at Rafe's house tomorrow.

Before we make it to the exit, Virginia comes after us, calling, "Rafe, wait."

He stops and turns back to face her, glancing at the billfold she's clutching. "What?" he asks.

Grimacing, she asks, "Is there any chance I could get a slightly bigger tip?"

He laughs, startled. "What?"

"I'm working on a side project, trying to help someone out, and I have to invest a little money into it since he doesn't have it."

Now he scowls. "Who? Is some asshole trying to take you for a ride?"

Scoffing, she asks, "Please. You think I'd let some asshole take me for a ride? Been there, done that. I learn from my mistakes, thank you very much. No, this is a business thing. Nothing shady. Anyway, my coffers aren't exactly overflowing, and I feel weird asking, but—"

He shakes his head dismissively, drawing out his wallet. "Coffers. What are you, Scrooge McDuck? Nobody says coffers. How much do you need?"

"I mean, I could use somewhere in the neighborhood of $300, but I'll take literally anything you can give me."

He counts out a lot of bills—definitely $300, maybe more, I don't keep track. "Will that suffice?" he asks her.

"I would hug you if it wouldn't be weird. Thank you," she tells him, smiling at the cash, then up at him.

"No problem," he tells her, sliding his wallet back into his pocket, then coming over and draping an arm around my shoulders. "Next time wait for my damn order."

———

I wait for Rafe to say he's going out, but it never happens. Of course he chooses tonight to stay in. He goes upstairs and takes a shower, and comes back down shirtless and with pajama pants slung low on his hips.

"Do you want to watch your show?" he asks casually, clicking on the TV.

I shake my head. "I'm not really in the mood tonight."

Since we left the restaurant, I haven't been able to stop worrying. A stray thought occurred to me and I couldn't shake it. Sin told me everything changed tomorrow. I took that to mean he would act tomorrow, but what if he acts tonight? What if he even told me tomorrow just to throw me off, and his real plan is to sneak in tonight and kill Rafe?

We're supposed to be on the same side of this situation, but I'm struggling with keeping to my side of the line. I want to straddle the line. I want to protect both of them.

I can't rest easy, and Rafe is so relaxed that I ache with how completely he would be taken off guard if Sin showed up tonight. It's all I can think about through every channel change. It's not like I want the fight to be fair anyway, it's not like I want Rafe armed and knowing what is going to happen, because while I *want* Rafe to be okay, I *need* Sin to be okay, but man... betrayal is not for me. I'm not cut out for it. It's low-down, dirty, and not right.

Since Rafe can't read my mind as he channel surfs, his lips curve up faintly. "You know, I sort of had my own *Smallville*," he tells me.

"What do you mean?" I ask, glancing over at him.

"Your sister made you start watching it, right? That's how you got hooked? My dad had a show like that. Watched the hell out of it when I was a kid, and we'd always watch it together so I came to feel like I liked it, too."

"What show?" I inquire.

"You may not even know what this is," he says dryly, looking over at me. "You're such a baby."

I can't help rolling my eyes. "Yeah, yeah, yeah. I'm the baby you knocked up, Humbert. What's the show?"

"*Walker, Texas Ranger*," he tells me.

"The Chuck Norris one? Yeah, I've heard of that." Pointedly glancing at my nails in a haughty manner, I add, "I mean, I've never watched an episode of it because I'm not 80, but I've heard of it."

"You little shit," he says, reaching over and catching me around the neck, yanking my head into his side.

"No roughhousing with the pregnant chick," I tell him, trying to sit up, but he keeps me locked in.

"I'm just going to leave you right here for the rest of the night," he informs me, casually turning his attention back to the television as he continues to flip channels. "Jesus, I have a lot of channels. I almost never watch TV, surely I don't need this many."

I huff out a sigh and claw at his arm, trying to free my neck so my face isn't stuck against his pectoral muscle. "Let me go, jerkface."

He doesn't. "What should we watch?" he inquires, casually as ever. "Can you see the TV from down there? I'll let you
out of the chokehold if you wanna earn your freedom."

His tone alone tells me his dick is involved in that scenario,
and my blood turns to ice water in my veins. Sin telling me not
to let Rafe kiss me floods back into my mind, and with it comes
a wave of remorse.

To Rafe, this is just another night of tomfoolery, and once
more I'm hit with the guilt of this terrible thing I am participating in. Just by keeping my mouth shut, I am participating,
but there's no palatable alternative. If I came clean to Rafe
now and warned him, I would be signing Sin's death warrant. I
don't have to think like them to know that—it's common sense.

For the briefest, most horrible moment, I run through what
that would mean. Sin would be dead, that's the gut-wrenching
part. That's the part that causes feelings to clog my throat so I
can scarcely breathe. I would have no one to distract me from
Rafe, so maybe I could grow feelings for him. I probably could.
He's much more likable tonight, and that's even knowing whatever it is he knows. He has so many secrets locked away inside
his head, it's impossible to know how impressive it is that he
can be so nice to me right now, that he can play around with
me like nothing is wrong when he knows *everything* is wrong.

Then earlier tonight at the restaurant flashes through my
mind, him going to find Marlena. That was incredibly annoying. I knew he wouldn't find her, but his interest strayed to her
as a direct result of my pissing him off, and I am going to piss
him off in the future, even if Sin isn't in the picture. I'm not
cotton candy, I'm a person with substance and my own thing
going on, and all people clash sometimes. At the first clashing
of horns, will he be casual and friendly at home, then go fuck
some piece of cotton candy to get his frustrations out? I

struggle to envision a future where Rafe wouldn't cheat on me. I don't think he would be cruel about it, I don't think he would even let me find out, but then I would live in a constant state of paranoia. Every time a woman looked at him with lust—which will happen—I'll wonder if that's the one he's fucking when he goes out to a club and I'm at home rocking our baby to sleep.

Even without Sin as a valid alternative, that's not how I want to live. I'm sure someone would be content with that, someone with less emotional investment. But I don't want an arrangement, I want a family. I don't want to raise a baby adjacent to a man I like, each of us leading more or less separate lives; I want to raise a baby with a man I love, a partner who will support me in every area of our life together.

If I want that, I have to be willing to reciprocate. If I want Sin to always love, support, and be loyal to me, I have to give the same thing back.

I know I'll carry the guilt for the rest of my life, but I can't be responsible for the alternative.

I have to let this happen.

40

SIN

When Laurel thinks of my job, I bet she thinks it's exciting. For such a good girl, she certainly has an acceptance of my lifestyle I wouldn't have expected, a fascination with the violent side of my work.

This is the part she doesn't consider. The boring part. It has been boring as hell sitting here in this trendy, cushioned dining chair, all alone in the dark. Waiting. I spend a good deal of my life waiting, and it's not glamorous. It is boring as all hell.

All there is, is time. Time to think, time to stew; time to consider the woman you love lying in someone else's bed, probably with his goddamned arms wrapped around her. At least it's for the last time, but that doesn't make it any easier. It certainly doesn't make it easier that she's mine now, and she still wants to protect his ass. I know Laurel has a good heart, but it would make me feel a hell of a lot better if she could get behind me killing him. Not because she wants him dead, but because she trusts me to do what needs to be done, even if it sucks.

The telltale creak of the floorboards draw me out of my

stewing and lets me know the excitement is about to begin. They're out of bed and moving around upstairs.

I flick a glance out the window—still dark. I don't expect Gio to linger, since he has to get back home to his wife before she wakes up. Asshole.

I take my gun out and lay it on the table in case I need to grab it quick. I hear them come down the stairs. Since it's so early, the house is so silent, I hear the smack of their lips as they kiss goodbye at the door in the other room.

I can't stop my head from shaking. I don't know whether to be more pissed off or disgusted that Gio would fall into Cassandra's trap after watching her blow through Rafe. Did he really think he could handle a woman *Rafe* couldn't manage?

No matter. *I* can handle all types of people. Men or women, smart or dumb, cocky or insecure, doesn't matter. Cassandra has never liked me because she's never been able to interest me. Whether it's her ego or her lust for power that is most offended, she has always considered me useless at best, and an obstacle at worst. Cassandra uses her looks and her body to handle men, but when she comes up against one who doesn't want her, she gets a little bitchy about it. She should stay cool. A smarter woman would just find another way, but she lets her ego have a heavy hand on the wheel. That's not smart.

Not that it matters anymore. Now I'm here waiting in her kitchen while it's still dark outside, and that never means anything good. Maybe the bosses of this family are dumb enough to fall for her bullshit, but they're also smart enough to hire someone like me who won't, so I guess it all evens out.

Someday this family will have a great boss. A steady boss who will earn the respect of his men, use his fucking head, and be a great leader of the Morelli family. I know that, because

I'm the one who's going to raise him. Assuming Laurel has a boy, anyway.

Fortunately, Cassandra doesn't head back upstairs now that her pawn has left, she comes to the kitchen like I figured she would. She's getting older, and all the maintenance she does to herself probably costs a little more effort now than it did a few years ago, so she won't have time to dawdle in bed.

The kitchen light flicks on and Cassandra freezes, her blue eyes widening as she spots me sitting at her kitchen table. Her relief is misplaced, but when she realizes it's me, she offers a thin little smile.

"Took you long enough. Is Rafe's little mouse distracting you, too?"

"No, I just thought Gio's brain resided in his head and he only used his cock for fun."

Smiling like we're co-conspirators, she meanders over to the kitchen counter. "Your mistake. All men think with their dicks, sweetie."

"Not *all* men."

"Fine," she says, purposely dismissive as she opens a cabinet and grabs a coffee cup. "You're special, is that what you need to hear?"

God, she is a pain in the ass.

Immediately, she turns back with a conciliatory look on her face. "I'm sorry; this isn't how I wanted to start things off between us. Truly, I'm just so used to us on opposite sides. I'm happy you found out about me and Gio. The sooner we got all that out in the open, the better. He wasn't ready to tell you yet, thought it might spook you and he needed to reel you in first."

I don't say a goddamn word.

Turning back to face me and holding up a black coffee mug, she asks, "Would you like me to make you some coffee?"

I shake my head.

She shrugs and goes about making some for herself. I watch as she calmly measures out the coffee grounds and dumps them into the filter. "So, why are you in my kitchen, Sin?" Glancing back over her shoulder with a suggestive smile, she asks, "I don't suppose you're here to kneel for your new queen?"

I can't help smiling at her dumb ass. "You'll never be my queen, Cassandra."

"Oh, come on. Give me a chance. You'll like working under me—I promise," she teases.

She already knows I'm not interested in her toxic vagina, but she can't seem to stop herself from trying. Just to annoy her, I offer back, "You know Gio already *has* a queen, right? Even if he takes power, you're just a side dish, not the main course."

"Ugh, his wife? Please. She's a joyless shrew. I'm getting rid of her."

"The same way you tried to get rid of Laurel?" I question.

Turning sharply, she points her finger at me. "I did *not* try to get rid of Laurel. I had no intention of killing her, only ridding her of Rafe's genetic material." Turning back to the counter, she grabs a knife and begins cutting into an avocado. "Would have been saving the bitch a trip to the clinic, but then you had to interfere. A dark knight with shining handcuffs," she says, mockingly. Her tone more normal, she says, "A twist on the tale, certainly, but I like it. Wouldn't have pegged you for the type, but I'm not used to working with men like you."

Because men like me are smart enough to stay out of her snake pit, but I don't bother saying what we both already know.

"Anyway, it doesn't matter now. Gio doesn't like potentially leaving Rafe's heir alive, but we've discussed it, and we both think you're worth the price. If you want to keep Rafe's little mouse and play daddy to her baby, go for it. His line should have never taken power before Gio's anyway, so there will be no issue down the line when my sons take over."

Now that's a fucking horror show, right there. Even if I didn't despise her, the prospect of working for Cassandra's sons would not be appealing. She'd rule them just like she plans to rule Gio now.

"You never loved Rafe, did you?"

"Love is for suckers and charlatans, Sin," she informs me. "You choose which side you want to be on, and I'm no sucker."

Short-sighted bitch. I've always known she thought an awful lot of herself, but right now I'm frankly floored at how honest she's being with me. Maybe it's a relief to expel her real self when she's so used to putting on a show, or maybe she figures I'm more apt to trust her if her cards are on the table, even if they're nasty, unpleasant cards.

Problem is, she's wrong. There's no trusting someone like Cassandra, because she has no principles. She's out for herself, and she doesn't care who gets caught under the tires. The same would apply to me, if I got in her way—regardless of whatever value she has assigned to me for now. Cassandra Carmichael will turn on anyone on a dime, and while she thinks she's flaunting how above it all she is, that's what she's cementing in my mind. Hungry dogs may not be loyal, but snakes don't *have* any loyalty, period. I won't work with people like that, and I don't admire it, even though it's clear she thinks I should. I'd rather be a dog than a snake any day.

"I'm surprised you don't know that by now," she continues, since I haven't spoken. "I thought Paula cured you of that sort of romantic bullshit. Four years of solitude and disinterest, now you're ready to overthrow the man you helped take power for some stupid girl. What's so special about Rafe's little mouse, anyway?"

"You wouldn't understand, trust me."

It's only a mild curiosity, nothing she'll lose sleep over, so she shrugs and spreads avocado over some unappetizing crackers. "Well, if you get bored with your teenager and start craving a real woman, Gio isn't as possessive as Rafe. I *would* like to be manhandled by you. Sounds like a good time."

"No thanks."

"Suit yourself. I'm excellent in bed."

"You're not my type. I'm attracted to non-psychopaths."

Smiling, she murmurs, "Opposites attract, huh? Okay, I get it. Well, anyway, everything Gio said to you still stands. We haven't been tricking you, only omitting my involvement. I had a hunch you wouldn't approve."

"When you're right, you're right. He has a daughter," I add, without preamble. "After you kill her mother, you planning to take her place?"

"I'll obviously have my own children, but Skylar is just a girl, so I don't need to kill her off, if that's what you're asking. She's still a baby, there's really no reason she ever need know I'm not her mother. I'm not anticipating any problems on the domestic side of this takeover; I figured you would have more questions about the business side."

If I had any questions about the business side, I certainly wouldn't be asking her. Her ego still gets in the way so she can't see the simple truth: I'd never let her be involved. I'd never bow to a snake. She still thinks she's more fascinating than she is, and she's so in love with her own vision of herself with all that power, she's not thinking clearly.

Power has seduced greater people than her, so I shouldn't be surprised.

"Did Rafe see this side of you? You were together for a while; you must have slipped up at least once or twice."

"All men with power have blind spots, sweetie, but *Morelli* men with power turn a blind *eye*. They never consider that they're tangling with a woman who might be smarter than they are. I let him have every bit of power in the bedroom, and he didn't look for what he didn't want to find." Smiling, she looks at me serenely. "Maybe that's why you both like the little mouse. You don't like tangling with women who are smarter than you."

"Laurel *is* smarter than me," I inform her. "But you're not."

"No?" As she turns to face me with her avocado cracker in her hand, she asks, "How do you know?"

My answer comes in the form of a bullet shot straight between her eyes. As special as she thinks she is, her body hits the ground just as fast as every other scumbag I've dropped. I adjust the black leather glove on my hand, then push up out of the chair and cross the room.

As I stand over her, I tell her, "Here are a few things you'd know if you were smarter than me." I fire another bullet into her head. "One: always double tap; make sure they're good and dead. Two: never turn your back to your enemy. Three: always know who your enemy *is*. Four: do not waste your time on villain monologues. You might be pretty fucking proud of yourself and your bullshit plans, but I'm not impressed."

I fire a third bullet into her, even though she's already gone.

"That one is just for pissing me off."

41

LAUREL

I make Rafe breakfast instead of having Juanita do it. That's not too far out of the ordinary, so he doesn't seem to think much of it as he sits at the island, eating his eggs and bacon, periodically grabbing a sliced strawberry as he scrolls through his phone and prepares to start his day, just like he would any other.

He trusts me, and that makes this so much worse.

Granted, he doesn't have many reasons not to. It's not like I'm the kind of asshole he thinks would participate in a betrayal, even if he thinks I am the kind of asshole who will actively lust after his hired muscle.

I am that kind of asshole. I'm exactly that level of asshole. I wish I had Sin here now to remind me why I'm letting this awful thing happen, because every time I think I have my shit together and I can do this, something happens and my dumbass heart grabs the reins, telling me nobly there *are* other ways, this is wholly unnecessary, and if I could just sit both of these men down and appeal to their senses of reason, I could stop this.

I don't want to trust Sin to handle it, I want to handle it myself. I know I could get the job done without any blood being spilled, if only these two assholes would cooperate.

Unfortunately, they are not terribly cooperative assholes. They are both pig-headed and they make life hard. Seeing how quickly I got *both* of them to the point they were willing to kill one another, I don't know how they worked together in harmony for so long. I know I'm biased, but Sin is just too fucking alpha to work under Rafe, who has a tendency to be a dickhead.

Sin is probably right; Chicago would have been a bad idea.

This is a bad idea too, though.

My idea is best. We all make nice and live the rest of our lives as friends, all of us alive and there for the baby, all being more or less a family. When I look out the window at Rafe's giant-ass pool, I envision a future where hot dogs are on the grill, Rafe and Sin are shirtless, drinking together on loungers, and I'm in the pool with the baby lounging in a floatie with a sunhat on, dragging his or her little fingers through the water and giving me a toothless grin.

I want *that*.

We could *all* be happy with that.

Goddamn their testosterone.

Since that vision appeals to me so much, I excuse myself to the bathroom and sneak out my phone, texting Sin to tell him about my vision. I leave out the part where I made them both shirtless, that's just for me, but I paint the rest of the picture for him. Surely he can see how perfect that would be.

Apparently not, because he texts back, "For the love of God, Laurel. Enough."

I scowl at the screen. "It can work! I know it can."

He does not respond.

My stomach aches when Rafe leaves the house after breakfast, because I don't know if it will be for the last time. I surprise the hell out of him when I follow him to the foyer like a puppy chasing after its master, then throw my arms around him and hug him forever before I let him leave.

For the first time, my odd behavior finally seems to trigger his suspicion. As he tugs me back, he regards me carefully. My arms are still around his neck, his hands remain on my waist, and even that is suspicious. Normally I wouldn't linger like this, because I'd be afraid he might try to kiss me or escalate things. Right now I just want to hug him, keep him close, and keep him from walking out that damn door.

"Is everything okay, kitten?" he asks, seriously.

All my insides feel wobbly, but I force myself to nod my head. I can't summon any words, though. My voice would shake if I tried.

Keeping his voice reassuring, he ducks his head a little, bringing himself down closer to my height. "You can tell me if something is wrong, Laurel. I won't be mad."

I shake my head, still unable to muster words to accompany the gesture.

"It's not too late," he tells me.

My blood runs cold. *What does that mean?* He couldn't *know* Sin is coming for him, right? There is no way he could know that. Is there? Goddammit, Sin, this keeping me in the dark bullshit is for the birds.

Swallowing down all the feelings lodged in my throat, I ask, "What do you mean by that?"

"Just what I said," he answers, without really answering anything at all.

I know he's giving me a chance to come clean, but I don't know for what. I don't want to play these dark, twisted games today. My stomach can't handle it.

"I just want everyone to be happy," I murmur, not meeting his gaze.

Touching his fingers just beneath my chin, he lifts it so I have to look at him. "Not everyone can win, kitten. That's not how games work."

"I don't want to play games," I state, echoing the thoughts I was just having. "I just want to live a happy life with the people I care about."

He sighs, his clenched jaw tightening, then he nods. Something like irritation flickers through his gaze, and it makes me worry all over again. Is he irritated because he knows what is coming, and he wanted me to tell him?

There aren't really stakes for *me* in this situation, only the people I love. Even in the absolute worst scenario that could play out, if Rafe does know Sin is coming, if he *is* ready for him, if *Rafe* emerges the victor today instead of Sin, I won't be harmed. Sin will be, but Rafe won't hurt me. I don't even think he'll send me away. I think he would just lock me up in his room and wait for me to settle down. Nothing would really change. He wouldn't kill me because I'm pregnant, and by the time the baby is here, he would be over it and we would already have a routine. A routine where I'm sad and he's barely present, but a routine, nonetheless. I would be safe, despite what I let happen. I would be another one of Rafe's many possessions, like this gigantic house or the pool full of glittering water outside.

I let Rafe leave.

As soon as he's gone, I text Sin. Not a plea this time, just a simple, "I miss you."

"I miss you too," he sends back. "I know today is hard. I'm sorry."

His unsolicited second text makes me tear up. It's not like I can stop thinking about all this for a single second anyway, but every time he says something that verifies his plan is still on, it hurts. I want him to change his mind. I want my sadness to matter, I want my will to make a difference. Maybe it's unreasonable. Maybe there's more to the story that I don't know about, and this really is the only way. I just wish I felt sure of that. I wish he had time to explain to me every facet of this situation, then maybe I could get on the same page. Maybe then I would see there is no alternative, and that for whatever reason, the future I want cannot happen.

There is no more time, though. Sin is surely busy setting up whatever he has planned, and he doesn't need me in his head distracting him.

So, instead of dumping more of my feelings on him, I text back something that will make at least one of us feel a little better.

"It's okay. I trust you."

To my surprise and confusion, Rafe comes home. It's dinnertime and I hope my confusion isn't plain to see, but when Rafe strides through the archway connecting the foyer and the living area, my heart nearly drops out of my body.

I didn't expect him to come home.

I set aside my book and rise from the couch, hesitantly following him into the kitchen where Juanita has already started preparing dinner. He must have let her know he was on his way. Nothing is cooking yet, she's still chopping and washing vegetables, so I hadn't realized she was in here making dinner. Since Rafe's schedule is irregular, she usually waits to hear from him. I should have noticed that, but in a desperate attempt to get out of my own head, I thought I could immerse myself in a novel.

Since I'm not sure how to ask why he's here, I go instead with, "How was your day?"

"Fine," he returns with an easy smile. He peels off his jacket and drapes it over the back of his chair at the island, then starts to loosen his tie.

"Are you home for the rest of the night?" I ask.

"Yep, all yours tonight. We should go for a swim after dinner. It's nice outside."

Why is this day just like any other? This is The Bad Day. Something terrible was supposed to happen. Why didn't it?

Oh, my God. What if it did? What if he handled it? What if I wasn't being paranoid this morning and Rafe *did* know what was happening? I didn't warn him, bad Laurel, but he handled it anyway and now he's going to ignore it?

Filled with a sudden, claustrophobic need to hear from Sin, I excuse myself to the bathroom and claw my phone out of my pocket. My fingers shake as I open up the text message chain between us. I don't even know what to say, I just need to know he's all right.

"Is everything okay?" I ask.

Then I wait. He has been responding pretty promptly, but after two minutes that feel like two hours, I want to throw up.

I text again. "Rafe just came home. He said he's home for the night. Is everything okay?"

No response. I wait as long as I can without arousing Rafe's suspicion, and he never texts me back. My heart stutters in my chest, dread filling every part of me. I've been so worried about protecting Rafe, I wasn't worried enough about Sin. I expected that if he had a plan, it would work. I expected that if he planned to take down Rafe, he would.

What if I was wrong?

What if Sin tried and failed?

Oh, my God.

How in the hell will I find out?

My poor stomach is a jumble of nerves when I rejoin Rafe in the kitchen. He looks up as soon as I enter the room, his gaze lingering on me. "You all right?"

I nod my head, trying to think of what to ask. I don't want to set off any alarms in case Sin *hasn't* acted yet, but if something went wrong, I have to know. I know absolutely nothing about Sin's plan though, so I don't even know what to ask. I can't ask if he has seen Sin today, because Sin is obviously a sore subject. I have no idea if anyone else is involved.

In the dark, that's where Sin wanted to keep me, and that's right where I am.

Someone needs to drop me a flashlight, because this fucking sucks.

Sin's face flashes to mind. A memory of him in bed with me yesterday, my naked body snuggled up against his. A searing vision of how powerful he looked standing above me in the shower, my wrists trapped in his cuffs.

My eyes sting and even though I'm in the kitchen and Rafe is standing right in front of me, I pull my cell phone out to see if Sin texted me back. Still nothing.

Rafe's gaze drops to my phone, then comes back to my face and he lifts an eyebrow. "What are you doing?"

"I don't know," I murmur, suddenly overwhelmed. This is all too much. I want the most stressful thing in my life to be finals week, not a possible showdown between my two most recent lovers that has to result in one of their deaths.

I shove the phone back in my pocket and leave the room. I can't be around Rafe right now. Even if he felt like boasting now, even if he would tell me exactly how his day went, I don't think I have the emotional capacity left to handle it.

42

LAUREL

The rest of the day passes by in a slog. A foggy slog. Sin never texts me back, and Rafe never expands on how his day went. It feels like verification that everything that *could* go wrong in my world has, and I don't want to face it anymore.

I don't know if Sin played and lost, but I know *I* feel defeated. All I want to do is cry, so I spend as much of the evening alone as I can. I take a bath instead of a shower. I can cry alone in the bath tub. I check my phone obsessively for something, anything from Sin. If he's okay, I don't understand why he isn't texting me back.

Day turns to night and I feel sicker and sadder than at any other point today. I am exhausted from dealing with all my emotions, but if tomorrow comes and I still haven't heard from Sin, I guess I'll just ask. Maybe he'll disappear just like Marlena did. Maybe I've said the last words I'll ever get to say to him.

I can't keep tears from welling up and spilling down my face.

I can't live this life. If Rafe killed Sin, I'm calling Mia for sanctuary. I won't be able to bear being with Rafe, knowing what he did. I know Mia will protect me. I don't know why I'm so sure, but I know she will. Carly says she protected Vince from Mateo, and everyone who knows more about their story than I do insists Vince wronged her horribly.

I've never done anything bad to her, and when I tell her what Rafe did, she'll understand why I can't be with him.

As soon as I know for sure, I'm getting the fuck out of this godforsaken town. I'll never step foot here again.

Since Rafe has already been tried and found guilty in my mind, I can't bear to be around him. I have to be for tonight, just until The Bad Day is over, just until I can be sure about what happened, but I don't have to like it.

He went for a swim without me since I hibernated inside, and now he sits next to me on the couch with damp hair, a pair of gray sweats slung low on his hips. If he notices how crabby I am tonight—especially juxtaposed with how caring I was this morning—he doesn't mention it.

I'm a ball of resentment curled up on my side of the couch, as far away from him as I can be when there's not so much as an empty cushion between us. I'm angry at him and angrier at myself. I can't keep checking my phone in front of him, but I wait for it to vibrate in my pocket. It just never does.

We're both stunned when Sin comes strolling in from the kitchen. For a split second, my heart stops, then fills up with joy. He's alive. Rafe didn't kill him.

My joy crashes a moment later when I realize that means he's here for Rafe, and I have been mean to Rafe all night long because I thought he had outsmarted Sin.

I don't know if it's the fact that Sin entered through the

424 | SINNING IN VEGAS

back door, my general weirdness over the past day, or pure instinct, but Rafe knows this isn't a normal visit.

The back door isn't normally unlocked, but then Rafe doesn't normally go for a swim. Sin's presence in Rafe's living room isn't normally anything to get worked up over, but today we all know why he's here.

Rafe lunges forward, reaching under the table.

Sin draws his gun and says, "Laurel, move."

I can't even breathe, adrenaline is rushing through my body so violently. I try to comply quickly, clumsily uncurling my legs and going to move off the couch, but before I can, Rafe's arm locks around my neck and he yanks my body back against him like a shield. He had a gun stashed under the coffee table and he has it now, but instead of training it on Sin, he points the weapon at my temple.

"Take another fucking step, Sin. I dare you."

My eyes bulge out and I claw at Rafe's arm locked around my neck, trying to get him away from me.

"Are you fucking kidding me?" Sin demands lowly.

"If you're not sure, take another step and find out," Rafe says calmly.

Sin doesn't move.

"This is disappointing," Rafe states, almost casually. "All the way around. I'm disappointed in both of you."

I'm so angry at myself for being so worried about him, I want to claw his face off. I know my anger won't help anything, but Rafe is so calm, I *want* to kill him. "Fuck you," I spit.

"Now, now, we'll get to that later," Rafe assures me, then he kisses the side of my face just to be a dick.

An idea occurs to me out of nowhere. I'm not sure from where, I have *no idea* if I can pull it off, or if it will work, but what do any of us have to lose at this point?

"Not you," I practically growl, jabbing a finger at Sin. "Him."

Up until now, Sin was vibrating with anger. His eyes were cold, his lip was curled with dislike, but now he blinks in real surprise. "Me?"

"I have been texting you all goddamn day. I thought you were *dead*."

Sin stares at me for a second, then says, "This isn't really the time, Laurel."

"I'm sick of both of you playing with my emotions," I rage. "Enough is enough."

As calmly as ever, Rafe tells me, "This isn't going to work, kitten."

"You're not going to work," I shoot back. "I'm done with both of you assholes. I've got news for you, I'm going back to Chicago and I'm never coming back. You don't think your men would respect you if you let me be with your enforcer, just wait. See how impressed they are when you can't keep me here even without competition. They're going to laugh at you when you can't even get me back from your own cousin. Mia will protect me, Mateo won't let you have me back, then they'll realize how powerless you really are. They'll know what a fucking shitty ass boss you are—"

His arm tightens around my throat, momentarily stealing the breath from lungs and the angry words from my mouth. "If your strategy right now is to remind me why I *don't* want to shoot you, you're doing a very poor job."

"Go ahead and shoot me," I tell him. "Then Sin will kill you and maybe a *real* boss can take over Vegas."

Instead of responding to my anger, Rafe just chuckles. "Your claws are adorable, kitten. Ineffective, but adorable. Is that as mean as you can get? I can get a lot meaner," he promises. "Want me to show you?"

Dread consumes me at the thought of how mean he could get. I'm not worried he would be mean to *me*, but now I know Sin has some tender spots and Rafe surely knows about them, too.

My mind races, desperately grabbing for words to throw against the wall. I don't know where any of Rafe's weak spots are—

Oh wait. Yes, I do.

"That's why Cassandra left you, you know." His arm tightens even more, but I keep going. "She knew you were weak. Look at this, you can't even take Sin on man-to-man, you have to use me as your human shield. That's pathetic, Rafe. No wonder she couldn't get wet for you anymore."

Even Sin cringes when I add that last part, so I know I'm hitting the right spot.

I can't see Rafe's face. I wait to hear fury in his tone when he speaks. He's quiet for several long, silent beats, then he asks calmly, "Are you done trying to goad me, Laurel? If not, keep going. I'll wait."

I'm so mad that my words didn't work, I do the only thing I can think of. Rafe has one arm locked around my neck and one hand on the gun. Since he doesn't have a third arm, he can't move quickly enough to stop me.

I reach back and punch him in the dick.

He grunts like he just got the air knocked out of him, then growls into my ear, his body hunching over mine. "That was fucking mean."

"I hate you," I inform him.

"So I've fucking heard," he mutters, dragging me off the couch. He keeps an eye on Sin as he drags me around the coffee table, but now that he's experiencing so much physical discomfort, he is less gentle with me. Less patient. As I'm scrambling for what to try next, Sin catches my attention.

His head falls back briefly and he mutters a low, angry, "Motherfucking fuck." Raising his gun, he points it at a spot beyond me. It's beyond me, but it's not Rafe, it's past him, too. He's looking behind both of us, at the arch between the living room and the foyer. His voice rises with helpless anger. "I asked you to wait in the fucking car. I'm so fucking sorry for this, Virginia."

Then he fires his gun.

"No!" Rafe lets me go and turns to lunge, as pointless a gesture as it is. He freezes, his gaze dropping to the ground, but she's not there.

I barely get out of the way before Sin attacks him. I stumble back, then kick into gear and run. My legs shake, but they carry me into the next room. Breath bursts in and out of my lungs as I run to the armoire and rip the door open. There are so many weapons in here, some I can't even name, but I don't know how to use any of them. There are guns, but they're probably not loaded. I pull open a drawer and find plenty of ammunition, but I don't know which bullets even go to which gun. I don't know how to load them, or how to check if any *are* loaded. Fuck.

There are simpler weapons hanging on the door—probably more for décor than any practical reason, since I can't exactly see Rafe brandishing a sword for real combat.

He has *swords* in this armoire. Jesus Christ. This whole thing would have had to go before the baby learned to crawl. This is just a cabinet full of danger.

Focus, Laurel!

I go to lift one of the swords, but I'm taken off guard by

how heavy the damn thing is. I'm not going to be able to swing this with confidence, I'm going to be clumsy and he'll get the damn thing away from me if it comes down to it.

All right, you know what, the sword is big, but bigger isn't always better. A small blade can be just as effective as this monster. If I slip a knife between his ribs, that'll hurt just as much.

The gun would be much easier, but even if I figure out how to load it right and don't shoot my own face off, I've never fired one. I might aim for Rafe and hit Sin.

I grab a knife. Something sharp-looking and shiny, then I close the armoire and rush back to the living room. At least for the moment, I needn't have worried. Sin is on top of Rafe, raining punches down on him. Rafe has his arms up, trying to protect his head, but Sin is laying into him. My stomach lurches. I stay back, but my fingers flex around the handle of the knife.

I'm hesitant to call out, not wanting to distract him, but I ask Sin, "Should I do anything?"

"Stay the fuck out of my way," he answers.

Okay then, I can do that. I keep a coffee table's length between them and me, then jump when Rafe lands a hit to Sin's jaw. Now that he found an opening, he hits him again. Sin shifts and Rafe takes advantage, throwing him off his body and leaping to his feet with the grace of a fucking bobcat.

Holy shit.

Rafe's ready now. Sin gets up just as quickly, lunging at Rafe, fists flying. Rafe ducks and charges Sin's torso, forcing him back a few steps. They spin, hit, charge, it all happens at such a fast pace, I can't keep up. I don't know who is winning— or if anyone is winning.

"What's wrong, Sin?" Rafe goads, arms up, guarding his

face as he moves. "Did seeing me with a gun to Laurel's head jog a few memories?"

Sin doesn't respond, but he tries to hit him.

Rafe blocks. "Did it make you think of Paula? Did it make you think of Ellie? You couldn't save them, could you?"

"Stop it," I scream, glaring at Rafe.

"You thought you were gonna get a second chance with the girl I knocked up, then, damn, you almost lost another one. You must not be a very good fucking protector, Sin."

Sin ignores all the bait Rafe is dangling. He ducks, charges, and sweeps Rafe's legs, knocking him on the ground again. He's on him fast, hitting Rafe in the face before he can get his arms up this time. His hands move so fast, even though I'm not in this fight, my heart pounds. I can't keep track of how many times he hits him, the only reason I know to be alarmed is that Rafe stops defending himself as well as he was and now there's blood on Sin's fists, blood on Rafe's face—blood all over the place. It starts to look less like a fight and more like Sin beating a human punching bag, and I recall his story about bludgeoning Paula's lover to death. Did he use his hands? Jesus Christ, I don't know why I assumed he used an object.

Just in case he's in a blind fury, I call out, "Um, I think you could probably stop and use the gun now."

"Ya think?" Sin asks casually, before landing another punch.

"I think you might kill him if you keep going," I suggest.

"I think he held a fucking gun to your head, so the bastard gets what he gets." He hits him again. "I don't even fucking care anymore, I'll call Vince up, train that little asshole to be my figurehead. I'll run this fucking city myself. Fuck this family."

Despite his words, Sin finally stops hitting him.

430 | SINNING IN VEGAS

He cocks his gun and pushes the barrel against Rafe's forehead. "You still in there, motherfucker?"

"Fuck you," Rafe grunts.

Pressing the gun harder into Rafe's forehead, Sin says, "No, fuck *you*. You're the one with a gun to your head, asshole. It won't take much at this point to convince me to pull the trigger, but I guess I should tell you, that's not why I fucking came here tonight."

"Bullshit," Rafe bites back. "Do I look like a fucking idiot?"

"No, you look like shit." Raising his voice, he says, "Laurel, go get this asshole an ice pack to put on his face."

What?

I don't know, but I don't want to miss anything, so I run to the fridge, grab an ice pack, a hand towel, and hasten back to the living room. Sin is still sitting on top of Rafe, still with the gun to his head, so I don't try to shove the stuff at him. It's cold, so I use the towel to hold the ice pack and wait.

"Now, if you can stop making me want to kill for five fucking seconds, I'm going to give you your options. Cool?" Sin asks, cocking an eyebrow at Rafe.

Rafe doesn't respond, he just casts me a mean look.

Sin punches him again, then puts the gun back against his forehead. "Try again, dickbag. She's the only reason you even stand a chance at walking out of here."

"Just say what you need to say," Rafe tells him.

"You have a big problem on your hands," Sin informs him. "Not me—a bigger problem. There's a mutiny brewing. I have a list as long as my arm of people who want you out of power, and at the top of that list is Gio. He wants your seat. Offered to bring me up if I turned on you."

"Offered that right out of the blue, huh?" Rafe asks, not nearly as cowed as a man in his position should be.

"No, not out of the blue. Right on the heels of you telling Theo to take me out," Sin replies. "Guess it seemed like an opportune time."

My eyes widen, but Rafe doesn't even deny it. Sighing, he reaches a hand out at me. "Give me the fucking towel."

"I'm not sure I want to give you the towel now," I inform him. "You sent someone to kill Sin?"

"Sin killed him first, don't worry."

"Good," I snap.

"Give me the towel," he says.

"No."

Rafe sighs, thumping his head against the hardwood floor. "Fucking Christ."

"Now, before the barrel of your gun touched Laurel, I came up with a different idea. She has this yearning to keep you around, though right now I can't think why," Sin informs Rafe.

"Right now I am also not married to that idea. Maybe you should kill him and we'll just keep his house," I suggest. "Just us playing by the pool with the baby also sounds fine, if he's going to be a murdery bastard."

"Thanks," Rafe says dryly. "You're a lot of help."

"I'm not taking that off the table just yet," Sin murmurs. "My first idea was this: I'm going to help you clean house. Wipe out all the assholes who want you gone—all of them. Attack with an iron fist. No more of this salvaging shit. If they were willing to flip, they're gone, no matter who they are. One final round of housecleaning and clear out all the bad apples. It's not going to be a small job. We're going to need help. You're going to have to call Mateo and ask if he can send us some guys, not necessarily to help us wipe them all out, but to help us keep the ship steady in the meantime while the ripples from this shit hit our crew. Other crews are going to hear about it. I have to kill Gio, he's in too deep. He was in bed with Cassandra Carmichael—literally. She's dead now."

That gets Rafe's attention. He tries to sit up. "What?"

"She tried to have Laurel poisoned. Abortion pill or some shit, didn't want her to have your baby. Marlena did the drop. She's dead, too."

Rafe's head falls back against the floor and he brings his hands up to cover his face.

"Yeah, I've been busy. Anyway," Sin says, his gun moved away from Rafe's face, but not putting it away yet. "This shit between us? It has to be over. We've gotta squash it. After you apologize to Laurel for that bullshit you just pulled," he adds. "You're gonna have to do that first. Then, once I help you get your crew cleaned up, you're going to need a new number two to help you run shit. I'm giving myself a promotion since you never got around to it. I'm your new number two. I also get Laurel. She's mine now. If you can accept these terms, great, let's get to work. If you can't, I'll feed you a couple bullets and persuade Carly to move Vince out here so there's a Morelli technically on the throne, but I'll be the one calling the shots. I can do a better fucking job. I don't *want* that job necessarily, but having her sister nearby would probably make Laurel pretty damn happy, so I can go for either option. We can work together and be stronger, or we can take each other on, but I'd caution you to notice which one of us is pinned to the floor with a bloody everything if you're leaning toward the latter option. Do not try to fake me out. I've already done that shit with Gio, and I'll see right through it. If I'm gonna have to kill you, I'd just as soon do it now and get it over with. If you agree to my terms, you better mean it. If you even think about double crossing me, I'll kill Virginia. I know that matters to you now."

"Fuck off," Rafe mutters. "You already killed every other fucking woman I know."

Sin shrugs. "You need to have better taste when it comes to women. I like Virginia. You should see if you can make it work with her. She could keep you busy. Laurel likes her, too, and if I'm not moving Vince and Carly out here, we're gonna need couple friends."

"I'm not fucking Virginia. And unless *you're* trying to fuck *me*, you wanna get the fuck off me?" Rafe adds.

Now Sin nods at me as he climbs off Rafe. "Give him the towel."

Since Sin asked, I do. Rafe levels me an unimpressed look as if to call me out on it, but I'm not a bit sorry. If Sin told me clean Rafe's wounds, I would. If Rafe asked me for a Kleenex, I would tell him to fuck off.

"Wait," Sin says, pointing at Rafe. "Apologize to Laurel."

Rafe rolls his eyes. "I'm sorry I held a gun to your head, Laurel."

"I forgive you for that, but not for sending someone to kill Sin," I inform him primly. "You can fuck right off for that."

Rafe shakes his head, wiping the blood off his face, then turning the towel over and wrapping up the ice pack. "I don't even know where to put this. Fuck, if you're not beating the shit out of people anymore, we're wasting your talents."

"I liked Theo to replace me, but now I guess it has to be Shane. Your fucking fault. Shouldn't have sent one of our best guys after me, you dick," Sin mutters.

Nodding at me, Rafe says, "We shouldn't be talking about any of this in front of her."

Sin cocks an eyebrow. "Laurel?" He wraps his arm around my waist, yanking me against his side. "She was gonna stab you. She's my little badass. She's fine."

"Only if absolutely necessary," I add, but I can't help beaming under Sin's praise. Plus he just called me his again, and this time in front of Rafe. After beating the living shit out of him and forcing him to apologize to me. My man is the hottest.

43

LAUREL

Sin doesn't do a thorough check of the house tonight. It's sexy because I know that means he's not worried, that he's taken care of every threat, that he's made sure we're safe.

Also I'm just finding everything he does tonight insanely hot. When we talked in bed about his job, I never expected I'd get to see anything like what I saw tonight. It was terrifying at the time, of course, but seeing what he's capable of ignites a fire in my belly that can only be smothered by his magnificent body. I don't like that he takes such big risks with his life, but God, his danger does things to me.

Sin's just as hungry for me. We barely get inside the house and he pushes me back against the wall, kicking the door shut. He plants a hand on the wall and leans so close I can smell him. He has his regular Sin scent, but more tonight. He's dirty and bloody and sweaty. Maybe the primitive scent of him is another reason I'm so damn turned on, but I'm near to humping the man's perfectly muscled thigh.

Then he crushes his mouth against mine and I'm gone. I

wrap my arms around him, clinging to his powerful shoulders to keep myself up as he carries me away with everything Sin. His scent, his danger, his kisses, his heart. After years of being cold and mean, bitter and closed off, I knocked out some of his walls. His fault. He shouldn't have cuffed me to one and expected I wouldn't do any damage.

Breaking away from my mouth, his lips travel down my neck. We're standing here making out in the dark, too caught up in each other to even hit a light switch.

"Upstairs," I tell him, when I catch my breath enough to speak.

Sin smiles, pulling back just enough to look at me, but staying close. Gesturing to his overall appearance with the hand not braced against the wall, he says, "I killed a bitch and beat the shit out of your sorta-ex today. I'm filthy. I can't fuck you for the first time like this."

"Um, yes you can," I assure him.

His smile drifts to a smirk. "You give me permission, huh?"

"I give you all the permission. All the deeds. All the agreements. I accept your terms of service. Show me the box, I'll click it."

"You are such a fucking nerd," he tells me.

I poke him in the chest, smiling. "Don't even pretend you don't love it."

He smiles and nuzzles into my neck, then surprises me by planting his hands under my ass and lifting me. "Wrap your legs. We're going to take a shower."

Excitement leaps low in my belly as I lock my legs around him. "Mm, I like showering together," I murmur with approval.

"I like having you home," he states.

All my feelings are out of whack. Now heat blossoms

within me and I wrap my arms around him as he carries me upstairs. "I like that, too."

Once we're shut inside the bathroom together, he lets me slide down his hard body. My nipples ache against the fabric of my bra, wanting out, yearning for his attention. Sin reaches for the hem of my T-shirt, immediately lifting it and drawing it over my head. I lift my arms to help him. It fills me up inside when his dark eyes rake over my body, then he grabs me, planting a hand on my back, and pulls me close so he can kiss my breasts.

I'm already needy and throbbing, desperate for his touch, but I need more than his touch. It feels like I've waited for-fucking-ever for this man; I want his dick. I want it inside me. I don't want to wait another minute.

He knows that, but he makes me wait anyway.

"I bet you're so fucking wet right now, aren't you, pretty girl?" he murmurs.

I feel like I've swallowed my heart. "Why don't you find out for yourself?"

His grin is wolfish, then he backs me up against the bathroom door and kisses me again. I tangle my fingers in his hair, closing my eyes and hooking a leg around his thigh, trying to pull him closer. I can't even get him any closer—I'm already plastered to the wall—but I want him closer anyway. He kisses me hard, with brutal lips and a forceful tongue. I can't get enough. There's a fire in my heart, in my soul, between my legs —I'm on fire everywhere with want for this man.

After kissing the fuck out of me, he breaks away suddenly and strips off his clothes. I squeeze my thighs together, needing friction, needing him. I want to taste him, so, so badly, but more than that I want to make sure he fucks me this time, so I'm not about to get on my knees.

Well, unless he tells me to. If I'm being honest, he could just look at the ground pointedly and I'd probably drop to my knees, but dammit, I'm trying to hold out.

It gets even harder because he's even sexy when he undresses. Forget the shower; I want to lick every inch of his incredible body. Right now he's so much scarier than usual, in the sexy way I like. As he strips off his bloody shirt, he may as well be a conquering soldier stripping off his battle armor. He could be a bawdy Scottish warrior (no doubt there are a few of those somewhere in his bloodline), returning home from battle to slake his lusts inside his ladylove.

I can't help smirking at my own thoughts. I'm basically his old timey tavern wench in my head right now. I like it a lot. I know what we're going to be for Halloween this year.

"What?" Sin asks.

I shake my head. "I'm just glad you can't hear my thoughts. I'm taking nerd to a new level over here, and also objectifying you a lot."

"Objectify away," he says, chuckling as he tosses the last of his clothing.

"I know an Anglophile is a person who loves the English, but is there a Scottish equivalent? A Scotophile? Maybe Celtophile? Is that a thing? I think you might have turned me into one."

"You're not seriously asking me, right?" he asks.

"I'll Google it tomorrow," I assure him.

"You do that." Nodding at my shorts, he asks, "Why are you still wearing clothes?"

"Oh, great question. I'm such a naughty tavern wench," I mutter, my fingers deftly pushing the button through the button hole.

He looks a little afraid. "What?"

I shake my head. "Don't worry about it now. We'll revisit come Halloween. You're gonna like it."

"You can dress up as a naughty tavern wench for Halloween," he says. "I have no problem with that."

I flash him a smile as I step out of my shorts. "You might when you see your corresponding costume."

"No," he replies instantly.

"We'll talk about it later," I assure him.

"We won't."

"I'm going to serve you ale. Or mead? I don't know much about alcohol. I'll do some research to make sure I'm historically accurate. I can't have any, because for the sake of our costumes and the character back stories I'm cooking up, you knocked me up." I rub my tummy. "Put your wee bairn in my belly."

"Stop. I'm not going to participate in whatever this is."

"You don't even have to wear it outside the house. Just for me," I promise.

"This isn't going to happen."

I nod my head. "It is. It's okay. Accept it. I'm going to reward you for it. So many rewards. Trust me, you're going to want to be buried in that costume by the time I'm done with you."

He does not appear convinced, but rather than waste time telling me no now, he turns his attention to my body as I shimmy out of my panties. When I reach back to unhook my bra, Sin spins me around, tenderly pressing his lips to the ball of my shoulder, then leaves a trail of kisses all the way to my neck.

I sigh, dropping my bra and wrapping my arms around him just in time for his lips to find mine. He breaks away and turns to the tub so he can turn on the water and adjust the temperature. I reach up and grab a clean wash cloth and a pair of towels off the rack on the wall. I leave the towels on the sink and bring the wash cloth with me.

"Let's get you clean," I say, pulling the curtain shut behind me.

Sin smiles, wrapping an arm around my waist and tugging me close. "I'm beginning to think you only want me for my body."

"I definitely want you for your body. I would sacrifice goats on a mountain top at midnight for this body. I want all the rest of you too, though, so it's okay."

Since we're standing under the spray together, we're both soaking wet already. I hold the cloth over my shoulder and catch some water in it until it's soaked through, then I look around for his soap. He grabs a bar from behind me and hands it over.

"Thank you," I say, rubbing it in the cloth to soap it up.

Looking faintly amused, he asks, "Are you going to clean me?"

I nod my head, handing back the soap. "Mm hmm. I'm gonna take good care of you."

"I think taking care of you is my job," he states.

"It's both our jobs. We'll take care of each other." My body craves his and I can't stay away, so I push my chest against his, reaching behind his back and running the cloth along his spine. He bends his head and kisses my neck as I continue to soap up his back. He doesn't point out that his back is probably the part of him least in need of washing. He knows I just want to hold him and he lets me.

For once, there's no rush. We're not running from anything, we're not stealing moments. This moment is ours. Every moment after this is ours. We belong to each other now.

We always have from the moment he stormed across the threshold into Rafe's house and his eyes met mine, but now we know it, and the whole world knows it, too.

If that's not a reason to just stand here in his arms and soak him up, I don't know what is.

"I'm gonna marry you," he tells me.

Between the sound of the water beating down on us and thundering of my heart, I can't be sure I heard him right. Pulling back, I meet his gaze. "What did you say?"

"You heard me," he murmurs, nipping at my neck with his teeth.

My stomach feels all wonky, full of butterflies and also in a freefall. A butterfly-filled freefall. Yeah, that sounds right.

"You're going to marry me," I repeat, flushing even though the words were his.

"That's right," he tells me, snatching the cloth out of my hand and pulling back so he can soap his chest. "You have a problem with that?"

I can't help laughing at this crazy man. "I mean, that's not how people traditionally ask, so I'm not entirely sure how to respond to it. Yes? Try again with a question mark in there somewhere?"

Sin just smirks at me. "Wasn't a question."

"You are so fucking cocky, I can't even handle it," I inform him.

"Tell me no then," he challenges.

Yeah, right. I roll my eyes at him. "You just said it wasn't a question."

"Good, we agree then," he surmises, his hand sliding down his abdomen.

I'm trying to pay attention, but now that soapy cloth is moving lower and I can't keep my eyes from following. "I think we should discuss this when I have a higher capacity for decision-making," I tell him.

"We could," he offers. "Or I could just refuse to fuck you until you agree to my terms."

My eyes jerk from his dick back to his face. "You wouldn't dare."

He cocks an eyebrow at me. "Wouldn't I?"

He totally would.

"You're crazy," I tell him. "You haven't even fucked me yet."

"Then call me honorable," he says dryly. "I'm protecting my virtue here."

"Yeah, right. Your nickname is *Sin*. I'm sorry to be the one to tell you this, but your virtue is long gone."

"I already told you once I fuck you, I'll never let anyone else touch you. Really, you're agreeing to forever the minute you open your legs for me."

I shake my head at him as he reaches for my hips and turns me around, then pulls me flush against him. "You're such a brute," I inform him.

"An oppressive caveman, yes, I remember," he says, kissing the damp skin along the curve of my neck.

"I am a woman of logic and science," I inform him. "People can't just get married this fast."

"Says who?" he asks.

"Says logic," I reply dryly.

"Fuck that. I want to make you mine forever. What's so illogical about that?"

I reach back and caress his neck as he kisses mine. "You can have me forever. Doesn't mean we have to do the paperwork yet."

"If it's just paperwork, let's get it out of the way," he counters.

I can't help grinning. "You're so persistent."

"I persuade people to give me what I want for a living. Just relent now and save us both some time."

"Not anymore," I tell him, turning back to face him, running my hands down his chest. "You promoted yourself, remember?"

"Oh, yeah." He cracks a smile. "I forgot for a minute. It'll take a little getting used to."

I wrap my arms around his neck, pressing my lips against his jaw. "I'm so proud of you."

"Yeah?" he murmurs, running his hand up my back and sending a delightful shiver through my body.

"Mm hmm. Did you change your plan to accommodate me when I told you I was sad?"

"I'll never tell," he informs me.

I grin, taking that as verification, then bury my face in his shoulder and lightly biting him the way he bites me.

He growls, fisting a hand in my hair and yanking my head back. He follows up with a tender assault, scraping his teeth down the side of my neck and backing me up against the tiled wall. I brace my hands against the cool wall and wait for more, but once he gets me there, he backs away, lifting a dark eyebrow and pointing at me.

"You stay put and stop distracting me. Let me finish getting clean so I can take you the bedroom."

"Mm, yes, sir," I tease.

44

LAUREL

I've never been so happy to see a bed in my life.

On one hand, I want to let Sin kiss me and do his standing-up sexiness like he did before, but I am also so fucking excited to be back in this bed, as soon as I see it, I can't help running over and jumping on it, rolling around in the blankets and just sighing with pure happiness.

Sin appears to be amused as he discards his towel in the laundry basket and comes over to climb on the bed with me. "You really like my bed, huh?"

"Our bed," I tell him.

"That's right, I guess it is now," he says, snaking an arm under me and pulling me close.

"And yes, I'm a huge fan of this bed. Mainly because I'm a huge fan of its owner. I'm even excited that your laundry basket is full and that means I get to do domestic things here tomorrow while you work. How crazy is that?"

"Pretty crazy," he tells me.

"I hate Rafe's house. I like the pool, if I ever stop hating him, I still want to take the baby to the pool, but your house is so much better than his."

"That is objectively untrue, but that's okay. I like this one better, too." Leaning in, he nips me on the shoulder. "Remember what I said about saying his name in this bed? Still applies."

"Ooh, you'll get mean?" I ask, with interest. "Rafe, Rafe, Rafe, Rafe."

His eyes narrow and I grin at him. He smothers my grin with his mouth, yanking me underneath him and climbing on top of me. "You're a little troublemaker," he informs me.

"I'm a perfect angel," I insist.

"You should be. I don't want to go hard on you the first time."

"I'm not a virgin, remember? I am *pregnant*. I have done this before."

"Don't remind me," he grumbles, leaning down and pressing his lips against mine.

"I'm sorry I'm not a virgin for you, my lord. You should have met me sooner. Swept me off my feet and demanded my virtue. Ravished me if I refused."

"When did you lose your virginity?"

"I was 17."

He cocks his head left and right. "Might've gone to jail."

"Only if you got caught," I tell him, wiggling my eyebrows. "Would you still fuck me, jailbait and all?"

"I'm starting to think you're into roleplay," he states.

I shrug. "Maybe. Never tried it before. Young guys aren't that interesting to have sex with."

Covering my mouth with his hand, he says, "All right, new rule. Stop referring to anyone else you've had sex with unless you want me to hunt them down and kill them. Then I'll be the only one *alive* who has ever fucked you, so I'll be the only one who counts."

I'm not *completely* sure he's joking, so I nod my agreement and murmur against his palm. "Gotcha."

"Good," he says, removing his hand.

"It won't even be hard to pretend you're the only one I've ever had sex with," I assure him. "You're already the best, and you haven't even completely fucked me yet. Speaking of..." I roll my hips forward, in an attempt to urge him on. "We gonna do this?"

"Not until you tell me what I want to hear," he tells me, sitting on my hips and crossing his arms.

"Seriously? I almost stabbed a guy for you."

"I won't tell you how many people I have murdered to protect you or keep you happy. Especially after tomorrow, when that count is a lot higher."

I shake my head at him. "That's not even fair. You can just pull out 'I've killed for you' and win any argument. 'What should we watch tonight, Laurel? Your show or mine? While you're deciding, I want to remind you, I've killed for you.'"

Smirking, he tells me, "I wouldn't waste the 'I've killed for you' card on which show we should watch."

"'Let's have one more baby, Laurel. Oh, you don't want to? I'd like to take this opportunity to remind you I've killed for you.'"

Sin nods. "You done yet?"

"'You want to go to your sister's for Thanksgiving this year? I don't want to do that, and since I have killed for you...'"

He cuts me off, tickling the fuck out of my sides until I can't breathe and my face hurts from laughing. I try to swat him away but it does not work. Tickling is the ultimate evil, but it does get his hands on me, so we've taken a step in the right direction.

Once he relents, he keeps his hands on me, and my helpless laughter turns to tender smiles as his scarred hands move across my tummy, and finally to flushed cheeks and moans of pleasure as he palms my breasts, his rough thumbs stimulating my nipples.

He ducks his beautiful head and takes one of my nipples into his mouth. Pleasure and tenderness mix together and fill me up with so much adoration, it's hard to keep it all in. I feel like it's seeping out of me, pouring from my eyes, floating around me like a cloud. He's lying between my legs, resting on top of me, his body plastered against mine, so if there is a cloud, I have him enveloped in it. I want to envelope him in all my love, and fill up all the empty spots he's made himself feel for so long.

I'm so happy we found each other.

And for *that* reason, not the very real possibility that he might not fuck me otherwise, I run my fingers through his hair, my heart filling up as he looks up at me with those intense dark eyes of his, and I tell him, "If you're serious about this, I will marry you."

He pops off my nipple, grins victoriously, and takes my mouth instead. His kiss makes me dizzy, or maybe it's what I just agreed to. Maybe it's both, but what the hell? I'm already going to move here, move in with him, and have a baby with him—a wedding band on my left hand isn't the most outrageous decision I'm making where this man is concerned. I like the idea of being committed to him, I already planned to be, so why not make it official?

Plus I like the idea of him wearing my ring while he's out in the world as much as I like the idea of wearing his. Yes, this belongs to me, now move along, skanks.

Not that I have to worry about that with him. It's a relief, and it lets me know I'm with the right person. I've never felt as appreciated as I do with Sin, as treasured. To Rafe, I was an amusing toy someone else wanted more but whose directions he couldn't even be bothered to read. To the guys who came before them, guys I've practically forgotten since Sin takes up so much space in my heart, I was just an ordinary girl they eventually lost interest in and stopped liking.

I'm so much more than that to Sin. I'm not one of many to him. I'm *it* for him, and damn, that is sexy.

And damn, I am lucky. I didn't think I was very lucky when that pregnancy test came back positive, but it may have been the best thing to ever happen to me. Maybe instead of cursing Mateo Morelli's name to the wind, I should send the man a thank you card.

"Does that mean we're engaged now?" I ask, bending my neck to give him better access.

"It does." Pulling back, he looks down at me. "Now when you send me grocery shopping, it'll actually be my job."

"You're going to be a great husband," I state, with absolute confidence.

"Let's do it this weekend," he says, before diving back into my neck.

"What?" I ask, rearing back, eyes wide. "This weekend? That's fast."

"You complain when I move slow, you complain when I move fast. You've got this wife thing down already, let me tell you."

I grin up at him. "I won't be a fishwife, I promise. But this weekend isn't enough time. I want my sister here. We'll have to clear it with Rafe for Vince to come back into town. We should have a real wedding, even if it's a small one, we should have our family and friends here. I've never even met your parents."

"They probably won't come," he tells me.

My eyes widen in disbelief. "They're not going to come to their son's wedding? They don't even live that far away."

"It's not about how far away they live. They've kept their distance from me since—since the funerals. It's not a big deal. It doesn't matter to me. But they probably won't come, so don't take it personally. I don't really have anyone to invite, so a quick Vegas wedding would be just fine with me. If you want a real one, that's up to you."

Well, I do... but I also don't want to make Sin feel badly for not having anyone. "You don't have *anyone* to invite? Friends? Cousins?"

His lips curve up faintly. "I can invite Rafe."

"God," I murmur, covering my face with my hands. "All right, well, we could do something small. A Vegas wedding, but I at least need Vince and Carly to be here with me. I would have liked to invite Mia too, but Mateo and Vince despise each other, so if we're not having a big enough wedding for them to stay on separate ends of the room, I don't know if I'll invite them."

"Probably should, I hear Mateo gives good gifts," Sin jokes. "I can keep them from killing one another. Invite whoever you want. Don't worry about that."

"You're the groom; I'm not going to have you working at our wedding."

"I care about the marriage, not the wedding." He shrugs. "We'll do whatever you want."

I smile, leaning up to kiss his perfect lips. "I'm excited. I want to tell everyone."

"Tomorrow," he tells me. "Tonight, you're all mine."

45

LAUREL

I'm caught completely off-guard when Sin's strong hands close around my wrists like the sexiest of shackles. It's no light, tender grasp—it's tight like a vice, and the suddenness knocks my heart right out of my chest. He presses me into the soft mattress, his heated gaze sweeping over me with a casual sense of ownership.

"All mine," he murmurs, his tone low and gruff.

"Always," I assure him quietly.

He releases my wrists now, skimming my sides with the tips of his fingers as he moves down my body. "Let's see how wet you are for me, pretty girl."

Flushing with anticipation, I have to fight to restrain the shy urge to turn my face. It still makes me flushed when he does this. When he spreads my legs and looks at my pussy the way he does. I don't want to look, but I can't resist the peek at his face while he looks at me. He looks so hungry, so reverent, like he's looking at something he wants so desperately.

I guess maybe it's the same way I feel when I look at his

cock. Really, any part of his body turns my body into a pit of flames, my insides into liquid need. The idea that he wants me even half as much as I want him makes me feel powerful. No amount of worshiping his body could ever adequately express how I feel when I look at him, how much I want him with every part of me. Maybe he feels that way, too.

Tonight he's not just here to look, he's here to touch. He's here to taste. He leans down and kisses the outside of my pussy like he would kiss my mouth. This is something new to me, not something I experienced before Sin. I've experienced oral sex before, but not the way Sin does it. Not like he truly wants to be doing it, like there's nowhere else he'd rather be than between my legs. There's no rush to the orgasm so he can get his—he treats this like he *is* getting his. Like this is all he's here for. Like we could do this all night and he'd be happy.

As his tongue breaches my entrance and rubs against my clit, I writhe, reaching above me to hold onto the pillow. His dark eyes shoot up to me. He looks so mischievous. It's adorable. I can't help smiling at him, but then he gets more aggressive, sucking on my clit, and I lose my smile, my breath hitching as my hips roll forward.

Sin's grip drops to my hips, holding me in place while he licks me. Every stroke of his tongue makes me shudder with delight. One of his hands remains on my hip, but he moves the other between my legs, pushing a finger inside me while he licks at my clit. His finger moves deeper into my pussy, stretching me, preparing me for him.

The thought sends a streak of excitement coursing through me. I'm finally going to have him inside me. God, I want it so much. I've never had someone inside me bare before. I wonder how it will feel.

Sin sidetracks my thoughts when he shoves a second finger

inside me, when the pressure building becomes hard to ignore. He licks, he sucks, he nips. He drives me crazy with his mouth, pumping his fingers inside me all the while, leading my mind toward the scary, sexy thought of him finally invading me. His attention between my thighs together with the sensual thoughts swirling through my head—it's too much. I cry out as an orgasm hits my body hard and violent pleasure bursts inside me. I can feel him watching me come, and God, that's hot, too.

Gratitude sweeps over me, desperate gratitude. I need him in my mouth. Getting a little aggressive myself, I try to push him off me so I can crawl down and suck on him, but he grabs a fistful of my hair and yanks my head back, dragging me down on the bed.

"Nope," he says, moving on top of me.

"Just a little taste," I beg. "Please. I'll be good. I'll do whatever you want after."

"It's sexy as hell how much you like going down on me, did I ever tell you that?"

Reaching between his legs, I grab his cock and rub the head with my fingers. "Then let me have a taste."

He shakes his head. "Not tonight. Tonight I'm saving every drop for when I'm inside you."

"Mm," I murmur, my lips parting in anticipation as his face moves closer. His perfect lips brush mine, but he doesn't deepen the kiss. Even now he's teasing me, dropping soft kisses all over my face. It makes me feel so loved. I want to give back, so as soon as he stops kissing my face, I bend my head and start kissing him. I'm so in love with every sexy inch of his body, I need the whole night to properly worship it. I need to kiss every inch, to taste him—even though he won't let me, because he's being stingy—and admire every plane of his body. I want to show him how lucky I feel that he's mine by giving him as much pleasure as possible.

He's still on top of me so I can't reach him everywhere, but I can wrap my arms around him—one over his broad, muscled shoulder, one around his back, my nails lightly scoring his skin. His eyes smolder when I do that, and excitement jumps in my belly. That look warns me of so many things, and I want every last one of them.

I want to know every desire he keeps locked away inside him, the darkest, dirtiest corners. I want to know him inside and out, know him as well as I know myself. I can't believe I get to have him. I can't believe he's mine for the rest of my life.

"What are you going to do to me, captor?" I tease.

He smiles darkly, sending a thrill through my belly. Then he leans down to drag kisses along my jaw as he tells me, "I liked being your captor. You should have seen your face the first time you saw me naked."

I flush at the memory of him standing bedside, this beautiful body a scary, dark fantasy. "You were so gorgeous, but so scary. I thought you were going to murder me."

Smirking, he mocks me. "Yeah, *that's* what you were afraid I was going to do."

I bite my lip, recalling the thoughts that went through my head. "Everything about you is part scary, part sexy," I inform him.

"Yeah?" he murmurs, nipping at my neck.

I nod, holding him close. "And 100 percent perfect, of course."

"Oh, of course," he murmurs lightly, before showcasing that perfection. Gathering my hair in his fist, he uses it to drag my head to the side. "You wanted a taste then, didn't you, pretty girl? You liked being at my mercy. You wanted me to use this sweet little mouth."

Oh, God, his words. I arch against him, closing my eyes and nodding my head. I'm not even altogether clear on what I'm agreeing to. He's filling my mind with his gravelly tone, his rough touch, his body pressing into mine.

He keeps a hold of my hair, but his body lifts off mine and then he's moving until he's on his knees beside me, stroking his cock with his free hand.

"Tell me you want it."

"I want it," I tell him, need clear in my tone. "I need it. Please."

"You want to taste it?"

My gaze darts to his. "You said I couldn't."

He smiles, liking that I'm respecting his orders even when *he* isn't. "You can have a little taste, just none of my cum. I'm saving all that. Think you can follow that rule?"

I nod eagerly, leaning my head toward him and opening my mouth.

"You're so good at sucking cock, aren't you?" he asks evenly, stroking himself, then guiding it to my mouth. I open wide and stick out my tongue like I'm trying to catch rain. It reminds me of our first time in the shower when he came on my body. Fuck, that was hot. I close my eyes, thinking of it now as he rests his heavy cock against my tongue. Now that he's moved his hands, I bring one of mine up to stroke him, to hold him while I run my tongue along the underside and use my lips to leave kisses along his whole length.

When I get to the soft tip, I moan, looking up at him prettily, wordlessly begging for just a little bit. I want him in my mouth. I want to suck him, and then I want him in my throat, but he told me no. I hold his cock and move my head, swiping my tongue around

456 | SINNING IN VEGAS

the sides of the tip, but carefully avoiding the indent where I already see a drop of pre-cum. It's almost painful, having to deny myself when I see it right there. Just one swift move of my tongue and I could taste him—he wouldn't be able to stop me in time.

Then he'd punish me. I want him to punish me. I should be a brat and disobey.

As if he can sense the direction of my thoughts, he tugs my head and takes his cock away.

"No, that was barely a taste," I object.

"I see that look in your eye," he tells me. "You wanted to break my only rule."

"I'm too hungry for you," I inform him. "It's a mean rule."

Ignoring me, he moves between my legs, lifts them high, and leans down to kiss my pussy again. Arousal flutters in my core and as ridiculous as it is, I almost hope he'll eat me again. He licks, sucks, and enjoys all the tastes he wants, but I'm not allowed. Big jerkface.

Looking up at me as he slides two fingers deep inside me, he tells me, "Last chance to come to your senses."

"And suck your cock even though you told me no?" I ask, since that's the only thing I'm ready to change my mind about.

His lips curve up faintly. "And stop me from claiming this for myself."

I shake my head. "Nope. You can keep us here for the next year and I won't change my mind about that."

Withdrawing his fingers from my core, he grasps his cock and nudges the head between my lips. I clutch the bed sheets, preparing for impact, but he doesn't move any deeper just yet. He rubs the bare head of his cock against my clit, undoubtedly smearing that first drop of pre-cum inside of me. The thought gets me hot and needy. I want every drop of him inside me. I want him to fuck me, claim me, mark me. I shudder with pleasure as he does it again, at the feel of his smooth skin as he teases my sensitive clit. I look down, wanting to watch. Wanting to see him disappear inside me.

"Fuck me, Sin," I whisper.

I watch as he fits his cock lower and I feel him at my entrance. I tense up for a second, then remind myself to relax. It only *looks* like it doesn't fit; I know it will. He pushes forward a few inches, watching my face as I watch him join us together. Then he shoves forward slowly, until he's buried all the way to the hilt. I gasp, feeling so fucking full. And I *am* full —full of Sin. I reach for him and he leans in close. I grab his face and yank him in for a kiss.

"You're finally inside me," I murmur against his lips.

His voice is low and rough with need. "I need to move, baby."

I steal one more kiss, then break away, nodding my head. He pulls his hips back, the aching fullness ebbing, leaving me feeling nearly empty until he thrusts forward and buries himself inside me again. This feels so perfect. He does it a third time and it still stings. I'm so aroused I thought it would be easy passage, but he's thick and his bare cock doesn't slide in as easily without a condom. I feel my skin stretching to accommodate him each time he pushes inside me. I need to hold onto him.

I'm greedy for his mouth, so I coax him close again and pepper the corners with kisses, nibbling on his bottom lip. His gaze falls to my breasts, jiggling rapidly with the force of his thrusts. He palms one with his rough hand, running his thumb across the hard nipple.

"All of this belongs to me now. Say it."

"I belong to you, Sin. Every inch. All of this is yours, only yours."

"That's right," he says, satisfaction heavy in his tone.

"Fuck, you feel so good inside me," I tell him, lifting my hips to meet his thrust.

"Yeah?" he practically growls. "Tell me more."

"I want you to stay inside me forever. I never want you to leave."

"Trust me, pretty girl, I'm not going anywhere. I should've done this a long time ago. I should've done this the first time I laid eyes on you."

I bite back a smile as he pumps into me again, filling me up with his hard cock and another spike of pleasure along with it. "That might've been awkward, considering I was fucking Rafe that weekend."

The tenderness is gone in a flash and he pulls out of me, flips me over so fast I lose my breath, and locks his arm around my neck. Even though I know he'd never hurt me, fear shoots through me and my hands fly to his arm, trying to pry the unforgiving bar off me.

"Three strikes," he says simply.

"What—?"

Then his hand comes down hard and he smacks my ass so hard it stings. I gasp and squirm, instinctively trying to wiggle away.

"Sin—"

A second hard swat comes down in the same place and it stings worse. That one sends a shudder of excitement traveling up my spine, though. My fingers tighten on his arm around my throat, but I don't try to pry it off, I just hold on, bracing for the third swat.

Instead of a swat, that time he runs his palm across my ass, over the spot where he just spanked me. Then, just when I think he's soothing me, he draws his hand back and smacks me again.

I cry out at the impact, at the burn that comes with it. *Three strikes*, he said. I think he's done. I crane my head back to see, and the sight of him makes my heart drop right out of my rib cage. He's magnificent when he's angry, and he looks legitimately livid. His perfect jaw is locked tight, his dark eyes are narrowed with intensity, and his cock, oh, God, his perfect cock is jutting out, prepared to invade me again.

I can't breathe. I need him inside me again. "I'm sorry," I tell him, my gaze bouncing from his face to his cock. "I'm sorry, I didn't mean to say it."

If he believes me or even cares, I can't tell. My words make no difference. He yanks one thigh to the side, then the other, and I let out a low, tortured moan as he shoves inside me again. It's different this time, with me on my belly and his arm locked around my neck. Less tender, but oh, so much hotter. I'm pinned here, helpless, and his thrusts are angry, bruising, punishing.

"Oh, God," I murmur mindlessly, pleasure spiking as he uses his cock to punish my pussy the way his hand punished my ass. It's the greatest punishment of all time. I'm panting, desperate for every brutal thrust. He thrusts so hard it hurts, but it feels so good, too. "Oh, Sin."

"That's right, *my* fucking name. That's the only name you say in this bed."

I consider apologizing again, but damn, I'm not actually sorry, not if his punishments feel this good. I might start pissing him off more often.

His arm across my throat should feel threatening, but as he ravages my pussy, his strong arm is my anchor. I hold onto it, hold it close, even bite him when the tension gets to be too much.

As his cock batters my walls, his grunts of pleasure send me soaring. The evidence that my body feels as good to him as his feels to me is intoxicating. My throat is dry from sucking in breaths, from crying out with every powerful thrust. He labors over me so hard, so fast, so angry, so magnificent. My senses are overwhelmed, the tension in my body ratcheted up to the point that I want to cry. Still, he thrusts. Still, he punishes. It never stops feeling so fucking good, but I need release.

Sudden terror overcomes me. What if he stops? He's a tease, and this is a punishment. I'll cry. I will *literally* sob.

"Please, please, please," I cry senselessly. I need to add more. I need to cry *please don't stop*, but I can't get out more words. My lungs burn with the effort to drag in breaths, to keep up with his frantic pace. I'm barely hanging onto my grasp on sanity, so great is my need.

"Say my name," he barks.

Another thrill shoots through my already overly stimulated body. "Sin. Sin. Sin," I cry it over and over and over.

He batters me again, and again, and again. The heat spreading through my body singes my nerve endings. Then finally, it hits—an orgasm I can only describe as violent, ripping right through me, hitting so much harder than the first one. It is so intense that my mind blanks, my body shudders uncontrollably, and I can only cry out and whimper incoherently. Sin's arm around my neck tightens and he groans, shoving deep and pumping me full of his cum. "Aw, fuck, Laurel."

My name on his lips extends the pleasure, extends the high. A sob wracks through me, then another. I feel tears leaking down my face, but I don't know why. I'm just trying to draw air into my lungs. Sin collapses beside me on the bed, but his face freezes immediately when he sees my tears.

"Are you okay? Did I hurt you?"

I shake my head, still not capable of words.

"Why are you crying?" he demands, grabbing me and gathering me close.

I don't know. I'm not crying on purpose. I'm just... I don't have the mental capacity to figure it out right now. I caress his face, trying to steady my breathing, and burrow close to his chest.

His arms tighten around me protectively and he presses his lips to my forehead. He gives me a minute to get my shit together, holding me tightly. Once I can function on a semi-normal level, I tip my head up and worship him, dragging my lips along his jaw, kissing every inch of him I encounter.

"I love you, I love you, I love you," I tell him.

"What was that?" he asks, still mildly concerned.

"I don't know," I tell him, shaking my head. "My body was just—I was feeling so many things. It's nothing you did—nothing bad, anyway. That was perfect. Absolutely perfect," I assure him.

"Yeah?" he asks, still sounding a little unsure. "I didn't mean to make you cry."

"It was a good cry, if that makes sense."

"You could've stopped me if you didn't like it," he tells me.

"I *did*," I assure him, my eyes widening. "Don't think that. I did like it. I want to do it again soon. I promise. I loved every minute."

That seems to mollify him, but he still mutters, "I told you I didn't want to go hard on you the first time."

I kiss his lips, then snuggle against his chest. "I'm glad you did. I want to experience every kind of lovemaking with you. I want it hard, tender, and everywhere in between. I want every single piece of you, Sin. I never want you to hold anything back from me."

Affection glistens in his dark eyes as he looks down at me, his big, beautifully scarred hand tenderly caressing my jaw. "Same here."

46

LAUREL

When my eyes drift open, the room is still fairly dark due to Sin's black-out curtains, but I hear him moving around the room quietly, getting ready for the day.

Contentment rolls over me as flashes of last night shoot across my mind—his powerful body moving over mine, how great it felt to finally have him inside me. There's a vague ache between my legs from how rough he was. I squeeze the muscles, relishing the faint soreness. I want more.

"Come back to bed," I request, lazily reaching an arm toward him. "I want more sex and more cuddles."

Chuckling lightly, he crosses the room and comes to stand by my side of the bed. "As tempting as that sounds, I can't. I was actually just about to wake you up."

"To give me more sex and cuddles?" I ask hopefully.

"No, to tell you to get your cute little ass in the kitchen and make breakfast."

Groaning, I ask, "Why does your sexist bullshit turn me on? You've broken my brain."

"Breakfast and coffee for nine," he tells me, smacking me on the ass. "Get up."

I roll over and throw the blankets off me, but instead of getting up, I start massaging my breasts. His dark eyes narrow, but he pauses in preparing to button his shirt and lets it hang open. I sigh, letting my hand drift down my abdomen, squeezing my thighs together. "Sin, don't you want to play with me?"

His nostrils flare and he all but glares at me. It startles me briefly, but then he comes over, grabs my ankle, and yanks me halfway off the bed. I squeal in surprise, grabbing onto the bedding to keep from falling. He doesn't pull me all the way off though, just close to the edge, and I feel him behind me.

"Ass up," he tells me.

Excitement floods me and I climb to my knees, putting my butt in the air and clutching a fistful of blankets. The sound of his zipper gets me short of breath, and before I can even look back at him, he shoves into me. I'm a little raw from last night and he didn't prepare me, so there's a little resistance, a little burn, but my eyes roll back and I sink back onto him, craving his possession.

"That what you want?" he asks lowly.

"Yes," I murmur, my head jerking back as he fists my hair and yanks it.

"Rafe's gonna be here in a few minutes," he murmurs, pounding into me again. "Every time he looks at you, he's gonna think about me doing this."

I'm not sure if this talk is for him or for me, but as long as he keeps riding me like he is, he can say whatever he wants.

"He'll know I made you mine last night," he adds, thrusting deep.

"I've always been yours," I tell him.

He releases my hair and pushes on my back, urging my upper body closer to the mattress, then tilting my ass a little higher. When he slides into me again, I gasp, squeezing the fistful of bedding closest to me. Anchoring one hand on my hip, he slips the other one between my thighs and starts teasing my clit while he fucks me.

"Oh, God," I murmur, closing my eyes.

"Spread your legs a little wider," he tells me.

I inch each knee out a little more before he slams into me again. My clit seems more sensitive now as he plays with it. He's relentless and it's hard to stay still, but when I start to move, he lets go of his hip anchor and swats me on the ass. Excitement jumps in my belly at the unexpected spanking.

"Ass up. It drops, I smack it," he tells me.

Pleasure moves through my loins in waves just from his words, then combined with his finger inside me and his dick pounding into my pussy, I'm stuck in a controlled pleasure vortex. Trying to obey, but so tempted not to. I like when he spanks me, but I like when he holds onto my hip and fucks me, too. The force of his thrusts makes it impossible to stay in one spot on the bed, so the fabric chafes my nipples as he fucks me. It all feels so good.

My legs begin to shake as his finger against my clit gets to be too much. The shaking causes my ass to drop. His finger abandons my clit and I gasp, my eyes popping open. Before I can object, he smacks my ass again.

"What did I tell you?" he asks.

"Oh, God, I was so close."

He pulls his dick out of me, grabs a fistful of hair, and uses it to drag me upright against his chest. I gasp as his arm moves around my neck like a bar, locking across my throat. "Only good girls get orgasms."

My heart stalls and I melt back against him, reaching back to loop my arm around his neck. "I am your good girl."

"Yeah?" he murmurs.

I nod my head and turn my face, needing a kiss. He bends just enough to claim my lips, then he breaks away and shoves me back down on the bed.

"Last chance. Ass up, pretty girl."

I plant my hands on the bed and thrust my ass in the air. I want that damn orgasm, but more than that, I want to please him. He grabs my hips and shoves his hard cock back into me, pushing on my back to remind me to lower my upper body. I drop lower, keeping my ass up, and once I hit the magic angle, his dick sliding against my walls feels incredible. Every thrust pushes me higher, then he locks in, fucking me hard and fast. My heart races in my chest. I clutch at the sheets and he mercilessly assaults what must be my G-spot, because my whole vagina explodes and sends pleasure shrapnel shooting all over my body.

"Sin, oh my God," I cry out, grasping helplessly at the bedding like it can help me.

"Fuck, you feel good," he tells me. "Hang in there, baby."

"Oh, God," I whine.

With a few more thrusts, he groans and pushes deep, emptying himself inside me. There's almost no strength left in my body, but I use what I have to keep my ass up until he releases my hip and pulls out of me.

Then I collapse on my side, rolling over to look at him. God, he's beautiful. I don't know how he's still standing, but his shirt hangs open so I can see his toned abs. He didn't even take his pants off, just unzipped and pulled his cock out. Now he's tucking himself back inside his slacks and zipping up, his eyes on me.

"See, I'm up now," I murmur.

His lips curve up faintly as he buttons his shirt up. "Good. Now, get your pretty little ass in the kitchen."

"Still hot," I tell him. He starts to walk away, so I call after him, "Wait, what about my cuddles?"

"I'll cuddle the shit out of you later," he promises. "Right now I have a meeting."

"Here?" I question, pushing myself up into a sitting position.

"Yep," he says, already on his way out of the bedroom.

I give myself another minute to recover from Sin's equivalent of 'good morning' before I drag myself out of bed. I'm the one who could use coffee, but I'm not allowed to have any. I grab my robe and go to the bathroom, attempting to make myself look less like a girl who was just mauled by a randy tiger. It doesn't work, but I splash some water on my face, do what I can to tame my hair, then pile it on top of my head and tie it up in a bun anyway. I put on some lip balm and mascara, pull on my robe and some panties, and head for the kitchen.

Breakfast for nine, huh? That's a lot of fucking people to cook for. I open the refrigerator and grab his carton of eggs. There are six eggs. I check for other breakfast possibilities and see he has five slices of bread, two bananas, and an orange.

What the hell am I supposed to serve these nine men for breakfast? I guess I'm going to have to go grocery shopping today. That's normally a boring chore, but I like the idea of stocking Sin's house with food. I like taking care of him. I need to find out everything he likes to eat and everything he hates.

I have cheese, milk, eggs, and a whole host of things on the counter as I attempt to throw together something I can call breakfast when the doorbell rings. Ordinarily I wouldn't answer the door at Sin's house, but since I already know he has people coming for this meeting, I assume that's probably Rafe. He has seen me in a robe before. No big deal.

When I swing open the door, however, it is not Rafe Morelli standing on the other side. It's a Morelli, all right, just not the one I expected to see.

My eyes narrow as Alec Morelli has the audacity to stand on my doorstep, a swarm of unfamiliar men trailing down the stairs behind him.

"What are you doing here?" I demand.

Looking past me dismissively, he says, "I'm not here for you, troublemaker. Where's your—I don't know what the fuck to call him. Where's your keeper?"

"My *keeper*?" I demand, glaring at him.

"Move aside, sweetheart," he says, practically shooing me as he steps inside.

To keep his stupid arm from touching me, I move out of the way. As he walks past, I tell him, "If I had known this breakfast was for you, I would have poisoned it."

"Don't poison me just yet," he calls back as he heads up the stairs. "Your keeper needs my help."

By the time Rafe shows up, Alec and all the men I don't know are assembled around my kitchen table. I've managed to put together a plate for everyone, but I didn't save one for Rafe. For one thing, he is still on my shit list. Also, I miscounted plates and I only dished out enough for the guys already present. If he asks, I'm only going to tell him the first part.

When he strides into the dining area, hands shoved into

his pockets, he looks at the men eating and drinking their coffee, then looks at me.

"Look at you, already getting your mob wife hostess skills sharpened up."

"I didn't make any for you," I inform him.

"That's all right. I have a maid," he informs me. Then he smiles, but promptly tones it down a little. My gaze drops to his split lip. It might hurt to smile. He's wearing the evidence of his fight with Sin last night. In addition to the split lip, one eye is swollen and discolored. I almost feel bad for him until I remember he sent someone to kill Sin—then I want to bring my palm up and smack him right in the eye to make him hurt some more.

"I was going to apologize to you for all the really mean things I said to you yesterday, but after finding out the things I found out, I rescind my apology," I tell him.

"You rescind the apology you never gave me?" Rafe asks, sounding faintly amused.

"Yes," I state decisively.

"All right, kitten."

"Don't call me that."

His lips curve up again. "You can't hate me forever."

Completely uninvited, Alec butts into our conversation. "Yes, she can."

"No one asked you, Alec," I inform him.

Lifting his dark eyebrows, he addresses Rafe and points to me. "This one holds lifelong grudges. I went on half a date with her before either of you ever met her. To this day, she hates me so much she would shoot me in the face for a piece of fuzzy floor-candy. She's gonna hate you forever. Welcome to the club."

Sin is seated at the head of the table. Upon hearing Alec's

summary of our relationship, he scowls and demands, "Half a date? How the hell did you go on half a date?"

Alec shrugs. "I bailed halfway through. A work thing came up, I had to leave."

"Bullshit," I accuse, pointing at him. "You're such a liar. No wonder you're still single."

Sin shakes his head, gesturing to Alec. "This asshole clearly has shitty judgment. This is who Mateo sent me?"

Rafe shrugs his broad shoulders. "What, you expected him to send Adrian? He's not going to send his best guys and leave his own business unprotected. You know what a paranoid motherfucker he is."

Wide-eyed, Alec objects. "Are you serious? I brought my guys out here to help you assholes; you want to be a little appreciative?"

"I think you should apologize to Laurel," Rafe suggests.

Sin nods, leaning back in his chair. "Sounds good to me. You apologize to her, then we'll be nicer to you."

"Are you fucking kidding me?" Alec demands.

I smirk, crossing my arms over my chest. "They're not. I'm waiting."

Alec laughs lowly, shaking his head. "I'm glad to see this family is as fucking crazy in Vegas as Chicago."

"That didn't sound like an apology to me," Rafe says with a mock-grimace.

Sin nods his agreement. "Decidedly not an apology. And we asked so nicely."

Rafe taps his black eye. "See this, Alec? Know how I got it?"

I don't know where he's going with this. Surely he's not going to admit Sin just beat his ass yesterday, right?

Alec shrugs like he's not sure why he should care.

"Pissed Laurel off and didn't apologize fast enough. She'll punch you right in the face. You want to join *my* club?"

That makes me snort. Rafe looks back at me and winks with his good eye. Damn him. I probably won't be able to hate him forever.

Alec rolls his eyes. "This clearly means a lot more to you people than it does to me. Laurel, I apologize profusely for not falling madly in love and marrying you after our half-date. I don't know what I was thinking. I will live the rest of my days in miserable regret."

I nod my head. "I accept your incredibly insincere apology. I still don't like you though."

Alec waves me off, taking his seat. "Whatever. Let's get back to work before I change my mind about helping you dick-heads and go back home."

I smile, feeling a little more cheerful now and grab the coffee pot. I didn't make Rafe any breakfast, but now I pour him some coffee and take it over to him.

"I get coffee?" he asks, as I hold out the mug to him.

"Baby steps," I tell him.

He smiles faintly and nods his head, taking a sip of my peace offering. I retrieve the pot and take it around the table, topping off cups to empty the pot so I can make more. I'm all out by the time I get to Sin.

I put the coffee pot down on the table and straddle him. Then I drape my arms around his neck, and his hands move to my ass. "Can I help you with something?" he asks.

"I ran out of coffee. I can't refill your cup."

"How *will* I survive?" he inquires.

"I thought I'd make up for it with kisses."

He smirks at me. "You just wanted kisses. You probably dumped the coffee so you had an excuse."

"I *would* do that, but since we have 85 men here today, I didn't have to. Anyway, about this kiss situation. Am I allowed to kiss you when you're working?"

"In this setting, yes. If I have my gun out, maybe wait until later."

"Good," I murmur, leaning in to steal a kiss. His grip on me tightens and he tugs me close, one of his hands roaming down to cup my ass. He gives it a squeeze, briefly deepening the kiss before pulling back.

I sigh and nuzzle into his neck, nipping him one more time before climbing off his lap. "All right, now I'll make some more coffee."

Sin swats me on the ass, then leans forward and gets back to work.

47

LAUREL

After all the men leave, I make a grocery list, take a shower, and promptly realize I have no idea where to get groceries. I also have no money to buy said groceries. Sin didn't leave me anything, so all I have is the pocket money I have left from Rafe. I hesitate for a minute to use that, but then I decide, screw it, I will. It's only $40, but it should get some staples in the house. Breakfast completely cleaned us out.

I don't want to contact Lydia. I have her number in my phone, but she's so terrible, I can't stomach the idea of actually calling her. The only other woman in Vegas I can reach out to is Virginia, so I shoot her a text and ask how she's doing and what she's up to.

Instead of texting me, she calls. I am initially alarmed—who the hell answers a text with a phone call?—but I answer anyway. "Hey."

"Hey," she says brightly. "What's up?"

"Um, not much. I actually wanted to ask you a weird question. I'm obviously new to Vegas, so I don't really know where anything is. I need to buy some groceries, but I don't even know where to tell the Uber person to take me."

"You have an Uber?"

"Not yet, but I will once I know where to tell them to take me."

"Oh, God, don't waste your money like that. I'm off today, I can swing by and pick you up. I need to pick up a few things anyway. My refrigerator looks like it belongs to a sad bachelor. Are you at home?"

"Yes—Um, not Rafe's. I'm at Sin's. Do you know where he lives?"

"I do. Why are you at Sin's?"

I hesitate, realizing she's not caught up. "Um, we're actually together now. I'm going to be living here with him."

"You and Rafe aren't—That's over?"

"Yep," I verify, nodding even though she can't see me. "Sin and I are official. Sorry, is that weird? I know you and Rafe... Actually, I don't understand what you are at all, but I know if sides are being taken, you'd be on his. Not that this is a side-taking situation. It's not. At all. He was just at my house for breakfast. I mean, things aren't back to normal yet, but, you know, I'm still pregnant, and he's still the father, so they probably will be."

"You're a nervous talker, huh?"

"Yeah, sorry," I mutter.

"No sweat. We're cool. I can pick you up at Sin's if you'd like a ride."

I'm not convinced it won't be weird, but since I have my heart set on making Sin dinner for our first official night living together, I also really need the groceries.

Shortly after we hang up, she pulls into the driveway. I

invite her inside while I try to figure out where Sin put my house key, then I go to set the alarm. Virginia turns away.

"You should be more careful setting that when people are around," she informs me. "Sin would kick your ass if he knew you pushed in the alarm code in front of anyone who isn't him."

Lifting my eyebrows as it beeps that it's secure, I ask her, "Are you planning to break into my house?"

"No, but someone else could be. I'm just saying, you can't be too careful. Don't trust people. People generally suck. I don't suck, but you haven't known me long enough to know that."

Thinking back to last night, I have to agree. "Good point, people do suck."

"The Morellis have a lot of power around here," she tells me, as I pull the front door shut behind me and follow her to her car. "If you're going to be involved with them now, that puts you with them. Thankfully you're not with Rafe now—that was bound to be a headache. Ambitious, money-grabbing bitches trying to kill you for your spot in his bed. It would have been a hassle. You're probably better off with Sin, really. He's dangerous as fuck, but also mean, and all the women in the know basically understand he'd just as soon kill them as fuck them, so he's not really the guy a scheming ho will go after. Rafe, though? There's basically a bull's eye painted right on that muscular back of his. A single boss? It has literally never happened before."

"You know an awful lot about the Morellis," I tell her, sliding into the car. It's still faintly cool, so she must blast the air conditioner.

"Yeah, I do," she murmurs. "I get bored easily. I research things, but I absorb so fast I'm on to the next thing. I run out of things, so... lots of idle research. Plus, I technically knew about the Morelli family before I came out here. When I was lost down one of my rabbit holes I stumbled across a news story online—one thing led to the next, I was researching as much as I could online. Then I moved out here for school and, what do you know, I ended up working for one of them."

Casting her a skeptical look, I remark, "That's an odd coincidence."

"Isn't it?" She flashes me a smile. "Don't worry, I'm on your side. I heard how faintly suspicious all that sounded once it was out of my mouth, but I would never do anything to hurt Rafe."

That I can believe. I don't know why, but her voice softens anytime she says his name. She was nice to me even when I was the one he was snuggling at dinner—while she served us— so whatever fondness she has for him, it has to be pretty pure. She's even above jealousy, and God knows I never was.

"Well, I'm glad," I tell her. "It looks like I'm going to be staying out here for good now, and I'm going to need a friend. I don't even know how much my sister will be able to visit, because Rafe won't let her husband come to town."

Virginia nods. "Vince. He seemed volatile. Very touchy. Like the smallest thing could set him off. Your sister sure is a lucky gal," she adds dryly.

I wave off her concerns. "He's fine. He's calmer at home; being around his family just gets him all riled up. He doesn't like Rafe. I think Rafe slept with his ex-girlfriend or something."

"Probably," Virginia agrees with a nod. "That sounds like something Rafe would do."

S pending the afternoon out with Virginia was nice. All day I've been fitting together pieces of my new life in my head, thinking about how lovely it can all be. I never found myself doing this with Rafe. Now that I'm in the right relationship with someone I actually want, I can see that I never really wanted it to work out with him. Rafe was never right for me, while Sin is *so* right for me. I know it's new, and it won't always be exciting, but I was moved into a literal mansion when I had to stay with Rafe and I couldn't muster enthusiasm for anything. Today I am excited to do Sin's *laundry*.

I'm grossly, disgustingly in love, and I couldn't be happier about it.

I don't hear from him much today, though. Since his job is obviously non-traditional, I have no idea what kind of hours to expect him to keep. I figure he'll send me a text to let me know when he's coming home for dinner.

What I *don't* expect when the phone finally rings and it's Sin, is for him to greet my pleasant "hello, handsome" with a short, to the point, "Get to Rafe's. Now."

"What?" I ask, my face falling. There's urgency in his tone —maybe more than that. Maybe actual fear. "Sin, is everything okay?"

"Laurel, get the hell out of the house."

I jump up off the couch and run to grab the purse I left on the counter, my heart hammering in my chest. "I don't have a car," I tell him, my voice shaking. "Where am I supposed to go?"

"I'm sending someone to pick you up, I just don't want you in the house alone. Rafe's at his house, he can keep you safe."

"Are we positive we want to trust the guy who held a gun to my head last night?" I inquire.

"He's not behind this. It wouldn't benefit him. Listen, I know you're nervous, but I need you to get out of the house now. Walk around back and keep walking until you're on the next street over. I'm going to send Rex to pick you up there. He'll be in a silver car. He'll be looking for you, but stay out of sight, just in case, okay?"

"Is someone coming here?" I demand.

"I don't know, okay? I just need you out of the house in case. Gio knows I turned on him, and he knows how to hurt me. I need to know you're safe or I can't concentrate."

"Okay, I'll be safe," I assure him, setting the alarm and heading down the stairs, turning off the lights.

I feel paranoid the moment I step outside. I follow his directions, going around the house and walking until I get to the road behind ours. I keep stealing looks back toward Sin's house as I walk, looking at the road to make sure no one pulls in. Sin stays on the phone, but he doesn't talk. There are noises, voices in the background. Periodically he breaks away to say something to someone, but he comes right back.

After a few minutes, I hear a car and turn to see headlights. My heart drops clear out of my chest, because I don't know if it's a good guy or a bad guy. "Someone is coming up the road."

"A silver car?" he snaps.

"I can't tell."

"I'm going to send you a picture," he tells me. "This is the guy picking you up. Do not get in the car with anyone but him."

I keep an eye on the car as it comes up the road. Sin's picture comes through and it's a dark-haired guy who looks to be around my age with dark hair, a strong jaw, and dark, bushy brows, slanting deviously so he looks like he's up to no good. Not someone I would get into a car with, if I'm being honest. It occurs to me that given the side of society I'm on now, all my knights in shining armor from here on out will always be the bad guys. Good guys no longer have a place in my life.

"I texted him and told him to slow to a stop," Sin tells me.

A few seconds later, the car slows to a stop. I breathe a little easier. "Okay. The car stopped. Should I approach it then?"

"Hang on." There's a pause, so Sin must be texting him. Then the car moves forward slowly. "Is he moving? I told him to move slow."

"Yes. Okay, it's him."

"Stay on the phone until you're in the car," he tells me.

Gripping the phone tightly, as if Sin can protect me through it if shit gets dicey, I approach the car. It stops and I lean down to look in the window. Thankfully, it is the guy from the picture. Just to be safe, I say, "Name?"

"Rex Donati," he offers.

"It's him," I tell Sin, opening up the car door and sliding in.

"Put him on real quick," Sin tells me.

I hand Rex the phone. He takes it, calming me slightly because while Sin scared the fuck out of me, Rex seems relaxed, like we're just going for a Sunday drive.

"Yeah?" he says to Sin. I can't hear what Sin says, but Rex hits the locks and starts driving. His large hand grips the wheel naturally, like he was born with a steering wheel in his hand. His air of aptitude has me settling down a little bit. He doesn't say much to Sin, just listens, then says, "Got it," and hands the phone back to me.

As soon as I get the phone back, Sin tells me, "I'm sorry if I scared you. I just... I had this fucking flashback feeling, and I had to get you out of that house."

"It's totally fine," I assure him. "No harm done. I'm out now, so we're all good."

"Text me when you're inside Rafe's house so I know you're safe."

"Are *you* safe?" I ask.

"I'll be fine. Don't worry about me. Eat Rafe's food and watch some *Smallville* or something," he tells me.

Cracking a smile, I tell him, "I can do that."

"I gotta go. I love you."

"I love you, too."

I end the call and flatten myself against the seat of the car, taking a breath and staring out the windshield. It takes a minute for the adrenaline to slow down, for me to get my bearings. Once I can hold my hand out without it trembling, I think I should probably introduce myself.

"I'm Laurel Price, by the way."

He nods his head once like he already knew that, his gaze slicing my way before moving back to the road. "You okay? Everything good over there?"

"Yeah, I just... I don't really know what's going on."

"Yeah, I think that's usually how it works for the ladies," he says casually. "Don't worry about it. You're safe now. I'm an excellent getaway driver. You're in good hands."

I don't mean to look so surprised, but I still don't think he could be very old. How does someone my age even get into this line of work? This guy was at breakfast this morning, so he's one of the guys Alec brought with him. "Um, you're from Chicago?"

"Yep. Well, New York way back, but Chicago now."

"How are you old enough to have worked for that many crime families?" I ask.

He cracks a smile. "I'm not. I didn't work for a crime family in New York, I was just a kid. I got away with some petty theft, but nothing that would impress a Morelli. I work for the Chicago family. I'm here to help with the clean-up. I'm the best driver, so I knew I could get to you quickest. I go where I'm needed."

"How old are you?"

"Almost 19."

My God, he's even younger than me. That makes me think about when Sin got mixed up in all this. He said he has worked for the family since he was 21, so I guess he was just a couple of years older.

Given the lifetime sentence this job is, though, it's almost sad to think of guys getting involved so young. Then again, Vince got involved at the same age.

If I have a son, will he be expected to get involved in this shit when he's my age?

My phone chimes and I check it. It's Sin. I must have got in his head when I mentioned Rafe holding the gun to my head last night, because now he sends me a text that reads, "Tell Rex he needs to stay with you. I told him to leave you with Rafe and come back, tell him I changed my mind."

"Okay...?" I send back.

"Do you trust Mia?" he sends back.

I frown at the phone. "Yes. Why?"

"Text her. Tell her to send you a text that says this. Rex, your main priority is keeping Laurel safe at all costs."

"I got in your head about Rafe, didn't I?" I ask.

"Just send her the damn text. Then show Rex. If Rafe does try any shit, Mateo's wife's word will hold more weight than Rafe's. Rex is only here because Mateo told him to be."

God, this is going to be so awkward to explain. I type out a

quick text to Mia, begging her not to make me explain why I
need this right now, then I copy and paste Sin's message.

A few minutes later, I get a video message. I tap it and
Mia's face fills the screen. "Hi Rex, this is Mateo's wife, Mia. I
just wanted to make sure you understand that your main job
right now is to keep Laurel safe at *all* costs, all right? Top priority. Thanks!"

Rex grins over at me. "Wow, your boyfriend is a paranoid
motherfucker, isn't he?"

"He's had some bad experiences," I explain. "When we get
to Rafe's, he wants you to stay there with me."

"So, I'm your bodyguard now."

"Yes. Against everyone, Rafe included. Not that it will
come up," I rush to assure him. "I'm sure it won't. Things have
been a little rocky lately, so Sin just wants to make extra sure."

"Got it. So, I'm there in case Rafe turns on you?"

Grimacing, I say, "No, not... I don't expect that, I just—"

"You don't have to tiptoe," he assures me. "My lips are
sealed. Just trying to understand the situation I'm walking into
so I know what to be prepared for."

Placing a hand on my tummy, I tell him, "I'm pregnant.
The baby is Rafe's. But now I'm obviously with Sin. It caused a
little bit of friction. We are in the early stages of rebuilding."

"Got it," he says with a nod. "So, Sin gave him that
shiner, huh?"

I bite my tongue, remembering Virginia's earlier words
about not trusting everyone I meet. This new way of life is
going to have a learning curve, but I would rather be safe
than sorry.

Instead of sharing, I tell him, "They're supposed to be
working together, but since the truce is so new, Sin just wants
to be sure. It's possible that during a prior dust-up, Rafe may

have grabbed me and put a gun to my head. We don't think he would have actually pulled the trigger, and we don't think he is in any way involved with whatever is happening tonight, but just in case we're wrong, we aren't going to bet my life on it."

"I understand," he says, like a good soldier. "You'll be safe with me, don't worry."

48

LAUREL

The wait is agonizing.

I don't even know exactly what we're waiting for, and it isn't the most comfortable wait in the world, because Rafe tried to dismiss Rex with a handshake and a "thanks, now you can get back to work" but Rex refused to leave.

Rafe saw right through it, so he knows Rex is here to make sure I'm safe from him. I'm sure it's at least faintly offensive, but I refuse to feel bad. If he doesn't want me to have a body-guard around him, then he should have never pulled a gun on me in the first place.

So, it's just me and these two gangsters, waiting.

Juanita makes us all dinner, but I'm too nervous to do more than pick at it.

"This isn't how I thought you'd next visit me, kitten, but if you want to keep yourself busy, you can pack up the rest of your things. Obviously you left in a rush last night, so you left a lot here," Rafe tells me, stabbing a piece of asparagus.

"Oh, yeah, I suppose I should do that," I murmur, my face

flushing faintly. It's weird that I'm already so thoroughly Sin's, but I still have stuff at Rafe's house.

"I packed up your books last night," he tells me. "You can take them with you when you leave."

"My books?"

"Your Brontë books," he specifies.

"Oh, no, I can't take those," I tell him, shaking my head. "They're too expensive."

Smiling faintly, he says, "I'd have to unpack them now. Seems like a hassle. Just take them with you. I won't miss them, trust me. Besides, I bought them for you."

"When you thought I would be..." I trail off, since Rex is sitting here, and I feel weird talking about this in front of him, given he is a complete stranger to me.

"It's fine, Laurel," Rafe assures me. "I bought them for you, no strings attached."

As I stare at my plate, I'm suddenly hit with a horrible mental image of Rafe all by himself in this giant house. I had abandoned him to run off with Sin, and while Sin and I were finally making love for the first time, Rafe was here all by himself, packing up books he bought me when he thought I would stay with him and we would have a family together.

Both men are equally alarmed when I suddenly burst into tears.

Rafe's eyes widen and he looks around, as if for something that would have caused this. "What's wrong? What's happening right now?"

"I didn't mean to make you lonely," I blubber.

He blinks, thoroughly confused. "What?"

"That's so sad," I bawl, grabbing the cloth napkin in my lap and wiping my face. "That makes me feel horrible. You packed up my books. Oh, my God, why am I crying so much?"

Looking more lost than he ever has, Rafe tells me, "I haven't the faintest idea."

Rex was initially concerned, but now he resumes cutting into his fish filet. "Pregnancy hormones. One time I met Mateo in his office, and Mia burst into the room, sobbing hysterically. Just sobbing her head off, talking about how horrible she felt for some woman and how lonely this woman would be. Mateo rubbed her back and tried to comfort her, but he had no fucking idea what was happening, you know? He's just standing there like 'tell me who I have to kill to make these tears stop'. Finally, she explains it was a commercial. There was a *fictional* couple on an insurance commercial, and the husband died in a car crash right before they bought their first home. She was so upset, I thought someone she *knew* died, so when she said it was a commercial, I just thought she'd lost her fucking mind. Crying over these fucking people that aren't even real. They live in a 90 second commercial. Who cries over shit like that? Adrian explained the situation. The hormones make women emotionally unstable. Apparently pregnancy is pretty hardcore."

"I am not emotionally unstable," I say, scowling at him, while also still crying.

Rex lifts an eyebrow and nods at me. "Right. Clearly not. My mistake."

None of this makes me feel better. Instead of being a normal human being, I get off the chair and go over to hug Rafe. He is understandably surprised, since last night I wanted to stab him, but now I'm crying because he packed up my books all alone in his giant library.

"Kitten, it's okay," he assures me, kissing the top of my head and rubbing my back. "You just live across town, not in another country. You'll see me all the time, for God's sake."

Sniffling, I tell him, "I want us to all be friends. I want you and Sin hanging out like you did before you met me, and I want to take the baby in the pool. I don't know why I'm so attached to this pool scene in my head, but I am. Also, our baby in my head is adorable."

"You can bring the baby to the pool anytime. My pool is your pool. You're still the mother of my child, and obviously I'm stuck with Sin, that asshole isn't going anywhere. We'll all see as much of each other as we want to see. More than we want to see, probably. We're good. Everything is good. I promise."

"I don't want you to be lonely," I say, looking up at him.

"I'm never lonely," he assures me, dragging his thumb across my check to wipe away tears. "You know that. It was one of our problems."

"I don't mean stupid, empty hook-ups. It sounds like packing up my books was sad."

Tenderly brushing my hair behind my ear, he tells me, "You're making it sad in your head because you want to feel guilty. Don't feel guilty. I don't want that. I'm glad you're with Sin if he makes you happy. I certainly didn't. It's not sad. We didn't even break up; we were never really together."

"I still feel icky."

"Stop feeling icky," he commands, like it's just that simple.

"That's not how this works."

"Well, pregnancy sounds terrible," he informs me. "I apologize."

"I'm still mad at you for trying to kill Sin," I tell him, frowning at him now.

"I know. I won't do it again. Does that help?"

I shake my head. It should help, he's taking away the

logical basis of all the reasons I'm sad, but I still feel terrible. "Why are you being nice? You're an impossible man to trust."

"I know," he murmurs, rubbing my back. "I'm being nice because I like you, and I don't want to make you sad anymore. That's simple, right?"

"You didn't care about making me sad yesterday," I point out. "What changed?"

He taps the discolored skin around his eye. "Remember this?"

"You gave up because Sin punched you?" I ask skeptically.

"No, I gave up because I lost. Only a fool keeps fighting once the fight is over. The wise man moves on. You let a man sneak into my house thinking he was here to kill me yesterday, kitten. You knew he was coming and you didn't warn me. I remained interested in you when I thought there was still something to work with, but there's nothing left. You aren't loyal to me, and that means you and I have no romantic future. It couldn't be clearer. You can't build a relationship with a woman who tries to kill you. If someone wants to disagree with me, fine, but I never would. Not in a million years. Once a woman tries to help someone else kill me, strangely enough, I don't want to pursue a romantic relationship with her anymore."

"Now you're just making me feel mean again," I tell him, my face crumbling.

Sighing heavily, he hugs me tighter. "That was not my intention. I'm not mad; I understand why you did it. I was only trying to explain so you know you can trust my retreat. There's plenty of blame on me for this not working out, too. Like you said, it just didn't work, that's all. There's no need for either of us to feel badly about it. We'll still have a relationship, just not a romantic one."

"See, now I'm back to worrying you're lonely."

"How about a distraction?" Rex suggests. "You got any playing cards? Let's play some poker."

"I don't know how to play poker," I mutter, still a little peeved at him for calling me emotionally unstable.

"Good idea, Rex. I'll teach you," Rafe tells me.

"I don't have any money, either. I spent it all on groceries."

"I'll give you some money, too. Who knows? Maybe you'll beat us both and take home all the winnings."

"I wouldn't count on that," I tell him.

"I wouldn't either, you're a shitty liar. I'm just trying to make you less irrationally upset. Is it working at all? I'll pay you to stop sniffling, if that will help."

So, after dinner, we play poker. I lose all the money Rafe gave me to play with, but they're both so afraid I'll burst into tears again that they spot me enough to play one more hand, then shamelessly let me win so it ends on a positive note.

I feel ridiculous, but my nerves have just had it. Between the hell of yesterday, the high of last night and this morning, and then the fear of tonight—plus not knowing where Sin is or what is happening even now—I just can't take anymore. After poker, I curl up on the couch and Rex keeps watch while I drift off.

49

LAUREL

y eyes fly open with some kind of urgency, like
it's my first day of work and I've slept past my
alarm. There's movement in the living room—a
lot more movement than when I went to sleep.

My heart leaps at the sound of Sin's voice. "Put it right
there."

I blink and smile, relief washing over me as I see him
standing in the living room with his back to me. He's safe.
Everything must have gone according to plan.

Rex's voice joins in next. He sounds unsure. "I don't know
what to do with it."

"*Her*, not it," Sin snaps. "Just fucking hold her, what do
you mean?"

Her? I look over at Rex and see him looking down at a baby
on his chest like he expects her to bite him. She's starting to
fuss at him, because he is not working Sin magic.

Wait, why is Skylar here?

Pushing myself upright, I say, "You're back."

Sin turns around at the sound of my voice, smiling faintly and coming over to tenderly caress my face. "Yeah, I'm back."

"Why is Skylar here? Gio isn't here, is he? I thought..."

Sin shakes his head. "Long story. No, Gio isn't here. Skylar...we're gonna have to keep her tonight while we figure some stuff out."

"Keep her? Why? Where's Lydia?"

Rafe answers that one, striding across the room to hand Sin some gauze and tape. "Dead."

Gauze and tape?

It's then that I notice the dark stain covering Sin's left arm. "Oh, my God, you're bleeding," I say, leaping up off the couch. I'm not sure what to do, exactly, but apparently the whole damn world changed while I took a nap.

Sin peels his jacket off. "I'm fine. Flesh wound, it's nothing."

"Flesh wound?" I ask, bug-eyed. "Like, you got *shot?*"

"Fucking Lydia," he mutters. "I'm gonna go clean this. You can help me tape it if you want to."

"We need to get you to a hospital," I state, floored by how calm he is being about this.

His eyebrows shoot up like I just suggested we go for a promenade through the park in our Sunday finest. "A hospital? For this? No."

Then he's gone, heading into the kitchen and leaving me to gape at his back. Since Rafe is still here and he didn't sleep through everything, I turn to him for an explanation. "What the hell is going on?"

Rafe puts a reassuring hand on my back and gives it a little rub. "He'll be fine. I'll make our doctor check it out tomorrow, but it's a clean wound, superficial. He got lucky. Well, and Lydia's a terrible shot."

My eyes bug out again. "Lydia *shot* him?"

"It's over now. Don't bug him about it tonight, all right? Today was a slaughter. He'll be fine, he knows how to take care of himself, but let him have the rest of the night off." Gesturing to Rex and Skylar he says, "I can't take care of a baby though, so you're going to have to handle that. Tomorrow I'll talk to my cousins and see who wants to take her."

"Take her?"

Sighing, Rafe rakes a hand through his golden hair. "Her parents are both dead. Sin brought her here because he couldn't just leave her in the house alone. Technically, I'm her godfather, but I think we both know I did not anticipate ever having to carry out that responsibility."

"Oh, my God." I walk over to check on Skylar. Of course she's just a little baby, so she has no idea what's going on. She looks over at me and smiles when I rub her cheek. "Hey, little girl."

Rex is still holding her awkwardly, so he asks hopefully, "You wanna take her?"

"In a minute. I have to go take care of Sin first. Between the way you hold a baby and calling pregnant women emotionally unstable, you better not knock anyone up anytime soon. Free life advice."

"I always take life advice from someone who's clearly killing it in the good decision department, so thanks," he offers back.

I shoot him a humorless look and rub Skylar's tiny hand one more time, then I go to the kitchen to help Sin with his wound.

I still want to demand he go to a hospital and make sure he's okay, but since Rafe is fairly calm too, I guess he probably has it under control. I'm still nervous about it, so I Google it on my phone as I walk into the kitchen. Sin is standing shirtless at the sink, washing up. He turns his head to look at me when I walk in.

Armed with my 40 seconds of medical training, I glance at the wound. "It's not swollen, is it?"

"Get off WebMD," he tells me.

I smile faintly. "I'm not *on* WebMD, so ha."

"I'm fine. I've handled far worse wounds than this one without medical assistance." Nodding at the sink as he takes a step back, he tells me, "Wash your hands and you can play nurse."

"Sounds much sexier than it is," I inform him, tucking my phone in my back pocket.

He smirks. "I knew you were into roleplay."

"I mean, I would rather be medically assisting you with a raging hard-on than a gunshot wound, but I work with what I'm given," I tell him, turning on the faucet and scrubbing my hands clean.

Once we're both clean and germ-free, I help him clean up the wound a little better and layer a bunch of gauze over it before taping it down. His shirt is ruined, so he bundles it up and tosses it in Rafe's trash can. I try hard not to ogle him, but that danger is leaking out of him again, tonight with a battle-hardened edge. He's clearly worn out from today, but he carries on, like he always does. Rafe was sitting here eating seasoned fish with vegetables and playing cards while Sin was out getting shit done, and now apparently we have to take a baby home because Rafe doesn't feel like doing that, either.

"Gio and Lydia both, huh?" I ask.

"It wasn't the plan, but yeah. She fucking shot at me. I didn't even have time to think, I just..."

"Of course. You had to defend yourself."

"I made that poor kid parentless."

I sigh, wrapping my arm around his unwounded side and hugging him. "You had no choice. Gio and Lydia were terrible anyway."

"You're always defending me," he says, lightly tugging my hair back to tip my head up so he can kiss me.

"I always will," I assure him. "You can do pretty much no wrong in my eyes."

"Got yourself a pair of rose-colored glasses, huh?"

"Hey, I knew which side you were on going into this. I'm not some fragile flower who can't hang. I'm taking mob wife lessons. It's gonna be fine. I've got this."

"You're a natural," he assures me.

"I beat Rafe and Rex at poker tonight," I tell him, as we head back toward the living room.

"Bullshit," he answers. "I can't speak to Rex's skill, but there's no way you beat Rafe. He let you win."

"Well, yeah," I allow. "They wiped the floor with me a bunch of times first, but then they let me win so I didn't start crying."

Sin cocks an eyebrow. "Because you're four?"

"Because I'm pregnant," I correct. "Rex says it makes women emotionally unstable."

"Rex better learn to be more tactful before he gets married," Sin advises.

I grin up at him. "I gave him some variation of the same advice."

When we get back to the living room, Sin relieves Rex of his baby burden. Skylar seems to recognize him, and she promptly pats his face with her tiny hand.

I sigh shamelessly, watching him stand there shirtless with a baby on his chest, tattooed and bandaged like a hardass, but pressing his lips to Skylar's forehead and giving her a kiss, murmuring an apology to her and calling her shortcake. My heart is so full, it aches.

"I should get him a shirt," Rafe volunteers.

Rex smirks and glances over at me. "You okay over there? You look a little flushed."

"I'm allowed to stare," I inform them both. "I'm marrying him, so all that belongs to me."

Rafe's eyes widen. "Back up. What was that?"

Sin walks over and bends down to grab his jacket. "That reminds me, I made a stop this morning before today went to hell."

My heart leaps as he opens his hand and there's a little square jewelry box in his palm. Bringing my wide eyes to his face, I say, "You didn't."

He hands me the box and nods. "Open it."

"You aren't seriously doing this in front of me," Rafe says. "You *are* an asshole. You're not even doing it right; you're supposed to get down on one knee."

"Yeah, but he's standing here like a badass at the end of an action flick with a baby on his chest," Rex reasons. "I don't think he has to. Pretty sure that starry-eyed look on her face pretty much answers his question."

"Thanks," Rafe says dryly.

Rex shrugs. "Just saying."

"I'm not proposing," Sin says.

"Thank God," Rafe replies.

"Already did," Sin adds. "Just didn't have the ring yet."

"Jesus Christ," Rafe mutters. "Where's the fucking fire? You've been together for three and a half minutes."

"Shh," I tell Rafe, my fingers a little unsteady as I pop open the lid. The breath quite literally leaves my lungs at the sight of the loveliest ring I've ever seen. It's a rose gold band with diamond accents on each side of a big oval stone that glitters in the light. It's absolutely stunning. I would have been happy with anything as long as it symbolized that I belong to Sin, but this is truly beautiful. I would have picked it out myself if I saw it.

"Like it?" Sin asks.

I'm tearing up again. Before anyone can make fun of me, I rush forward and hug him, carefully accommodating his arm and Skylar. "I love it so much. It's perfect. Thank you." I kiss him, then lean my head on the shoulder Skylar isn't currently occupying. "You're the best."

"Put it on, I wanna see."

I grin, drawing the ring out of its velvet bed. "I can't believe how perfect it is."

"I have good taste," he tells me, with exaggerated cockiness.

"Hell yeah, you do," I agree. Looking up at Skylar, I say, "Whoops, sorry, baby. Heck yeah, you do." I slide the ring past my knuckle and it settles perfectly on my finger. I flex it a few times, tilting my hand so it catches the light. I lean my head on his shoulder again and sigh. "It's so perfect. I love it so much."

He presses a kiss to my forehead. "Good."

"All right, you guys need to slow the fuck down," Rafe informs us. "What the hell is the rush? You can't get engaged this quickly."

"We can do whatever we want," I inform him. "We're going to get married soon, too, like this weekend. If you don't like it, don't come."

"For the love of God. What is with you Prices and your impulsive lifelong commitments? Date first, for Christ's sake. There's no need to rush into anything."

"The decision has been made," I inform him, immovably. "Nothing you say will sway me."

"Yeah?" Cocking a golden grow, he asks, "Have you told Carly?"

Damn, okay, that one gives me pause. I know Carly is not going to be happy about this.

Rafe nods his head, pulling his phone out of his pocket. "All right, let's call her."

"Don't you dare," I tell him.

"I'm gonna *video* call her," he states, swiping his finger across the screen.

"Rafe, no," I whine, moving away from Sin and going over to try to steal his phone. "Come on, let me be excited for a night first. I'll tell her tomorrow."

"Too late," he informs me.

I groan, covering my face with my hands. This is going to be so bad. Sin shouldn't be here for this.

My sister's voice rings out. "What do you want now, Satan?"

"I have great news," Rafe tells her. "Or, Laurel does. Here, I'll give her the phone."

"News?" Carly asks, already cautious.

I glare at Rafe, then smile as the phone turns to me and Carly can see me. "Hi!"

She is already prepared for some fuckery, I see it on her face. "What's going on, Laurel?"

"Good things," I assure her. "Great things. Lots of things that make me happy, so... great things."

She says nothing.

Swallowing, I smile with even more enthusiasm and hold up my left hand to show her my new ring.

"What the hell is that?" she asks.

"That is an engagement ring. Isn't it gorgeous? Can you tell through the phone? It's really beautiful in person."

Her blue eyes widen in horror. "Laurel, no. Oh my God, do not marry him. Don't do this. This is—I can't keep my mouth shut. It's bad enough he knocked you up—"

I interrupt her. "Um, actually... Plot twist. Not Rafe."

"What?" she asks sharply.

"Not marrying Rafe. I'm marrying Sin."

"Who the *fuck* is Sin? That's not even a name, it's a biblical bad idea. What the hell is going on out there, Laurel?"

"It's a nickname. Short for Sinclair. That's not the point," I say, reminding myself, trying to focus because I'm starting to get the urge to chatter nervously. "I didn't tell you everything and I'm not going to right now because I have an audience, and Rafe is a dick, but just trust me, okay? We're in love and we're happy. He's great, you'll love him. He's good to me—amazing."

"Honey, great. Wonderful. I love all of that. So, *date* him, don't *marry* him."

Since I want to melt her a little and make her nicer about all this, I turn the phone so she can see Sin.

"Aw, jeeze," he mutters, sighing. "Well, this isn't how I thought I'd meet you."

"Okay," Carly says, her tone knowing. "Turn me back around."

I do, and then I start talking before she can. "I think we're just going to do a quickie Vegas wedding, but of course—"

"Laurel, honey, I don't want to rain on your parade here, and I'm not even going to ask why he has a baby on his chest, but you're in lust, not love."

My shoulders sag. She was supposed to melt, not undermine my feelings. "Don't be like that."

"I'm trying to keep my shit together, but this isn't you,

Laurel. You don't do things like this. Think about it. And I bet he works for Rafe, doesn't he?"

"Well, yes."

She nods. "Rafe foisted you. You've been foisted. This is all a sham. That guy doesn't want to marry you, Rafe just doesn't want to play daddy anymore so he called in an alternate to handle it for him. Rafe is *Lexing* you, Laurel. This is all an exercise in manipulation. We need to get you the fuck out of there. I'm done with this. Rafe, go ahead and tell Vince all you want to tell him, I don't give a damn. The only reason I got involved with this fucking family in the first place was to protect my sister, and now you're systematically dismantling her life. Nope. Over the line. We're done. Rip my life apart, I don't care. I'm getting my sister out of this bullshit right now."

"This is not Rafe's doing, and you're not being fair," I tell her. "I was happy for you when you and Vince decided to get married on a whim."

"We had already been dating for over six months! You've only known this guy for six *days*."

"It's been longer than that." Shaking my head, I tell her, "Look, I understand where you're coming from; I know they're tricky bastards, but I haven't been foisted. This is not what you think it is. Sin and I really are in love."

"Do you remember the scene where Anna lost her shit for a minute and decided it would be a good idea to marry Hans even though she didn't know him at all, and Elsa had to be a queen bitch and tell her misguided little sister, um, no, that's not going to happen? That's where we are right now. You've been hypnotized by killer abs and an undoubtedly convincing performance, and you're in full-on brain-dead Anna mode. I get it, I do, I know hot guys are your kryptonite, but honey, he's Hans."

I sigh, rolling my eyes. "He is *not* Hans. Rafe is Hans."

"I don't understand anything either one of you are saying right now," Rafe volunteers.

Massaging the bridge of his nose, Sin approaches. "I actually do."

I can't help lifting my eyebrows at that. "You've seen *Frozen*?"

"It was Ellie's first movie." Grabbing the phone out of my hand, he tells Carly, "Look, if we absolutely must compare this situation to a kid's movie, I'm not the calculating dickhead she fucked up with, I'm the one with the reindeer who talked some sense into her. This is not a sham. I am in love with your sister. And Laurel is an adult, so she doesn't need your permission; she can make her own decisions. Now, I've had a long day and I don't have the patience for this tonight. Goodbye, Carly."

Then he ends the call.

I gape at the phone in horror. "What have you done?"

"I fixed it," he tells me, handing Rafe back his phone.

"You just hung up on my sister," I say, still staring at the phone, expecting her to burst through it and punch Sin in the face.

"She was being a pain in the ass," he reasons.

"Oh, my God," I mutter, drawing my own phone out of my back pocket so I can text her with further explanations. "Do you think I can convince her the call dropped?"

"Definitely not," Rafe says, barely holding back laughter. "I'm gonna go grab this asshole a shirt."

50

SIN

By the time we get home, I'm beat. Then we walk up to my front door and all my worst fears attack at the sight of my door. The wood is busted open. Looks like someone took an axe to it, trying to get inside. I have bullet-proof windows and metal bars on some of them, too, in the rooms I wanted to work as panic rooms. Upon realizing that, someone must have figured the door would be easier to get through.

Would be, except I already accounted for that and I ordered a steel reinforced front door. So while the wood is split open and the steel exposed, the door is still standing and my house is still secure.

That's good to know. Never tested it out before. It was too little too late anyway. After Paula and Ellie were killed, I didn't have anything worth protecting, but it became an obses-sion. I needed to make sure it couldn't happen again, even though making the house safe a few months too late did nothing to save them. It was better than drinking myself stupid every night and praying to a God I don't believe in not to make me wake up the next day.

I drop the folded up bassinet and diaper bag I carried to the front door, take the car seat out of Laurel's hand, and just grab her, pulling her close. She wraps her arms around me, hugging me back as tightly as I'm hugging her.

"Someone tried to break into the house," she says, sounding a little stunned.

I can't fucking believe Gio actually stooped that low. I wish I could kill the bastard all over again—I'd do it slower this time.

"Yeah, but they couldn't get in," I point out. "I'm still glad you left. That would have been terrifying."

"Holy shit," she mutters, still looking at the door, even as she hugs me. "They came to kill me?"

"I would never let that happen," I assure her.

"But... they tried."

She's stunned. I guess this is the first time she knows anyone has ever tried to kill her, so that's bound to be a little upsetting. I release her, digging the key out of my pocket. "Let's get inside."

She nods, looking around warily. It must scare her right now, all the shadows and darkness, spots in the yards where people could be hiding. Now that I know my house is as secure as I hoped it was, I feel a lot better, but I doubt she does.

Once we're inside, I lock up and set the alarm. I hit the lights since Laurel is still skittish. I glance down at Skylar to see if the sudden brightness caused her to stir, but she's out. After Laurel fed her and burped her, Skylar fell asleep in the car on the way home. It felt like the ride was a million hours long. When I left Gio's, I only grabbed the diaper bag, the blanket out of her crib so she'd have something familiar to sleep with, and this rectangular bassinet contraption he brought the night Laurel babysat. There wasn't enough formula to last tomorrow in the diaper bag, so I stopped at a drug store on the way home for that and diapers. Been a long damn time since I've had to go down that aisle.

I'm drained, but Laurel turns and smiles at me, and I feel a little better.

"Do you need help setting that thing up?" she whispers, pointing at the portable baby furniture I'm lugging with me.

"Nope, I've done it before."

Laurel puts Skylar's carrier down in the living room and kneels on the ground beside her, rooting through the diaper bag to see what we actually have for this baby. I put down the bag from the drug store and proceed upstairs to the bedroom next to mine—Ellie's old bedroom. I always kept the door closed and I told Laurel not to snoop the day I left her home uncuffed. Maybe she listened, or maybe Rafe just got here before she got around to it. If she had seen it, she probably would have had questions. When I bought the house, the walls were white like all the rest, but Paula fell in love with elephants when she was pregnant. I painted the walls in this room a pale pink and gray, and in the corner where Ellie's toy box used to be, there's a cartoon elephant decal on the wall. I packed up all her stuff, but I never took that down. Occasionally I would drink a lot, lie down on the floor in this room, and just stare at that elephant to make myself hurt.

A ball of grief remains nestled in my gut as I stand in this empty room, but I shake it off and get to work assembling the playpen so we can put Skylar to bed.

I hear noise and glance back just as Laurel steps inside the room. She's carrying the pink blanket I brought with Skylar, her eyes drifting around. She takes in the color on the walls, the elephant decal in the corner.

"Ellie's room?" she asks quietly.

I nod wordlessly and stand, leaning down to press my hand along the mat and make sure it's pressed down good. I think there's a SIDs risk if not. Or maybe that's for cribs. I don't remember. Better safe than sorry.

Laurel comes up behind me, wrapping her arms around me and hugging my back. She doesn't say anything, just holds onto me, comforts me the only way she can.

I use my good arm to reach back and drag her around to my side so I can kiss the top of her head. Pointing at the open, empty closet, I tell her, "A bunch of little dresses and sleepers used to hang right there." I glance around at the empty nails on the walls. "We had some pictures of her hanging up in here, too, but I had to take 'em all down. It was too much."

She nods her head, then presses herself even closer to me. "I know I said it before, but I'm so, so sorry, Sin."

"I know."

Sighing, she says, "Now I'm feeling really stupid for pitying Rafe because he had to pack up books. You had to pack up your daughter's whole life."

I frown, a little lost. "Books? What?"

She shakes her head. "Never mind. It's not important. Next time you're at Rafe's, tell him you want to bring my books home. We were supposed to tonight, but then you got shot and Skylar was there... Long story short, the books didn't matter anymore."

I don't know what she's talking about, but I don't really have the energy to find out, so I just nod. "All right."

"We could put her in a different room, if it's too hard to be in here," she tells me. "I don't have a baby monitor yet anyway, so we could even put her in our room for tonight."

"I can move it in there if you want."

"Only our second night living together and you're already getting cockblocked by a baby," she states.

I smile faintly at that. "You can owe me one."

Laurel leaves me to go grab Skylar while I move this thing to our bedroom. For the first few months after Ellie was born, we kept her in our room, too. I don't know if my heart's ready for it though—if she wakes up in the middle of the night, and I open my eyes to see Laurel sitting up in bed, wearing my ring and snuggling a baby. I thought I had a few months to work up to that.

Once Skylar is in bed, I need a shower. I know eventually I'm going to have to shower without her, but tonight I don't want to. I grab Laurel's wrist and drag her in the bathroom with me, stripping off my clothes and climbing in. She already knows the drill by now, so she follows suit, closing the shower curtain and wrapping her arms around me from behind, pressing her face against my back.

"I love you, Sin."

Instead of telling her, I show her. I reach back and bring her around front. I back her up against the wall, lift her leg, and sink myself inside her. I know she likes it hard and fast— hell, so do I—but tonight I just want to stay inside her. Tonight I'm slow and tender, kissing her and making it last. I'm already exhausted, might as well empty the last of my energies inside her.

Even though it's been the day from hell, it feels like my own little slice of heaven when I walk into a bedroom that doesn't even feel like mine anymore. The scent of Laurel's shampoo lingers in the air, there's a baby sleeping in the corner, a beautiful woman climbing in my bed. I shake my head, drop my towel in the otherwise empty laundry basket, and climb in bed with her. I must be the luckiest bastard around as I secure my arms around Laurel's waist and tug her as close to my chest as I can get her.

Leaning in and pressing a kiss against my lips, she whispers, "How many kids do you want?"

"A bunch. Maybe four. You?"

Her eyebrows rise and fall. "Four, okay. That's probably doable. I thought more like two, but I'm flexible. Do you mean four *after* this one?" she asks, placing a hand on her tummy.

"Four total. If you haven't noticed, I'm not a stickler about biology."

"I have noticed," she says, smiling and caressing my face with her soft hand. "You're such a great man."

I don't know how she can say that after all the terrible shit I did today, but I don't bother arguing. I just tug her closer and appreciate her perspective. I hope she can keep it.

"Who do you think will take Skylar?" she asks.

"No idea."

"Rafe said he's her godfather," she tells me. "Obviously he isn't going to take her; he didn't even want to raise his own kid. I don't know the other Morellis out here."

I'm too tired to think about all this. "That's a problem for tomorrow," I tell her.

She nods and curls close. "I'll let you go to sleep. You need the rest. Wake me up in the morning and I'll make you breakfast before you leave. I bought groceries."

"We'll see if Skylar wakes you up. I'm not going to wake you up to cook if you're up with a baby all night long."

"You're wounded. Let me take care of you, dammit," she says, playfully stern, before pecking me on the lips.

"Wounded, my ass." I let my hand slide down so I can grope her ass. "Go to sleep."

"What will you do to me if I don't?" she teases.

I can't help grinning, shaking my head at her as I close my eyes. "Insatiable."

"Your fault. You teased me forever."

"I did not tease you *forever*, I teased you very briefly. I just teased you hard."

"So hard. Fifty years into our marriage I'm still going to be convinced I have to earn dick privileges."

Grinning, I tell her, "Sounds good to me."

She swats me in the stomach, then curls closer. "Good night, Sin."

"Good night, Laurel."

51

LAUREL

Skylar woke me up twice during the night. Both times, Sin woke up, too. Both times, he laid there watching while I fed and soothed her. I apologized that she woke him up, but he didn't seem to mind. I imagine it must be weird, maybe even a little haunting, witnessing something like this again. Surely he saw it plenty when Ellie was the baby. He clearly adored Ellie, whether she was his or not. It breaks my heart for him, but it also reassures me that my baby will never be less loved for not being biologically his.

When Skylar wakes me up the following morning, Sin is already gone. It's later than I thought it would be, and Skylar has a fresh diaper, so Sin must have changed her before he left. God, he's great. I feed Skylar a bottle and then we laze in bed for a little while longer. She's only a few months old, so she can't do much anyway. I rub her belly, tickle her toes, count her gummy little grins, and snuggle her. She doesn't flip her shit on me at all, so Sin must be right, she must have smelled my fear the first time.

There are no toys here, except for the mirror one in the

diaper bag, but I remember that I bought a board book the day Rafe took me to the bookstore, so I dig it out and read it to her.

After I read her a story, I snuggle her against my chest facing forward and pose both of us peeking over the book, snap a selfie, and send it to Sin.

"You're lucky there's a baby in you already," he informs me. "If not, I'd put one in you tonight."

I send him a winking emoji. "Promises, promises."

"Keep it up, we'll have six," he tells me.

I laugh. "Be kind to my vagina!"

"Oh, I'll be kind to it all right."

Even though Sin would kill me, and I'm pretty sure I convinced her not to immediately board a plane to Vegas last night, I take a screen shot and attach it in a message to Carly. "See why I want to marry him?"

"OMG, where did you get that adorable baby?" she demands.

"One of Rafe's cousins. Babysitting," I say, for simplicity's sake. I'm trying to warm her to Sin, and while my sister is no goody two shoes, I'm not positive telling her my fiancé technically orphaned this child yesterday is a great way to accomplish that.

Much the same as we avoided talking about Rafe when I was trying to make it work with him, Carly avoids talking about Sin. It makes me nervous, but I tell myself she will get over it. I don't know if she'll *love* Sin—that may have been a bit of an oversell—but once she sees how happy he makes me, I know she'll see the light. Once she sees the way he looks at me like I'm the only woman in the world, she'll lose her skepticism. She just hasn't seen us together yet, that's all. I called her up and told her I was marrying someone she has never met, and she understandably freaked out. I get it. A month ago, I would have probably had the same reaction, because I had never experienced anything like that before. I don't think Carly has, either. She and Vince didn't fall hard and fast the way Sin and I did, their relationship is completely different. Sin and I consume each other. Carly always stays in control.

I wonder if that's okay. I wonder if she ever gets to feel the way I feel. Knowing she and Vince are happy together, I never really put much energy into dissecting their dynamic, but now I sort of wish my sister understood the depths of my feelings. Am I crazy?

My mind drifts to Mia. I've seen the way she and Mateo look at each other, and even though I should probably let Rafe be the one to tell her since she is more his family than mine, right now I need more than my sister's opinion. Maybe I *have* lost my mind. Maybe even Mia will tell me that.

So I text her, "I need to tell you something."

And then I do. I tell her everything. Every single thing. I even tell her things Rafe doesn't know—the night Sin helped me watch Skylar, the note he wrote in my book. I'll ask her to delete the messages afterward, just to be safe, but I need *someone* to tell me I'm not crazy, and she can only get it if she has the whole story.

I conclude by sending her a picture of my engagement ring and the question. "So, am I crazy?"

She texts back immediately, "If you are, who wants to be sane?! I love that so much. I don't blame you at all. You 100% made the right choice. Congratulations!!"

Oh, thank God.

"I can't wait to meet him!" she adds. "If you don't want us to come to the wedding because of Vince and Carly, I totally get it. Make sure you let me know when it is anyway though, I want to send you a gift. I don't think Scotophile IS a thing, but

I'm going to take this love into consideration when picking your gift," she adds with a wink.

"I really DO want you to come to the wedding. I just have to convince Sin that we should wait and have a bigger wedding, but that it doesn't mean I'm having second thoughts."

"I'm sure you'll come up with a way," she tells me. "Give me your address, I'll send you an engagement present that might help."

"Oh, you don't have to send me an engagement present, silly. I just wanted someone to tell me I'm not crazy."

"If you don't give it to me, I will get it from Adrian. I'm trying to be less creepy about this," she informs me.

I laugh, relenting, and sending her my address. I guess I shouldn't feel guilty. Her husband has more money than God, so she can afford to send me a present.

Skylar and I go downstairs and bum around the house. I talk to her and she coos back. I make myself some lunch and ask Sin when he'll be home, but he doesn't know.

At some point I should probably text Rafe to ask for an update about who is taking Skylar, but I'm enjoying having her here, so I don't.

A few hours later, around the time I'm hoping Sin will arrive, the doorbell rings. I'm not answering the door after last night, but I go to the window and look out. It's Rex, and he seemed safe, so I go down and ease open the door.

He doesn't look terribly impressed to be playing delivery boy, but he hauls a huge box and a Nordstrom bag into the house.

"Um, what is all this?" I ask.

Once he puts it all down, he indicates the box. "A stroller, in case you wanted to take Skylar for a walk. There are some clothes in the bag. Do you need me to put this thing together?"

"No," I say, staring at the box. "I don't even know if I'll have Skylar here long enough to ever need this."

Rex shrugs. "If you don't want it, donate it. Mia can't look at baby stuff and not buy it. If she could, she probably wouldn't have 800 kids."

"I'll be honest, when she said she was sending me an engagement gift, I kinda thought she meant a simple lingerie set."

"It's probably in the bag. I did not go digging through it to find out."

I give him a thumbs up. "Good call."

Since his job is done, Rex goes to leave, but he doesn't quite get the door open and Sin is storming in, glaring at him.

"Whoa," Rex says, stumbling back a step in surprise.

"Why are you at my house when I'm not here?" Sin demands.

I glance down, seeing poor Rex cornered, and tell Sin, "Look, baby, Mia sent us presents."

Jerking his thumb up in my direction, Rex explains, "That's why."

Sin narrows his eyes at Rex just for good measure, and Rex eases around him and slips out the door. Sin is still in intimidating mode when he gets up to me, glaring down at me with leftover annoyance at Rex. At least, I assume so, but his thunderous scowl gets my blood pumping anyway. I'm already on the floor, so it doesn't take much to climb to my knees and crawl over to him so I can hug his legs. "I'm glad you're home."

"Why was he here?"

I release him and turn back to the bag I haven't opened yet. "I told Mia about our engagement. She's thrilled for us, by the way. She told me she wanted to send me a present. I assumed she meant in the mail, but I guess since Mateo already had an errand boy in Vegas, she made him go pick it up for faster delivery. Look at this, she's crazy. She sent us a stroller—for *Skylar*. I doubt we'll use it for her, but we can definitely save it for when the baby comes. That's one less thing we'll have to buy, and it looks like a *really* nice one. I probably would have got something a lot cheaper, but look at this thing."

Nodding at the bag, he asks, "What's in there?"

"Not sure yet."

I dig out the first item, right on top, and gasp with delight. It's a white satin robe similar to mine, but the back says "the bride."

"Look, look, look," I say, holding it up to show him.

He's already over the gifts and onto Skylar, getting down on the floor and picking her up off the pillow I propped her up on. He transfers her to his chest and she coos at him in approval.

The next item must be the gift Mia was talking about—I don't show that to Sin, just yet. While he's distracted with Skylar, I set it aside. It's black, sexy, and sheer, so I'll surprise him with that later.

There's still more in the bag though. I nearly die when I pull out the cutest little pink and blue baby swimsuit with a matching pink sun hat. It's exactly the kind of adorable thing I envisioned when I had my daydreams of taking the baby in the pool, but this is obviously for a girl. The last thing in the bag is another adorable baby girl outfit in Skylar's size.

"Not sure if Mia is super sure we're having a girl, or she thinks we're keeping Skylar."

I glance up at Sin and see Skylar playing with his face again, him gazing down at her tenderly. Uh oh. Not sure if *Sin* thinks we're keeping Skylar.

"Any word from Rafe about who might be taking care of

Skylar now?" I ask, wondering if he knows something I don't. It would be just like him to go and agree to raise a kid without telling me.

"Not yet," he says, unconcerned. Then he plays like he's going to eat Skylar's fingers and she squeals, delighted.

I think I have lost my fiancé to a much younger woman. Smiling faintly, I take the pink sun hat and crawl over to join them on the floor. "Lookie what Aunt Mia sent you. Is that pretty?"

"I think she's a second cousin by marriage," Sin says.

"Second cousin Mia sounds weird, we'll go with Aunt Mia," I say, fitting the little hat on Skylar's head. She tries to look up and the hat falls off, so I put it back on. "I mentioned my pool fantasy to Mia, so she sent me a bathing suit for Skylar. She's an enabler."

"Well, she's happily married to Mateo, so I would have guessed that," Sin reasons.

I crawl back over to grab my phone. "Hang on, I have to send her a picture."

Sin turns her around so I can get a picture. I take advantage of the opportunity to take his picture, too. Mia asked a long time ago what he looked like, and I never got to show her.

She immediately texts back somewhere in the neighborhood of 30 heart-eyed emojis.

Looking up at them over there playing, I can't help feeling a little heart-eyed, myself.

I don't know if Sin is angry because we are at Rafe's house to hand off Skylar and he's not ready, or if he's angry that this dude and his wife are currently complaining about having to go back to caring for a baby in diapers now that theirs are finally potty-trained.

It might be both. He's got her snug against his chest like he's not going to give her up. I'm low key preparing for him to get up and storm out with her, the same way he did with my purse the night I met him.

Apparently, Vince has a much older sister. He has never once mentioned her, only his sister Cherie, but Rafe tells me the woman who agreed to take Skylar in is Vince's half-sister. She's 37 and married—and her husband is an asshole, if this first impression is an accurate picture of him. But she's Skylar's family, in the strictest technical sense. Sin doesn't seem to think that's important. I get it. Better that she is with someone who will happily take care of her than someone who happens to share some common ancestry. I'm not going to tell Rafe how to run his family though, not in this regard.

It doesn't help Sin's mood that when Roseanna and her husband were offered Skylar, they said things like, "Of course no one wants to take her, she's just a girl." Even Sin with his oppressive caveman bullshit looked like he wanted to punch these people in the face with a brick.

He's a ticking time bomb, and I'm just sitting here waiting for him to go off.

I don't have to wait long. When Roseanna comes over to retrieve Skylar, the moment I knew was coming finally arrives.

"Nope," Sin says firmly.

The woman frowns. "Excuse me?"

Sin shakes his head, pushing up off the couch. "Nope. I'm not giving her to you. You don't even want her."

"Well, someone killed her parents," the husband says pointedly. "So now somebody has to take her in."

"That's right, but it doesn't have to be you."

"No one else was knocking down the door to take her in," he replies.

Sin shakes his head, looking over at me. He doesn't say anything, but he doesn't have to. I know exactly what he wants. Nodding my agreement, I place my hand on his thigh to show my support.

Now that I'm on board, he looks to Rafe. "We'll keep her."

"Are you serious?" the husband asks. "This isn't even your problem."

"She's not a fucking problem," Sin snaps. "Jesus Christ, you people. Babies are not problems."

Putting a hand up to keep the peace, Rafe nods his head. "All right. That's fine with me if it's fine with everyone else."

Rafe's jerky cousin and her dumb husband seem irritated, but not by the loss of Skylar. They leave grumbling under their breath, but Sin doesn't care. I don't either. No wonder Vince doesn't associate with that sister; she sucks.

Sin looks down at Skylar on his chest, and she holds onto his finger while she naps.

My heart fills up, aches, bottoms out, and fills up again. I hope the sight of him in daddy mode breaks my heart a little less once I get used to it, but right now it all feels very dramatic. My heart splits in half because I can't help thinking of Ellie, but then adheres together again because he seems so much more at peace already. He may be snarling at Rafe's asshole family members, but overall, he's calmer with Skylar around.

Tonight when we take her home, he's the most at peace he has been since I met him. I've seen him stoic, passionate, mean, happy, in love—I see love shining in his eyes each night when he holds me in bed, but the peace, that feels like something new. I thought the measure of peace I brought him was as good as it got, but now I get the feeling his missing pieces are finally all filled in. No one can ever take the place of Ellie, naturally, but Skylar gives him back something he lost. Something he never thought he could get back.

I get teary thinking about it, but most of them are happy tears.

The little family we are piecing together may not be entirely conventional, but it's ours. As long as we all fit together, it really doesn't matter where we came from.

52

LAUREL

FOUR MONTHS LATER

The hot Vegas sun beats down on every inch of my exposed skin—and it's a lot of inches, because I'm six months pregnant and wearing a hot pink bikini. I absently rub my baby bump, wondering if I should get out of the lounger and into the pool with Sin and Skylar. I love soaking up the sun with Rafe while Sin plays in the water with our little one, but I've been relaxing here for a while and I don't want to accidentally bake my unborn son.

"I'm thirsty. Get me a drink."

I lift my eyebrows and turn my head, looking at Rafe like he's lost his damn mind. "Get it yourself, lazy ass."

"Remember when you were so dazzled by me that you served me without question?" he asks.

Pointedly sticking my nose in the air, I say, "Not really. I think you're remembering wrong."

Sighing, he folds his hands over his washboard abs and laments, "I should have knocked up a nicer girl."

"Hey! I'm a nice girl." I scrunch my nose up at him and reach into the lemonade glass beside my lounger, grabbing a few fingers full of ice and flinging them at him. He jerks at the sudden cold hitting his side, but smirks nonetheless. "I'm the one growing a human being inside my body," I inform him. "If anything, you should be catering to me."

"Not really my thing. You have a fiancé for that."

Eagerly anticipating the wrath I'm about to incur, I say, "Not really his thing, either. We should start inviting Rex to Sunday dinner. He'll make sure all my needs are met."

A violent wave of chlorinated water suddenly surges out of the pool and hits my legs as Sin splashes me. "That's not fuckin' funny."

I grin at him. "Yes, it is. You know I don't go for guys my own age anymore, baby."

Keeping one hand on Skylar's baby float to keep her stabilized, he uses his other one to point at me. With a warning look that makes me tingle, he states, "Your ass is gonna pay for that bullshit tonight, mark my words."

"My ass is looking forward to it," I tell him with a wink.

I chuckle to myself, grabbing my lemonade and sipping through the straw. It's a source of much amusement for Rafe—and sure, me—that Sin gets possessive when it comes to Rex. After Mateo's guys helped clean up Rafe's mess, a few of them stayed behind to help him and Sin rebuild. Rex was one of them, and since he's a nice guy (for a thug), sure, he makes a point to catch up with me when he's around. Since he's also physically attractive and age-appropriate, and because Sin is an absolute caveman, it makes him salty.

It's laughable, but I can't even button my jeans anymore, so I can't complain about the ego boost.

Sin shakes his head at me. "It's all fun and games until the little bastard disappears."

My amused smile slips, because while he knows I'm

joking, I can't be sure he is. "You know I'm only teasing. You know I have eyes for no man but you. All the rest might as well be eunuchs, for all my romantic interest in them."

"Too late, you already said it." Leaning down over Skylar's float, he pretends to be a shark, 'eating' her toes and earning a squeal of delight from her. When he leans down, I see the expansion of his back tattoo. Below Ellie's sun there's now a ripple of water and a sandy shore, Skylar's sun hat resting on the beach, and two little foot prints in the sand. Originally, he wanted a spider, since *The Itsy Bitsy Spider* is Skylar's favorite song, but I vetoed that one. I love his tattoo tributes, but I'm not going to wake up in the middle of the night and freak out about the huge spider on his back before I fully wake up and realize it's just a tattoo. "Mommy should use her big brain before she opens her mouth and lets crazy things slip out, shouldn't she?"

Skylar grins at him with unabashed adoration. She's such a daddy's girl, it's not even funny. She answers him to the best of her ability, saying, "Mama!" She's probably agreeing I should use my brain. She's always going to take his side—even if he's wrong. Little monster.

"Sin," I whine. "Promise Rex won't disappear."

"Nope."

"You can't kill Rex," Rafe tells him, backing me up. "Mateo wants him back when we're done with him."

Holding up his hands with mock innocence, Sin said, "Who said anything about killing the kid? I'm just suggesting he might get lost and never be seen or heard from again."

"Sin, don't be crazy. You know I'm only playing with you."

"Yeah, well, you're not the only one who's got jokes," he says smugly, since he knows he has me squirming.

"As long as you promise you're only joking. You know I

can't be held responsible for everything I say. The baby is eating my brain. Remember the other day when you found my car keys in the cereal cupboard? I'm running at half-power over here."

"Half-power, my ass. Hanging out over there with Rafe is making you ornery, that's the problem. Bring your pretty little ass over here and get in the pool where I can keep you in line."

"Yes, master," I tease, nonetheless putting my lemonade down and standing. I adjust the ass of my bikini pointlessly, since I'm about to get in the water anyway, and take the hat off my head, dropping it on my lounger.

Before I make it to the steps, Sin casually commands, "Go get me a drink first."

I halt and turn around obediently. "Sure, what would you like?"

Sin doesn't answer me.

"You're a dick," Rafe states, his tone dry as hell.

I turn around, confused, until I see Sin is laughing.

Belatedly realizing he just wanted to show up Rafe, I roll my eyes and go back to the steps. "You're both huge dicks."

Sin smirks at me as I wade into the water. Once I'm close enough, he reaches out his free arm and grabs me around the waist, tugging me so close I can feel his body heat. "You like when I'm a huge dick."

Wickedly letting my hand drop down into the water, I cup that much-loved piece of equipment right in the palm of my hand. "I like that you *have* a huge dick."

His eyes darken as I caress him through the fabric of his swim trunks. He leans in to kiss me. "You like when I am one, too."

Leaning my forehead against his, I assure him, "I like you all the time, no matter what you're being."

Sin moves Skylar's pool float and I naturally reach a hand out to steady it, freeing his up so he can wrap both arms around me. He catches me under the ass and lifts me, so I wrap my legs around his waist.

"Dada, dada, dada," Skylar says, jealous of all the attention Mommy is getting.

Sin breaks away, grinning against my mouth. "She hates when I kiss you."

"I think Rafe put her up to it," I insist, looping my free arm around his neck and tickling Skylar's tiny feet.

She giggles and crosses her hands on her tummy like the cutest little person ever.

Rafe calls from his lounger, "I would have, if I'd have thought of it. You two are making me lose my appetite, and dinner's in an hour."

"You should invite Virginia to come over next Sunday," I tell him. "Now, *she* would serve you without complaint. She's already used to it."

"Give it up, kitten," he tells me, closing his eyes and leaning his head back against the lounger to indicate he's ignoring me now.

I shake my head at Sin. "Why is he such a pain in the ass?"

"It's in his blood," Sin answers.

Rafe still blithely ignores the fact that Virginia clearly cares about him. When he first informed me he was taking a break from dating, I didn't believe him. I figured it would last a couple weeks, at most. I was glad he was trying, though. A lot had happened to him in a short time on a personal level. Not only did I leave him and get engaged immediately, but Sin killed that Marlena girl he liked and the ex he had all that history with. I understood that he felt like he needed a breather

—I just didn't think he could actually give up women for any length of time. I don't even think he completely gave up women when we were trying to date, though I've never asked. I really don't want to know. It doesn't matter at this point.

He followed through, though. To my knowledge, there have been zero scantily clad platinum blondes hanging from his arm. He still flirts when he goes out, of course. I saw that firsthand when Rafe convinced me that we needed to go out and be adults. We asked Virginia to babysit Skylar and went out with Rafe to a club he likes. The whole time we were out, I kept thinking about how much I would prefer to be sitting on the couch at home between Sin's legs, wearing my robe instead of real clothes, with Skylar napping on her Boppy pillow in my lap.

Eventually we will implement date nights so we can spend some time together baby-free, but for now, we like our family routine. And I think we're both definitely over going to Rafe's clubs. I was over those the first time I stepped foot inside one. If no one is feeding me, why am I even dressing up? Hell, why am I even *showing* up?

I guess maybe it's more fun if you're not pregnant and you can actually drink, but for me, it's a big no thanks.

We incorporated the Chicago Morelli tradition of having family dinners every Sunday, though. I initially suggested it because I was afraid Rafe might be lonely. He would never admit it, but I thought since he's taking a breather from women for the first time in his adult life, we should do what we can to fill the void. Then it just turned out to be really nice. On Sundays, we sleep in at home, then we get ready and come straight to Rafe's house. We'll have a light lunch, play by the pool, catch up on my pregnancy if we've been out of touch that week—whatever we want, the important thing is we spend time together.

The main difference for us, though, is that we don't have dinner *at* Rafe's house—we have it at Rafe's restaurant. Virginia always works Sundays, so it feels like a way of including her in our Sunday family day, even if she is the one serving our food.

Now that Rafe has shown he can abstain from fucking everything in sight without incentive, though, I'm starting to see more potential in him as someone's mate. I literally didn't think he could do it before, and I didn't want him to cheat on Virginia and break her heart, but now I have seen he is capable. His break has to end eventually, and I'm hoping he ends it with her.

I already asked her to be a bridesmaid in our wedding. While we were still trying to figure out when to get married, I stopped at a bridal store. Seeing all the beautiful gowns, veils and tiaras, I realized whether we had a big or small wedding, the day I marry this wonderful man, I want to feel like a princess. I would marry him in a tacky Vegas chapel or a common courthouse, but it's a celebration, and as such, I'd like to do it in front of our family and friends. So, we agreed to wait until after baby Nicholas is born, that way our whole family (at the moment) can be present. Sin is still planning to put two more babies in me eventually, but I'm just getting settled in at my new school right now, plus soon I'll be juggling two babies. It's a lot, so I think we will wait a little while before we start having bouncing baby Sinclairs.

Plus, I need to actually *become* a Sinclair first.

Professor Laurel Sinclair. Yep, that's gonna be perfect.

53

RAFE

I am struck by a sense of déjà vu as I look over at Laurel, her hair lighter and wavier after playing in the pool this afternoon. Her sunkissed skin glows, probably from the sun she got today and the "pregnancy glow," if that's a real thing. She's wearing a flowy white dress with the pink straps from her swimsuit visible, so I can't see the bump as clearly as I could when she was in the bikini. Now that her bump is visible, it feels more real. There is physical evidence of my child growing inside her, and it's fucking crazy.

Then there's Sin's arm draped over her shoulders, casually marking his possession. The baby inside might be half mine, but the host belongs entirely to Sin. Laurel is so accustomed to his arm around her by now that her hand absently caresses it as she peruses the dessert menu.

Finally, with a heavy sigh, she says, "No dessert today."

"What? Why?" Sin asks, since she always gets dessert on Sundays.

"I'm getting fat," she states.

Sin's eyebrows rise. "You're too smart to say dumb shit like that."

"I can't button my jeans anymore," she informs him solemnly.

"So we'll get you those maternity ones. You're pregnant, for Christ's sake. Of course you were going to get to a point where you couldn't button your jeans."

"Yes, the fat point," she agrees.

"I don't want to hear that bullshit again. You're gorgeous. Your body is perfect. If your jeans make you doubt that for even a minute, I'll throw the fucking things in the garbage."

Laurel grins, leaning against his side and hugging him. "I love that you think you can punish my jeans for being mean to me."

"Damn right I can," he mutters, his arm around her tightening.

She glows some more and leans in to steal a kiss. "You're the best."

God, someone fucking shoot me. I like having these family days with them, but a man can only take so much. Virginia must see me over here hoping someone puts me out of my misery, because she appears like a fucking angel with a new drink for me.

"Have I told you lately you're my favorite waitress?" I ask her with a charming smile.

Grinning back at me, she says, "I know I am. Drink up." Looking at the lovebirds beside me, she asks, "Dessert?"

"No," Laurel says.

"Yes," Sin says, more firmly. "Bring her a piece of cheesecake."

"To-go," Laurel adds. "I'm too full of food right now."

As it always does, Sin's gaze drifts to Skylar's carrier in the booth on his other side. He always needs to check on her, even if she's asleep—which she is right now. Has been since ten minutes into dinner, but still he checks every five minutes like she might have stopped breathing since he last looked.

Virginia brings Laurel's cheesecake, but not the bill yet since I'm still drinking. I always pick up the tab on Sundays anyway, so Sin looks over at Laurel. "You ready to get out of here?"

Shaking her head, Laurel sits back in the seat. "Rafe hasn't finished his drink yet."

"You don't have to wait for me," I tell her, taking a sip. "I'll probably have one more after this. Go on home; I'll see you next week."

"You sure?" she asks, giving me that damned look. That "I don't want you to be lonely" look.

Smiling softly, I tell her, "I'm sure, kitten."

"We really don't mind waiting."

"I insist you leave," I reply.

They finally do. I have mixed feelings about it—on one hand, I don't feel like being alone tonight. I spend a lot more time alone now than I used to, and while that was the point of this pussy-cleanse, it's beginning to get old.

On the other hand, I've endured too much of their lovey-dovey bullshit today, so one of them had to go. If one wanted to take the baby home and one wanted to stay, I would have said great, but that never happens anymore unless Sin and I have business to discuss. He'd much rather be home with Laurel and Skylar than out with me. I don't take it personally. Sin's a family man, and now he has one. Good for him.

Less good for me, since I'm the one he used to spend most evenings with.

Wouldn't matter if I'd stop this self-imposed celibacy, I

528 | SINNING IN VEGAS

suppose. I draw out my phone, looking at the names of the women who have messaged me lately. Not quite as many as it used to be, but only because I'm not putting out the signal. If I really wanted to, I could end the loneliness and the lack of sex all in one fell swoop.

Instead, I drink.

I drink and I drink, and then I drink some more. Like the loneliest bastard in the world, I drink until the place closes. The funny thing is, they can't make me leave. Perks of owning the fucking place.

The manager keeps shooting me looks, the little bastard. He wants me to clear out of here. It's not because I'm being a pain in the ass, it's not even because he wants to go home. It's because Virginia should have left already, but she's waiting for me. She's going to give me a ride home like she always does when I drink too much. She's fanatical about none of us driving home drunk. She quotes statistics and tells horrifyingly detailed stories about little kids killed by drunk drivers until none of us would even *think* to tell her no when she offers us a safe ride home. I'm fine with her offering me a ride, but I don't like that she does the same thing for the other guys. Guys in my family, guys that work for me. She used to give Gio rides home, even, and now that I know all I know about Gio, I feel retroactively nervous about it. Drunk assholes aren't the best company, and late at night, all alone—any one of them could hurt her. Then I'd have to kill 'em. It'd be a whole damn thing.

Trent knows she's gonna offer to give me a ride home and he doesn't want her to. I'm surprised he doesn't do the smart thing and offer to give me a ride before she can. Knowing Virginia, she would offer anyway, but hell, he could at least try. Dumbass. I catch him looking at me again, second time in the space of a minute. I tip my glass at him and wink before I throw the rest of it back.

He's so fucking mad at me right now. He should be; I'm an asshole. Nothing he can do about it, though. Storm in the back and kick a cleaning bucket across the kitchen in a fit of impotent rage.

I laugh a little, picturing him doing just that.

Virginia has nothing left she can even pretend she has to do. She's just leaning on the counter, waiting me out. Now she sees me laughing at nothing, so she walks over to check on me.

"Hey, looks like you're done with that," she tells me, nodding at the glass.

"Looks that way," I agree.

"Want me to take it and clean it?" she offers.

Trent appears around the corner like a little weasel. "I'll take it so we can get out of here."

Virginia lets him take the glass, and instead she takes a seat in my booth, sliding in next to me. She keeps a little distance between us, where most women would slide all the way until our thighs are touching. I'm looking at her thigh covered in the sturdy fabric of her work pants when she touches my arm and steals my attention. My gaze snaps to her face a little too fast, and I have to blink to steady my vision.

"Are you okay?" she asks softly.

Virginia's not ordinarily soft-spoken. She used to be, back when she started working here, but no one ever listened to her and it started pissing her off. I used to rag on her for being too meek, and boy did that light a fire under her ass. She wasn't meek, people just thought that because she was quiet. Eventually, she learned to dress for the job she wanted—in this case, the job of making people do whatever the fuck you tell them to do. Started carrying herself with authority. No one fucks with her now, not even that little bastard Trent, even though he's technically her manager.

It's different for me, though. She kept a soft spot for me.

I try to nod my head, but it fucks me up, so I stop. I probably should have stopped before that last drink. "Yep. I'm good."

"You don't look good," she tells me.

"Thanks," I say, dryly.

Rolling her eyes at me, she says, "You know that's not what I meant. You don't need *me* to tell you that you look good. You're too well aware of that already."

My head feels heavy, so I rest it back against the cushioned seat of the booth. "How crazy is it that they went from o to family like that? From nothing. Just... cobbled together a fucking family out of pieces and parts. I had all the parts, they were actually mine, and I couldn't do that. It's like I had the flour and the water, and I couldn't make bread if my life depended on it. Sin had fucking sawdust, and he made a basket full of dinner rolls."

"Yeast."

I look over at her. "What?"

"You don't make bread out of just flour and water, you need yeast—never mind, that wasn't the point." She pauses. "Using your bread analogy, Sin and Laurel may not have had the right ingredients, but they knew what they wanted to make. They *knew* they wanted bread, so they found a way. You had a counter full of ingredients and no idea what to do with them. Or maybe no *desire* to do anything with them. You didn't want to make bread, so all the ingredients and recipes in the world wouldn't have helped you."

"It didn't work because I didn't want it to work."

She nods. "Exactly. Sin wanted it. You didn't. You just like playing with other people's toys."

I grin, turning my head to look at her. "That's true, I do."

Instead of being annoyed at me, her eyes shine with indulgent fondness. "You're such a rogue."

"That's a nice word for what I am," I tell her.

"Yeah, well, I'm a nice girl," she says dryly.

"You *are* a nice girl," I agree, with much less irony. "Too nice. You should have kicked me out of here an hour ago."

Amusement twinkles in her brown eyes. "I should kick you out? You own the restaurant. I'm a waitress. I don't have the authority to kick you out."

"You never know. I might listen to you if you tried."

"Well, I didn't, and here we are. You wanna go home? It's late and I'm tired. I worked a double."

"A double? That doesn't sound fun."

"It's not," she agrees, poking me in the arm playfully. "Some of us actually have to work for a living."

"You don't *have* to. You could hook yourself an old millionaire and be a trophy wife if you set your mind to it."

She snorts, and it's fucking adorable. "Yeah, right. Let me get right on that."

Trent comes storming back on the floor, mean-mugging the shit out of me. "Back's closed up. I open in the morning, so it'd be really nice if we could leave."

"See yourself out then, pal," I tell him. "I have a key."

Turning to look back at Trent, Virginia shoos him. "Go on. I'll make sure the place is locked up before I leave."

Since that is not his motive at all, he tries to stall. "It's dark. I don't want you to go outside alone. I'll wait and walk you out so I know you're safe."

"I'm going to give him a ride home," she tells Trent. "I

won't be alone. Unless you want to make the argument that someone is going to fuck with me on my way to the car with Rafe Morelli walking next to me?" she suggests, making no attempt whatsoever to mask the ridicule in her question.

Trent leaves, but he grumbles all the way. Amuses the fuck out of me. Sorry bastard.

Leaning close as if to tell her a secret, I loudly whisper, "He wants to bang you."

She doesn't bother playing coy. "Yeah. But he wants to bang every decent-looking woman who comes through here, so it's nothing to write home about."

Since I'm already this close, I lean a little closer. I can't tell what she smells like, and suddenly I need to know. She's been working all day long and her dark hair is pulled back in a severe pony tail. Without thought, I reach behind her head and tug it free. She jerks in surprise, her eyes darting to my hand as I offer her the elastic that was just holding her hair in place.

"Was my ponytail offending you?"

Hardly paying attention to her response, I push my hand into her hair and shake it out. The part of her hair where her ponytail was tied is somehow still damp, so she must have tied it back straight out of the shower and come directly to work. What a fucking drag.

"Your hair is too pretty to be tied back in a ponytail 12 hours a day," I inform her.

I hear her swallow, but then I remember the reason I took her ponytail out in the first place. I wanted to smell her hair. I want to know what she smells like when she steps out of the shower and wraps a towel around her bare breasts.

My hand automatically moves to her chest as I think about her breasts, wondering what they look like. She gasps, stunned, and a breath shudders out of her, but still she doesn't speak. I definitely shouldn't touch her, but since she lets me, I palm the soft globe through the fabric.

God, it has been a long time. Way too long. Since Laurel left, since Cassandra died—too much happened all at once, and I started to wonder if the man looking back at me in the mirror each morning was the man I wanted to be. The man who had wrought such destruction. I needed to be alone for a little while to get my own head straight. Given I am currently drunk off my ass, groping the only woman I have ever been able to maintain a non-sexual relationship with in my adult life, I'm not sure I managed to get my head on straight in these few months alone, after all.

Finally, Virginia clears her throat. "Why don't I get you home?"

"Come with me," I murmur, my lips grazing the shell of her ear.

"Oh, my God." Her voice is more tortured than it should be. "Rafe, come on."

I cup her jaw in my hand and draw her close to me. "I don't want to sleep alone tonight."

"That is not a good idea," she says, looking anywhere but at me.

"It feels like one," I assure her.

"Because you're drunk," she says, far too soberly. "You're drunk, and you're feeling sad tonight. You just watched the mother of your unborn child go home to live her happily ever after with someone else. I get it, I would be sad, too. But I'm not a tumbler full of alcohol. You can't consume me and then go about your life casually as can be like it didn't happen. And even if you can, I can't. I want to stay in your life, and that means I need to stay out of your bed. We both know that."

"I won't fuck you," I promise. Her eyes narrow skeptically,

534 | SINNING IN VEGAS

but she doesn't outright shoot me down, so I go on. "I won't. I just don't want to sleep alone. That's all."

Now her shoulders sag, and I know I have her. I don't even know if she believes me, but she has a soft heart underneath it all, and an even softer spot for me. If she makes me go to sleep alone tonight, she'll feel worse about it than I will.

Swallowing, she says, "Why don't I think about it on the way to your house?"

"Why don't you say yes now and save us both the suspense?" I suggest.

Rolling her eyes, she says, "You're a piece of work, you know that?"

"I know what I bring to the table."

"Commitment issues and a dreamy smile? Yeah, we all know what you bring to the table."

As I drag my ass out of the booth, I mutter, "I don't have commitment issues."

"Fine, a deeply-seated certainty that everyone is unreliable," she offers, watching me grab onto the back of the booth to get my bearings. "Is that a more palatable summary?"

"Now that's more like it. That's just the truth, not me having commitment issues."

"Like I said," she murmurs, walking ahead, preparing to hit the light switch once I'm out the door.

"You don't think people are unreliable?" I ask her.

Rocking her head back and forth, she says, "It's complex. If you mean disappointing, then yes. People are consistently disappointing, but that's usually because we trick ourselves. We use hope to set our expectations, thereby setting ourselves up for inevitable disappointment. People show us exactly who they are, and we ignore that reality in favor of who we want them to be. For instance, you and Laurel. I could have told you the first night she came in here with Sin that you were wasting your time trying with her. You're wasting your time with most of the women you bring in here. Without even being present for more than snippets of conversations, I can tell they're terrible matches for you. I think that's why you pick them. I don't know what your love life was like before Cassandra, but since her, you have consistently chosen women who would prove what you wanted to believe—that they will always let you down."

Now she hits the lights, slips out the door, and holds out of her hand for my key.

"Laurel wasn't a terrible match," I murmur, as I dig the keys out of my pocket.

"For you, she was. Aside from the facts that she was clearly into someone else *and* she wanted kids, she's territorial. The only way you could possibly live a mutually happy life with a territorial woman is if you lived alone on a desert island with no hope of rescue."

That makes me laugh. I can't really argue with that.

Virginia smiles faintly, using my key to lock up, pulling the handle to double-check, then handing me the key.

"You don't think I'd come to Jesus for the right woman?" I tease.

Shaking her head firmly, Virginia says, "People don't change. Not like that, anyway. They obviously change over time and as life happens to them, but they don't experience personality transplants because they fall in love—and if they do, when the limerence wears off, they'll get tired of selling themselves out and revert to their old ways. Sometimes people shift in subtle ways to accommodate one another, to grow together instead of apart, but not the way you're talking about —not permanently, anyway. People need to already be compatible, not change to fit one another. That's not a recipe for lasting happiness. No woman will ever change you, and it would be a shame if one tried. You're great; you just don't go out with women who match your personality."

"Sometimes I do."

"No," she says decisively. "Not once. Not here, anyway."

"Mia would have been a pretty good fit."

"She's *married*. I've never met her myself, so I don't know if you're right, but if you are, surely I don't have to explain why her emotional unavailability is the only reason you even looked twice at her. You're drawn to women who disappoint you—the *only* exception is women you can't have. You like Mia because she loves your high-maintenance cousin. In your eyes, she has probably already proven by being happy with him you could depend on her, that she's a safer pick than most women, but it probably isn't true. Mateo might be difficult, but you're completely different people. I'm sure he has his issues, but they're not the same as yours. Mia and Mateo have kids, don't they? So, clearly she wanted kids, and you don't. Would you have compromised to make her happy? If so, would you have resented her for it and felt trapped later on? Is Mateo a flirt? If not, she might be territorial. Could she have handled going out to dinner and having you shamelessly flirt with the waitress? Even if she gritted her teeth and sat there through it, would it slowly erode her feelings for you and breed resentment? There are all kinds of ways she probably doesn't fit you that you gloss over because you can, because she can be an untouchable idea in your head, but even if I'm off and she is a paragon of perfection designed specifically to suit you, that's not what you look for. If Mia *is* perfect for you and you had met her when she was single, you would have walked right past her. You look for reassurance that your viewpoint about relationships is accurate, not someone who can prove you wrong."

I'm not sure if all of that seems really insightful because I'm drunk, or because it is. "You have an awful lot of information about me. Do you have a 'Rafe Morelli' dossier tucked away in your apartment somewhere?"

Smiling faintly, she taps her temple. "I keep it all up here, whether I want to or not."

"I like to observe people, too," I tell her.

"I know," she says indulgently.

"Of course you do," I murmur. "Seems like you know more about me than I know about myself."

"Probably. People can never see themselves as clearly as they think. I see you, though. That's why I will not fuck you tonight and make everything weird forever, so don't even try it. I'm wise to your tricks."

I shoot her a harmless smile. "Oh, come on. Surely a hand job wouldn't make things weird?"

Smothering her laughter, she unlocks her car and opens the driver seat. "Get your drunken ass in the car."

I open her passenger door and drop into the seat, yanking the door shut. "Do you like bookstores?" I ask her.

She hits the locks, then pushes her key into the ignition. "I love bookstores. Do you?"

"I liked going to them with Laurel. As you mentioned, bookstore dates are a little too serious for me."

I say it like I'm joking, but now that she's called me on it, I can't deny it. I can invite a woman to a club for drinks, or my restaurant for dinner, and it doesn't have to mean anything. But taking a girl out during daytime hours to a bookstore? They'd start getting ideas about seriousness. That's a damned shame. I don't think Sin will let Laurel go to the bookstore alone with me until the baby gets here, and then there's a kid tagging along. Not the same.

I want someone to go to bookstores with, but not someone who's going to be a pain in the ass and start wanting things I won't want to give.

Maybe I just want a friend.

Huh. I haven't tried being friends with a woman since... Nope, I can't remember. Grade school, probably.

"Where do you fall on the 'can men and women be friends' theory?" I ask her.

"Depends. Personally, I have had zero lasting male friendships, but I'm sure they're possible between the right people." Glancing over at me, she asks, "You?"

I would invariably screw it up by wanting to fuck her. Laurel is trying like hell to be my friend now, but I have to keep her at a distance. I still think about fucking her most Sundays, especially when she wears that tiny ass bikini by the pool. Only reason it hasn't happened is because of Sin. Obviously it never will as long as Sin is around, but a single female friend wouldn't have Sin to fend me off.

"I'd be bad at it," I admit.

Virginia cracks a smile. "Hey, at least you're honest. That's one of the things I admire most about you. You pretty much know who you are and you don't try to hide it. It would be really easy for you to be sleazy, but I've never seen you pretend to be anything you're not."

"Are you territorial?" I ask, though I can't say why. Curiosity. I've always thought of Virginia as incredibly bright, but right now I want her to tell me more things. She should stay at my house all night and keep telling me all her thoughts and observations.

"I don't date, so it's not really an issue for me," she tells me.

"Why don't you date?"

Cracking a smile, she says, "Because most people are disappointing, and I don't feel like dealing with it at this point in time."

Side-eyeing her, I tell her, "Isn't that my thing?"

"You have to share your thing," she states.

"Hey, I'm damn good at sharing my thing," I inform her.

"Of course you had to make it dirty," she says, sighing at my antics.

"If you have all the answers, you should take your own advice," I tell her, leaning my head against her car door.

"Are your ears broken? I'm not lost. I don't need advice. I don't *desire* a relationship, so I don't have one. Simple."

Now she's speaking my language. "See? We could fuck and it wouldn't be a big deal."

"No," she says, shaking her head. "And if you keep bringing that up, I'm for sure not going to spend the night platonically."

I'm tempted to keep her talking, but I'm more interested in convincing her to stay the night, so I lean my head back against the seat and close my eyes while she drives me home.

I already know she'll come in, so I don't bother asking, and I don't waste my time floating an insincere "good night" to see if she needs convincing. Once we're in my driveway, I just open the car door and climb out, expecting her to follow.

She does, but she balks a little bit. "I still think this is a terrible idea. How about I'll make sure you make it all the way up to your bed, but then you pass out and I leave?"

I smirk at her attempt to make me compromise. "How about no?" I counter.

"I've been working all day. I'm gross. I don't want to sleep on your undoubtedly nice bed in my stinky work clothes."

540 | SINNING IN VEGAS

"So shower and wear one of my shirts."

Appearing to choke on nothing, she looks horrified. "No."

"Haven't you ever had a platonic sleepover before, Virginia? Didn't you have girlfriends growing up?"

"Sure, but they lacked dicks, so it was a little different."

"Dicks make everything better," I assure her.

Laughing, she tells me, "You have that very wrong."

I push open my front door and gesture for her to walk in ahead of me. She stares at the inside of my house like it's an elevator to hell, her feet seemingly rooted to the stoop outside.

"Are you a vampire?" I ask. "Do I have to vocalize the invitation?"

"Maybe," she says, nodding. "Let's go with that. I'm a vampire. It's impossible for me to step over that threshold."

"Nothing is impossible," I assure her. "Virginia, I would like to invite you inside my house. Go on in. There, all better."

"Well, now I'm going to suck you dry, so that was a bad idea."

My head lolls back. "Jesus Christ, woman."

She snorts, realizing what she said. "Sorry. No, I'm not going to do that. I meant your blood. It's not a good idea to invite supernatural predators into your house."

Following her inside, I say, "Since there's no such thing, I think I'll be okay."

"You're lucky I'm not really a vampire, you'd be so dead."

Gesturing to my weapons armoire, I tell her, "I keep my wooden stakes in there. I'd be all right."

"You'd have to train a new waitress though. Can you imagine trying to replace me? It would be a nightmare. You could never enjoy dinner properly again."

"She wouldn't anticipate my needs. I would have to actually *ask* for drinks." I shudder theatrically. "Unbearable."

Virginia grins. "All right, let's get you to bed. I'm tired. I want to go home."

"You're not going home," I remind her.

"You're going to pass out in three minutes flat. You consumed enough tonight alcohol to tranquilize a large horse."

"I'm not going to make the obvious joke about my dick," I tell her.

"Much appreciated," she replies, following me up the stairs.

"What's your favorite book?" I ask her.

"My favorite book? You're really hung up on this bookstore thing, aren't you? That's probably the first real date you've been on in a long time, huh? That makes sense. You put in some effort and still lost. That must sting."

"I did not ask for more psychoanalysis," I point out. "I asked about your favorite book."

"I have a lot of favorite books. I don't see how I could pick just one," she answers.

"What about music?"

"I don't have a favorite band."

"Favorite song?"

She shakes her head wordlessly.

I cock an eyebrow. "TV show?"

She smiles. "Nope."

The little pain in the ass isn't going to answer any of my damn questions. I'm too drunk to pursue it right now. I'll find out eventually.

My bedroom door is open already. She hesitates outside, but I already see it coming, so I grab her arm and drag her inside.

She sighs like I'm murdering her. I have half a mind to tell her how many women would trade their left tit to have me this adamant they spend the night, but she already knows.

I'm frustrated for a moment, the goddamn alcohol clouding my senses as I kick off my shoes and try to figure out why she's being a pain in the ass. Normally she accommodates me. Obviously she doesn't want to be here, but she is. It takes me a minute to work through it. She stays close to the door like she's preparing to run and watches me warily. This isn't going to work. Gotta disarm her. Too much alcohol sloshing around to think clearly.

"Unbutton my shirt," I tell her.

"Why?" she inquires, looking mildly horrified again.

"There's two of every button. It's gonna take me a minute and I'm going to look like a drunken asshole."

Her horror gives way to mild amusement, but she finally walks closer, since I'm in need. "You are a drunken asshole," she tells me. Her tone is pleasant, though, and her fingers are already popping the buttons through holes, so that's okay.

My gaze drifts from her fingers to her face. I watch intently as she unbuttons my shirt. She's focusing too hard, like she's the one seeing two of every button. Like it's a complex task I've assigned her, and it requires every bit of her mental acumen to accomplish. The scent of her shampoo wafts up to me and I lean in to keep it coming. Virginia swallows audibly, quickly popping the last button through the hole. I know she's about to step back, so I grab her before she can.

"Rafe..."

There's a warning in her tone, but I don't believe it. I know she finds me attractive. If she's not looking for a relationship, why can't we fuck around? I wonder what she'd do if I just took the decision out of her hands, tossed her little ass on the bed, and stripped off her clothes. Could she keep saying no when she feels that much tension unbuttoning my shirt?

"I don't believe you," I tell her, dragging her against my chest.

"You don't believe you're a drunken asshole?" she asks, still trying to maintain levity, but struggling hard. Physical contact shorts out her circuits. Is it like that with all men, or just me? Is it real discomfort, or attraction she's trying hard to ignore? I think it's the latter.

"I think you shouldn't follow drunken assholes to their bedroom," I tell her, keeping her close, my fingers slipping the first button on her black dress shirt through the hole.

"Huh. Seems like you've recovered from your inability to work buttons," she tells me, catching my hand and pushing it away.

"It's a miracle," I tell her, blinking and reaching for the next button on her shirt.

"Someone add a chapter to the bible so we can share this inspirational story with the masses." Barely missing a beat, she looks up at me and says firmly, "Let me go."

"Why?"

"Because I asked you to. Because even drunk, you know this is not okay. Because you're fumbling, and you have an image to protect. Pick a reason."

"I am not fumbling," I mutter, even as I fumble with the third button.

"Rafe," she says again, shoving my hand away and re-buttoning the shirt. "I'm not going to fuck you."

"No?" I ask, grabbing her again and tugging her close. Closer this time. I grab her hips and pull them against me, making her feel the outline of my cock in my pants. It's hard, and it wants to come out to play.

"Do you know how I usually respond to aggressive drunks? By hurting their dicks. Do you want me to hurt your dick?"

"Go ahead," I challenge, knowing she won't do it. Just to egg her on, I lock my arms around her, truly trapping her against my chest. She swallows and refuses to look at me, but she won't speak, and she certainly doesn't try to fight back. "Go on," I tell her. "Get out of my hold. Punch me in the dick. Knee me in the face. I'll deserve it, I won't be mad."

"I'm not going to do that," she mutters.

"Who got aggressive with you?" I ask.

"What? You, right now."

I roll my eyes. "You said aggressive drunks. Do you mean my guys, when you've given them a ride home? I need names, I'll have a talk with them."

"Sin took care of it."

"Good ol' Sin," I mutter dryly. "You should've told me. I would have handled it myself."

"You would have told me to stop giving people rides home, and I wouldn't have listened. Telling Sin worked out nicely. They're mostly dead now anyway—or, missing," she says, her tone obviously unconvinced. "Most of them don't come around since Gio disappeared, so I drew the logical conclusion."

"Mm." I don't confirm or deny that, but she doesn't expect me to. Sin may share more than he should with Laurel, but that's not how I was raised.

Seeing an opening, she brings her hands up against my chest and pushes me back. "Now, get in bed."

"Belt," I tell her, nodding down toward my hips.

She sighs, but nonetheless unbuckles my belt and draws it off. "Pants?" she questions, glancing up at me.

I nod my head.

She swallows again. I swear, I hear it every fucking time. I wonder if I would hear her swallowing my cum. I wonder how she looks kneeling, those big brown eyes gazing up at me.

"What do you like in the bedroom?" I ask her.

"Sleeping," she replies, giving me a shove toward the bed. "On the bed, come on. I don't have all night."

Luckily for her, I wore boxer briefs tonight, but my cock is still at the ready. She avoids looking down and lets go of me to pull back my blankets, like a maid.

I should hire her. I should make her be my maid, not just my waitress. Then she'd be stuck here all the time. I could follow her around the fucking house making her answer my questions. Then again, I have a rule about not fucking my employees.

Oh, wait, she is my employee. Whoops. How did that slip my mind? Oh well. I fall into the bed and sigh. I love my fucking bed.

Virginia smiles softly and pulls the blanket up over me, tucking me in like I'm a little kid. "Now, get some sleep. Want me to get you a glass of water for the bedside table before I go?"

"I told you to stay."

"Yes, but then you did all sorts of things that made me decide against it," she reminds me.

I don't know why she lingers close when she knows I have no qualms about grabbing her, but she does, so I reach out, grab her hips, and drag her on top of me.

"Rafe," she complains again.

"Rafe," I mock her. "If you don't like it, don't stand so close."

"I didn't realize I needed to treat you like a sexual predator," she informs me, primly.

546 | SINNING IN VEGAS

Grinning, I roll her onto her back and move on top of her. "I *am* a sexual predator. Come from a long line of 'em. I'm actually one of the more decent ones out of the bunch."

Unintimidated, she pokes me in the chest with her finger. "Off. Now."

"I wanna play," I tell her, eyeing up her neck.

She must be able to see my intentions, because her voice is suddenly much firmer. "If you kiss me, I'll quit."

"Quit?"

"My job. Effective immediately."

Her job.

Because she works for me.

I should not be on top of her right now.

I frown, feeling mildly confused, but I'm not sure about what. How the fuck did I get here?

It's manipulative as hell, but I can't stop myself. "Why do you want to leave me?"

Her whole face falls, like I just killed her dog right in front of her. She's struck momentarily speechless, her mouth opening, then closing before she can utter a single syllable. It takes her a minute before she can formulate words, and I almost feel bad about the guilty look on her face when she finally does. "I'll stay until you fall asleep. Just don't try to kiss me, okay? Please?"

"Why?"

"Because I asked you not to."

I shake my head at her. "No. Come on, give me this. You've dodged every single question I've asked tonight. You won't even tell me your favorite fucking song. Give me one real answer, Virginia. Just one."

Her face flushes, like I've asked much more of her than I have. The silence stretches on for such a long moment, I don't think she's going to answer me. I'm just about to push a little harder when she finally speaks.

"Because you're drunk, and you'll be able to forget all about it. But I won't. I'll never be able to forget. I will memorize all of it. I'll remember the way your lips feel against mine, and the way you smell, and the look in your eyes. I will remember *everything*. A kiss wouldn't cost you anything, but it would cost me a lot. It would mean too much to me, and not enough to you." She shakes her head, her eyes glistening with unshed tears that make me feel a little more sober. I know I'm the reason the tears are there, but I don't know why. I don't know what I did this time.

I swallow, rolling off her and back to my own spot. "Okay. I'm sorry."

"No need to apologize," she assures me, blinking, trying to disguise the fact that she teared up. "I sort of wish I could. I do wonder what it would be like, just... not curious enough to foot that bill."

Since I don't want her to be upset, I try to joke with her. "Maybe we need to get you drunk first."

Chuckling faintly, she shakes her head. "That doesn't work. I've tried. The most memorable time, I was standing on a wooden chair, leading a room of drunken strangers in a heartfelt rendition of *I Believe I Can Fly*. It was... not a night of good decision-making."

"Oh, my God, I want to see that," I tell her, grinning.

"If I could play the memory for you... no, actually, I wouldn't share it."

"R. Kelly, huh? My life will be meaningless if I never get to see you drunkenly bumping to R. Kelly."

"Then I apologize in advance for the meaninglessness of your life," she says solemnly.

"You should, it's entirely your fault." Closing my eyes, I start to hum the music, a helpless smile creeping across my face as I envision Virginia standing on the table at the restaurant, drunkenly belting it out. "You know what? Never mind, I can see it."

"No," she says, reaching over and covering my closed eyes. "Stop looking. Stop imagining it. It's terrible."

I shove her hand away. "Wait, it's getting good."

"Rafe," she whines.

"Did you spread your arms like wings? I bet you did, didn't you? Yep, you are now, I can see it. Oh, shit, you stumbled. That's okay, no one noticed."

Growling at me, she swats me in the stomach. "I'm glad you're drunk. You won't remember this. That's the only good thing I can take away from this right now."

"Oh, I'll remember. I'll let you think I don't, and just when you think you're safe, I'm going to walk up behind you while you're making a salad for your table and start singing it in your ear."

She covers her face, trying to hide her grin. "Oh, God. I'll die."

"I've got you now," I tell her, smugly.

I'm caught completely off guard, and somehow it hits me in the gut, but she *giggles*. Actually giggles. Then she peeks over at me, affection in her eyes, and all of a sudden my chest feels really fucking weird. That's the cutest fucking sound I've ever heard in my life. I've heard lots of giggles, most of them fake, but that's the purest sound of enjoyment I've ever triggered in another person, I know that for a fact.

Since she doesn't know that, and I've finally stopped harassing her long enough for her to have an opening, she curls up on her side of the bed, on top of the covers. Her body placement seems deliberate to keep me from trying to grab her and drag her close, but I wouldn't now anyway. I made her almost cry, and I made her laugh, and I like the last one a whole lot better. I'll keep my hands to myself and let her keep looking at me like I'm the funniest man she's ever met.

"Want me to go get you that water?" she asks.

I shake my head. "Nah. I'm good."

"Okay." With one more fond smile, she says, "Good night, Rafe."

"Good night, Virginia."

Stay tuned for the conclusion of the Vegas Morelli trilogy—Submitting in Vegas, available for pre-order now!

IF YOU HAVEN'T READ THE ORIGINAL
MORELLI FAMILY SERIES YET…

WHAT ARE YOU WAITING FOR? PICK UP
ACCIDENTAL WITNESS NOW!

ABOUT THE AUTHOR

Sam Mariano loves to write edgy, twisty reads with complicated characters you're left thinking about long after you turn the last page. Her favorite thing about indie publishing is the ability to play by your own rules! If she isn't reading one of the thousands of books on her to-read list, writing her next book, or playing with her adorable preschooler... actually, that's about all she has time for these days.

Feel free to find Sam on Facebook, Goodreads, Twitter, or her blog—she loves hearing from readers! She's also available on Instagram now @sammarianobooks, and you can sign up for her totally-not-spammy newsletter HERE

If you have the time and inclination to leave a review, however short or long, she would greatly appreciate it! :)

Made in United States
Orlando, FL
15 July 2022

19820014R00333